BROKEN LINES

JAMES HUNT

BROKEN LINES: EMP SURVIVAL

By James Hunt

THE STEEL MILL

The floorboards creaked when Mike stumbled from the bed to the bathroom. He tripped over one of Anne's heels and cursed under his breath, kicking the shoe out of his path. He turned around to make sure he hadn't woken her up. She was still drooling on her pillow.

Mike crammed himself into the tiny bathroom. His legs smashed up against the side of the tub when he closed the door. He splashed water on his face, letting the cold shock him awake. Droplets of water speckled his reflection in the small mirror above the sink. He cracked his knuckles, wincing with each pop.

He showered, shaved, threw his boots on, kissed Anne on her forehead, and did the same with his daughter, Kalen, and son, Freddy, then was out the door.

Dirt and bits of rust and metal flew up from the cloth seats of his truck's cab when Mike sat down. He pulled the handle of the glove box open. He shoved a small bag out of the way and pulled out a badge. He pinned "Yard's Steel Mill" to his chest. Scraps of metal and steel rods rolled and clanked in the truck bed as he reversed out of the driveway.

The blue digital lights of the dashboard clock glowed 6:11 a.m. The view of the Pittsburgh skyline from the interstate was still outlined in gray without the morning sun. Mike's fingers twisted the radio tuner, searching for a station. Static and scramble came through until he finally landed on an AM radio station.

"Good morning, Pittsburgh. It's a beautiful Wednesday morning here at 560 WFRB. Traffic right now is clear on Highway 62. The first day of summer should be a hot one as temperatures are expected to get into the mid-eighties this afternoon, so taking the kiddies to the pool to cool off might be in order now that school is officially over."

Mike pulled into the parking space of an empty lot outside a small, fading brown one-story building. He walked through the empty parking lot up to the automatic sliding glass doors. A smiling receptionist gave him a wave when he entered.

"Hey, Mike."

"Hey, Nicole," he said. "Is my dad ready to go?"

"Should be. He was finishing getting ready when I walked past him this morning. I'll give him a buzz."

"Thanks."

A few elderly folks with walkers emerged from the hallway into the waiting room where Mike sat. Their liver-spotted hands gripped the steel-gray handles of their walkers. The green tennis balls at the bottom slid across the carpet, propelled by their slowly shuffling feet.

Ulysses walked down the hallway, weaving in and out of the shrunken, hunched over, elderly obstacles and walked right past Mike without looking at him. The automatic sliding glass doors chimed open when Ulysses passed through them and headed for Mike's truck.

Mike's eyes went from the exit back to Nicole, whose lower lip was protruding, still watching Ulysses walking to the truck.

"Pirates lose last night?" Mike asked.

"Yeah," Nicole replied.

The sun was rising in the east, coming up over the skyscrapers in the foreground. Beams of orange light hit Mike's and Ulysses's faces through the windshield of the truck. Blinkers and taillights flashed in front of them in the thickening traffic. Mike flipped on his left blinker to merge. A horn blared and sent Mike swerving back into his own lane and sending Ulysses's shoulder slamming against the door.

"Jesus Christ," Ulysses said, adjusting his seat belt.

"You all right, Dad?"

"I could have driven myself."

"The doctor said you wouldn't be able to drive after the tests."

"Tests. Pills. Needles. Activity time. You know I helped construct half the buildings in this city?"

"Dad, I told you to just come and stay with us. We have the spare bedroom."

Ulysses waved him off. He twisted a thick gold band around his wrinkled fingers.

"I won't be anybody's burden."

The clock dashboard flashed 6:55 a.m when Mike pulled into the hospital's drop-off lane.

"The doctor said the tests should only take a few hours. I'll come and grab you on my lunch hour and take you back to the retireme —" Mike started, but Ulysses spun his head around. Mike knew he hated that word.

"Back to your place, okay?" Mike finished.

"Yeah, okay," Ulysses said.

"Hey, and don't give the staff any trouble if they have to bring you out in a wheelchair this time."

"If I can walk out on my own steam, I'm going to do it. I don't need a goddamn wheelchair."

Ulysses flung the passenger door open, climbed out, and slammed the heavy metal truck door behind him.

* * *

THE STEEL MILL was already filled with the sounds of cranes, trucks, and the shouts of supervisors giving orders. Mike joined the line of men waiting to clock in. A solid row of hardhats and baseball caps were ahead of him.

Paul White, an elderly man almost his father's age, squinted down at a computer screen. His large hands fumbled with the icons on the touch screen.

Don, a twenty-something man in a greasy jumpsuit, shifted from side to side. His eyes drilled into the back of the old man's head.

"You just hit clock-in, grandpa," Don shouted.

Paul stayed focused on the screen. His finger hovered over dozens of tiny icons. He jumped a bit when Mike grabbed his shoulder.

"It's usually easy to find my name, but I've never seen this screen before," Paul said.

"It's all right, Paul," Mike said.

Mike pressed a few different icons and pulled up Paul's name. He hit "clock-in," and a large green check mark appeared.

"Thanks, Mike," Paul said.

Paul hobbled off into the yard, and Mike walked back to his spot in line.

"I'm surprised you were able to figure it out, Mike. I figured once they got rid of that old punch-card reader half the plant would retire," Don said.

"Let me know if you need help getting your welder running, Don. I wouldn't want you to burn your hand again."

Mike grinned while walking back into place, listening to the rest of the line chuckling behind him.

* * *

WHITE, yellow, and orange sparks flew into the air from Mike's torch. Two pieces of metal he was working on fused together. He turned the torch off and flipped his welder's mask up. He tore off his gloves and wiped the dripping sweat from his eyes, smearing dirt and soot onto his cheeks.

The lunch whistle blew. The continuous motion of loading steel girders, pouring lava-hot metals, and welding ceased.

The cafeteria's tables were crowded with men, shoulder to shoulder. They dug into the lunch pails packed with sandwiches and leftovers. Their heads, hair flattened from their hard hats, bobbed up and down over their food as they ate. Mouths full and laughing.

Mike bit into his BLT, the crunching of bacon and crisp lettuce filling his ears, when suddenly the lights shut off and the cafeteria went dark. The humming of lights and machinery went silent. The men groaned collectively.

Mike pulled out a small flashlight on his keychain and pressed the power button. Nothing. He could hear the clicking of the button, but no light came on, no matter how many times he hit it.

Once Mike's eyes adjusted to the darkness, he joined the rest of the workers exiting the cafeteria. He looked up into the corners of the walls where the emergency lights were installed. *Why didn't the emergency power go on?*

The yard was eerily quiet. Steel beams being moved from the yard to trucks teetered in midair from cranes. The hum of the furnaces was silent. Workers opened truck hoods, checking the engines that stopped. A gathering crowd formed around Glenn, the foreman. He had his hands up, trying to calm the men around him.

"Hey, everybody, listen up. Power's down for the entire block. By the looks of it, we're probably going to be closed for the rest of the day, so everybody goes home," Glenn said.

"Is this gonna be paid leave?" Don asked.

"Are you working?"

"No."

"Then no."

The workers started heading for their cars. Mike walked among them, watching everyone shake and tap their mobile devices. Don cursed, shoving the phone into his pocket.

"Goddamn thing never stays charged."

Mike pulled out his own phone. The screen was completely black. He held the power button down, but the phone wouldn't turn on. He knew it had a full charge that morning when he left for work.

One of Mike's coworkers smacked into his shoulder, rushing past him. He looked up from his phone and saw some men in the front of the group rushing toward the parking lot. Soon the rest of the group started running, and Mike was caught up in the current of people herding forward. Mike pushed his way to the front of the pack next to Don.

All of the cars along the highway were completely still. Wrecks dotted the road for miles. People were outside their vehicles, checking the engines. Some were walking toward the city while others sat on the side of the road, expecting someone to come and get them.

"What the hell?" Don asked.

Mike thought of the backup generators that hadn't turned on, the machines in the yard that had shut off, and the dead cell phones. All of it added up to one thing.

EMP burst.

THE STREETS

$\mathcal{M}$ike was the first to break for his truck. A few other people followed him, but most people stood in the yard staring at the stalled cars along the highway. Gravel kicked up behind him. He stuck his hands in his pocket, fumbling for his keys in mid-stride. The truck door flew open, and he reached for the glove box then yanked out the small bag inside. The hospital where he dropped his dad off was a few miles away. If he kept up a steady pace, he could be there in thirty minutes.

The factories and warehouses on the edge of the city slowly morphed into office buildings and small businesses the closer he moved to the hospital. The silence of everything was eerie. No engines running. No horns blaring. No power lines buzzing. There was only the low murmur of crowds piling into the streets, looking confused in the motionless city.

People held their cell phones in the air, looking around, asking questions to one another. Growing crowds surrounded the police officers stationed on corners. Mike could hear the bombardment of questions and pleas:

"What's going on?"

"When is the power coming back on?"

"Why isn't my phone working?"

"My car got hit back on Fourth Street and the guy took off!"

"Help me."

Mike's pace slowed. He squeezed in and out of the growing crowds piling into the streets. He could feel the restlessness growing in the people around him. He thought of what this mob would start doing once they realized what he already knew.

Yesterday Mike watched two men get into a shoving match over a fender bender. On Monday when he was standing in line for coffee, the woman at the front had an outburst because the barista said they were out of the white chocolate creamer she liked.

Now, there were wrecks on every corner. There wasn't Internet, or transportation, or a way to keep people's food from spoiling. There weren't any ATMs that were working, no way to call for help or to check to see if someone's friend or family member was okay. There wasn't even any power to turn on the barista's coffee machines. The whole city was shut down.

After twenty minutes of running, Mike clutched his ribs. A knife-like pain was digging into his side, running from his hip to his shoulder. The ring of sweat from the summer heat formed around the collar of his shirt. The crowds had grown so thick now there wasn't enough space for him to run. He slowed to a brisk walk. He stared down at his feet, feeling the throbbing ache of running in boots.

Mike stepped up on the platform of a street lamp to get a better view of what was in front of him. A large crowd had gathered in front of the precinct a block away. A line of police stationed outside was attempting to control the hordes of people rushing to get inside.

Just beyond the precinct he could see the front of Allegheny General. Behind the crowd in front of the police station, on the other side of the street, a space opened up where Mike could get by. He jumped down from the lamppost and made his way toward the opening.

Mike pushed his way through crowds of people on the other side of the street, his fingers gripping the small bag in his hand. Elbows jabbed his side, shoes stepped over his boots, and shoulders collided with him. The summer heat combined with the sweaty bodies around him made the air thick and hard to breathe. The crowd was hot, uncomfortable, and irritable.

An officer's voice boomed through a bullhorn outside the station. He kept his hands up in the air addressing the crowd. Officers in riot gear appeared from the side of the station, wielding shields and batons. The crowd hadn't noticed them yet.

"I need everyone to please remain calm. We are working with state and federal officials to figure out what's going on and when the power's coming back on. I need everyone to make an orderly line, and I assure you one of our officers will be available to address each of your concerns individually. Anyone that does not comply and becomes disruptive will be arrested."

People on the outside of the crowd in front of the station started pushing their way to the front. One man grabbed a woman's shoulders and threw her backwards. An officer in riot gear subdued him before he made it into the crowd. A teenaged girl had a backpack on, and the woman behind her pulled the backpack down, smacking the girl into the pavement. The riot officers grabbed the woman's arm and cuffed her as well. All around the outskirts of the crowd, shoves and punches started to break out.

One by one the mob outside the station was being curtailed, but others were showing up, gathering behind the riot police and trying to get in the station.

The shouts from the bullhorn faded behind Mike. He glanced back and could see the swarm of bodies overwhelming the officers. He still had his eyes on a man being thrown to the ground and handcuffed when the gunshot rang out in the alley behind him.

A solid ringing went through Mike's ears. The shot was close. Mike dropped to his knee, and the crowd around him ducked and scattered like cockroaches being discovered when a kitchen light turns on. He rose from his knee and was smacked in the face by a stray elbow from the crowd around him. More bodies ran into him, tossing him around like a pinball machine. He could see a man in the alleyway, clutching his stomach, sliding down the wall of the building behind him.

Mike pushed through the crowd, the ground seeming uneven beneath him from the blow to his head. The ringing in his ears subsided and was replaced by screams and cries for help.

"Guy f-fucking shot me. I d-didn't even have any c-cash on me," the young man said.

"What's your name?" Mike asked.

Mike opened the bag he brought with him. He rummaged through it, pulling out white bandages.

"G-Garry," he said.

Garry's entire body was shaking. Mike lifted Garry's hands off the wound he was covering and shoved bandages in its place to staunch the bleeding.

"Garry, I need you to keep pressure on this, okay?" Mike said.

Blood soaked Garry's shirt, and the red stain was growing larger.

Mike kept both his hands over the wound, helping to keep pressure on it. Color faded from Garry's face.

"Am I gonna die?" Garry asked.

Mike felt the spasms of Garry's body against his hands, the struggle to stay alive. The eyes staring back at him were scared, tired, and losing their fight. Garry's green eyes seemed brighter against the pale flesh of his cheeks. Mike's son's eyes were green.

"Allegheny General is just a few more blocks. I need to move you there now, but you'll need to keep pressure on the wound," Mike said.

Blood spilled from Garry's gut when Mike removed his hands from Garry's stomach. Mike threw his arm around his shoulder and took the bulk of Garry's weight onto it.

Mike pulled Garry from the alleyway, his feet dragging behind him, drips of blood splattering against the concrete underneath.

When they appeared out of the alleyway, people just stared at the two of them. Everyone took a few steps back. Nobody was sure what to do. Mike stared into faces filled with fear, panic, and uncertainty. A guy in a business suit came up and threw the young man's other arm over his shoulder.

"Thanks," Mike said.

The crowds outside the hospital were enormous. The shouts, cries, and pleas for help drowned out any sound or ability to hear. The three of them kept moving forward. Each bump into the person in front of them cleared a path to the hospital's doors.

People jumped back in revulsion. Most people had minor injuries, and the sight of blood dripping from Garry's stomach, his head hanging limp on his neck, caused them to get out of the way.

Nurses and doctors ran around the lobby. Patients were being treated in the chairs in the waiting room. Trails of blood stained the hospital's tile. The only light visible shone through the glass doors from the entrance. Mike could see a few candles down the hallways, offering a slight glow in the darkness.

Mike reached out and grabbed a doctor's arm passing him.

"I've got a critical patient with a gunshot wound to the abdomen," Mike said.

The doctor's eyes fell on Mike, Garry, and the man helping them. He lifted Garry's head up and opened his eyes. He placed his fingers on the side of Garry's neck. The doctor shook his head.

"I'm sorry, boys. He's gone."

The room around Mike went into slow motion. The frantic

nurse that rushed up and stole the doctor, family members begging with the medical staff to do more, and the blood dripping onto the tile from Garry's stomach seemed unreal. Ten minutes ago the man he was holding up was alive.

They dragged Garry's body over to a corner of the room next to a door with "MAINTENANCE" written in white bold letters and set him down. Mike grabbed a sheet off a stretcher and tossed it over Garry's body. Mike turned around, and the man that had helped him was gone. Garry's blood was still warm, lingering on Mike's hands. He smeared his shirt, attempting to wipe the red from his fingers.

No matter how hard he wiped, the blood wouldn't come off. The metallic stench filled his nose. He could feel it, taste it. He had to get out. Mike made a beeline for the door, savagely pushing people out of his way, and then he stopped suddenly.

"Dad," he whispered.

Mike turned on his heel and grabbed another nurse rushing past him. He held her by both of her arms.

"I'm looking for my father," he said.

The nurse squirmed to free herself from Mike's grip. Her face twisted from the uncomfortable feeling of the unfamiliar touching her.

"Sir, please let me go," she said.

"He came in for a blood test this morning."

"I have to get ready for surgery."

"Where is he?"

"I-I think they put all the non-critical patients on the third floor."

Mike let her go and sprinted for the stairwell. The door was propped open. The light from the lobby doors and windows flooded the first flight of stairs. He could see faint rays of light above him from the open doors in the stairwell.

Two large orderlies carried an elderly man on a stretcher and were making their way down to Mike as he reached the second floor. Mike could see the white wisps of hair on the old man's head, the limp hand hanging off the stretcher with a gold band around the ring finger, but couldn't see his face. Mike's heart leapt, and he pushed the orderly aside to get a better look.

"Hey, what the hell are you doing, man?" the orderly asked.

It wasn't his dad. Mike let out a breath he didn't realize he'd been holding.

"Sorry," Mike said.

Mike moved to the side of the stairs and let them pass. On his way up the last flight of stairs, he could overhear the two orderlies below talking.

"You think he's gonna make it?"

"You kidding me? You see what's happening right now? Anybody who's dependent on modern medicine ain't gonna last much longer. The old man's a goner."

3

HOSPITAL

*M*ike leaped the steps two at a time. He burst through the open door into a hallway on the third floor. He looked left, and bright sunlight shone in from a window down the hallway. To his right, the hallway faded from the light into darkness. He rushed past nurses, doctors, and patients, scouring the floor for his father. Shouts from hospital staff filled the hallway.

"We need IV drips going in rooms twelve, nineteen, and seven."

"We need a doctor in here now!"

"Ma'am, please, we're doing everything we can to help your husband."

"Any spare candles should be put in the operating rooms."

Mike squinted, trying to make out the signs hanging from the ceiling. He read "ICU", "ADMINSTRATIVE DESK" and "BLOOD LAB" on the bottom with an arrow pointing farther down the hallway.

Mike weaved in and out of the traffic of people clogging his path. He passed room and saw the figures in bed, unmoving. He saw nurses huddling around candles, filling syringes by their light. He walked past the intensive-care unit. The silence of machines was replaced by the sobs and screams of mothers, fathers, wives, and husbands slumped over lifeless bodies.

Beyond the ICU, Mike passed the blood-soaked operating tables with doctors frantically trying to keep their patients alive. All of the technology used to aid them in surgery was now gone.

The sign of the blood lab was plastered on the door. Mike bolted inside. The room was pitch-black.

"Dad?" Mike whispered, but no answer.

Mike exited the lab. He stood motionless in the hallway. The hospital staff rushed past him. He had no idea where to look next.

"Michael!"

The light from the window down the hall outlined Ulysses's silhouette. Mike couldn't make out the reaction on his father's face upon seeing him, but Mike knew Ulysses could see the relief spreading across his own.

"Dad," Mike said, running toward him. He took his father in both arms, pinning him against his chest.

"I thought I'd lost you, old man," Mike said.

"Not yet," Ulysses replied. "I need your help."

Mike tried to keep up with his father. He noticed the red bandage around Ulysses's arm.

"Are you all right?" Mike asked.

"There are some people trapped in the elevator down the hall. I don't know how many," Ulysses said.

"Dad, did they give you any insulin?"

"I'll need you to hold the doors open until I can pin them in place."

"Dad!"

Mike seized his father's arm. He whipped him around, and the two stopped dead in their tracks. The flow of people moving through the hall rushed around them like water breaking on rocks in a river.

"Michael, I'm fine," Ulysses said.

"Did they already give you your insulin?" Mike asked.

"The lights went out before they could give it to me."

"We need to get you that medicine now."

Ulysses jerked his arm out of his son's grip.

"After we get those people out of the elevator."

Ulysses marched back down the hallway, and Mike turned his head back to the direction of the blood lab. He should have tried to grab the insulin before he left.

The shouts coming from the elevator shaft roared louder the closer they moved to it.

"You sure they're below us?" Mike asked.

"Yeah, we need a drop key to get the doors open. I went looking for the maintenance room, but I couldn't find it," Ulysses replied.

"It's downstairs. I saw it on my way up," Mike said.

Mike flew down the hallway and rushed back down the stairs. When he reached the first floor, the number of people inside had doubled.

Mike stepped forward, and his boot slid on the tile; he stuck his arms out, trying to steady himself. He looked down and saw his boot print smeared in blood. His eyes followed the trail to other fluids staining the white hospital tile.

Mike pushed his way through the growing masses in the hospital's lobby. When he reached the maintenance door, he saw Garry was right where he left him. Mike paused, glancing at the covered heap of flesh.

The maintenance room was chaotic and unkempt. Mike hunted through drawers with mixed tools, light bulbs, and spare screws. Blue jumpsuits hung on a rack along the wall. He searched the pockets, turning them inside out. He reached the last jumpsuit on the rack, and as his hand dug into the outer pocket, he could hear the jingle of keys. Mike flipped through them until he found the three-inch-long rod with a hinge piece hiding amidst the rest of the silver and bronze keys surrounding it.

* * *

Ulysses had gathered more candles and was joined by two stocky-built men, Adam and Sam. Mike handed Ulysses the elevator key, and he jammed it into the hole, letting it fall into place. The elevator doors' locks released.

Adam and Sam pulled the doors open. Mike glanced down and saw the elevator was stuck between the second and third floor five feet below them. The shouts were more audible.

"Help us!"

Ulysses stretched out his hand to grab the cable, and Mike knocked it away.

"I'll go down and check first," Mike said.

Before Ulysses could protest, Mike shimmied down the cable. His landing shook the elevator car a bit, and he yanked the service hatch open.

A nurse in scrubs was furiously pumping a patient's chest on a gurney while a young girl squeezed an air mask over the patient's face.

"What happened?" Mike asked.

"His pacemaker went out when I was taking him upstairs for some tests. We need to get this guy out of here and into surgery now," the nurse said while continuing to pump the man's chest.

"Adam, I'll need your help getting him out," Mike said then looked over to his dad. "As soon as we get this guy out of here, you'll need to start CPR on him."

"Okay," Ulysses said.

Adam took Mike's place on top of the elevator, and Mike slid through the service hatch. Mike noticed the trembling hands of the young girl holding the mask. Her face was down and her hair hovered over the patient's head. Mike placed his hands over the young girl's. She looked up when their hands touched. Her eyes were misty.

The nurse brought the straps from the side of the gurney and tightened them over the patient's body.

"We'll move him on three. One, two, three," Mike said, and he and the nurse lifted the patient to Adam's extended hand.

Mike pushed the patient up through the service hatch with the nurse's help and watched him disappear out of sight. He folded his hands like a step and motioned to the young girl.

"C'mon, you're next," he said.

The girl placed her Converse sneakers into Mike's hands and he lifted her up to the ledge of the service hatch above. He could see Adam's hands grab under her arms and pull her the rest of the way.

"Thank you," the nurse said.

"Up you go," Mike said and thrust the nurse up to freedom.

Once everyone was out of the shaft, Sam jumped down to the top of the elevator next to Adam and the two of them lowered their arms inside the service hatch. Mike jumped and grasped both of their hands. He felt himself being yanked up through the hole in the ceiling and then his feet landing on the metal casing on top of the elevator.

The nurse and patient had already disappeared. The young girl wrapped her arms around Mike when he stepped back into the hallway. She couldn't have been older than fifteen. His hand held the back of her head gently, and then, without a word, she left.

"Appreciate your help, boys," Ulysses said, shaking Sam's and Adam's hands.

"Yeah, thank you," Mike said.

The two men nodded and disappeared into the crowd. Ulysses pocketed the maintenance keys. Mike gave him a frown.

"They might come in handy later," Ulysses said.

"Dad, we need to find the pharmacy here," Mike said once the others had left.

"What for?"

"We need to grab you as much insulin and needles as we can."

Beyond the busy operating rooms and ICU, the rest of the hospital was eerily quiet. Mike could see shadows moving in the rooms he passed and hushed murmurs coming from the inside. The deeper they went into the center of the hospital, the quieter it became. Patients sat in the darkness, some with loved ones, others completely alone.

Finally, Mike saw "PHARMACY" painted in bold black letters across a door window. Inside he found a twelve-pack of ten-milliliter bottles. Mike found a backpack and emptied the contents. He stuffed the pack full of insulin and disposable needles. He tossed one to Ulysses.

"Take one now before we leave," Mike said.

"I have that stuff back at my place. You don't need to steal it, Michael," Ulysses said.

Mike's gut turned sour. That's what he was doing, wasn't it? He'd never stolen anything in his entire life. Then he remembered the hordes of people trampling each other to get into the police station. He saw the young man with the gunshot wound. He wasn't going to let his father die when he had the means to save him.

"C'mon, Dad. We need to get out of here," Mike said.

Mike peeked around the corner outside the lab. The hallway was empty. He motioned for his father to follow, and he walked briskly down the hall.

On their way back to the stairs, Mike noticed a large group crowded around the window. He pushed his way through the crowd and made it to the edge of the windowpane.

The streets were chaos. Looters smashed windows and ran from stores with whatever they could carry in their hands. People were jumping and stomping on car roofs. Police officers were in full force in their riot gear, trying to calm the riots breaking out everywhere, while those not joining in the riots searched for places to hide.

Mike pushed his way back to his father.

"What's going on out there?" Ulysses asked.

"Nothing good. We'll have to take the back way out of here. I-279 is right behind us. We can hop on that and take it to 65 back to my place. I'm not sure how safe it'll be, but we should be fine as long as we make it back before dark," Mike replied.

Mike and Ulysses rushed down the stairwell and burst out onto the first floor. Almost everyone that wasn't dead or dying had crowded near the large lobby windows to watch the events outside.

They hurried down the hallways, turning left and right around corners, searching for the back exit of the hospital. Around every turn was death. All of the failed equipment in the hospital had turned the place into a morgue. There were so many individuals that couldn't survive without the aid of machines and the computer chips that powered them.

When Mike and Ulysses finally made it out the back, they shielded their eyes from the sun. Mike could hear the shouts of voices coming from the other side of the hospital, voices with a mindless purpose of chaos.

4

THE HIGHWAY

*T*he summer sun was brutal. Even the asphalt was sweating. Mike and Ulysses trudged between the abandoned cars on the highway. Other travelers were spread out on the road, heading to whatever home they still hoped was there.

It'd been three hours since they left the hospital. Mike pulled the water bottle from the bugout bag he grabbed from his truck at the steel mill. The rays shining through the plastic hitting the water shimmered like crystals. He had to keep reminding himself to drink, while restraining himself not to down the entire bottle in one chug.

Mike pressed the bottle to his forehead, attempting to cool down. The water felt hot against his head. He reached out his hand to Ulysses, but the bottle hung in the air, and when Mike looked over, Ulysses was gone. He spun around searching behind him.

"Dad?" Mike asked.

Ulysses was bent over on his knees and slowly slid down the driver's side door of a car and collapsed on the pavement.

"Dad!"

Ulysses sprawled out on the ground. He was breathing quickly, panting like a dog trying to cool off, but with no success. Mike lifted his father's head up and felt his forehead. He was burning up.

Mike tipped the bottle into Ulysses's mouth. The water spilled over his lips and dribbled down his chin. Ulysses coughed and pushed the bottle away from his face.

"Dad, you have to drink," Mike said.

"I'm fine."

"Goddammit, Dad, now's not the time to be stubborn."

Ulysses put his hand down and took a few more gulps of water. Mike dropped the bottle in Ulysses's lap. His eyes fell on the bandage around his arm where the hospital staff had drawn blood.

"Did you take that shot I gave you before we left the hospital?" Mike asked.

Ulysses took another sip of water, avoiding his son's face. Mike ripped open his pack and pulled one of the bottles of insulin out of his bag. He ripped one of the needles out of the packet. He pulled the syringe back, filling it with the insulin from the bottle. Mike jammed the needle into his father's arm and emptied it.

That was typical of his father. Never thinking he needed outside help. He'd never needed it before. He'd worked two jobs while going to school finishing his engineering degree. He'd lived in a broken-down apartment in the slums of the city when he was first starting out, with barely enough money to feed himself, and ended up as head engineer for one of the most prestigious firms in the city.

When Mike was little, his dad was superman. He could lift him up in the air with one arm. Now, just like the patients in the hospital on life support, without this tiny bottle of liquid he'd be dead.

Mike joined his dad under the shade of the car. The two of them sat there in silence for a while. The people passing them didn't bother to stop. They didn't think to ask what was wrong. They just kept moving toward their destinations, mindlessly. Mike thought about his destination. He needed to get back to his family.

"You and I both know that those insulin bottles are only good for another month," Ulysses said.

Mike's heart dropped. He'd never heard his father talk like that before. His dad had always been the one to push forward, find solutions, and get it done. It was the first time in his life he'd heard his father hint about the inevitability that comes to all men.

"Insulin isn't the only thing that can help fight diabetes, Dad," Mike said.

"It's the only kind that can fight the type I have, and you know it."

"Think you can walk?" Mike asked.

"Yeah," Ulysses replied.

Ulysses handed the bottle back to Mike, and the two headed down the path toward home. Mike's eyes kept wandering to the windows of the cars he passed. Items left behind in the vehicles that he could easily take. Flashlights, emergency flares, food, water, all sitting in back seats, cupholders, and glove boxes.

Stop it. His eyes went back to the road. He wasn't a looter. He only took the insulin because without it, his father would have died.

Two men one car over from Mike were talking in whispers, trying not to be too loud. One wore a gray Steelers jersey and shorts. The other was dressed in a short-sleeve polo and kaki pants.

"I'm tellin' you, man, this was an EMP," said Polo Shirt.

"It's just a power outage," said Steelers Jersey.

"A power outage doesn't cause your phone and car to break down."

"You really think it's the whole country?"

"Why haven't we seen the national guard roll in yet? You saw what was happening in the city; people were going nuts."

"You think it's safer in Philly?"

"I guess we'll find out when we get there."

"Stay out of the cities," Mike said.

The two men glanced over at Mike, who was looking at them.

"Your best bet is to head to a town with a small population. Gather whatever supplies you can and get to somewhere remote."

"You think it was one of these EMPs that did all of this?" Steeler's Jersey asked.

"Yeah, I do," Mike replied.

"Is that what you're doing, survivor man? Going to get supplies?" Polo asked.

Then Mike heard it behind him, the low roar of an engine and the stiff shifting of gears. A light-blue Chevy truck rumbled up the emergency lane.

People froze. Mouths dropped, and then arms flew up in the air. People made a sprint toward the car. Their frantic hands hit the side of the car, pounding on the windows, begging for a ride.

"Can you take us to New York?"

"I'm trying to get to Dayton."

"Please, we've been walking for hours."

"I'll pay you, just please let us get in."

The truck crawled to a stop from the blockade of people. Mike could see the young man and elderly couple inside the truck cab. The young man rolled the windows down.

"Hey, get off the truck," the driver called, turning toward the back.

Everyone was jumping in the truck bed, shoving each other out of the way savagely to make room for themselves. The unwanted passengers banged on the roof and sides of the truck demanding that they move forward.

"Get out of there! Now!" the driver said, getting out of the truck cab.

The elderly couple held onto each other, their eyes wide with fear. One of the crowd members tried to climb in the driver's seat when the driver got out, but he shoved him away.

Ulysses sprinted for the truck.

"Dad!" Mike said.

Ulysses had pushed his way through the crowd to the passenger-side door. The truck started to rock back and forth. The driver turned around and saw Ulysses trying to pull the young man's mother out.

"Don't you dare touch her, asshole!" he said.

The young man leaped over the hood of the truck, shoving Ulysses back. The crowd around them had grown to at least sixty people. Mike came up from behind and subdued the driver in a headlock.

"Dad, get them out," Mike shouted.

Mike dragged the young man away from the crowd while Ulysses helped the elderly couple out of the cab. When they were finally clear of the chaos around the truck, Mike let the young man go.

People crammed themselves into the truck. Someone finally jumped behind the wheel and slammed on the gas. The truck hit several people before they were able to get out of the way. It swerved, smashing into cars and the concrete wall along the highway. People in the truck bed were falling out and smacking onto the pavement.

The truck drove farther down the road with more people chasing after it. The young man started after it but stopped when he realized his parents wouldn't be able to keep up. He came back and took a swing at Mike's head, but Mike ducked out of the way.

"What the hell, you piece of shit!" the young man shouted.

"Calm down, boy," Ulysses said.

"Calm down? Our truck is fucking gone!"

"Somebody would have shot you, stabbed you, or hurt your parent to get that truck," Mike said.

"It's okay, Chris," the boy's father said, putting his hand on his son's shoulder, and with that the fight went out of him.

"We made it all this way," Chris said.

"You should have stayed off the highways. That's where most people will turn to when they travel. It's large, familiar, and if other people are traveling, it's possible for them to get a ride," Mike said.

"There were so many people begging us for rides. My parents kept yelling for me to stop, to pick some of them up, but I knew what would happen if I did," Chris said.

"You did the right thing," Mike replied.

As the five of them walked along the road, Mike saw him glance back at his parents, shuffling along the highway next to Ulysses. The boy's father had his arm around his mom while Ulysses chewed their ear off about last night's Pirates game.

"They're not going to make it," Chris said.

"Don't count them out just yet," Mike said.

Mike was speaking about Chris's parents but looking at his dad.

The sun sank lower in the sky the farther they moved west. The orange ball in front of them spread its colors across the sky in pinks, reds, and fading blues. Chris's exit came up, and they parted ways.

"Good luck, Mike," Chris said.

"You too."

Ulysses shook both of Chris's parents' hands. They turned onto the off ramp that would take them to Chris's girlfriend's house. Mike watched the couple grasp each other's hands and follow their son's lead. He wanted them to make it. He wanted them to survive.

Mike and Ulysses were about an hour away from home when they came across the blue Chevy truck turned on its side. Blood and bullet holes riddled the windshield. The mob that had attacked it didn't know why the car was working—they just saw it and panicked—but Mike knew.

The truck that had worked was too old to have any computer chips in it. That's why it ran, but the masses didn't care about that. They just wanted something to work, without understanding why.

Across the dashboard, slumped over the wheel of the truck, Mike recognized the back of the Steelers jersey. Mike kept his eyes forward, and the smoke rising from the wreckage grew smaller behind them.

5

HOME

*T*he sun had completely disappeared from the sky when Mike and Ulysses turned onto 24th Street. Most of the driveways were empty. The windows along the street were dark. There was only one dim light coming from down the street: his house.

Mike felt himself running. His feet lost their pain. His face lost its weariness. His body lost its fatigue. He ran up the driveway, digging into his pockets for the keys, fumbling them in the lock and thrusting the door open.

"Anne? Kalen? Freddy?" Mike shouted.

Mike looked up and saw Anne lean over the railing on the second floor. He watched her face fade from a smile to shock. Her feet thumped against the steps as she rushed down to him.

"Oh my God. Mike, are you all right? What happened?" she asked.

Her hands touched the dried blood on his shirt. She touched gingerly, looking for a wound that wasn't there.

"I'm fine. The blood's not mi—"

Mike stopped. He pictured Garry's lifeless body covered with the white sheet where underneath his green eyes were open, unmoving, frozen.

"It's not mine," he finished

Mike gently leaned his forehead against hers. The candles in the foyer barely lighted the features on her face, but he already knew every line of it with his eyes closed.

"Are you and the kids okay?" Mike asked.

"Yeah, we're fine. The kids are a little restless. Mike, what's going on? Nothing's working. The phones, laptops, cars, everything's dead."

"I know. You didn't try and take the Jeep out, did you?" Mike asked.

"No, why? Would it work?"

"Yes, but let's keep that to ourselves for now, okay?"

"What makes you think it will work?"

"It doesn't have any computer chips in it."

He watched her face process what he said, then saw her hand slowly cover her mouth in realization of what that meant.

"Jesus," she said.

"I hope you've got room for one more," Ulysses said, finally catching up with Mike.

Anne composed herself and hurried over to Ulysses, wrapping her arms around him.

"I'm glad you're okay," Anne said.

Ulysses kissed the top of her head.

"Still breathing. How are you and the kids holding up?" he asked.

"Well, Freddy went over to Sean's house, and Kalen's at Malory's," Anne said.

"Shouldn't Kalen be here? She's grounded," Mike said.

"What's she going to do over there, Mike? Everything she's grounded from doesn't work," Anne replied. "And besides, she was driving me nuts."

"I'm going to change upstairs and then bring the kids home. Will you set up the guest room for Dad?" Mike asked.

"The couch will suit me just fine," Ulysses replied.

"I'll have the spare room ready in no time," Anne said.

* * *

MIKE WALKED down to Sean's house to grab his son. He didn't mind Sean, but his father, Nelson, was a man he could never understand. They just didn't have anything in common.

When Mike rapped his knuckles on the front door, he could hear the shouts of the two boys running around inside the house. Nelson answered and smiled.

"Mike!"

"Hi, Nelson. I've come to collect Frankenstein's monster."

Freddy came running by the front door. His head was hidden inside a cardboard box that had two eyeholes cut out and a wide, toothy mouth drawn across it.

"Dad!"

Freddy rushed toward his father. Mike lifted him up in the air and tilted the box up to see his son's face.

"Hey, buddy."

"Dad, the power went out and then Kalen got really mad because she couldn't look at pictures of James, the boy she likes, and then I told her that she should just stand outside of his window and drool at him there and then she threw her phone at me and Mom yelled at her and then she screamed about how she hated living here and that when she moves to New York the power will never go out, but I don't mind the power being out because I got to be outside all day."

"I'm glad you're making the best of it."

Mike turned to Nelson.

"I appreciate you watching him, Nelson."

"It's no trouble. He's welcome to come over any time, but umm, Mike, before you go," Nelson said, stepping outside the house and closing the door behind him.

Mike stood, still holding Freddy in his arm. He watched Nelson fold his arms across his chest. He was worried.

"Do you know what's going on?" Nelson asked.

"No."

Mike wasn't sure why he lied, or why he answered so quickly, but when the words left him, he felt a pang of guilt in his stomach.

"It's just… I haven't been able to reach Katie on her cell. It's like everything's fried," Nelson replied.

The flashbacks from the mobs in the streets popped into Mike's mind. He remembered the smell of blood and heat from the hospital, the rush of panic spreading through everyone in the city.

"I'm sure she's fine, Nelson."

"I know. I just worry."

Mike knew that Katie was some sort of vice president at a company. It was a large corporation, so he figured she must have had some sort of security detail with her. He thought that would at least give her a chance.

"Well, you guys have a good night," Nelson said.

"You too," Mike said.

"Bye, Sean," Freddy said, waving his arm wildly at his friend through the front window.

"Now, it's time to go and get your sister," Mike said.

"Do we have to?" Freddy asked.

* * *

MIKE'S DAUGHTER seemed less pleased to see him. When Malory's mother, Genie, came to the door and called her name, letting Kalen know that her father was here for her, she trudged downstairs, marched out of the house without looking at him, and walked down the street.

"I hope she didn't break anything while she was here," Mike said.

"Oh, Mike, she's fine. She's just a teenager. No worse than mine," Genie replied.

She bit her lower lip, looking at Mike.

"You know, if you ever need any advice or anything, you can always come over," she said.

Freddy's eyes opened wide. Mike smiled awkwardly.

"Have a good night, Genie," he said.

"You too," she replied.

Mike shook his head, and Freddy mimicked him.

"I think she's crazy, Dad."

"Me too, bud. Me too."

* * *

ULYSSES HAD MADE the best argument he could, but by the time Mike and the kids got back to the house, Anne had already set him up in the spare bedroom downstairs.

"Your daughter was thrilled to see me," Mike said.

"*My* daughter?" Anne asked.

"She's got *you* written all over her."

"If by that you mean she's smart, independent, and beautiful, then yes. Those little gems were mine. The stubbornness, well let's just say I almost had to get violent with your father before he agreed to sleep in the guest room."

Anne kissed his cheek and headed into the living room and plopped on the couch. Mike took Freddy upstairs and tucked him in. On his way back down to the living room, he passed his daughter's room and knocked on the door.

"Yeah?"

Mike opened it up, and his daughter was on the floor flipping through the pages of a magazine.

"Hey," Mike said.

She didn't look up at him.

"Hey," she said.

"Everything all right?"

"I can't use my phone, laptop, car, or listen to music, so no, everything is not all right."

"Kalen, I just wanted to—"

"I'm going to bed, Dad."

She glanced up at him and walked to the door.

"Goodnight," he said.

A burst of air hit Mike as Kalen slammed the door shut. He lingered there for a moment and then headed back downstairs.

Mike lay down across the couch and rested his head in Anne's lap. She ran her hands through his hair and circled the small bald spot on the top of his head.

"Just because it's there doesn't mean you have to point it out," Mike said.

"What? It makes you look tough."

"It makes me look old."

"Hey, if *you're* old, then what does that make me?"

"If the boot fits."

Anne smacked his chest. Mike winced and snatched her hand in his. He ran his fingers along her soft hands, gently rubbing them, and then he brought them to his lips and kissed them.

"What's wrong?" Anne asked.

"It's going to get worse," Mike said.

"Aren't there measures for stuff like this?"

"Not on a scale this large. I don't think there's a single piece of technology left in the country that's still working. If it had a computer chip in it, then it's toast."

"What are we going to do?"

"I'm going to start getting everything ready in the Jeep tomorrow, but we'll stay here as long as we can. We have enough food and water to last us a while, but we won't be able to take all of it with us."

"The cabin?"

"Yeah."

The two of them glanced around the living room. Pictures of holidays, vacations, the kids' sport events, snapshots of the history of their lives, all here in this house. He got up from her lap and put his arm around her. She leaned her head onto his shoulder and they sat there in silence, holding each other while the candles in the room flickered, casting their shadows on the walls around them.

6

THE SECOND DAY

*T*here really wasn't a breeze, but Mike had opened the windows of the house anyway. The heat was intense. Even Freddy, who never complained about anything, was starting to feel it.

"Is the power *ever* going to come back on?" Freddy asked.

Kalen was still on her "not speaking to anyone" strike, unless it was asking when the next time food would be served.

Mike spent most of his morning in the cellar. The walls were lined with shelves of canned goods. He had bags scattered along the floor, half-filled with food.

A tall gray safe sat in the corner. Mike unlocked the door and revealed two twelve-gauge shotguns, a .223 lever-action rifle, a 9mm Smith & Wesson, and a .45 Colt revolver. Boxes of ammo for each lined the sides and bottom of the safe.

He heard a knock from upstairs, and Mike grabbed the 9mm and tucked it behind his shirt. He closed and locked the safe and headed upstairs.

When Mike opened the door, he was greeted with Nelson flashing a neighborly grin.

"Hey, Mike, how are you doing?" he asked.

"I'm fine, Nelson. What can I do for you?"

"Well, since it's been about a day since the power's gone out and we're not sure when it's coming back on, we all thought we'd get the neighborhood together for a grill-out. It was Bessie Beachum's idea.

The food won't last much longer, and she figured it'd be a nice way to get everyone together."

"I don't think that's something we can be a part of today. We've got a lot of chores around the house to do."

"Oh, come on, Mike. We already have the grills going. It'll be fun. Oh, hi, Anne."

Mike felt Anne come up behind him.

"Nelson, how are you?" she asked.

"Well, I'd be better if you could convince Mike to join the barbeque today."

"Barbeque?" she asked.

"Yeah, we're getting the whole neighborhood involved."

"Sounds great. What time?"

"In about an hour."

"I'll bring some patties out of the freezer."

"That'd be great! I'll see you guys in a bit."

Nelson trotted off to the other neighbors, and Mike shut the door. Anne stood there grinning at him.

"It's going to get worse, huh? Armageddon's barbeque. How will we survive?" she asked.

Mike waited until she was out of earshot before he said anything.

"And you think our daughter gets the attitude from me."

* * *

THE TURNOUT for the barbeque was huge. Bessie Beachum had gathered the whole neighborhood and had coordinated anything and everything people could want. Burgers, ribs, hot dogs, beers, liquor, ice cream, popsicles, anything that wasn't going to last in the freezers and fridges was on the menu.

The whole setup was a makeshift combination of picnic tables, lawn chairs, and card tables. Everything was parked at the end of the cul-de-sac.

Ray Gears even had an old record player he brought out. Everyone munched on their hamburgers while listening to the sounds of the Beach Boys.

It almost felt like a normal Saturday during the summer. Mike allowed himself a moment to actually enjoy himself and even managed to get a smile out of his daughter by drawing a smiley face on Freddy's forehead with the tip of his fudge pop.

Nothing felt as if the city behind them was being ravaged with violence and despair. Here they seemed out of its reach, but Mike knew what would eventually come, and the momentary joy he felt slowly disappeared.

The lower the sun sank in the sky, the drunker most of the parents became. With the party winding down, Mike helped organize the cleanup. He was clearing one of the tables when Bessie Beachum started walking toward him.

"Mike, you don't have to do that," Bessie said.

Bessie had her hair done up, fresh makeup caked on her face, and that wide unnaturally forced smile you see people use when they're pissed about something but want to hide it, and Bessie could get mad about anything.

A few years ago, there was a family that moved in down the street. Their kids were in a band together, and they were pretty good. They'd practice every chance they could in their garage, but Bessie managed to get a petition signed banning them from practicing because the "noise pollution" was detrimental to the neighborhood's reputation. The family moved out a month later.

"It's fine, Bessie," Mike answered.

"Well, I appreciate you helping out. I think it was a great turnout, don't you?"

"Yeah, it seems like everyone enjoyed it."

Mike looked up and saw that she was lingering. Her arms were folded, and she was squinting at him.

"Is there something else I can help you with?" Mike asked.

"It's just that, well, I find it odd that *everything* isn't working. I mean, it would be one thing if it were just the power, but our car, phones, laptops; things that aren't plugged in aren't working. Do you happen to know what's going on?"

"Not really."

"I know that you're one of those people who… prepare, so I was just curious to hear your thoughts. You must have *some* idea of what's happening, right?"

Mike changed the subject.

"We should get all of the garbage cans together, centralize the trash. It's going to build up fast."

Bessie flashed another forced smile.

"I'll get Ted to round them up," she said.

Bessie trotted off, her heels clacking against the pavement. With her back to Mike, the plastic smile faded. She found her husband, Ted, cleaning his grill and holding a beer can.

"Mike knows something," Bessie said.

"Knows about what?"

"He knows why nothing's working. I mean they go once a month to that stupid cabin of theirs in Ohio practicing their survival skills. He's hiding something."

"Why wouldn't he tell us if he knew? Maybe he really doesn't know."

Bessie's arms slumped to her sides. She cocked her head to the side and looked at her husband, who was putting some serious elbow grease onto one of the blackened spots on the grill. She snapped her fingers, and he finally looked up.

"Ted!"

"What?"

"Just get the trash cans together and put them in between Nelson's and Mike's house."

* * *

MIKE TOSSED the last bag in the pile of garbage, and then he felt his hand curl and begin to shake. He grimaced and started massaging the inside of his palm. Anne saw him wince and grabbed his wrist.

"Are they acting up again?" she asked.

"Yeah, a little."

When Mike looked up, he saw Kalen talking to the Sturgis boy, James. They both had their hands in their pockets laughing at everything they were saying to each other.

"What's all this about?" he asked, motioning over to Kalen.

"Well, from how much time she spends on his Facebook page, I had an inkling she might like him."

Anne put her hand on Mike's back and then recoiled when she felt the gun tucked in his belt.

"What is that?" she asked.

Before Mike could stop her, Anne lifted his shirt, then gasped and yanked it back down.

"Jesus, Mike. You brought your gun to the barbeque?"

"Keep your voice down. Yes, I did, and I want you to start carrying too."

"Mike... We'll be fine. Now, let's go home before you shoot Kalen's new boyfriend."

"Boyfriend?"

The conversations happening around them stopped, and the only thing you could hear was the Beach Boys' "Little Deuce Coupe" playing in the background. James looked terrified, Kalen looked mortified, and both were flushed red.

"Dad!" Kalen said.

Freddy rolled off the bench of the picnic table he was sitting on, roaring with laughter. Kalen stomped off past Mike and stormed into the house.

Ray Gears, dressed in a Hawaiian shirt, cargo shorts, and white tennis shoes packed up his record player along with the Beach Boys.

"Sorry about that. Mike Love has been known to increase the hormone levels in teenagers. At least that's what it did to me at that age," Ray said.

"Hi, Ray," Anne said.

"Anne. Mike. How are you guys holding up?" Ray asked.

"We're all right. How about you?" Mike asked.

"I'm fine, but I don't think all this was the best idea," Ray said.

"Why?" Anne asked.

"The cars? Cell phones? They're all off. This isn't just a power outage, but you already knew that, didn't you, Mike?" Ray said.

"I know," Mike said.

"People keep saying somebody's coming to fix this, but no one's coming. People are happy now, but come tomorrow things will start to turn. I saw a few people stupid enough to bring some canned goods," Ray said.

"I saw," Mike replied.

"Look, I don't know how much supplies you have, but now might be a good time to start thinking of teaming up."

"We might be getting ahead of ourselves, Ray."

"Is that why you decided to carry your 9mm tonight?"

"I always carry."

"Look, Mike, you know just as well as I do that when people start to get hungry, they're going to turn on each other, and unless you have an escape plan or a castle that can protect you, you're not going to make it out of here alive. But I guess that's what your Jeep's for."

"How do you know my Jeep will run?"

"Because you're a man who carries a gun when he knows when shit's about to hit the fan."

Mike and Anne watched Ray grab the rest of his vinyl and head for the dark shape of his house in the distance.

"What are you thinking?" Anne asked.

"I'm thinking Ray might be the only friend we have left when things turn bad."

7

DAY THREE

*M*ike dipped the pot into the bathtub and filled it halfway. Before he went to bed last night, he filled all of the tubs and sinks in the house, collecting as much of the water left in the pipes as he could. He'd gathered enough water to last them three or four days.

Mike pounded on both of his children's bedroom doors on his way back to the kitchen.

"Wake up! Everybody downstairs. Family meeting time."

Mike lit the gas stove and set the water to boil. Freddy trudged into the kitchen with his hair sticking straight up on one side of his head while the other lay completely flat.

Kalen came in next wearing sweatpants, her makeup from the day before, and her hair pulled in a ponytail.

"Dad, I need to take a shower. I feel disgusting," Kalen said.

"You smell disgusting too," Freddy said.

"Shut up, Freddy!"

"Okay, that's enough, you two," Anne said, entering the kitchen and giving Freddy a slight pat on the bum.

"I drained all of the water in the pipes last night. No more showers for a while," Mike said.

"Yay!" "What?" Freddy and Kalen shouted simultaneously.

"Everybody sit down. We all need to talk about a few things," Mike said.

Kalen folded her arms and dropped into the seat at the opposite end of the table where Mike sat. Anne and Freddy sat on either side of him. Mike reached for Anne's hand and gave it a squeeze.

"Everything we talk about here stays with the family. Understand?" Mike said.

Freddy nodded. Kalen rolled her eyes.

"The power's not coming back on," Mike said.

Freddy and Kalen looked at each other, making sure they heard their father correctly.

"Why?" Freddy asked.

"What we're experiencing isn't a power outage. It's the effects of an EMP burst. Anything that has a microprocessor in it is completely useless," Mike explained.

"The whole country can't be like this," Kalen said.

"I think it is. If it weren't, we would have heard from someone by now," Mike said.

"W-what does that mean?" Freddy asked.

"We're going to be fine," Anne said.

"We're going to stay here as long as we can, but we'll probably need to head to the cabin in a few days," Mike said.

Kalen shot up out of her chair.

"In Ohio?" she asked.

"Yes," Mike said.

"We should leave now," Ulysses said.

Mike hadn't heard him enter the kitchen. His father wiped some grease from his hands with a rag and threw it over his shirt.

"Dad, what are you doing?" Mike asked.

"Changing the oil in your Jeep. Want to make sure it's good to go in case we have to leave in a hurry."

"Why do we have to leave at all? What about James? What about school? My friends? What about my life!" Kalen screamed.

"Kalen, sit down," Anne snapped.

Kalen dropped into her chair.

"Look, we don't know when or how bad this is going to get, but we all need to be ready. From here on out, we always walk in pairs. Freddy. Kalen. You two aren't allowed anywhere without your mom, Grandpa, or me," Mike said.

"Noooo."

This time the cries of both Freddy and Kalen were unanimous.

"No exceptions," Mike said. "We also need to keep what we have to ourselves. I don't want people knowing about the Jeep, or our provisions in the cellar, okay?"

"Why can't we tell anyone, Dad?" Freddy asked.

"Because we can't help—"

Mike cut himself off. He thought back to the young man who was shot, the hospital, and the walk home. All of those moments were sacrifices of his time and energy to help people in need around him. The man looking at him with greasy hands standing in the kitchen taught him that. What was he teaching his own son now?

"We need to make sure we protect our family first. We're a team. All of us," Mike said.

"Yeah, and we'll need all the food we can get with those hollow legs of yours," Ulysses said, coming up behind Freddy and patting his grandson's leg. Freddy giggled.

"First things first," Mike said. "I want everyone to have an emergency bag with anything you'd want to bring with you ready and packed in case we need to get out quickly. Go."

Freddy ran enthusiastically up the stairs. Kalen dragged herself back to her room.

"You too," Mike said to Anne. They kissed, and she walked back to their room.

Mike walked back over to the stove. The pot was boiling now. He added the hot water to a bowl of oatmeal and stirred.

"Michael," Ulysses said.

"Dad, I can't turn our house into the Salvation Army," Mike said.

"You're doing the right thing, son."

Mike dropped the spoon back down into the mush of oats in front of him. He looked up at his father. The face he was staring at wasn't the face of iron he remembered as a child. It was a face of understanding.

"You think so?" Mike asked.

"I do. You have to take care of your own before you take care of someone else. I know sometimes I wasn't the best with feelings, but I was only that way because I knew I didn't have to worry about you. You can take care of yourself. Now, you can take care of your family."

"Thanks, Dad."

8

DAY FOUR

"*D*on't hold out on me, Frank, I know you have some!"

"I'm telling you, Adam, I don't have any."

Mike dropped the saw from the plywood he was cutting when he heard the shouts from the neighbor's house. His tool belt hung from his waist. He pushed the side gate open from the backyard. The shouting became louder the closer he moved to the front yard.

"My whole family is starving, and you've got enough to feed two families for a week!"

"Adam, I'm telling you I don't have as much as you think I do. I'm just trying to keep my family going on what I have."

Mike turned the corner and saw Adam Stahls's red face beaming with anger. Adam's nose was pressed against the screen door that Frank Minks was hiding behind.

"Hey, what's going on?" Mike asked.

Adam marched toward Mike, focusing his rage on a new target.

"This prick is holding out on us, Mike," Adam said.

"Easy, Adam," Mike said.

Mike kept his hand close to the hammer around his belt. Adam paced back and forth in the driveway.

"Where the hell are the relief efforts, huh? Why hasn't everything turned back on? Why the fuck can't I turn my car on and drive to the grocery store!" Adam screamed.

Adam collapsed to his hands and knees on the concrete. A few tears splashed the driveway.

"My boy said he was hungry and I can't… I don't have anything to give him."

Frank came out from behind the screen door. He and Mike knelt down to Adam and helped him up.

"Frank, why don't we go around and get a pool going for anything that can be spared. I bet we could get a little something from everyone," Mike said.

"Yeah, we can do that," Frank replied.

"Adam, you head back home. Frank and I will see what we can put together, okay?" Mike said.

Adam wiped the embarrassment from his eyes and nodded. Mike watched him shuffle back over to his home. Mike noticed faces peering out from behind blinds from the front windows of a few of the houses, checking out the commotion.

Anne came out the front door and joined them.

"What's going on?" she asked.

"Put together some goods for the Stahls," Mike said.

"Anne, wait," Frank said.

He rushed back inside and came out with a few cans of peaches.

"For Adam," Frank said.

* * *

THE SUN DIPPED below the horizon when Mike finally finished cutting the plywood. He started labeling each one: Living room. Kitchen. Bedroom. Each piece had small holes cut close to the corners that would allow them to look outside. He brought them in the house and rested each piece of plywood at its corresponding location.

"What are you doing?" Anne asked.

"For the windows. In case things get bad," he said.

"I gave those supplies to Adam. He broke down when he saw them. I've never seen him like that before."

"Nobody was ready for this."

"You were."

Anne grabbed his arm and pulled him over to her. She rested her face on his chest, and he rested his chin on the top of her head. Her hair was still warm from the sun, and there was still the faint scent of her shampoo, lingering under his nose.

The two of them rocked slowly back and forth. The room

around them was still and quiet. The light breaking through the windows caught the swirls of dust flying around in the room.

"You know... I think I'm going to have to overrule your no shower rule," she said.

Mike pinched her, and she squealed. She threw her head back laughing.

"You smell really bad," she said.

"Better get used to it," he said.

"You're a good man," she said.

A knock from the front door interrupted their kiss. Mike lifted the back of his shirt, revealing the pistol, and checked the peephole. When he saw who it was, he flipped his shirt down and opened the door.

Nelson's eyes went to his feet. His hands fidgeted awkwardly at his sides.

"It's just. Well, I heard about what you did for Adam and I..."

"How much do you need?" Mike asked.

There wasn't any malice in Mike's words, no sense of mockery or "I told you so," just a genuine concern. Nelson kept his head down.

"Just a few days' worth. You know, until all this blows over."

"Is Sean allergic to anything?" Anne asked.

"No, but he doesn't like Brussels sprouts," he answered.

"Who does?" She smiled.

"Come on in," Mike said.

Mike and Nelson sat on the couch while Anne put together a package downstairs. Mike unhooked his tool belt to get a little more comfortable and laid it next to the plywood on the floor.

"Been busy today?" Nelson asked, pointing at the plywood.

"A little," Mike said.

"You know if you're working on any projects around the house, I'd be happy to help. It's the least I could do. I used to be a foreman before I met Katie—"

Nelson's throat caught at the sound of his wife's name.

"Sorry," he said.

"How long were you a foreman?" Mike asked.

"Five years, but I was doing construction since I was eighteen. Never really thought I was the college type, so I got the first job I could after high school and just worked my way up."

"I had no idea."

"Most people don't. I miss it some days, but most days I don't.

Seeing you covered from head to toe in sweat and sawdust doesn't bring back any fond memories."

"Yeah, I'd love to take a shower."

"No water pressure?"

"Not anymore."

"I might be able to help with that."

Mike took him downstairs to the water heater, and they located the water pressure regulator. Nelson took a look at the configuration of pipes, gauges, and valves spread around the basement.

"The water pressure coming into the house from outside is more powerful than most homes need, so contractors use a pressure valve to decrease the water flow coming through the pipes. If I open up the pressure on the house's end, it should squeeze out more pressure for another shower or two."

Nelson opened the valve up, and the pipes hissed and rattled from the water rushing through.

"That should give you a little modern comfort. For a while at least," Nelson said.

"Thanks, Nelson."

Anne met them back upstairs with a bag of canned goods: corn, peaches, green beans, and beef.

"I can't thank you two enough," Nelson said.

"It's our pleasure," Anne said.

Nelson left, and Mike headed upstairs. He knocked on Kalen's door. She cracked it open.

"What?" she asked.

"Oh, nothing. I just wanted to see if you should take the first shower, but if you're busy…"

The door flew open, and she nearly knocked him down on her way to the bathroom.

"Are you serious?" she screamed.

"Hold on. Make sure you have everything ready before you turn it on. And be quick. I'm not sure how long it's going to last."

"Dad, you're amazing."

She ran back over to him and wrapped her arms around him. When she dug her face into his chest, she pulled back.

"And you smell terrible."

"I know, so make it quick, huh? I'd like to take one too."

"You can have my shower time, Dad!" Freddy screamed from his bedroom across the hall.

"Thanks, buddy," Mike called.

DAY FIVE

*A*t least ten families crammed into the living room. Most of them stood, while a few others sat stiffly on couches and chairs. Ted Beachum stood at the front of the living room. He paced back and forth in front of his audience, rubbing his hands together, searching for words.

"I think it's safe to say that the power's not coming back on, and nobody's coming to help. It's time we get organized," Ted said.

Heads nodded in agreement with the exception of one. Ray Gears stood silent in the back corner.

"We need to pull everyone's resources on the block and see who has what to offer. From there we'll divide it up based on the size of each family and their needs," Ted said.

Bessie Beachum, Ted's wife, came up behind him. She placed her hand on his back. She was a woman who was always well-groomed, meticulous about her entire appearance, but the past five days had left stray hairs sticking out and old makeup flaking off her cheeks. The tired bags under her eyes aged her, and the attempt to reapply the blush on her cheeks was the equivalent of trying to hide an ugly picture in a beautiful frame.

"There are some people in this neighborhood that had no idea that this could happen. How were we supposed to prepare for something like this? How were we supposed to know this would happen?" she asked.

"Nobody could have known," a woman cried.

"Exactly. These are circumstances that are beyond our control, so the only way to survive now is by whatever means is necessary," Bessie said.

"And who will decide what means to use on whom?" Ray asked.

Everyone in the room turned to look at Ray, who was leaning against the back wall of the living room with his hands in his pockets.

"The neighborhood will," Bessie replied.

"The neighborhood?" Ray asked.

"It's the only way we'll survive this, Ray," Ted said.

Ray rocked his chin in his hand, mulling the response over.

"Well, if it's the neighborhood that's deciding, I think we're missing a few members, aren't we?" Ray asked.

Most of the neighbors' faces wore looks of surprise and innocent ignorance, but out of all the faces Ray watched, Bessie's was the one that frightened him most.

"We extended the invitation for everyone to come. I can't force everyone to be a part of this," Bessie said.

"You can't force people to be a part of your community of help and survival, but you can force people to give you the supplies to keep it going?" Ray asked.

The heads in the room were swiveling back and forth from Ray to Bessie. Even Ted's face went back and forth. They were all searching for some unnamed enemy to point their fingers at, but the real enemy was their own ignorance. And they knew it.

"I'm sure that those who see someone in need will be more than willing to participate if they're able to," Bessie replied.

"Just like any good Samaritan would," Ray said.

"Now, why don't we start with everyone that's already here?" Ted asked. "Bessie and I will head over to everyone's house for an inventory check and see what we have, and then divide it up amongst ourselves. Then we can spread out to the other houses and see if they want to join in. Tim, we'll start with your place."

The crowd dispersed and headed back to their homes. Ray was the only one that didn't go home. His feet took him to Mike's house.

* * *

MIKE SMACKED the last nail in place for the upstairs bedroom window. He brushed some of the plaster off the bed that had fallen from the wall and stood back to examine his work. He worried that the nails wouldn't be strong enough to hold the plywood in place covering the windows if someone wanted to force their way in, but he did the best he could. At the very least it would give him and his family time to escape.

He gathered up his nails when he heard muffled voices coming from downstairs. When Mike walked over to the stairs, he saw Ray and Anne in the foyer below.

"It happened today? Bessie told me that it was tomorrow," Anne said.

"Mike, we need to talk," Ray said.

The three of them sat in the living room and were joined by Ulysses. Ray recounted what had happened at the meeting with the Beachums.

"So, what? They're going to try and steal our supplies if we don't hand them over?" Anne asked.

"Everyone's starting to feel the pressure. There were at least ten families at that meeting," Ray said.

"They're being driven by fear. Ray's right; it won't be long before they start stealing instead of asking," Ulysses said.

With the windows sealed shut, they had lit candles to help illuminate the house. Mike looked at shadows being cast across half-visible faces. *Men can't survive in the dark.*

"We leave tomorrow," Mike said.

"You got room for one more in that Jeep?" Ray asked.

"What if we don't?" Ulysses asked.

"Relax, Ulysses. I just need to know if I should wait around or not," Ray said.

Mike mulled it over. Ray had known about his Jeep and, to his knowledge, hadn't told anyone else about it.

"Pack all of the food you can. Do you have a gun?" Mike asked.

"Yeah."

"Bring it and all the ammo you have."

After Ray had left, Anne ran upstairs to gather the kids. Ulysses walked over to Mike.

"You trust that guy?" Ulysses asked.

"I'll find out soon enough," Mike said.

Mike made five trips from the cellar to the Jeep in the garage. He threw packs of food, ammo, and first aid kits in the back of the Jeep. He strapped everything down with a few cargo belts, checking to make sure it was secure.

He heard shouts coming from upstairs. Mike made it to the

second floor, and Anne was standing outside Kalen's door with both her hands on her hips.

"Kalen Grace Grant, you open this door right now!" Anne said.

"What's going on?" Mike asked.

"She's locked herself in her room, because she doesn't want to leave."

"Let me talk to her. You make sure Freddy's good to go," Mike said.

Anne threw her hands up and walked into Freddy's room. Mike knocked on the door.

"Kalen, open up," Mike said.

"No! I'm not leaving."

"C'mon, Kay, open the door. You owe me that much for the shower."

There was a pause and then the sound of footsteps and the door unlocking.

When Mike entered, Kalen had her legs crossed, sitting on top of her bed and scratching the paint from her nails.

"I'm not going," she said.

"Well, Freddy will be devastated."

Mike ignored the eye roll and focused on the smile instead. He sat down beside her, putting his hand on her leg.

"What's going on?" Mike asked.

"It's just not fair, Dad! Why did this have to happen now? Why couldn't this have happened after I was dead, or at least after college? What am I supposed to do now? What am I going to do with my life? What has the past three years of high school meant if it doesn't exist anymore? James was just starting to like me."

Mike cringed at the sound of James's name, so he was glad she wasn't looking at him. He didn't think it would help the situation.

"Kalen, we can't control everything that happens to us. The best we can do is prepare and hope for the best."

Her shoulders began to shake. Mike walked up behind her, and she spun around into his arms, her tears soaking through his shirt.

"I'm scared, Dad."

"We'll be fine. I promise."

10

THE NIGHT OF THE FIFTH DAY

*T*welve families brought all of the canned goods and water they could find. The measly collection of their combined efforts lay scattered across the floor of the Beachums' living room. It was enough to feed each family for another day. After that they would have nothing.

"This is everything?" Ted asked.

"That's all we had," Rusty said.

"We were down to our last can," Sam replied.

"We brought more than everyone else. I just want to point that out," Brian said.

The families were restless. Everyone's eyes drifted from the food and supplies in the middle of the room to the faces circling it. Family members whispered in each other's ears.

"I bet Frank has more than what he brought."

"There's no way they only had one can."

"Just because they're fat asses and don't know how to ration, we've got to give them our food?"

Bessie checked each house she visited from top to bottom. She spent all afternoon going door to door, scouring every cabinet, cupboard, cellar, attic, and shed to find what she could.

"I think it's safe to say that everyone here contributed as much as they could," Bessie said.

Everyone stopped talking and looked at Bessie.

"However, it does seem that a few of our neighbors are in a better situation than we are and aren't matching our… generosity," she said.

Bessie made her way over to Adam. He kept his head down and avoided looking at her the entire night. She knew that Mike had given Adam supplies.

"Adam," she said.

Adam kept his face down. His feet shuffled awkwardly in place. He fiddled with his hands, pulling at his fingers. Bessie walked slowly to him, showing motherly concern.

"Don't you think that Mike and his family should help the rest of us like they helped you?" Bessie asked.

"I... I don't know," Adam answered.

"But you're the one who told us they gave you that basket of food. Are you saying that's all they have?"

"I didn't see how much they had. They just gave it to me."

"Well, then. That settles it. If they're able to hand out food like that on a whim, then they should have enough for all of us. Now, we'll divide up what we have here, and then everyone should head home. We'll start fresh in the morning," Bessie said.

The families lined up, and everything was rationed equally. People either received fewer goods than what they brought, or more than they were able to offer.

Bessie pulled Adam aside from the line. She brought him into the kitchen. Ted followed.

Bessie sat him down at the kitchen table and joined him. Ted stood by the stove, watching both of them.

"Adam, I appreciate what you told me about the Grants. It was very helpful, but I was curious to know if they had anything else. Did they have any other provisions, any modes of transportation, any...weapons?" Bessie asked.

"I told you I never went inside. They brought everything to me."

"Well, it's well-known that Mike has always been one to prepare for these types of things."

"If he hadn't given me that food, my boy would still be hungry."

"Adam, if Mike really cared about making sure your boy was okay, why didn't he come today? Wouldn't he have tried everything he could to make sure your boy didn't go hungry again?"

"Yeah. Yeah, you're right. He should have been here tonight," Adam said.

Bessie watched his hands curl into fists and then pound on the kitchen table, knocking the saltshaker to its side.

"Why the hell didn't he come?" Adam said.

"Do you still have your brother's guns and ammo?" she asked.

* * *

MIKE LOADED the 12-gauge shells into the shotgun. He checked the safety and put it in the large duffle bag he pulled from storage. Voices coming from upstairs made him freeze; he was holding a handful of 9mm shells. He threw on his holster and shoved the pistol inside.

The stairs creaked with each step up from the basement. When Mike made it to the top, he could hear two voices in the foyer.

"Anne, it's so wonderful to see you. You seem to be holding up well."

"Thank you, Bessie. Is there something I can help you with?"

"Well, I was hoping to—oh, hello, Mike."

Mike watched her eyes fall to the pistol at his side. Her fake astonishment didn't have the effect she intended.

"Do you really think it's necessary to carry a gun around like that? I mean, really, Anne, what if Freddy got a hold of one," Bessie asked.

"What do you want, Bessie?" Mike asked.

"I'm sure you know a few of the families in the neighborhood are in a bad spot with what's been happening. Some of us have decided to pool our resources for the benefit of the neighborhood. I wanted to see if you and Anne would like to join us."

"Who needs help?" Anne asked.

"Well, everyone really, but there are some folks worse off than others… and a few that are better off than most."

Mike saw her eyes land on the open basement door that Mike had left. They were only there for a moment, but Mike saw her notice it.

"I'll run downstairs and see what I can put together," Anne said.

"Oh, let me help you."

"No, it's all right. I'll only be a minute."

Anne slid behind Mike and left him alone with Bessie.

"It's very kind of you to help the way you have, Mike. Not everyone is as fortunate as you are," Bessie said.

Mike followed her to the edge of the living room. She leaned in without moving her feet from the hardwood floor of the foyer to the brown carpet of the living room.

"Redecorating?" she asked, motioning to the plywood over the windows.

"Just making sure the things that belong outside stay outside," Mike said.

Bessie backed closer to the front door when Anne returned from downstairs with a bag of goods, almost spilling over at the top.

"Oh, Anne, this is too much," Bessie said.

"No, take it. I hope it helps with what you're trying to do," Anne said.

"It surely will."

Bessie clutched the bag to her chest with both hands. Her shoes clacked against the pavement as she walked back to her home. The moon highlighted her hair along with the slight outline of her downturned mouth, furrowed brow, and creases in her forehead. She entered through her back door into the kitchen and dumped the cans from the bag, sending them clanking and rolling onto the countertops.

Tim and Adam sat at the kitchen table. Both were emptying boxes of bullets and filling magazines. Both of them froze at the sight of the goods spilling onto the counter.

"They have all that?" Adam asked.

"That's a fraction of what they have. They're holding out on us, and they're boarding up their house so no one can get in. They're creating a fortress over there," Bessie said.

Adam shoved one of the loaded magazines into his pistol. The click brought a smile to Bessie's face.

"We hit them in the morning," Bessie said.

11

DAY SIX

*M*ike rolled out of bed. The room was pitch-black. He stumbled to the bathroom, tripping over one of Anne's shoes again. His hands ran along the dresser until they wrapped around the pocket watch that his grandfather had given him. It was the only thing that still kept time in the house.

He lit a candle in the bathroom and held the clock face up to the light. Six a.m. The watch snapped shut, and he scooped some of the water in the sink into his hands, splashing it on his face. He walked back out to the bedroom, candle in hand, and let the glow fill the room.

The light hit Anne curled up under the sheets. Mike stood there staring at his wife, just like he had done for the past twenty-six years, every day, before he left for work.

The second-story floorboards creaked under Mike's steps. He tiptoed to Freddy's room and cracked the door open. His son lay still, quiet on his bed with all of the covers thrown off and his shirt up, exposing his belly. Freddy had his mouth open, and all of his limbs were extended outwards like a starfish.

When he opened the door to his daughter's room, she looked just like her mother. Curled up under the covers. The sheets rising and falling from her calm, steady breath.

He stood in the center of the hallway among the three rooms. This could be the last time he watched them sleep in this house.

Pictures hung on all the walls around him. The memories came flooding back to him. The vacation to the Grand Canyon they took three summers ago. The Christmas mornings, Thanksgiving feasts, birthdays, anniversaries, all on display.

The tear he wiped from his cheeks wasn't one of sadness for having to leave, nor fear of what was ahead. It simply represented all of the joy he felt during those moments frozen in time along the walls, and the gratefulness he felt for still being able to remember them.

Mike stepped down into the cellar to grab the guns and ammo and check for any last items he may have missed. He had the duffle bag strap on his shoulder, walked back up the stairs, and headed for the garage.

* * *

"Don't you all want to keep your family alive?" Bessie asked.

Shouts and cheers filled Bessie's living room. Fifteen families crowded together. Bessie stood on top of her coffee table in the center of the group, Tim standing by her side.

"We tried to come together in a civilized manner, didn't we?"

Hands clenched into fists while others wrapped tightly around baseball bats, crowbars, tire irons, pistols, and rifles.

"Most of us answered that call, and for that my family, and every other family here, thanks you."

All of the animosity they had for each other the night before had transformed to a single point of hate. A universal cry of fear and hunger rose from the crowd.

"But one family did not answer that call. One family chose to keep what they had to themselves. One family is letting you starve."

She fed them hate.

"Your family can't survive without the food they have. We don't know when help is coming. Help may never come, so we have to help ourselves."

She fed them fear.

"But you can do something about it. You can make sure your family survives. You can make sure that they all have something to eat!"

She fed them the answers they wanted to hear.

Bessie threw her hands out, calming the crowd. The cheers slowly dissipated. She stepped down from the coffee table. Tim handed her the bullhorn, and she marched everyone out the front door.

* * *

MIKE FIRST HEARD the squeal of the bullhorn from inside the garage. He rushed to the front door; looking through the peephole, he saw twenty people standing out front in the morning light. Bats, crowbars, tire irons, and rifles were poised at the ready.

"Mike, we don't want to harm anyone. All we want you to do is the right thing. We know you have supplies, and there are people out here who need them," Bessie said.

Anne, Freddy, and Kalen rushed from their rooms and were leaning on the banister rail above Mike, listening to the words echo outside.

"Dad?" Kalen asked.

"Stay there," Mike said.

Ulysses came out of the guest bedroom fully dressed in a long-sleeve shirt, jeans, and boots. He grabbed the duffle bag off Mike's back and set it on the floor. He pulled out the .223 rifle. The clang of metal on metal rang through the foyer when he shoved a clip in.

"How many?" Ulysses asked.

Mike clicked the safety off the shotgun.

"Around twenty, but there could be more around the house."

Mike picked up a box of shells and slid them across the floor over to the base of the kitchen window.

"Anne, bring the kids downstairs." Mike said.

Anne grabbed both of their children's hands, pulling them down the steps. Freddy clung to Anne's leg all the way down.

"Dad, you take Freddy and Kalen to the Jeep. Get it ready. The moment we get a bad breach, I'm going to set the house on fire."

"What?" Anne asked.

"It will send them running and give us enough space to get away," Mike said.

Freddy started crying hysterically now.

"Shh, it's okay, buddy. Hey, you're gonna be fine," Mike said. "We're all going to be fine."

"C'mon, kids," Ulysses said.

Kalen grabbed her brother's hand and followed Ulysses into the garage.

Mike handed Anne the other shotgun and tossed her a few shells. She fumbled the first one to the ground after attempting to load it in the chamber.

"Shit," she said.

Mike picked it up and placed it back into her hand. When she went to take it, he held her hand in his and squeezed. He locked eyes with his wife. There was no fear in them. Only the stubborn will to survive.

"Take the kitchen window," Mike said.

Anne clicked her safety off and crawled over to the opening in the plywood at the corner of the window. Mike kept his head low heading for the living room. Bessie's voice boomed outside.

"We don't want any bloodshed, Mike. Your family will still get their fair share of food. Don't make this harder than it has to be," she said.

Mike put his eye up against the corner hole of the plywood, looking outside. He watched Bessie motion to a few of the people on the edges of the group. They scurried over to the sides of the house. Only one of them had a gun.

Mike hunched low as he moved to Anne, who was looking out her corner of the kitchen window through the hole in the plywood.

"A few broke off and went to the sides of the house. I'm going to head to the back."

He leaned in and kissed her. The moment had his adrenaline pumping. He felt like he could smash through the walls if he needed to, but even with all of that, his lips still hit hers with tenderness.

"I love you," Anne said.

"I love you, too."

At the back of the house, Mike peered through one of the plywood holes giving him a view of his backyard. He saw the barrel of a gun peek around the back corner of the house. The hand and arm came next, followed by the face.

Adam Stahl.

* * *

NELSON CAME RUNNING out of his house, his slippers nearly flying off his feet and his robe flapping in the wind.

"Bessie? What's… What's going on?" he asked.

"Nelson, go home. This will be over soon," she said.

"But, what are you doing? Where's Mike? Mike!"

"Quiet!"

"Mike! Are you okay?"

Bessie pulled a revolver from her side and shoved the barrel into

Nelson's face. Nelson threw his hands in the air and slowly backed away from her.

"Go home, Nelson. Now," she said.

Nelson ran back to his house. Bessie pulled the bullhorn back to her mouth.

"You have sixty seconds, Mike. If you don't come out by then, we're coming in."

A gunshot rang out. People ducked for cover, hiding behind cars, mailboxes, bushes, anything close that they could jump behind.

The bullhorn and pistol that Bessie held dropped to the ground, followed by her knees, and then her chest and face hit the grass of the front yard.

"Bessie?" Tim asked.

Tim rushed to his wife. Her mouth was spilling blood. She coughed and hacked, spitting it all over his shirt. She grabbed Tim's shirt desperately, wrenching his collar.

A few final coughs of blood and her hand slowly let go. Tim snatched it up before it fell to the ground.

Tim rocked her back and forth. He brought her lifeless body up to his chest. Both of their bodies shook, but he was the source of the shaking. He laid her gently back down and kissed her forehead. He looked up at the house. His face distorted from grief and pain to anger. He picked the revolver up from the ground and cocked the hammer back. The shrill screams of his voice were silenced by unloading the entire .45 revolver into Mike's front door.

* * *

WHEN THE FIRST gunshot went off, Mike watched Adam duck for cover. He took the opportunity to run back to the front of the house.

Anne had her shotgun through the plywood's hole and blasted through the glass. She pumped the shotgun, sending an empty shell flying to the floor, and squeezed the trigger again, the recoil from the blast knocking her shoulder into the chair behind her.

"You all right?" Mike asked.

"Somebody shot Bessie," Anne answered.

"What?"

Anne scooted out of the way to let Mike get a look outside. He could see Bessie's lifeless body sprawled across the lawn.

A few bullets came splintering through the plywood and into the kitchen. Mike threw his body over Anne's until the firing stopped, then aimed his shotgun through the window and squeezed the trigger, sending a dozen steel balls through James Sturgis's chest.

Mike pumped the shotgun and reloaded the chamber. He scanned the yard. He saw a few people hunched behind a car on the side of the street. He saw the pistols in their hands. He took aim and fired.

The blast from the shotgun shell shattered the car's windows and peppered the metal on the side doors.

"Anne! Get to the Jeep, now!" Mike screamed.

Anne nodded and ran, keeping herself low, through the kitchen into the garage. The front door thumped loud, and Mike could hear the wood starting to crack.

* * *

RAY WATCHED the crowd around Mike's house scatter with the exception of a few after he sent the bullet into Bessie's back. He sat hunched behind a car on the other side of the street behind everyone. He re-racked the bolt-action rifle, watching Tim make a beeline for Mike's front door.

RAY ADJUSTED the pack on his back and headed up the street, keeping low and out of sight behind the cars parked on the curb.

* * *

"GRANDPA!" Freddy screamed.

"JUST STAY DOWN!" Ulysses said.

THE GUNSHOTS outside echoed loud from inside the garage. When Anne rushed inside, she saw Freddy covering his ears and Kalen holding him tight.

"WHERE'S MIKE?" Ulysses said.

\. \. \.

"HE'S COMING."

* * *

MIKE SPLASHED the gasoline all over the basement. He poured it on the walls, the floor, the couches, shelves, everywhere. He threw the can in the center of the room and backed up all the way to the stairs. He pulled a match from his pocket.

The head of the match scratched across the box and ignited into a tiny, yellow flame. Mike tossed it on the ground and watched the fire spread in a red glow around the basement.

He rushed up the basement stairs and down the hallway to the kitchen, where the garage entrance was. Smoke rose from the basement, chasing him. He turned the corner into the kitchen when the front door finally gave way and Tim burst inside.

Before Mike could get a shot off, Tim threw his pistol at him, sending the gun ricocheting off Mike's shotgun. It gave Tim just enough time to fly into Mike, slamming him into the wall.

Tim sent his fists into Mike's ribs. Mike doubled over with each vicious blow.

Mike grabbed the butt of the shotgun and smacked it into Tim's head, relinquishing the assault on himself. Mike's fist landed against Tim's jaw. Tim countered with a left cross. Mike blocked it. Tim grabbed Mike's head with both hands and then head butted him. Blood spurted from Mike's nose, and he fell to his knees.

Tim came up behind Mike and put him in a headlock. Tim's arm muscles rippled as he squeezed Mike's neck, chocking the life out of him.

Mike stretched out his arms, trying to free himself, gasping for breath. The smoke from the basement was getting heavy now. The flames had crawled their way into the halls and were marching down toward the front of the house where the two men were.

"You kill my wife and think you can get away with it?" Tim asked.

* * *

THE SMOKE HAD FILTERED into the garage. Ulysses looked at Anne and then reached for the keys in the ignition. Anne's hand jolted forward to stop him.

"Wait!"

"Anne, we have to go now."

She looked at Freddy and Kalen in the back seat, both of whom were coughing from the smoke filling the garage. She let go of Ulysses's hand, and he started the engine.

Ulysses pumped the gas pedal a few times before the engine roared to life. Anne reached up to pull the cord above them that sent the garage door flying open, and Ulysses slammed on the gas.

The Jeep tore out of the driveway and into the street. The crowds around the house had scattered, and Anne looked behind her watching the smoke rising from all of the windows of the house into the early-morning sky.

They were almost to the end of the street when Ray popped out from behind one of the parked cars. He held both hands in the air, one clutching a rifle in his right hand.

Ulysses slammed on the brakes, coming inches from hitting him.

"Thought I'd offer my services," Ray said, running to the side of the Jeep.

Ulysses shook his head at Anne, but she unlocked the door and he climbed in the back seat with the kids. Ulysses jammed the shifter back into first, hit the clutch, and took off down the road.

* * *

MIKE GASPED FOR BREATH. He squirmed, thrashed, and elbowed Tim in the ribs, but nothing would loosen his grip.

THE WORLD around him was beginning to fade. He could feel the heat from the flames burning his flesh. He caught a glimpse of a picture of his family through the flames, the fire swallowing them up and crumpling the photo into ash and smoke.

THE POP that he heard sounded distant and faint when Mike's head hit the floor. The blackness started to clear a little. He felt a hand on the back of his shirt pulling him backwards. He could see the damage of the fire more clearly than before. The fire danced along the walls. The floor above the stairs collapsed, sending a flurry of sparks into the air. Then he saw blood dripping from the side of Tim's head and watched his body catch fire.

NIGHT OF DAY 6

*T*he heat was the first thing Mike felt. He was sweating profusely. He threw the covers off him and caught a glimpse of the bandage on his arm. He jerked his head up to get a better look but fell back down on the pillow. He placed his fingers gently onto his temple and felt the bandage wrapped around his head.

"Thank God. You're awake."

Nelson came in and set a tray down on the nightstand next to the bed. Mike watched him examine the bandages.

"Looks like they're in need of a fresh wrap," Nelson said.

"W-what? Where's Anne? Where are Freddy and Kalen? Where's my—"

Nelson pushed him back down when Mike started to rise. Mike tried to resist but was too weak.

"You need to rest. I was barely able to pull you out of the fire," Nelson replied. "Here, drink some of this."

Nelson tilted a glass to Mike's lips, and he drank thirstily. The water spilled, hitting his chin and rolling onto his chest. Nelson pulled the glass back and rested it on the table.

"What happened?" Mike said.

"When I heard the gunshots, I took Sean down to the cellar. When I saw the smoke coming from your house, I ran over. By the time I got over there, the whole place was on fire. The front door was knocked down, and I could see you and Tim on the floor. At first I thought the two of you were both unconscious, but then I saw

Tim choking you. There was a pistol on the ground, and I picked it up. When I got to the door I—"

His throat caught.

"I killed Tim and dragged you out of there," Nelson finished.

Mike watched Nelson close his eyes and take a few breaths before he looked at him again.

"Did you see my family get out?" Mike asked.

"No, but I heard a few people talk about it today. Most everybody left after what happened, but a few stuck around. I think a lot of people were afraid the fire would spread to the other houses, but it just collapsed on itself."

Nelson saw the stab of pain shoot through Mike's face.

"Sorry."

But Mike wasn't thinking about the house. He forced himself upright and swung his legs to the side of the bed.

"I have to get to Ohio," Mike said.

"Whoa, no, you need to rest. I think you have a concussion."

"Tim didn't hit me that hard."

Mike rose to his feet and then immediately fell back down on the bed. He felt dizzy. He clutched the sheets into a ball-sized fist on the bed, trying to anchor himself down.

"Look, whatever it is you want to do, there's no way you'll survive the trip in your current state. You need to rest, at least for tonight."

Mike eyed the tray on the nightstand. There was fresh gauze and an unopened can of peaches. It was one of the same cans Mike had given him a few days ago. He picked it up and rolled it in his hands.

"Hey, I'm just repaying a favor," Nelson said.

* * *

WHEN MIKE WALKED out in the afternoon heat the next day and took a look at the smoldering wreckage of his house, he wasn't sure what to expect. The roof and second floor had completely disintegrated. Only pieces of the couch, kitchen, and garage remained intact.

He sifted through some of the ashes, looking for anything that was salvageable. He looked for any food, tools, or ammo left behind that would still be useful, but had no luck. The one thing he really wanted to find though was a picture. He had hoped at least one of them survived. They hadn't.

"Find anything?" Nelson asked upon his return.

"No, but we need to get moving. It'll take us three days to make it to the cabin."

"We?"

"There's nothing left here, Nelson. If you and Sean stay, you'll starve to death, or be killed by the next gang of raiders that comes through here."

"You think we can make it?"

Mike closed his eyes and thought of the last glimpse of his wife. He could feel her lips on his and the whisper of "I love you." He saw his children lying in their beds, sleeping with the morning light cascading into their rooms.

"We'll make it."

13

DAY 7 (KATIE)

The smell in the room was unbearable. The number of people in the relief center, combined with no showers, no A/C, and the summer heat beating down on the building made the air thick with human stench.

Katie's hands were dried with dirt and grime. The white paint on her fingernails flaked off in chips. The only jewelry still on her was the wedding band around her left finger. The diamond ring was stolen, but she managed to keep the gold band.

Katie watched the bodies shuffle in between the cots spread out on the floor. The dark circles forming from the sleepless nights weighed heavy under her eyes. All she could think about was her family. She had no way of contacting them, no way of knowing if they were all right, no way of telling them that she was alive.

It had been almost two days without a fight breaking out, but people were getting edgy again. She knew it was just a matter of time before the fuse ran out. The food rations had decreased dramatically, along with access to the water tanks.

Guards armed with automatic rifles kept watch on them. They patrolled the border of the room, and two were stationed at the food and water counter.

An elderly man with hunched shoulders and liver spots dotting the top of his bald head approached the guards barricading the food rations. He looked two steps from death. He pointed toward the counter, his finger trembling in the air.

"Sir, dinner rations will be served at six p.m. We will notify the group when it's time to approach. Please return to your space."

The old man didn't walk back. He inched a few steps forward, still pointing at the counter behind the guards. Each of the guards was a good foot taller and one hundred pounds heavier than the old man.

The same guard that spoke to him let out a sigh. Keeping his rifle in one hand, he grabbed the old man with the other and walked him across the room. Everyone stared at them. The guard wasn't forceful, and the old man didn't resist, but the sight made everyone feel uncomfortable, some more than others.

"Hey, dick, just give him something to eat."

The comment came from a young man in his twenties. His shirt was stained with sweat rings. His hair was untamed, and his face was smudged with a week's worth of dirt.

The guard ignored him. He continued escorting the old man across the room.

"He's hungry!" the young man said.

The guard released his grip on the old man and brought both hands to his rifle. He brought the gun to his shoulder, aiming the barrel at the young man's head.

"We're all hungry, and all of us will eat, but not until six p.m. Understand?" the guard asked.

The young man didn't back down. A few others gathered around him. The other guards converged on them, their rifles aimed and ready to shoot.

Katie gripped the edge of her cot. Her knuckles turned white against the faded blue padding clutched in her hands.

Katie slowly rose from her cot and backed away from the center of the room. She inched her way to the back wall. A few people followed her lead, but most of the room gathered in the center, either out of defiance or wanting to see what would happen.

"Everyone disperse and return to your beds," the guard said.

"You think you have the right to tell us what to do?" the young man said.

"I'm warning you."

Katie's back bumped against the wall. She felt herself trying to push her way through the concrete. Her heart beat faster. She wanted to leave. She had to get out.

The crowd around the young man grew, and with it the young

man's boldness. He stepped closer to the guard. The rifle still aimed at his head.

"You're warning me?" the young man said.

"Stand down."

"You gonna shoot us?"

"Stay where you are and stand down!"

Katie jumped as a hand wrapped around her wrist.

"Mrs. Miller, we need to leave," Sam said.

Sam's jacket was off, exposing his shoulder holster, his pistol sitting in it. The top button to his collar was undone, and his tie hung loosely around his neck. Sweat collected on his forehead.

The young man continued to move toward the guard. Each step was slow, deliberate, testing the waters before moving forward.

"You have enough bullets for all of us?" the young man asked.

The young man reached his hand into his pocket slowly.

"Put your hands up!" the guard ordered.

Katie felt Sam pulling her along the edge of the wall. She could tell that he was heading for the door. Her eyes kept glancing to the center of the room.

The young man's hand lingered in his pocket. The crowd around him had grown to fifty-plus people. All six guards' fingers itched over their rifle's triggers.

The moment the young man jerked his hand out of his pocket, the guards open fired. A spray of bullets sent him hurtling backwards to the floor. Everyone outside the circle of guards ducked to the ground, while everyone inside the circle sprinted toward the closest guard to them.

The gunshots echoed through the room. The massive flood of people rushing to grab the guards' guns, or raid the food and water, sent the room into a frenzy.

Katie's arm almost pulled out of her socket once Sam started running. The two sprinted out the door with screams and gunfire exploding behind them.

The two of them ran through the herd of people fleeing the relief center. Outside, people scattered everywhere. They put as much distance between themselves and the Red Cross relief center as they could.

The streets of downtown Pittsburgh were dead. Abandoned cars filled the streets. Broken windows lined the storefronts, their shelves completely looted. Trash littered the sidewalk and overflowed.

After running a few blocks, Katie ripped her arm from Sam and stopped. She bent over, trying to catch her breath. She hadn't eaten anything since yesterday and was severely dehydrated. Bits of white crust formed at the corners of her mouth.

"Wait… Sam… I need… a break."

Sam pulled a half-full bottle of water from his pant pocket. He held it out to her. The water was warm, but she gulped it down. She let a mouthful linger for a moment, letting the water splash around her arid mouth. She handed the bottle back to Sam, who screwed the cap back on and returned the bottle to his pocket.

"How'd you get your gun back?" Katie asked.

"All of the guards disappeared except for the ones in the food hall. I rummaged through the weapons they confiscated and found my sidearm. I figured it was just a matter of time before the other guards took off or the place became overrun."

"What do we do now?"

"We need to keep moving."

"And go where, Sam? That place was supposed to be safe. Those people were supposed to help us!"

She threw her hands up in exhaustion, pointing at her surroundings.

"There isn't anything left, Sam."

Katie leaned against the vehicle behind her. Her purple blouse was torn and dirty, her pinstriped pants stained with the three-day-old blood she wiped from her hands.

"I'll get you back to your family, Mrs. Miller. I promise," Sam said.

14

DAY 7 (MIKE)

A trail of boot prints lay behind Mike. He stopped to kneel in the burnt wreckage of his home. He dug his hands into the gray ash and let it sift through his fingers. The particles formed tiny mounds under his hands, like an hourglass running out of time.

The roof sagged. The stairs leading to the second floor were charred and splintered, stained in shades of black. Pictures were burnt. His son's toys ruined from the heat. His daughter's clothes destroyed. The house was dead.

Tears hit the dusty floor, turning the gray ash into black. Mike wiped his eyes, causing a smudge to smear across his cheek. He retraced his steps the way he came, afraid of disturbing the burnt shrine that was his home.

The rest of the neighborhood wasn't in much better shape. Smashed windows and broken doors lined the street. Bullet holes peppered the fronts of homes. A breeze blew trash littered on the ground, piling it in different spots.

Mike glanced at the Beachums' house and the two crude grave markers set up in the front yard. He thought about leaving Bessie's body where she fell, but when he saw the cold, stiff corpse across the lawn, he couldn't bring himself to do it. No matter what she'd done, she wasn't always bad, just at the end. He buried her in the front yard, along with her husband's scorched body.

Mike pawed the bandage on his arm as he walked back to Nelson's house. He could still feel the heat from the fire burning through. He looked at the once well-kept lawns and houses now in shambles. The neighborhood he came home to from the steel mill for the past twenty-five years lost to despair and betrayal.

"What happened to us?" Mike asked.

The question was quiet, meant only for him, in the graveyard of 24th Street. It had only been a week since the EMP blast. Everything from simple modern conveniences like phones, laptops, and tablets to life-sustaining utilities like water and power were gone. They were back in the Stone Age.

The front door to Nelson's house was open. Nelson's home remained fairly unscathed after the neighborhood turned on Mike and his family. If it weren't for Nelson, he would have burned along with his house.

Two backpacks sat next to the front door when Mike entered. They'd gathered what they could from the abandoned houses. There wasn't much left, but they had enough to make it to Mike's cabin in Ohio.

The pounding upstairs grabbed Mike's attention. He walked up the stairs, looking at the family portraits on the wall: first days of school, vacations, holidays. The last picture Mike saw before watching Nelson bang his fist on his son's door was a family portrait of Nelson, Sean, and Katie, who never made it back from downtown Pittsburgh the day of the blast.

"Sean, we have to go," Nelson said.

Nelson jiggled the handle.

"Sean, open this door."

"No!" Sean said.

"We talked about this, Sean," Nelson said.

"We can't leave without her," Sean said.

Mike noticed the dark circles under Nelson's eyes, the stubble thickening to a beard on his face. It took Mike all of last night to convince Nelson they had to leave. There wasn't anything left for them here, and if he wanted him and Sean to survive, they had to leave.

Nelson pressed his left palm to the door, the contrast of the gold band around his finger against the blue paint.

"Mom would want us to go."

The door flung open. Tears ran down Sean's cheeks. The room behind him was messy. There were toys on the hardwood floors, his bed unmade, and piles of dirty clothes.

"She wouldn't want us to go. She'd want us to stay here and wait for her to come home," Sean said.

Nelson knelt down and scooped his son up in his arms. Sean threw his arms around his father's neck, burying his face in Nelson's shirt.

"It's okay. Shhhh. It's okay," Nelson said.

Nelson's voice cracked, and a tear rolled down his own cheek. Nelson set his son back down and brushed the hair off of his forehead.

"Mom loves you so much, and the thing she would want the most is to make sure you're safe. It's not safe here anymore. That's why we're going with Mike. Okay?" Nelson said.

"But if she comes back, how will she find us?"

"We're going to leave really good directions for her. Right, Mike?"

Mike looked at Sean's tear-soaked face. What he was asking the two of them to do was hard. He was asking them to leave their home, to leave their mother and wife, to leave all they knew on a chance to survive.

"Yes," Mike said.

"Now, get the rest of your stuff ready. We need to leave soon," Nelson said.

Nelson kissed Sean's cheek and set him back down on the ground. Sean disappeared back into his room, gathering a few more toys. He patted Mike on the shoulder.

"I appreciate you taking us with you," Nelson said.

"Of course."

"It's just hard on him, you know?"

"What about you?" Mike asked.

Nelson's voice dropped to a whisper.

"I'm fine."

Once Sean had finished packing his bag, Nelson and Sean moved all of the furniture in the living room into a circle. They placed a few rations of food and water in the center, hoping that if Katie were to come back to the house, the formation of the living room would catch her attention. Mike wrote down the coordinates of the cabin and left a map tucked under the supplies.

"Let's go," Mike said.

They'd packed their rations. They'd said their goodbyes. Now they walked down 24th Street toward the highway. It was a three-day walk from Pittsburgh to Mike's cabin in Ohio.

Mike's fingers reached for the pistol on his right side. He felt the outline of the gun, making sure it was still there. The fire had destroyed all of his weapons and supplies, but he'd found the 9mm pistol tucked away in a closet of one of the abandoned houses they ransacked yesterday in preparation for their journey.

Every time Mike busted through a locked door, pulled open a drawer, or opened up a cabinet that wasn't his, he felt a stab of guilt shoot through his conscience. This wasn't his house. These weren't his things. He hated every minute of it. He had no right.

No right? This neighborhood that turned on him and his family had no right to threaten them. They had no right to try and take what was his. Mike closed his eyes, wrapping his mind around the one solid thought propelling him forward. *He had to get to his family.*

"Dad, you think Mom will be able to find us?" Sean asked.

"Absolutely," Nelson answered.

Mike watched Nelson and Sean walk together, holding onto each other. If it hadn't been for Nelson, he'd be dead. Nelson pulled him from the flames, risking his life and never seeing his family again. Would he be able to do that? If the choice between saving Nelson or being with his family was presented to him, which path would he go down?

When they turned onto Highway 60, the sun peeked over the Pittsburgh skyline behind them. A breeze swirled trash and dust across their feet. They weaved in and out of the abandoned vehicles along the road. It was an endless parking lot.

"Look at all of them," Nelson said.

"Keep an eye out for any older models, prior to 1980. They won't have any microprocessors in them and wouldn't have been affected by the EMP."

"That's how your family got out? Because of the Jeep?"

"Yeah."

Mike thought about the once-a-month weekend trip where he and his family would go to get away from the city, enjoy the outdoors, and prepare for what was happening now. He reached into his pocket and felt the outline of the pocket watch that belonged to his father. His dad gave it to him when he was a boy. It was the only piece of technology he owned that still worked. It was as steady and reliable as the man who gave it to him.

15

DAY 6 (THE CABIN)

*T*he gears grinded in the Jeep. Ulysses threw the shifter into third gear. He pressed the clutch and weaved in and out of the massive blockage of cars along Highway 60. He glanced in the rearview mirror and saw the smoke rising from his son's house behind him.

Ulysses shifted his eyes from the smoke to his grandchildren in the back seat. Freddy clutched his sister, Kalen, in the back seat, and the two of them held on to each other. Ray sat next to them, his rifle propped up against his shoulder.

Anne sat in the front seat next to him. Her whole body was turned around. She dug her nails into the headrest to the point of almost puncturing it. Her eyes were glued to the smoke plume.

All of their bodies swayed back and forth. The top of the Jeep was off, and the wind flew everyone's hair around wildly. Bungee cords held down the supplies they packed the day before.

"Anne, I need you to tell me where I'm going," Ulysses said.

Anne didn't move. Her face was frozen. Ulysses downshifted back into second gear, narrowly missing a black Lexus. Anne didn't move. She held tight to the back of the seat, watching the smoke shrink in the distance.

"Anne!' Ulysses shouted.

With the combination of the roar from the engine, the wind, and the adrenaline coursing through his body, Ulysses's voice was harsh.

Anne sat down in the seat and pulled open the glove box. She flipped through the stacks of paper and pulled out a map, focusing every shred of her will on the task of getting her family to the cabin.

"You'll want to follow Highway 60 all the way to I-376 and take that north; from there we'll take 30 North to 39 West. That'll lead us all the way into Ohio by Carrollton, where the cabin is," she said.

The wind kept flipping the map closed. Anne shoved it on the ground and glanced back behind her. The street was no longer in view. Her eyes shifted to her children in the back seat. Tears rolled down both of Freddy's cheeks.

"Everything's going to be fine, sweetie," Anne said.

She gently cupped her hands around Freddy's face and kissed his forehead. Her eyes flitted up once more at the smoke behind her, the only thing still visible.

"Do we have enough gas to get us there?" Ray asked.

"We have a full tank now. The cabin's only seventy miles away. Even with the gas mileage this thing gets, we should have enough," Ulysses said.

The more distance they put between themselves and Pittsburgh, the fewer cars they ran into.

Ulysses watched the faces on the people they passed walking along the sides of the highway. Their mouths dropped at the sight of the Jeep. Each time the look was the same: shock followed by desperation. Arms waved, voices shouted, people ran for them, but they didn't stop. Ulysses's face was stone. There was no emotion upon hearing the shouts of their pleas. The fire that was consuming the home behind them was also ablaze inside him.

* * *

RAY WATCHED THE "WELCOME TO OHIO" sign flash by. His hands wrapped around the wood stock of the rifle. No one had said anything for the past hour. The howling wind was the only sound his ears had come across.

"How much further?" Ray asked.

"About forty miles," Anne said.

The abandoned cars became more sporadic. They hadn't seen anyone for a few miles. Ray shifted the gun to the other shoulder and leaned up between the two front seats.

"We should start checking some of these cars for supplies," Ray said.

"I don't want us to stop," Ulysses said.

"We might find something we could use in one of them."

"Mike has everything we need at the cabin."

"That doesn't mean there won't be something useful. We might not get a chance like this again."

"Drop it, Ray."

Ray fell back into his seat, shaking his head. It's not that he didn't believe Mike was well prepared. He was sure that the cabin would be well stocked with provisions. He just didn't want to miss an opportunity. Ray knew the longer this lasted, the more scarce resources would become, and while Mike was sure to have supplies, there was no way he would have enough supplies to last them the rest of their lives.

Freddy started to squirm in the seat next to Ray. He shifted in his seat, and his leg bounced up and down.

"You all right, Freddy?" Ray asked.

"I have to pee."

"Can you hold it?" Anne asked.

Freddy shook his head.

"Ulysses, pull over," Anne said.

"Anne," Ulysses said.

"Freddy has to go to the bathroom."

"I really have to go, Grandpa," Freddy said.

Freddy bounced up and down on the seat. The Jeep slowed to a crawl and pulled off onto the side of the road. Freddy climbed over Kalen and jumped over the side of the Jeep, landing on the pavement.

"Kalen, go with your brother and make sure he doesn't go too far," Anne said.

"Ew, gross! I'm not going to the bathroom with him."

"You're not going to the bathroom with him, just making sure he doesn't get lost. Now go."

Kalen rolled her eyes and jumped out of the back seat. She grabbed Freddy's hand, and the two walked toward a tree line twenty yards from the edge of the highway. The trees were tall, and the area was thick with bushes.

From the back seat, Ray could see an SUV parked fifty yards ahead of them. His feet hit the pavement and walked past Ulysses on the driver side.

"Where are you going?" Ulysses asked.

"I'm going to scout that car. Just pick me up when the kids get back."

Ray removed the rifle from his shoulder and tucked it under his shoulder. His feet stepped lightly on the pavement. He scanned the sides of the road, looking for any signs someone was still close by, but couldn't see anything through the thick brush.

The barrel of the rifle rose once he moved closer to the car. He peered through the back window, checking for anyone inside. He worked his way up to the driver-side door and pulled the handle. Locked. He walked around, checking each door, but all of them were closed.

The butt of the rifle smashed against the passenger-side window. The glass shattered but didn't break. Ray gave the window another blow, and the butt of the rifle crashed through the window. He cleared the crumbling bits of glass from the rest of the window and reached his hand through to unlock the door.

Ray brushed the glass off the seat and climbed inside. He searched the glove box, checked the back seat, under the seats, and the side door panel containers. A half-eaten packet of crackers, road flares, and a bottle of water were his rewards. He looked behind him and saw the Jeep still idling along the side of the road. He leaned the seat back and put his feet on the dash. He pinched the corners of one of the crackers in his fingers and tossed it in his mouth.

* * *

"Just do it over there, Freddy," Kalen said.

"I don't want anyone to see me," Freddy said.

"Well, by the time you pick a spot, Grandpa's gonna leave you."

"No!"

"Better hurry up then."

The thick layer of pine needles under Kalen's boots made each step soundless. She wandered through the trees, glancing back at the road every once in a while, making sure the Jeep was still in view. She could see her mom pacing back and forth through the leaves and branches.

The forest was quiet. She thought back to the many times her dad took her hunting. She remembered how much she fought him about it, how she complained that she didn't want to go, but grew to love it. She could still hear his voice. *Don't aim where the game is, aim where it's going to be.*

Kalen leaned her head back against the hard bark of the tree. Sunlight struggled to break through the dense leaves above. The trees' long shadows covered the ground. She closed her eyes, completing the darkness around her. The snap of a twig caused her to open her eyes again.

"Freddy, don't come over here and do it. I don't want to se—"

A hand came up from behind her and covered her mouth. Her arms were pinned at her sides, and she was pressed hard against a man's body she didn't know. She could feel his hot breath on her ear, whispering.

"Shhhhh."

Kalen couldn't see the attacker. Her breaths were sharp, sporadic. Her body shook. She could feel the grime of the man's hand on her lips. The sour stench from days of not bathing engulfed her.

"Scream and your family dies, understand?"

She slowly nodded her head.

"Good."

He turned her around against the trunk of the tree, keeping his hand over her mouth. She saw the yellow in his teeth, the bits of old food in his beard. The point of his blade dug into her chin.

"Kalen, I'm done," Freddy shouted.

The man put his finger to his lips. She watched his eyes move in the direction of Freddy's voice. She could feel her heart beating out of her chest, thumping faster.

"Kalen?" Freddy asked.

She could hear Freddy's feet shuffling through the pine needles and twigs on the ground. The man's face turned into a smile. He moved the blade from her chin and kept it poised in front of him. He wasn't looking at her anymore. She saw the side of his ribs exposed. Freddy's footsteps were just beyond the tree beside them.

"Kalen, whe—"

Before Freddy turned the corner, Kalen shoved her foot into the man's rib cage, knocking him down.

"Freddy, run!" Kalen screamed.

Her feet fell from under her, slipping on dead leaves. Her belly slapped against the ground, hard. Freddy stood frozen in shock. She got to her knees, and before she was able to stand up, she felt the grip of a hand around her ankle pulling her backwards.

"*Help!*" Kalen said.

Kalen's fingers clawed in the dirt as her assailant pulled her deeper into the forest. She felt his arms wrap around her stomach and lift her off the ground, carrying her. She thrashed her arms and legs in defiance, but he managed to subdue her. He wrapped his large hands around her throat and squeezed.

"Shut up!" the man said.

Kalen could see her mother and grandfather through the trees, rushing toward her from the distance.

"Kalen!"

She tried to call out, but the man's grip was too tight. She could barely breathe. The airflow was cut off and she gasped, coughing and choking for air. Then she felt her whole body being thrown to the ground.

The back of her head smacked against a tree root. Her body went limp, disoriented from the blow. She felt foreign hands grabbing her, ripping her shirt off, tugging at her jeans. When she started to regain her ability to fight back, a fist came barreling into the side of her cheek. A numbing, ringing sound went through her skull. She couldn't feel anything anymore. The forest around her spun in circles and faded in and out of her consciousness until everything went black.

* * *

KALEN'S HEAD THROBBED. Her face was sore, and she felt the scratch of the blanket covering her skin. She glanced down and saw that her shirt was gone and she was wearing only her jeans and bra. The cracks in the Jeep's seat scraped her bare back. She tried to get up but felt dizzy and fell back down.

"Kalen?" Freddy asked.

She hadn't noticed him sitting on the floorboard next to her. She turned her head and saw his eyes blinking up at her.

"What happened?" she asked.

"Grandpa and Ray pulled you out of the forest with some other man. You weren't moving, so Grandpa brought you to the Jeep. You didn't have your clothes on," he said, looking down at his knees.

"A man?" she asked to herself.

"He was scary looking. After Grandpa brought you back to the Jeep, he went with Ray, who took the man back into the woods."

A breeze lifted Kalen's hair. She shivered, but not from the wind. She couldn't remember what happened, and she was afraid to learn what did.

* * *

THE MAN LAY sprawled out on the ground. Blood dripped from Ulysses's and Ray's knuckles. Each of them had their turns beating him. The man's face was swollen, and blood poured from his broken nose.

ULYSSES SENT the toe of his boot into the man's side repeatedly, each blow causing the man to double over in pain. He cried out for mercy. He begged, but the punishment was relentless.

RAY PICKED up the same knife the man held to Kalen's throat. His fingers wrapped tightly around the handle. Ray knelt down and pressed the blade flat against the swollen bruises and cuts along his face.

"HOLD HIM DOWN, ULYSSES."

ULYSSES PINNED the man to the ground. Ray unbuckled the man's pants and pulled them down around his ankles.

"PLEASE. P-PLEASE, DON'T DO THIS," the man said.

RAY BROUGHT the blade below the man's waist. The bloodcurdling screams that followed were the tortured sounds of an animal.

16

DAY 5 (BIKER GANG)

*T*he ray of light coming in through the crack of the curtains hit the Diablos patch on Jake's cut hanging from the corner of the chair. Jake lay sprawled across the bed, his arm hanging over the side with his fingertip next to an empty bottle of tequila. Someone pounded on his room's door.

"Jake!" Frankie said.

Jake slowly rolled over, bumping into the naked girl lying next to him.

"Jake! We got a problem!" Frankie shouted.

Jake threw the door open, the president's patch flipping forward as he adjusted his cut.

"You better come see this, boss."

Jake followed Frankie down the hall and into the bar lounge. Pictures of motorcycles, girls, bands, and alcohol lined the walls.

A few of the motorcycle club members sat at the bar drinking beers. The crack of pool balls on the table and a few mumbles from the bikers were the only signs of life in the lounge.

Frankie opened the door from the bar to the garage. Candles were lit, casting light on two huddled masses on the floor with bags over their heads. Frankie ripped the paper bags off. Their eyes blinked, adjusting to the dim light in the garage.

"Meet Jimmy Fance and Bobby Turnt," Frankie said.

"Where'd you find them?" Jake asked.

"Sneaking around the back, looking for any supplies they could take. Isn't that right?"

Frankie kicked Jimmy in the leg, sending him collapsing to the floor.

"What do you wanna do with them?" Frankie asked.

Jake scanned the garage. His eyes rested on the tools and equipment he'd used for building and maintaining the bikes that came through. He grabbed a bolt wrench off the table.

"Stand them up," Jake said.

Frankie pulled Bobby up by the collar of his shirt. Bobby's hands were tied behind his back, and he kept his face pointing toward the grease-stained floor.

"Look at me," Jake said.

Bobby's face rose slowly. Jake's face was calm. His pronounced jaw was relaxed, the wrench gripped firmly in his hand.

"You think you can steal from me? From my brothers?"

"We didn't steal anything," Bobby said.

The force of the wrench hitting Bobby's kneecap crippled him, sending him to the floor in agony. Bobby cursed every name under the sun.

When the screams died down, Jake smashed the wrench into Bobby's other knee. Jimmy tried to make a run for it, but Frankie caught him before he got out.

"Wait your turn, asshole," Frankie said.

"C'mon, man, we didn't steal anything. You made your point, just let us go, man," Jimmy said.

"Not yet," Jake replied.

Jake swung the wrench high and sent it crashing down into Bobby's head. The skull caved from the force of the blow. Bobby lay motionless in a crumpled mess on the floor.

Jake dropped the wrench to the ground. He walked over to Jimmy, who was crying and shaking in Frankie's grip.

"You see this? You tell everyone you know that this is what happens to anyone who robs the Diablos. Got it?" Jake asked.

Jimmy nodded sharply.

"Get this piece of shit out of here," Jake said.

Frankie tossed him out of the back door of the garage, and the man took off running. Jake wiped the specks of blood from his hands on a rag.

"Why didn't we kill him?" Frankie asked.

"Fear," he said. "Fear grows with legend, Frankie. He tells the story to one person, they tell another, and each time they do, the story grows more intense, gruesome. When people see the Diablo patch, they'll know what they're dealing with."

Jake finished cleaning his hands and tossed the rag onto Bobby's body.

"Take out the trash," he said.

Jake walked back into the bar lounge and pulled a stool over to him. The bartender poured a glass of beer and handed it to Jake. Jake took half of it down in one swig.

The girl from Jake's bedroom walked out and sat on the barstool next to him. Her makeup was smeared across her face, and her hair was tangled. The bartender poured a drink for her and slid it down. Before she could grab it, Jake snatched it up.

"What the hell, Jake?" she asked.

Jake finished the beer he had, slammed it down on the counter, and then backhanded the girl. She flew off the stool and smacked the floor hard. Jake took a sip from the fresh beer and gently placed it down.

The girl crawled away from him. Blood dripped from her lower lip. Jake picked her up by her hair and jerked her head back.

"You don't get to drink until I'm not thirsty anymore," Jake said.

Jake tossed her forward. She stumbled in her heels and then disappeared to the back of the clubhouse.

The other members of the MC chuckled from the bar. Jake walked back over to his stool, sat down, and finished his drink.

* * *

THE LINE of bikes out front stretched twenty wide across the parking lot. You could see the door to the clubhouse was open from the street and the patches on the backs of members could be seen inside.

Jake stood in a circle surrounded by his MC. The worn faces of men who'd lived their lives in the wind, sun, and rain looked at their president, hungry.

"Diablos, this city is dead. If we want to make it, we have to keep moving. We scoured the city for as many working bikes as we could. They're all older models, but they run. Each of you is here because you're the strongest of our club. You represent who we are, and what we do," Jake said.

Frankie stood at Jake's side, his hands behind his back, watching his leader.

"We're riding south. We hit town after town and take what we find. This is our time, Diablos. The strong are powerful again."

The men around Jake were dangerous and wild. Pistols hung from their hips, and shotguns rested over their shoulders. The bikers shifted their weight on each foot with a vicious cadence, itching to wreak havoc.

"Let's ride," Jake said.

17

NIGHT OF DAY 7 (MIKE'S JOURNEY)

*W*hen Mike, Sean, and Nelson finally made out the sign for the airport sixty yards ahead of them, Mike knew they were making good progress.

The closer the three of them moved to Pittsburgh International, the more plane wreckage they saw. It looked like a few of the pilots were able to glide their aircraft in on its belly, but the majority of the planes were mangled heaps of metal. Seats, wings, jet engines, luggage, and fuselages littered the fields around them.

Other travelers along the road were scavenging through the wreckage, hunting through the luggage like grave robbers looking for a quick score.

Mike could see the sun sinking behind the airport itself. The tarmac was still and hauntingly quiet. He could make out the distress signals people painted on the outside of the terminals when the realization of being stuck finally came to fruition. "HELP" and "S.O.S." were painted in large, red letters.

"Hey, you think we should scope out some of this stuff? It might be a good idea to see what we can find in all this," Nelson asked.

"I'd rather not stop. We're still close to the city. I want to put as much distance between the masses and us as possible. We just need to focus on getting to the cabin," Mike said.

Sean tugged at his father's sleeve.

"Dad, I'm tired. Can we take a break?" he asked.

"We'll rest soon. We just need to go a little bit further," Nelson answered.

Mike could feel the burning in his feet from the long day of walking. Each step hit the blisters under his toes like knives. He couldn't imagine how Sean had kept up as well as he had.

"Let's keep an eye out for a good place to make camp tonight. The sun will be going down soon," Mike said.

A 727-jetliner fuselage sat a half mile up the road. The plane had crashed just outside the airport tarmac. Most of it was still intact. The pilot had a successful crash landing. The emergency doors were thrown open, and the plane was abandoned.

"Better than a Holiday Inn," Nelson said.

The sun finally disappeared under the horizon, and Mike checked the front and back of the plane for any food and water. The food cart was flipped on its side with each of its drawers pulled open and completely empty.

Mike moved to the first aid stations, but those had been wiped out. The only things that remained were a few small bottles of liquor that had rolled under the cart that nobody bothered to pick up and check underneath.

Nelson and Sean reclined a few seats up in first class and found a pair of pillows left behind from the passengers. Sean passed out within minutes of his head hitting the pillow.

Mike leaned back in the row across from Nelson and Sean. Mike leaned back, and Nelson tossed him a pillow, which hit him in the face by surprise.

"Get some rest. I'll take the first watch," Nelson said.

"I'm fine."

"No, you're not."

Mike could feel the weight of the day bearing down on him. The burn under the bandages on his arm was sore and in need of redressing. Nelson was right. He was in no shape to make it through the night without passing out. He was melting into the chair underneath him.

"Just wake me up when you need to rest," Mike said.

"I will," Nelson said.

Mike folded his arms in his lap and closed his eyes. His eyelids slammed shut like the steel doors of the mill at the end of the day.

* * *

IT WASN'T until Mike felt his wrists pinned to the arms of the seat and heard Sean's screams that he woke up. He jerked his arms, but they wouldn't budge. He squinted his eyes, trying to adjust to the darkness. Nelson's head was bent to the side, a massive lump forming across his temple.

Mike's eyes adjusted to the darkness. He couldn't make out the people in front of him. He could only hear the shuffling of feet and the murmur of voices.

"This is all they have?"

"Yeah, I searched these two and that's it."

"What about the other guy? What's he got?"

Before the man could get close, Mike kicked the man's knee, sending him to the floor with a thud.

"Goddamn asshole!"

"Grab his legs, Tim."

"Screw it. It's not worth it. Let's just grab the rest of this shit and go, man."

Tim sent a nice right cross to Mike's cheek before he left. Mike's ears rang. His mind went foggy with pain. He squeezed his eyes shut, trying to orient himself.

The sobs coming from Mike's left gave him a point to focus on. They grew louder until they completely replaced the ringing caused by the punch. He looked over at Sean, who was struggling to free himself.

"Sean, are you okay?" Mike asked.

"I can't move my arms," Sean replied.

"Just hang on, buddy. Nelson," Mike said. "Nelson!"

Nelson didn't move. Mike jerked his wrists, attempting to free himself, but it was useless. He bent over and started tearing the tape with his teeth. He picked at the tape over and over until he finally had a tear. He tore the piece, splitting the duct tape in half. He yanked his hand free and peeled the tape off his other wrist.

Sean was squirming, trying to get free. Mike had to climb over Nelson to reach Sean, whose tears were streaming down his face.

"Dad! Dad!" Sean cried.

"Hold on, Sean."

Once Sean was unbound, Mike pressed his fingers against Nelson's neck to check for a pulse. Mike leaned in and listened to see if Nelson was breathing. Nelson was breathing, and Mike could feel the faint beat of a pulse.

"Stay here, Sean," Mike said.

Mike tore out of the emergency exit and glanced around in the darkness, but the attackers had vanished. Lightning streaked across the sky followed by a deep, rolling thunder.

When Mike entered the plane, Sean was resting his head on Nelson's shoulder, hugging his dad.

"Sean," Mike said.

Sean ignored him. Mike reached his hand, placing it on Sean's arm, but Sean jerked it away violently.

"Leave me alone!" Sean said.

It wasn't any use trying to argue. The kid was scared, tired, and the one person who could help him was lying unconscious right in front of his eyes. Mike walked back over to the entrance of the plane to keep watch. He pulled the gun from the back of his waist and clicked the safety off. In between the cracks of thunder, he could hear Sean's faint whimpers.

* * *

"DAD?" Sean asked.

Mike's attention switched from the water dripping from the plane's emergency exit frame back to Sean and Nelson.

"What happened?" Nelson asked.

"How are you feeling?" Mike asked.

Nelson touched his finger to the outline of the lump on the left side of his head and winced when he made contact.

"It was a rough night," Mike said.

Nelson, still disoriented, turned to his son.

"You all right, buddy?" Nelson asked.

Sean wrapped his arms around his father, burying his face into his shirt. Nelson cradled the back of his son's head as he rested against him. His eyes looked up into Mike's.

"Did they take everything?" Nelson asked.

"All of our packs are gone," Mike answered.

"Well, I'm glad you two are okay. What are we going to do now?"

Mike had thought about that all night. He thought about how they were going to finish the trip to the cabin that was at least another three full days of walking without any food or water. He knew the farther they traveled into Ohio where the cabin was located, the fewer towns there'd be to try and gather supplies. Right now the only place that was close enough to do them any good was the one place Mike wanted to avoid.

Nelson noticed Mike glancing back toward Pittsburgh International and picked up on what he was thinking.

"I hope you printed our boarding passes before we left," Nelson said.

* * *

THE MUGGERS from last night confirmed what Mike already knew would happen: that people were getting desperate and traveling around, looking for easy scores. It wouldn't be long before people started organizing into gangs to survive.

That's what Mike feared awaited them in the airport. It had been a week since everything stopped working. No power, no water, no food, no modern conveniences, nothing. He'd already watched his neighbors turn on each other, and that was in the first week. He didn't want to imagine what would happen a month from now.

Mike tried to convince Nelson to stay in the plane with Sean, but he insisted on coming to help. Mike finally caved. If he did find a stash of supplies, he'd need all the help he could get carrying it.

Clothes, trash, and abandoned airport equipment littered the tarmac. The massive jetliners stood motionless. Some were lined up at the terminals, while others stood frozen on the runways, never leaving the ground.

Mike thought about how everyone on board started to complain the moment everything shut off. He could hear the mumbles and groans on the plane, people cursing under their breath that they'd been inconvenienced by what happened, but if they'd taken off thirty minutes earlier, they all would have crashed, and most likely would have died.

Mike kept his eyes alert. He scanned the tarmac for anything unusual or out of place. He couldn't afford anyone getting the drop on them now. As much as Nelson said he was okay, Mike knew that he wasn't going to be of much use if things went south.

"How do we get in there?" Nelson asked.

"We'll have to go up to the main entrance. I'm not sure how to get in from the tarmac," Mike said.

The three of them walked around the outside of the terminal and followed the monorail to the airport drop-off and pick-up area. A few of the monorails were stuck on the track in between destinations.

"Dad, what's that on the windows?" Sean asked.

When Mike looked up at one of the monorail windows, he could see dried bloodstains smeared across the glass.

"Dirt," Mike said.

Nothing moved. Mike still hadn't become used to that. All the times he'd complained about people moving too fast, and now he'd give anything to see a car speed around the corner of the building up ahead.

Then Mike saw him. It was only for a second, but he saw the flash of brown hair duck back into the airport. He pulled Nelson and Sean down behind a luggage carrier.

"What's wrong?" Nelson asked.

"There're people inside," Mike said.

"Do you think they're dangerous?"

"I don't know, but if they're keeping watch, then they must be protecting something."

Mike pulled the pistol from his waist and clicked the safety off. He peeked above the luggage carrier to the door the man had gone inside.

"We should move to the corner by the front of the building. Sean, you stay close to your dad, okay? If anything happens you two run, got it?"

Both of them nodded their heads.

"Stay behind me," Mike said.

Mike led the three of them in a single-file line. He kept the gun clutched in both hands, his eyes scanning the area. He slammed his back up against the corner of the building. Nelson and Sean followed suit, catching their breath. Mike placed his index finger over his lips.

"C'mon," Mike said.

Most of the automatic glass doors were shut. A few had been smashed, and the rest had been opened manually.

The crunch of the glass behind Mike made him freeze in his tracks. Nelson mouthed "Sorry" and stepped around the remaining shards.

Mike found one of the opened doors and stepped through. The airport was musty. A week of no air-conditioning and continually being baked in the sun caused everything to stink. Mike motioned for Nelson and Sean to move in close. His voice was barely above a whisper.

"Look for food. You'll want to take non-perishable items. Anything in a can or a wrapper should be okay. Bottled water is another good thing to grab. Also, be on the lookout for backpacks we can use to store what we find, okay?"

"What about weapons?" Nelson asked.

"I don't think we'll find anything like that here, but if you do, grab it."

Mike squinted his eyes, trying to see deeper into the depths of the airport, but he could only see as far as the light from outside would reach through the windows. No windows, no light. The only things visible were security lines and metal detectors.

Tables and chairs from the food court were flipped on their sides and backs. Broken glass from display cases and vending machines was scattered on the floor. Sean reached down and picked up a candy bar and showed it to his father. Nelson gave him a thumbs-up. Just as Sean pocketed it, they heard a crash coming from the back of the Burger King kitchen.

"Stay here," Mike said.

Mike climbed over the Burger King counter, landing quietly on the other side. He could feel his pulse beat faster. A dim light glowed under the crack of the door leading to the kitchen. He raised his weapon, his knuckles turning white against the black composite of his 9mm, and burst through the swinging door.

A group of people was huddled on the floor, all of them with their hands up in surrender. A family with two small children, a young woman, a middle-aged man, and an overweight man dressed in a TSA uniform looked at him.

"Hey, man. We don't want any trouble. Just take what you want and be on your way, okay?" the TSA agent said.

Mike kept his weapon aimed, but moved his finger from the trigger. He glanced around at the group. Each time he swept the pistol over them, they crouched lower to the ground. Finally, Mike lowered his gun, clicked the safety back on, and tucked the pistol in the belt of his pants.

"I'm not here to hurt anyone," Mike said.

"Mike?" Nelson called from the counter.

"We're good, Nelson. C'mon back," Mike answered.

The TSA man extended his hand.

"Clarence Furns," he said.

The two men shook hands.

"That's Tom Wrink, Fay Cam, Jung To, Jenna To, and their two little ones, Jung Jr. and Claire," Clarence said.

Tom wore the remnants of what was left of his business suit. His beard crept down along his neck. When Mike went to shake his hand, it was grimy with dirt, skin, and whatever he'd ate at his last meal.

Fay's hair was pulled back into a ponytail. Her nails were long, the nail polish flaking off. Mike noticed the tattoos along her arm, exposed from her tank top.

Jung and Jenna stayed close to one another. They were both dressed in what looked like comfortable clothing for a long trip. Jung Jr. and Claire hid behind their parents' legs, glancing up at Mike.

Mike introduced Nelson and Sean.

"So, what's for breakfast?" Nelson asked.

Clarence picked up the lantern and walked them back into the kitchen. The group had stacked the kitchen with boxes of food rations, vending machine boxes, and canned goods.

"You can take as much as you need and stay for as long as you'd like, but I don't know how much longer we're going to be able to last here," Clarence said.

"What are you talking about? There's enough food here to last you for the rest of the year," Nelson said.

"When everything stopped working, most of the airport was evacuated. They marched people to local hotels, into the city, wherever. There were quite a few that were just left here, and everything was fine for the first few days," Clarence said.

"Then people from the city started showing up. I guess they thought they could escape on a plane or something. They came in droves, and when they got here and found out that the airport was just as broken as the rest of the city, people started losing it," Tom said.

"It started off with small stuff: where they slept, about personal space, where they could keep their stuff, stupid things. But then people started arguing over food and water. A few of the TSA and law enforcement officers that stuck around tried to keep things in order, but it didn't take long for most of them to start causing trouble too," Clarence explained.

"How'd you manage to get all of this stuff in here with all of the looting going on?" Mike asked.

"I grabbed as many things as I could when I started seeing everything fall apart, but then after the first person was killed, it was a free-for-all. People just tore into each other. I grabbed these guys and locked us in the TSA security office. We were there for two days before I unlocked the door. When we came out, most of the airport was abandoned. A few other people who had survived by hiding in other spots stayed, but most had left. We decided to gather everything we could find and put it in a central location. This was the spot we chose. It has a good vantage point from the front, and if we need to get out quickly, there are multiple exits," Clarence said.

They did manage to find a large amount of supplies even after the looting. Nelson was right. They had enough food to last them for the rest of the year, and if Clarence were a TSA agent, he'd have access to the security weapons at the airport.

"You said that you didn't think you could stay here for long, but it sounds like most of the large groups have gone. If it's just you guys, why would you leave?" Mike asked.

"Gangs," Fay said.

"Gangs?" Nelson asked.

"A guy came through a few days ago raving about motorcycle gangs coming down from Michigan and Ohio. Groups from small towns roving around like Vikings, pillaging what they want. He was a little off his rocker if you ask me though, so I don't think he really knew what he was talking about," Tom said.

"And I haven't seen a single mechanical engine work in the past two weeks. Everything's down," Clarence said.

Mike thought about his 1975 Jeep. He could see his family piled in, supplies in the back, heading for the cabin. These people had no idea about the EMP blast and what it meant.

18

DAY 6 (THE CABIN)

*A*nne grabbed the side of the wall blindly trying to get her bearings. Her foot jammed into the corner of the chair, sending it crashing to the basement floor.

"Shit," she murmured to herself.

"Anne, you okay down there?" Ulysses yelled from upstairs.

"I'm fine."

She finally found one of the gas lanterns she was looking for. She lit the wick, and the lamp illuminated the rest of the basement.

Shelves of canned food lined one of the sidewalls. A gun safe stood anchored in one of the corners of the room, filled with assault rifles, pistols, shotguns, and ammo for each of them. Crates filled with medicine, bandages, spare clothing, blankets, sleeping bags, camping gear, fishing rods, and lures were stacked along the back wall. Anne grabbed one of the first aid kits out of one of the medical boxes and rushed back upstairs.

Kalen was still on the couch, lying on her side. Her eyes stared blankly at the floor. Dried blood flaked on the edge of her lip.

Anne dropped to her knees in front of her daughter. She opened up the first aid box and pulled out some cotton balls and a bottle of hydrogen peroxide.

"This might sting a little, sweetheart," Anne said.

She placed the cotton ball on the corner of her daughter's mouth, but Kalen didn't even flinch. Her eyes glazed over. Anne wiped Kalen's mouth, the white cotton ball turning a light pink.

Anne ran another fresh cotton ball along the cuts and scratches on Kalen's arms and neck. She kept watching her daughter's face, but Kalen didn't move, she didn't flinch, she didn't show any emotion.

Ray walked in and dropped a duffle bag to the floor. It hit the ground with a thud. Ulysses came in after him.

"Should be the last of it," Ray said.

"Let's take a walk around the perimeter and make sure everything's intact," Ulysses said.

Ray headed out the door first, and Ulysses glanced back at his granddaughter sitting on the couch. He walked over to her and kissed the top of her head. He looked at Anne.

"I'll be back in a second," he said.

The sun was sinking in the sky. The light broke through the leaves of the surrounding forest in fragments.

The two men walked around, checking the walls and windows, and then climbed up to examine the roof. A small well was out back, and Ulysses pulled a bucket of spring water up and handed it to Ray.

"Take it to the basement. There's a water testing kit down there. We'll see what we're dealing with," Ulysses said.

Ray carried the bucket back to the cabin, the water sloshing back and forth, splashing over the sides.

Ulysses examined the rope and pulley for the well. He checked for any cracks or wear, and once satisfied, set the rope back down.

A small piece of land had been plowed behind the cabin to be used as a garden. Ulysses dug his hands into the dirt and rubbed it between his palms. The soil was warm from the sun.

You really did think of everything, didn't you?

When he walked back inside the cabin, Kalen was gone from the couch. Anne was packing up the medical supplies, grabbing the pink-stained cotton balls lying on the floor and placing the unused materials back in the first aid box.

"How's she doing?" Ulysses asked.

"She's still not saying anything," Anne said.

Ulysses watched her lock the latches on the medical kit and then look up at him. The sweat from her forehead caused strands of her hair to stick to her face.

"Thank you," Anne said.

"I shouldn't have let them go off by themselves," Ulysses said.

"It wasn't your fault."

Ray popped his head up from the basement door.

"Hey, guys, can I get a little help down here?" he asked.

Downstairs, the glow from the lanterns lit up the bucket of water and workstation that Ray set up to test the water.

"I'm not sure I'm doing this right," Ray said.

"Here," Anne said, taking the kit from him.

She grabbed the finger-length tubes and dipped them in the bucket. She filled five of them and dropped test strips into each one. She shook the tubes and let them sit.

"Each tube checks for something different?" Ray asked.

"Lead, pesticides, chlorine, nitrates, and pH levels," Anne said, pointing at each of the tubes. "Blue means they're at a safe level. If they turn yellow, then they're not."

"How do you know how to do this?" Ray asked.

"Every time we came up to the cabin, Mike would assign us different tasks. This was one of mine," she said.

"If one of them does turn yellow, can we fix it?" Ray asked.

"No," Anne replied.

Anne looked at the pallets of bottled water by the food shelves. She counted them, doing the math in her head. If the well were tainted, then the four of them would only last a month before their water supply ran out.

When the test strips turned a light shade of blue, they all let out a sigh of relief.

"Well, that's one less thing we'll have to worry about," Ray said.

* * *

THE SUN WAS TURNING neon orange as it dipped into the horizon. Anne fired up the gas stove and placed a few pots with water on them to boil. Cans of green beans, corn, and chicken lined the counter.

Anne peeled the cans open and dumped them into the simmering water. She added a few spices to each and let them heat up. Ray and Ulysses sat in the living room playing chess, and Freddy had pulled out some of his toys he brought with him.

Anne walked down the hallway to Kalen's door. It was closed. She stood in front of the door for a moment, wiping her hands on the front of her apron. Her stomach was in knots. She let out a slow breath then knocked on the door.

"Kalen?" Anne asked.

No answer. Anne opened the door slowly. Kalen was on her bed, lying on top of the sheets, her back facing the door.

Anne shut the door behind her when she entered and softly sat herself down on the edge of Kalen's bed. She stroked her daughter's hair, letting the strands run through her fingertips.

"Honey, dinner will be ready soon."

Kalen remained motionless. Anne brought her lips to Kalen's ear.

"If you need anything, I'm here. Okay?"

Once dinner was ready, Freddy helped set the table, and he, Anne, Ray, and Ulysses gathered around. Anne put together a separate plate and handed it to Freddy.

"Go take that to your sister," she said.

Freddy grasped the plate with both hands and walked back down to his sister's room. The door was cracked, and he pushed it open with his shoulder.

"Kalen?" Freddy asked.

She was still curled up in a ball with her back to him. The curtains were drawn shut, blocking out what was left of the fading sunlight.

Freddy tiptoed into the room and placed the plate on the nightstand next to her, the steam rising from the piping-hot plate.

"Mom made you some dinner," he said.

Freddy stood there, his hands hanging awkwardly at his sides. He slowly walked up to the edge of her bed.

"I hope you feel better," he said.

Once Freddy was gone, Kalen turned around. She didn't touch her food. She couldn't remember a time in her life when she had felt worse.

* * *

THE THUNDER CRASHED OUTSIDE. The wind and rain battered the side of the cabin. Anne watched the rain smack against the window. The lighting flashed across the sky, reflecting in her eyes and illuminating the room.

She paced back and forth in the bedroom. She couldn't sit still. Every time she settled into one place, she became uncomfortable and had to move somewhere else. In between the cracks of thunder, she would close her eyes and see the red flames engulfing her home. She saw the faces of her neighbors, their eyes wild and crazy with rage and fear. She felt the warmth of Mike's lips on hers before she ran to the garage. Then she started to feel hot. She could feel the flames ripping through her as if she was there with Mike. She wrapped both of her arms around herself and fell onto the bed, the tears falling from her eyes.

Just when she felt exhausted, the entire cabin rumbled and shook. She swung the bedroom door open and could hear the faint screams coming from the living room over the cracks of thunder and the howl of the wind. One of the ceiling beams fell and landed on the couch in the living room where Ray was sleeping.

Anne rushed over to him. Blood gushed all over the couch and floor. Ray's shin was bent inward, snapped in half.

Ulysses came up from behind her and helped roll the log off Ray, and it thudded on the floor. Blood poured from Ray's leg onto the couch.

"Ulysses, help me take him downstairs," Anne said.

Anne lifted Ray onto her shoulder, supporting him. Ulysses came around and threw Ray's other arm over his shoulder. The three of them hobbled over to the basement. On the way there, Freddy poked his head out of his room.

"Stay in your room and keep the door shut," Anne yelled.

Anne and Ulysses kept Ray steady bringing him down the steps of the basement. The lower half of his shin swung back and forth with each step, and with each swing Ray dug his hand harder into Anne's shoulder.

Once they made it all the way down the steps, Anne cleared a table and lit a few lanterns while Ulysses helped Ray lie down. Ray kept glancing down at his mangled leg. Anne pushed his head back flat on the table.

"Don't look at it," she said.

"What do you need?" Ulysses asked.

"Scissors," Anne said.

Ray's breathing accelerated. His body was shaking. The muscle in his jaw flexed from grinding his teeth together.

"You got anything for the pain?" Ray asked.

"Are you allergic to anything?" Anne asked.

"No."

Ulysses handed Anne a pair of scissors. She hurried over to one of the medicine shelves, and she opened the box and pulled out a bottle of oxycodone. She tore a bottle of water out of the package holding it and fed Ray the pill. He choked a little bit but managed to get it down.

Anne ran the scissors across Ray's jeans and ripped them apart from his knee to his ankle, exposing the wound. Bits of bone poked out through the skin, which was a deep shade of black and blue.

"Ray, I'm going to have to push some of the bone back in and then try and set it. I don't know if it's a clean break or not, but the wound will get worse if I don't try," Anne said.

"Give me… more drugs," Ray said.

"I can't. You've lost a lot of blood, and if you have too much oxy, it could drop your blood pressure even further and put you in cardiac arrest. Ulysses, give him something to bite on."

Ulysses took his belt off, folded it a few times, then slid it into Ray's mouth. Ray's hands gripped the side of the table until his knuckles turned white.

Anne's finger hovered over the bone. She pressed down. Ray's body seized in tension on the table, his whole body shaking as the bone slid deeper into his leg until it disappeared. When the pressure from Anne's finger stopped, Ray went limp on the table, passed out.

The crack of the bone resetting into place triggered an unconscious spasm from Ray. Anne grabbed a splint from another first aid bag.

"Get those straps at the top, Ulysses," Anne instructed, tying the splint firmly to Ray's leg.

Anne cleaned the wound, wiping the blood away and dumping hydrogen peroxide over the cuts. She applied fresh bandages and checked Ray's pulse.

"We'll have to watch him through the night, make sure there wasn't any internal bleeding," Anne said.

She placed the back of her hand to Ray's forehead, checking his temperature. She took a rag and wiped the sweat from his face, patting him gently.

"If his temperature spikes within the next twenty-four hours, it means he has an infection. We should keep him down here tonight and move him as little as possible," Anne said.

Anne knew that Ray wouldn't be able to walk without assistance for the rest of his life. She did what she could, but without professional medical help, the bone wouldn't set right. If Ray got an infection, though, it wouldn't matter. They didn't have any antibiotics in their medical stash to fight it.

* * *

WHEN ULYSSES WALKED around the cabin the next morning, he could see the full devastation from the storm. Multiple trees had toppled over throughout the forest. The tree that had landed on the roof of the cabin was a thick pine.

Ulysses spent most of the morning clearing out the smaller branches on the roof. He chopped them down and tossed them to the ground to be used as firewood for later. Trimming the tree would also make it easier to move. With one of the support beams from the roof already damaged, he wasn't sure how well the roof would hold, or if the tree would come crashing through at any moment.

The afternoon heat was getting worse. Ulysses's shirt was drenched in sweat. He swung the axe high, digging deeper into the thick trunk of the pine. He felt the wood handle of the axe slide through his hands with each blow. The strain on his face, the tightening of his back, his muscles fatigued from the exertion and hot summer sun. Finally, the massive trunk snapped in half.

With half the tree now leaning at a more easily leveraged angle, Ulysses climbed up on the roof and crept around the area where the rest of the tree still remained. His knees cracked as he bent low trying to put his body behind the lift. He strained, pushing the log from the roof to the ground.

Just like the tree, Ulysses collapsed after the encounter. He lay on his back, sucking in air. His chest heaved up and down, the heat from the sun barreling down on him. He focused on slowing his breath to a steady rhythm and letting his heart rate come down.

Once Ulysses felt he had controlled his breathing, he pushed himself up and took a look where the tree had crashed into the roof.

It wasn't as bad as he thought. Only one of the logs on the roof had been cracked from the weight of the pine, and the only hole it created didn't penetrate all the way through the roof.

Ulysses climbed down the ladder and headed to the front of the cabin to grab some water. When he entered, Anne was coming up from the basement, her bloody hands holding dirty gauze.

"How's he doing?" Ulysses asked.

Anne tossed the old bandages into the waste bucket. The dark bags under her eyes dragged her face down.

"He's getting a little warm. I've been giving him Ibuprofen to help with the fever and I've been redoing the dressings on his wound, but it's still too soon to tell. How's the roof?"

"Not as bad as I thought."

Ulysses walked into the kitchen with a slight limp. He tried to play it off, but Anne noticed.

"Did you hurt yourself?" Anne asked.

"I'm fine."

"You're not fine. Here, sit down," she said, pulling a chair out for him.

Anne helped him into the chair and grabbed a bottle of water out of the cabinet. Ulysses gulped it down. She disappeared into the basement and came back holding two pills and extended her hand to him.

Ulysses popped the pills into his mouth and leaned back in the chair gingerly.

"Your back?" Anne asked.

"Just tired," Ulysses said.

"Ulysses, now's not the time to be a hero. I can't have two seriously injured men to take care of. I need you to be careful."

Ulysses twirled the gold band around his finger. He smiled to himself.

"You're just like her, you know."

"Like who?"

"My late wife Margaret."

The chair creaked as Ulysses leaned forward. He rubbed his fingers along the calluses covering his palms, the flesh still pink from the friction of the wooden handle on the axe.

"She was the strongest woman I ever met. I remember the first time I saw her. I had just started engineering school. The farm next to her family's needed a new barn and called the construction company I worked for. We went on our first date that night. Sandwiches by the river."

Ulysses could still smell the mud on the riverbank. He could feel his bare feet, squishing into the mud. His hand finding hers for the first time and remembering how warm her skin was. The moonlight danced off her hair, and her green eyes glowed in the darkness.

"I wish I could have met her," Anne said.

"She would have liked you," Ulysses answered.

Freddy came into the kitchen, yawning.

"Who would have liked you, Mom?" Freddy asked.

"Grandma," Anne said, lifting Freddy into her arms and kissing his temple.

"Do you think she would have liked me?" Freddy asked.

"She would have loved you," Ulysses replied.

"Well, I would love some breakfast," Freddy said.

Anne set him down, and he rushed over to the table behind Ulysses.

"I think we all would. Ulysses?" Anne asked.

"I'd love some," Ulysses replied.

19

DAY 6 (BIKER GANG)

*T*he motorcycles flew down the highway, scattered randomly along the road. Jake rode in front, leading his men to whatever town came next. They'd left Cleveland behind to rot. They'd been riding for forty miles before they came across Carrollton, a small town just west of Pennsylvania in the middle of nowhere.

Whatever cars the town had were parked right where they were when the EMP blast hit. Jake led the Diablos onto Carrollton's main street, past some of their local stores and the sheriff's office, to the motel. The bikers pulled into the motel's parking lot side by side. The locals came out of their shops. The sight of working transportation caused a lot of jaws to drop.

Jake cut the engine off and set the kickstand out, leaning the bike to the side. His face was red from the wind, and his hair was blown back. His dark sunglasses reflected the townspeople moving toward him.

"Afternoon, folks," Hank Murth said.

Hank Murth was an elderly man. He had walked out of the grocery store that bore his name. He had his apron on, and the pistol hanging at his hip seemed out of place. He extended his hand to Jake, who ignored it.

The crowd around them grew. None of Jake's men moved until he did, so they followed his lead, just waiting. Questions flooded the air:

"How did you guys get the bikes to work?"

"Is the rest of the country in trouble?"

"Where did you come from?"

"Is help on the way?"

Most of the townspeople were older. Their worn faces pleading for answers, worried about what the future would hold for them. Jake looked around and noticed more people leaving their stores, coming out in the street to meet them, but the only person he kept his eyes on was the sheriff strutting down the sidewalk.

Sheriff Barnes was a good ol' boy if Jake ever saw one, all the way from his cowboy hat to his boots and that polished badge shining in the sun. Two deputies dressed in similar fashion followed closely behind him.

"Well, I never thought I'd see the day where I'd be happy to have a group of bikers roll through my town," Barnes said.

Jake looked the officers up and down. Their bellies protruded over their waists, their gun holster straps still covering their pistols, slowing them down if they had to draw. They were kind. They were weak.

"How many people do you have in town, Sheriff?" Jake asked.

"Oh, I'd say there's probably fifty of us here right now, more if you count some of the surrounding farms."

"You and your deputies have any trouble lately? Any shortages of anything?"

"Well, no, so far we've been okay."

Jake pulled the knife from his side and jammed it into the sheriff's throat. The blood spurt over Jake's arm as he dug the blade deeper. Jake pulled the blade out, and the sheriff dropped to the ground. The sheriff's blood drenched his shirt and dimmed the shine on his badge.

Before the deputies could react, Frankie blasted them through the eyes with his pistol. Hank reached for his gun, but Jake drew his own pistol and shot Hank through the gut.

Hank barreled over to the ground, and the rest of the crowd scattered. They ran for their stores, their homes, whatever cover they could find.

With the town's law at Jake's feet and their blood pooling on the street, Jake turned to his men, specks of the sheriff's blood still fresh on his face.

"We take what we want, boys. This town is ours," Jake said.

The Diablos cheered and made their way down Main Street. Jake had his men hit the hunting store first. They smashed the windows, broke the glass cases housing the weapons, and hoarded all the ammo they could find.

They all spread out, hunting down the townspeople like dogs. A few fought back, but there weren't enough that did to cause any trouble. Jake and his club were twenty strong. They were hungry, vicious, and had nothing to lose.

Gunshots and screams filled the town's streets. Jake could see people running down the highway. He gathered six of his men around him.

"You three take the north end, and you three take the south. Anyone that tries to run for it, you gun down, understand?" Jake asked.

They nodded and took off toward the ends of town. Jake flagged down Frankie.

"Clear out the motel," Jake said.

Frankie ran through the small motel, smashing down doors. He cleared the first floor and made his way up to the second. Each room he checked was empty. He blasted the locks of the doors until he came across a family huddled in the corner of their room: a husband, wife, and three daughters.

The husband tried to keep his family behind him, shielding them from harm. They were all shaking. The husband was the first to stand and speak.

"P-please. We don't w-want any trouble," he said.

The smoke from Frankie's gun barrel rose in the air next to him. He holstered his pistol, smiling. His left hand went for the blade on his side. He ran his fingers across the flat end of the steel right up to the tip.

The husband stepped forward, his hands trying to form fists. Frankie toyed with him, jerking forward to scare the man, keeping him on his toes. Each time Frankie moved, the wife and daughters behind him let out a yelp, and with each yelp Frankie let out a throaty laugh.

When the husband finally made a move for the blade, Frankie knocked his hand out of the way and thrust the five inches of steel into the husband's stomach.

Frankie twisted and turned the knife in the husband's gut. The husband's hands groped Frankie, grasping onto him and trying to hold on to the last moments of life he had left.

Blood dribbled down the husband's chin and then he collapsed on the carpet, coughing up blood, clutching the knife wound and trying to staunch the bleeding with his hands.

The wife crawled to him with tears running down her face. She held his face in her hands. His eyes stared blankly up at her. His lungs gasped for breath until finally the gasps stopped, his body lying motionless before her.

Drops of blood from Frankie's knife dripped on the carpet next to him. He wiped the blood from the blade onto the bedsheets, smearing red stains at the foot of the bed.

"Well, aren't you a pretty bunch," Frankie said.

Frankie's ragged black hair hung in mangled strands across his face. A week without showering had let the grime on his skin build up, and a strong odor surrounded his body. He pointed at the oldest daughter, Mary, who was no older than sixteen.

"You. Come here," he said.

"No!" the mother cried, rushing back to her daughters.

Frankie moved slowly toward them. The daughters retreated farther into the corner of the room by the sink and bathroom. All three daughters were crying, their mother spreading her arms wide, offering her body as the only protection she had to give.

"Come here," Frankie repeated.

Frankie tossed the mother aside and seized Mary's arm. The girl flailed as he threw her onto the bed covered with the bloodstains of her father.

"Wait!" the mother screamed.

Frankie pointed the pistol at the youngest daughter, Erin, and the mother stopped.

"Wait," she said calmly. "Take me."

She slowly unbuttoned her blouse, her fingers trembling and fumbling with each button. She walked slowly to him, taking her shirt off.

"Take me," she repeated.

Frankie looked her up and down. The gun still pointed at Erin, while Mary lay on her back, frozen in fear on the bed.

"Just let them go," the mother said.

She was standing directly in front of him now. Frankie ran the tip of his blade gently across the mother's exposed flesh.

"Take off your pants," Frankie ordered.

She undid the clip on her skirt and let it slide down her legs onto the ground. She kicked the skirt off of her bare feet. Small spasms shook her body as she stood there awkwardly in front of him.

Frankie grabbed her by the hair and threw her on the bed next to her daughter. The mother tried to push Mary off the bed, but Frankie pointed the pistol at her.

"No. She watches," Frankie said, smiling.

Frankie's jeans dropped to the floor, and he climbed on top of the mother. She turned her head to her daughters, their faces red and wet with tears. Her face was calm. She slowly mouthed, "Close your eyes."

The mattress rocked back and forth. Frankie's grunts were loud and sharp. He kept his head down, his face buried into the mother's neck, forcing his body onto hers.

The door to the motel room still hung open. Outside the sounds of gunfire and screams echoed in the distance.

The mom saw the open door and used her free hand to grab Mary's arm. Mary opened her eyes, focusing only on her mother's face. The mother made a quick nod toward the door and pointed to her other daughters crouching on the floor.

Mary nodded and gently crawled off the bed. She rushed over to Erin and the middle sister, Nancy, and grabbed the two of them.

The mother wrapped her arms around Frankie's back, her lower lip quivering as she coaxed him on.

"Yes," she whispered

"You like that, bitch?"

Frankie thrust his body harder into her, and the mother cried in pain as she watched her daughters slip out the door.

The three girls ran down the concrete sidewalk outside the rooms, ducking below the windows when they saw the doors open and the sounds of other bikers inside.

Mary led the pack, checking each open door they passed, making sure it was safe. The only one that kept glancing back to where they'd left their mother was Erin.

All of them were barefoot, and once they made it to the parking lot, Mary picked up Erin and they sprinted across the cracked pavement, avoiding the line of bikes parked near the front.

They made it onto Main Street and ran inside the first store they came across. The windows were smashed to Murth's Grocery, and inside a body lay across the tile, a trail of blood following it from the street.

Hank Murth was on his back, gasping for breath when the three girls came in. The bell at the top of the glass door jingled when they entered. The girls gasped at the sight of the body.

"Mary, what are we going to do? What about Mom?" Nancy said.

Mary whipped around, her face angry, and grabbed Nancy by the shoulders and shook her violently.

"Will you shut up?" Mary screamed.

Nancy broke down. She collapsed to the floor, weeping.

"I'm sorry, Nancy. I just…" Mary said.

The crack in Mary's voice brought on sobs of her own. She had no idea where she was going, what she needed to do to protect her sisters, or how to help her mother. She closed her eyes, trying to get the picture of her mother lying on the bed out of her mind.

"In the back," Hank said.

Hank was lifting a bloody, shaking hand, pointing behind him. His breaths were short and sporadic. His lungs wheezed with effort, trying to stay alive.

"There's a… room… in the back… stay there," Hank said.

The back of the store was dimly lit.

"It's… safe," Hank said.

Mary was out of options. She grabbed her sisters and headed to the back of the store. A small sliver of light came from under the crack of a door. Mary turned the doorknob and pushed it open.

It must have been a room where the old man was living. There was a small cot on the far side of the room when they entered. A desk with a kerosene lamp on it, mirror, sink, and closet door filled the rest of the tiny space.

Mary locked the door behind her. Nancy picked Erin up and put her on the bed, while Mary paced back and forth.

"What do we do now?" Nancy asked.

"I don't know," Mary said.

"When do we get to see Mom and Dad again?" Erin asked.

Mary froze in the middle of the room. Nancy looked back at Erin, whose legs swung on the edge of the bed.

Erin's eyes had the uncertainty and naiveté only a four-year-old could have.

"Erin, did you see what happened?" Mary asked.

"I saw Daddy fall down and hold his stomach like he had a tummy ache, and then I saw Mom change her clothes when that man was talking to you," Erin said.

"Daddy did fall down, but it wasn't because he had a tummy ache. Erin, you won't see Daddy again."

"Why?"

"Dad's… dead. Do you know what that means?"

"Yes. Kimmy Sears in my class said her dad died of cancer and that she only gets to go and visit his grave. Is that what we have to do now?"

Nancy started crying. She buried her face in her hands, her shoulders shaking violently from her sobs.

Mary pulled Nancy to her. She wrapped her arms around her sister, holding her and stroking her hair.

"Yes, that's what we have to do now," Mary said.

The crash of glass hitting the floor spun all of them around to the door of the room. Mary dimmed the lamp.

"Shh," Mary said.

Mary unlocked the door and cracked it open, trying to see what happened.

Two bikers entered, crunching pieces of glass under their boots.

"Well, look here, Pete. This old bastard's still alive," Don said.

"Resilient bag of bones, isn't he?" Pete asked.

"Please…" Hank said.

One of the bikers pulled his pistol out. The hammer cocked back, and he pointed it right at the old man's face. Mary covered her mouth, her eyes watering. The biker squeezed the trigger, and the gunshot blasted through Hank's head. His body went limp. Mary gasped.

"Hey, did you hear that?" Pete asked.

"Hear what?"

"It came from the back."

Mary's heart beat faster. She retreated back into the room and told Erin and Nancy to hide under the cot. Mary ran to the closet and crammed herself inside. The closet was too small for her to close all of the way, so she had to leave a sliver of it open.

"It was in here," Pete said.

The door creaked open. Through the crack, she could see the barrels of their guns poking around the room.

"I didn't hear anything, Pete," Don said.

Pete let out a whistle.

"The old man didn't have much, did he? Look at this shit hole," Pete said.

Each step of their boots around the tiny room caused Mary to shudder. She breathed as softly as she could, scared to even move. She clutched the clothes hanging around her with both hands, making sure they stayed motionless.

She could only make out parts of their faces. One of the bikers turned, and she noticed a flaming devil on the back of his jacket. The devil had his head thrown back, laughing.

"C'mon, Pete, let's get out of here. The way this place looks, it was probably rats," Don said.

"All right."

Mary watched both of them leave through the cracked door of the closet. Once she couldn't hear the sound of their boots anymore, she exhaled. Nancy and Erin crawled out from under the bed.

"C'mon, we need to get out of here," Mary said.

They rushed out the back door of the grocery. They spilled out onto a small sidewalk next to a massive field of tall grass, five feet high. Mary led them behind the main street buildings, sprinting toward the end. Once they reached the edge of the buildings, Mary slowed down.

She peered her head around the brick wall and saw bikers smashing the storefront windows, carrying people to the middle of the street and executing them on their knees. Then two bikers spotted her.

"Hey!"

Mary grabbed Nancy's and Erin's hand. She pulled them along, searching for a place to hide behind the stores. She jiggled the handle of each door she passed. They were all locked.

The shouts from the bikers were getting closer. She didn't know where to go. She didn't know where to hide. She took her sisters and ran into the tall grass as far as she could and then dropped to the ground, pulling both of her sisters with her.

The grass was thick. Mary couldn't see anything around her or between the tall brown and green blades. She kept her hand over Erin's mouth to silence her sobs.

"Do you see them?"

"They're not in the buildings."

"Where'd they run off to?"

"Check the grass."

Mary brought her finger to her lips. She hushed them both quietly. All three of their bodies were shaking. Mary covered her own mouth with her hand, afraid she might give away their spot. The voices of the bikers taunted them.

"Come out, come out, wherever you are."

"We're not going to hurt you."

"Yeah, why don't you come out to play?"

Mary could hear the movement of grass being swept aside and

the steps of their boots on the blades, rocks, and dirt. All of a sudden, she could see the grass move and then...

"Hey!" a distant voice shouted.

"What?"

The biker's foot was only twelve inches away from Mary's face. She looked up but couldn't see the man's face through the blades of grass.

"Jake wants everybody back now. Quit jackin' off over there and head to the motel."

"All right."

The grass shifted but stopped as the sound of the biker's steps faded away from her. Mary kept her hand over her and Erin's mouth for a few more minutes until she was sure they were gone.

Mary rolled onto her back. The grass scratched against her exposed arms and legs. Erin crawled up next to her, and Nancy's breathing was quick as she hyperventilated.

"Mary," she said.

"Yeah."

"What do we do now? Where do we go?"

Erin rested her head on Mary's chest. Mary had her eyes closed and could feel the warm sun shining down on her. Her body felt tired, expended.

"Let's just lie here a few more minutes," Mary said.

20

DAY 9 (MIKE'S JOURNEY)

*T*he airport terminal was stuffy, and the springs in Mike's cot squeaked when he rolled over. It smelled like a musty towel, but it beat lying on the ground. He pushed himself off the cot and rested his boots on the floor. He'd slept with his shoes on ever since the fire at his house.

Nelson and Sean were still sleeping on their cots, and the To family, Fay, and Tom were sound asleep as well.

Mike lit a candle and weaved around the cots toward the kitchen door. He pulled his pocket watch out, running his fingers along the smooth surface before he opened it, checking the time. Seven a.m. The watch snapped shut, and he quietly pushed the door open and headed toward the front to meet Clarence.

Clarence sat crouched behind one of the check-in counters. He leaned up against the wall with a rifle over his lap. Whoever was on watch could see the entire front of the airport and could stay well hidden from the vantage point he had chosen.

"How was your shift?" Mike asked.

"Quiet. One guy walked by, but never came in."

"What would you have done if he had?"

"I... I don't know."

Mike could see the struggle on his face. It was something Mike had experienced himself, back in his neighborhood. He tried helping. He tried giving advice, but it fell against deaf ears. When the people around you begging for help resort to strangling you, it's time to fight back. Mike hoped that it wouldn't come to that for Clarence.

"The longer this goes on, the more desperate people will become," Mike said.

"I know."

Mike watched Clarence fumble the rifle awkwardly in his hands.

"You know I've never even fired one of these things before," Clarence said.

"You haven't?"

"Firearm training isn't a part of the TSA program."

Mike grabbed the rifle. He flipped it on its side, exposing the safety lever and making sure it was clicked on and pointed away from them.

"Rule number one when handling guns. Never point it at another person unless you're ready to pull the trigger."

Mike brought the rifle up to his shoulder and peered through the sights, scanning the front of the building.

"When you aim, you always want to bring the gun to your eyes, not the other way around. When you're handling a rifle or shotgun, keep the butt of the gun firmly tucked against your shoulder. It'll help with the recoil when you fire. When it's time to shoot, you want to squeeze the trigger. Don't pull it," Mike said.

Mike handed the gun back to Clarence. Mike watched him keep the end of the barrel away from the two of them, and he brought the rifle up to his shoulder.

"And know where the safety is. You don't want to be in a situation where you forget it's on and when you go to squeeze the trigger nothing happens," Mike said.

Clarence's thumb found the lever on the side of the rifle and flicked the safety off. He put his finger on the trigger.

"Wait," Mike said.

Clarence lowered the rifle, taking his hand off the trigger.

"Rule number two: never put your finger on the trigger unless you're ready to fire. Just keep your finger extended beyond the trigger until you're ready to shoot," Mike said.

"Right," Clarence said.

Mike grabbed the rifle out of Clarence's hand and clicked the safety back on. He threw the rifle strap over his shoulder and clapped Clarence on the back.

"We'll take it out back for target practice after breakfast," Mike said.

"You've taught people to shoot before?"

Mike paused, trying to overcome the lump forming in his throat. "Yes."

* * *

TOM AND FAY gathered the empty wrappers and cans from breakfast and threw them in the garbage, which was overflowing.

"It's your turn to take it out," Tom said.

"Fine," Fay replied.

Fay tied the open ends of the trash bag together and lifted it out of the can. The bag caught on a crack in the can and split open, dumping trash all over the floor.

"Goddamnit," Fay yelled.

Tom laughed. As he walked back through the kitchen, his laughter echoed through the food court.

Fay threw up a middle finger. She picked up the pieces of trash and dumped them back into the can. Once the mess was cleaned up she dragged the can to the front of the airport.

The can slid across the pavement until she reached the dumpster on the side of the building. She placed the can right next to it, and just then heard a gunshot go off. She immediately ducked for cover.

"Shit," she murmured.

She glanced around looking for the source of the shot, keeping her head covered. She squinted farther down the tarmac and saw Clarence, rifle in hand with Mike behind him, aiming at something in the distance.

Fay covered her ears as the gunshots continued to ring out. She walked to them and could see that both Mike and Clarence had ear protection on. She screamed their names, and when that didn't work, she threw an empty soup can at them. She hit Mike square in the back.

Mike took the earpieces off. Clarence clicked the safety on and leaned the rifle up against his shoulder.

"What the hell are you two doing?" Fay asked.

"Mike's teaching me how to shoot," Clarence said.

"He's pretty good," Mike said.

"Well, it took me a couple tries, but I finally got one."

Fay walked up to them and saw a row of soup cans set up thirty yards away on top of a luggage carrier.

"You really think this is a good idea? I thought we weren't supposed to bring attention to ourselves," Fay said.

"Most people run away from gunshots, not toward them," Mike said.

Fay grabbed the earpiece off Clarence's head.

"Where'd you get these?" Fay asked.

"Found them in the ground control locker rooms," Clarence said.

"Can I try?" Fay asked.

"Sure," Mike said.

Fay put the earpieces on, and Mike grabbed the rifle from Clarence. He showed her how to hold it and gave her the same advice he'd given to Clarence.

Fay brought the rifle up to her eyes. She kept the stock snug against her shoulder. Her finger hovered until she finally rested it gently over the trigger. The sights along the end of the rifle shook slightly as she tried to balance the gun. Once the gun felt steady, she lined up her shot, squeezed the trigger, and the can went flying.

"Shit," Clarence said.

"Nice shot. You're a natural," Mike said.

"What?" Fay screamed.

Mike patted her on the shoulder and gave her a thumbs-up. She smiled and then noticed the crowd behind her. Everyone had gathered outside. They were all looking at her and cheering. Fay's smile slowly faded. She handed the rifle back to Mike and took her ear protection off.

"Where are you going?" Clarence asked.

Fay ignored him. She ran between Jung and Jenna and headed for the side door, which led her to the food court. Once she was inside she sat on her cot, her shoulder feeling the strain from the recoil of the rifle.

Clarence walked in behind her, panting from the short jog he made running after her.

"What was that about?" he asked.

"Do we have any more Ibuprofen?" Fay asked.

"I think so, but Fay, why'd you leave like that?"

"Where is it? I don't want my shoulder to be too sore."

"Fay."

"What?"

Fay's voice was harsh, accusing. She saw the open look of apology across Clarence's face. He held his hands out and sat down on the cot next to her.

"What's going on?"

"I'm fine."

"You're not fine."

"It was a lucky shot. That's all."

"That's why you ran? Because you hit the can?"

"No."

"Then why'd you take off like that?"

"I don't want to talk about it."

"Fay…"

"I don't want to talk about it!"

Fay bolted from the cot, leaving Clarence by himself. She ran through the food court and past the check-in desks by the front entrance of the airport, her feet carrying her to the other side of the airport. She ran around security ropes and jumped over fallen displays until there wasn't anywhere left to run. She leaned her hands up against the wall, her chest heaving, trying to catch her breath.

She spun around and slammed her back against the wall and slid down. She wiped the sweat from her forehead and rested her head against her knees.

* * *

MIKE DROPPED small amounts of oil along the tip of the barrel then wiped it down with a rag. Nelson watched Mike's movements. They were precise, rhythmic.

"WHAT DO WE DO NOW?" Nelson asked.

"WE LEAVE TOMORROW. I can't afford to stay here another day," Mike said.

"BUT WHAT ABOUT THESE PEOPLE?"

"NELSON, the cabin was built for me and my family. It can hold five people at the most. Bringing you and Sean along with me is already pushing it. I can't show up with another seven people."

.   .   .

"THESE PEOPLE HELPED US. They fed us. Took us in."

"These people stayed here and hoarded as much food as they could."

"BUT THEY SAID they're leaving soon too. Why don't we ask where they're going? Maybe it's better than the cabin?"

"MY FAMILY ISN'T wherever it is they're going. My family is at the cabin. If you want to go with them, you're more than welcome, but tomorrow morning I'm leaving with or without you and Sean. End of discussion."

MIKE FINISHED WIPING down the rifle and slung it over his shoulder. He walked back into the food court through the side door. Jung and Jenna To were watching their two children play when he walked in. Jung saw him and made a beeline for him.

"MIKE," he said.

"I'M BUSY," Mike said, grabbing one of the lanterns from the Burger King counter.

"PLEASE, WAIT."

JUNG PUT his hand on Mike's chest, stopping him and blocking his path.

"LET MY FAMILY COME WITH YOU," Jung said.

"JUNG, I don't have anywhere for your family to go."

.   .   .

"The cabin, right? You're going to the cabin?"

Nelson.

"Look, Jung, whatever it is you think I can help you with, I can't. I'm sorry, but I can't," Mike said and then moved to the side and ran past him.

Jung caught up with him as Mike headed back to the weapons depot where Clarence had shown him the rifles.

"We were heading back home to China when everything stopped working."

"Isn't your wife American? Doesn't she have family here?"

"She does, but they're in Florida. We were here on vacation."

"You wanted to go vacation in Pittsburgh?"

"New York. We were here as part of a layover."

The deeper they went into the airport, the darker it became. Mike flicked on the lantern. The flame ignited, casting an orange glow around the two of them and lighting their path.

Clarence and the rest of the group hadn't ventured into the dark portions of the airport because of the bodies. When they came out of the TSA security room after the rioting started, they searched for supplies, and the only things they found deep within the terminals were corpses.

You could barely see them in the darkness, but the smell was overpowering. The rotting flesh baking for the past week in the unventilated, un-air-conditioned depths of the airport sent a foul stench in the air. The sour, bitter musk hit you like a brick wall.

By the time Mike and Jung reached the weapons holding, both of them were gagging, covering their noses and mouths with their shirts, but it did no good.

The inside of the weapons holding was practically barren when they checked it earlier. Most of the weapons had been picked over, but a few rifles, a stack of boxes with ammunition, and a cleaning kit still remained.

"Grab those rifles over there," Mike said.

"Mike, please. My family can't stay here. If there was help coming, it would have been here by now. If we can't get somewhere safe, we'll end up like those people out there."

The lantern swung in Mike's grip. The light danced across Jung's face, which was filled with desperation, a look he'd seen too often over the past week.

"You pull your weight, each of you. Everyone has a job. No one gets special treatment. Understand?"

Jung nodded.

. . .

"GOOD. NOW, GRAB THE RIFLES."

* * *

THE TO FAMILY, Nelson, Sean, Tom, Clarence, and Mike sat around one of the tables in the food court. The sun had gone down, and they were swallowing down cans of ham and black beans. Fay was on watch.

Mike chose to tell the rest of the group about the cabin. They all jumped at the chance. Mike instructed each of them to pack enough food and supplies for a two-day walk. Everyone dumped any luggage they had and immediately started packing.

"After we leave in the morning, it'll be important for us not to stop. I want to make sure we get there as quickly and safely as possible," Mike said.

"Will it really take two days?" Tom asked.

"Yes, and it could take more if anything slows us down," Mike answered.

"What's it like out there now?" Jenna asked.

"The road? Dangerous," Mike answered.

"Do you think we'll get mugged like you and Nelson?" Clarence asked.

"Not if we stay smart," Mike answered.

"Guys, we'll be fine. Mike knows what he's doing. Trust me," Nelson said.

Trust him. Mike looked at the faces staring at him, and a pang of guilt shot through him. The last time he helped people, they turned against him and separated him from his family. He wasn't going to let a gang of bandits stand between him and his family ever again. If it came down to it, he would sacrifice the lot of them to reach his family.

After dinner, it was time for Mike to relieve Fay of her watch. She was posted in the corner where she was supposed to be, vigilantly staring into the night.

"Grab some dinner," Mike said.

"Thanks."

Fay put her hand out, and Mike helped her up. She handed him the rifle, but before she turned to go, he stopped her.

"You sure you never used a rifle before?" Mike asked.

"No. That was my first time."

"Well, it was quite a shot."

"Thanks. And thanks for saving us."

"I haven't saved anyone."

"Well, you're doing more than most would... More than I would."

The last words were said to herself, and Mike could see from her reaction they weren't meant to be said aloud.

"Do you know why I took off today after I hit the can?" Fay asked.

"No."

"It was because I saw the look on everyone's faces. They saw that I could do something that they couldn't. They saw that I could be someone to protect them. They thought I was someone who could keep them safe."

"Why did that make you run?"

"Because if I didn't keep them safe, and I knew how to do it, then I failed. So, that's why you've already saved us. You're not afraid."

Mike sat down as Fay turned to leave. He stared out into the night. The moon was full, so he could see clearly. He thought about what Fay had said. She was wrong. He was afraid, but it wasn't the type of fear that comes with indifference. It was the fear that comes with action. He knew what he was capable of. He remembered how easily he had pulled the trigger on the neighbors attacking his house. He could see the blood spilling onto the grass of his lawn, turning everything crimson.

He cradled the rifle in his lap and rested his head back against the wall. He pushed the rest out of his mind with one single thought: *get to my family.*

DAY 9 (THE CABIN)

"*D*ammit, Ulysses, will you let me finish what I'm saying!" Ray screamed.

Ray propped himself up on his elbows from the couch. Sweat beaded on his forehead. Anne tried to ease him back down onto the couch, but he pushed her away.

"You have no idea what's in that town. It could be overrun," Ray said.

Ulysses put in a few bottles of water and a day's ration worth of food into the satchel. He pulled the strap of the bag over his head and let it fall across his chest. A holster rested on the counter, the pistol's grip sticking out. He slung it around his waist and clipped the belt together.

"Maybe I don't know what's in town, but I do know what'll happen if your fever keeps going the way it has," Ulysses said.

Ray's arms were shaking from the exertion of keeping himself upright. His elbow gave way, and he collapsed back on the couch. The room felt like it was spinning. His head swayed back and forth. He tried to collect his thoughts. Before he could come up with a rebuttal, he felt a hand on his chest and Ulysses's face came in and out of focus.

"I'm going, Raymond," Ulysses said.

"Remember what I told you," Anne said.

"I'll be fine."

Ulysses walked out the door and down the dirt path that winded up to the cabin. The town was only a mile and a half away.

The morning sun wasn't yet hot, and the trees around him provided nice shade. His boots crunched the twigs and leaves on the ground. Along the way, he saw a deer and a few turkeys. *Good hunting.*

Once Ulysses made it out of the tree line and back onto the highway, he headed west to the town of Carrollton. He could see the small outline of the buildings on Main Street in the distance. The tall fields of grass surrounding the town stretched out to the forest tree lines surrounding it.

The road was completely clear with the exception of a tractor that had shut down in the middle of the road, blocking both lanes. Ulysses glanced up into the cab window. He climbed up and opened the door, taking a look inside. Except for a pair of gloves on the seat, it was empty.

From his elevated position, he was able to see into the distance. He looked for signs of any farms in the distance, but was disappointed when he could find nothing. He jumped back down from the tractor and continued his journey into town.

The buildings grew larger the closer he came. The sun had crept higher into the sky, and the heat was bearing down on him now. The cool of the morning was disappearing. He reached into his pack and pulled out one of the bottles of water he packed. He took a sip. The town was only another hundred yards away.

Ulysses squinted his eyes at lumps scattered on Main Street. At first he couldn't tell what they were, then he glanced up into the sky and saw the buzzards circling. His pace slowed. He glanced around the buildings, looking for signs of any people. He edged along the side of the road, moving along in the tall grass for cover.

The only part of him exposed was the top of his head. His eyes scanned above the grass, looking for anyone that might have seen him coming. He approached the stores on the right side of Main Street and waited on the edge where the tall grass ended and the clearing began.

There was no movement in the town, so Ulysses kept low and ran up to the side of the first store. He followed the edge of the building's wall to the main road.

The buzzards overhead squawked, still circling the rotting flesh down below. Ulysses turned his focus to the storefronts. Most of their windows had been smashed in. None of those close by was a pharmacy.

Ulysses adjusted the strap along his chest and mapped out a

route in his mind. There were enough cars for him to hide behind, so he'd have to pass each store carefully, checking to see if there was anyone inside.

He sprinted to the other side of the street and knelt down by a car. He put his hands on the hood but then removed them quickly. The metal on the car was scorching.

Ulysses crept along the storefronts, checking inside each window before he passed. Each one he looked into was ransacked. He kept his eyes peeled for a pharmacy and then, halfway down Main Street, he finally saw it.

The pharmacy windows were smashed, but its green painted letters glistened in the sun. Ulysses kept his hand close to the holster on his hip as he moved toward the pharmacy.

As he approached the motel, he could hear voices in the distance. He couldn't make out what they were saying, but the murmuring grew louder. Ulysses stopped at the corner of the building right before the motel. Two bikers came into the parking lot.

"The dumb bitch is still here. I'm surprised she hasn't taken off yet."

"How the hell is she supposed to escape when she's got another guy on her every twenty minutes?"

"You try her out?"

"Yeah, I've had better, but it wasn't bad."

The sound of their boots and voices started to fade. Ulysses grabbed the pistol from his holster. He clicked the safety off and glanced around the corner. He saw the back side of the two men he had overheard heading to the far end of the motel, and then they disappeared through one of the doors.

Ulysses waited to see if someone else would come outside, but no one did. A car sat out front of the motel in the street, riddled with bullets. He made a dash for it, crouching behind the engine. His fingers gripped the gunshot holes in the passenger door.

Another car sat parked in front of the pharmacy. He glanced back through the window of the car, checking to see if anyone was watching. When he took off running, his knees popped, and when he reached the curb of the sidewalk, he tripped. The pistol flew from his hand and skidded across the sidewalk.

He pushed himself off the pavement, wincing. He grabbed the pistol and leaned back against a building wall. He looked to see if anyone saw him. Nothing. He panted heavily, trying to catch his breath. He looked down at his knee and his torn jeans. The skin peeled off, revealing a bloody spot. He reached out to touch it, then recoiled.

"Dammit."

He grabbed the side of the car for support and pushed himself up on his good leg. He limped over to the pharmacy door. The frame was busted, and it swung open crooked when he pushed it. Glass crunched under his boots. He kept the pistol up, scanning the abandoned store.

Most of the shelves were smashed. The tip of his boot kicked an empty prescription bottle, and it rolled across the floor. He grabbed the bag and pulled out the piece of paper with the name of the antibiotics that Anne told him to find.

His fingers fumbled through the bottles of pills. They rattled as he spun them around, holding each of them to the light from the window, checking the labels. He scanned the first wall, found nothing, then moved on to the next.

He went through all of the shelves, scraping his hands reaching through the broken glass cabinets that had been locked. Finally, Ulysses brought one of the bottles to the window, checked the label, and gave a sigh.

Ulysses tossed the bottle into his bag and made a step toward the exit when he saw three bikers head out of their room in the motel and walk across the parking lot. Ulysses slid behind the wall next to the door. He inched to the edge of the broken window and peered out through the jagged edges of glass.

"Hold on, Frankie, I'm gonna go grab some more of that shit out of the pharmacy. I'll meet you guys over there."

"All right, Garrett."

Two of them drifted off farther down the road, and Garrett made a beeline for the pharmacy. Ulysses tried to move, but his leg didn't respond fast enough to hide. When Garrett walked through the door, Ulysses hit him in the back of the head with his pistol.

Garrett stumbled into the counter and pulled out his piece. Ulysses squeezed his trigger and shot Garrett in the leg and stomach. He squeezed the trigger again, sending a bullet through Garrett's chest, dropping him to the floor.

Ulysses could hear the shouts and the sound of boots coming in his direction. He hobbled around Garrett's body and made his way to the back of the store. Each step sent a knife digging into his knee and then ran all the way up to his hip. He pushed himself as fast as he could go. He swung the back door open and stepped outside, the sun shining bright in the blue sky. He glanced around for any place he could hide. He looked to his left. Nothing. He looked right. Nothing. The tall grass in front of him was the only place that offered any cover.

Ulysses limped through the grass for twenty feet then dropped to the ground. He crawled, spreading the grass apart, trying to see in front of him when he found himself looking into the eyes of a young girl, frozen in shock, lying hidden in the grass.

"Spread out! I want the head of whatever prick did this on a steak before lunch!" Frankie said.

"All right, Frankie."

Ulysses brought his finger to his lips. The girl nodded. Ulysses saw some other movement behind her, and then Nancy's and Erin's eyes stared back at him through the grass.

The bikers swept through the tall grass, searching for them.

"Frankie, this shit is thick. It could take a while before we find them."

"Then you can be the one to tell Jake why you let someone get away with killing one of our brothers."

* * *

IT WAS an hour before the bikers gave up their search. The bikers disappeared, and Ulysses finally let his body relax. He let his head rest on the ground for a moment. He felt the cool earth, with its rocks and pebbles under his belly. He rolled onto his back, wincing from the pain in his knee.

"Are you girls okay?" Ulysses asked.

"We're not hurt," Mary said.

"If we can get to the edge of town, we can follow the highway to my cabin. You three can come with me," Ulysses said.

He saw her hesitation as she stared at the pistol in his hand. He holstered it.

"My family is there. It's safe. I promise."

"Mary, I don't know if we should go. What about Mom?" Nancy asked.

"We can come back for your mom, but we'll need help," Ulysses said.

"You promise we can come back for her?" Mary asked.

"Promise."

Ulysses noticed the dirt smeared on their faces, the scratches and cuts from the rocks and grass around them, the dark circles under their eyes, their sunburnt faces. These girls had been here for a while.

"Okay," Mary said.

"Stay low and follow me," Ulysses said.

Each time Ulysses's knee hit the ground while he crawled, a shot of pain shot through his entire leg. After thirty yards he collapsed on his side. It felt like a pad of spikes was sticking into his knee.

"Are you all right?" Mary asked.

Ulysses nodded. He led the girls through the grass, Ulysses having to stop every now and then to rest.

"How much longer?" Mary asked.

"Shouldn't be much further," Ulysses answered. He poked his head over the grass and saw they were even with the end of the stores on Main Street.

"The highway is just another twenty yards. We'll want to stay in the grass for a little ways before we start walking on the road in case they have people keeping watch," he said.

They traveled up the side of the highway a little further, crawling along the grass, avoiding rocks, and on the watch for snakes. Ulysses checked behind them one more time to see how far they were from the town. It was over a hundred yards behind them, so Ulysses motioned for them to get on the road. The three of them moved as fast as they could. Ulysses hobbled trying to keep up, and Mary went back and put his arm around her shoulder to help steady him.

* * *

JAKE SLAMMED the knife onto the table. The men around him had their heads down, not daring to look him in the face.

"You're telling me three girls did this?" Jake asked.

"Maybe they thought they could get their mom back," Frankie answered.

Jake stared Frankie down. He motioned for the other two bikers to leave the room, and they shut the door behind them. Jake walked over to Frankie, looking behind him at the closed door. The room was hot and stuffy. Jake put his hand on Frankie's shoulder.

"You're getting sloppy, Frankie," Jake said.

"Jake, I'm sorry."

Jake patted Frankie's cheeks softly and then turned his back to him.

"I know you are," Jake said.

Jake sent his fist to the side of Frankie's jaw, sending him to the ground with a thud. Jake picked him up by his cut and threw him into the mirror above the dresser, shattering it to pieces. Jake picked Frankie up by his hair and yanked his head back.

"You're letting a group of girls get the better of you? I want you to find them and bring them to me, do you understand?"

Frankie nodded. Jake let go of his hair and pushed him backwards.

"Tell the boys we'll have Garrett's wake tonight," Jake said.

* * *

KALEN SAT on the end of her bed, staring out the cabin window. The sun was breaking through the trees, sending beams of light into her room. Her fingers rubbed the bruises around her neck. The flesh was still tender. Whenever she moved, she could feel the strain of her muscles and tendons. Her lip was still slightly swollen on the bottom corner.

She fell back on the bed, recalling a faint memory of the day before, of the woods and being dragged into them by a strange man. She didn't feel like moving. She hadn't felt like talking. Every time her mom came in the room to speak with her, she shut down. She knew her mom was trying to help, but there wasn't anything that she could tell her that would make her feel better.

She hadn't slept for more than a few hours a night since they arrived at the cabin, and the hours she did rest were distressing. When she closed her eyes, all she could see was him on top of her. She could feel his hands gripping her neck, the weight of his body forcing himself on her, the feel of his unwanted hands.

Then, she would wake. Her heart would be pounding, her hands trying to free a grip that wasn't there. The attack replayed in her mind over and over. She tried to remember everything, but pieces were missing. Her last clear thought was of the man on top of her, his hands around her neck and the screams of her mother in the distance. After that she could only remember waking up in the Jeep with the blanket over her.

Kalen reached into the drawer of the nightstand next to her and pulled out a bottle of pills. Her hands were shaky as she opened the top of the bottle. The label on the side read "Oxycodone." The once full bottle was already half empty.

She popped three of the pills in her mouth, letting her body go numb. Her heart rate started to come back down; the rolling weight of dullness fell upon her. Her thoughts started to scramble. She couldn't remember what she was thinking about anymore. She could only feel herself sinking into the bed beneath her and the warm sun beating on her legs through the window.

The crash of the front door swinging open snapped her out of her daze. She could hear the shuffling of feet and the sliding of furniture. There were voices she didn't recognize.

Her legs felt heavy when she moved them. Her whole body was heavy. She moved toward the door of her room, swaying slightly back and forth. When she reached for the doorknob, everything seemed to move in slow motion.

Kalen's hands padded along the walls of the hallway as she tried to steady herself. She could see people moving in the living room. She saw two young girls staring back at her, their faces smudged in dirt and their nightgowns covered in grass and mud.

The two girls were holding each other's hands. That's all Kalen could focus on. Then there was a slight buzzing in her ears. Her eyes shifted from the two small hands laced together to her mother mouthing words at her, until finally the sound broke through the humming in her mind.

"Kalen!" Anne said.

"What?" Kalen asked.

"Grab the antibiotics out of Grandpa's bag and a bottle of water out of the kitchen and give them to Ray."

"Okay."

Kalen tried to focus on the task. She made herself walk to the bag, search it until she heard the sound of pills rattling in a bottle, then put one foot in front of the other to grab a bottle of water from the cabinet.

On the walk back, a third girl was staring at her. She was around Kalen's age, a little bit taller than she was though, and had the same dirt-smudged face as the younger girls. The three of them looked alike.

Kalen twisted the top of the bottle off. Ray's face was dripping with sweat. She could feel the heat coming off of his body just standing next to him. She shut her eyes hard. Her thoughts felt jumbled. She tried focusing on the task at hand.

Tilt his head up. Give him the pill. Have him drink the water.

She recited it a few more times in her head, making sure she had it correctly. She opened her eyes and tilted Ray's head up. His mouth opened, and she placed the pill on his tongue. She placed the bottle to his lips. She slowly tilted the water into his mouth. Most of it went down his chin and onto his shirt, but enough made it into his mouth for him to swallow the pill.

She fell onto the floor, her butt landing hard against the wooden planks. Her thoughts became jumbled again. She felt a hand pulling her up then pushing her down the hallway. She felt the hand guide her into bed, where she collapsed into a dreamless sleep she desperately needed.

* * *

THE ROOM WAS dark when Kalen opened her eyes. The sunlight that had come through the window earlier in the day had been replaced by the silver glow of the moon. The pills had worn off. She started to remember again. She reached for the drawer of the nightstand.

The familiar rattle of pills was gone. She pulled the drawer open farther, her hand running along the bare sides and bottom. Nothing.

A glow of light from under her door caught her attention. The glow faded, as if moving down the hall. When she opened the door, she saw a girl around her age, her face lit by candlelight. She looked familiar.

"Hi," Mary said.

"Hi."

"I didn't mean to wake you up. I was just getting some water."

"You came in with my grandfather earlier today, didn't you?"

"Yeah. He found us in town and brought us up here."

"I'm Kalen."

"Mary."

The two girls shook hands. Kalen could feel the dryness in her mouth. She followed Mary to the kitchen for some water.

Kalen tipped the bottle back and downed half of it immediately. She didn't realize how thirsty she was until the water hit her lips. Her stomach growled.

"I think there was still some meat left over from dinner," Mary said.

Anne had cooked some of the canned chicken from the supplies downstairs. Mary had saved some for a snack later but gave it to Kalen instead.

Kalen wolfed the food down. The fork scraped the sides of the bowl until there was nothing left, then she placed it on the counter. She wiped her mouth with the corners of her sleeve.

"Are you okay?" Mary asked.

"Yeah, why?"

"It's just I don't see how someone who has an entire basement stockpiled with food acts like they haven't eaten in days."

That's because she hadn't eaten in days. Her last meal had been in their old house. A house she watched go up in flames with her father inside.

"Who were the girls with you?" Kalen asked.

"My sisters."

"What about your parents?"

Kalen recognized the look on Mary's face. It was the same look she'd been wearing for the past three days. Kalen changed the subject.

"Where are you from?" Kalen asked.

"California."

"What are you doing in Ohio?"

"We were on vacation. My dad wanted to have his daughters experience the world of the small town. We've been on a road trip all summer. We were planning on heading back the day everything turned off."

Kalen watched Mary's eyes drift down when she mentioned her father. She had said "dad" very softly.

"What about you?" Mary asked.

"Pennsylvania."

"Were you guys here when everything went out?"

"No, we were back home in Pittsburgh."

"You walked all the way from Pittsburgh to here?"

"We drove."

Mary laughed.

"I'm serious," Kalen said. "The Jeep out front works. That's what we came here in," she said.

"You're telling me that you have a working car?"

"Yeah."

Mary's smile faded. Her face turned serious. She rushed over, seizing Kalen by her shoulders.

"We have to get out of here," Mary said.

Kalen felt Mary's fingers digging into her shoulders. She squeezed hard, pulling her closer.

"Why? We came here because it was safe. My grandfather brought you here because it's safe," Kalen said.

"You don't understand. That town, Carrollton, that's just a few miles from here, is overrun. There's this gang there. You want to know what happened to my parents? They killed my dad and raped my mom in front of me."

When the words hit Kalen's ears, she didn't have the reaction she thought she would. She'd been scared of facing what had happened to her in the woods. She didn't want to give it a name. She couldn't force the words from her lips. It wasn't until Mary had said the words that she finally felt something about what had happened.

She felt angry.

"They raped her?" Kalen asked.

Mary didn't cry. She kept the same rushed tone as before. She spoke not out of remorse for what happened to her mother, but of the fact that she didn't want it to happen to her sisters.

"One of them burst down the door of the room we were in. My dad tried to stop them, but the guy pulled a knife on him. After he stabbed my dad, he pulled a gun on me, my mom, and my sisters."

Kalen felt herself being drawn into Mary's story, her anger rising with every word leaving Mary's mouth.

"He grabbed my arm and threw me on the bed. Before he could do anything to me, my mom stepped in. She took her clothes off and let him..."

"Rape her," Kalen said.

It was the first time those words left Kalen's mouth. The man who had tried to rape her shared the same face in her mind as the man who raped Mary's mom. They were the same person. She never asked what her grandfather did to that man in the woods, but she had imagined a few scenarios. The satisfaction of revenge on her assailant by her hands could no longer come to fruition, but maybe she could do something about the man who hurt Mary's mom.

"He's still alive?" Kalen asked.

"I think so. I mean, I don't know what happened afterwards. I just grabbed my sisters and we ran. We hid in the fields for almost two days."

Kalen's grip on the water bottle tightened, causing the plastic to crack and crumple from the pressure.

"How many?" Kalen asked.

"How many?" Mary repeated.

"How many gang members were there?"

"I'm not sure. I only saw around ten, but there could be more. That's why we have to get out of here. We need to get in that Jeep and drive as far away from this place as fast as we can."

"And go where?"

"Someplace safe."

"There isn't any place safe anymore."

"We can't just stay here forever."

"No, but we'll stay here for as long as we can and do what we need to do to *make* this place safe."

"What are you talking about? Those people outnumber us. They have guns. They don't care who they kill. They don't care who they hurt. They're animals."

"Then we'll hunt them down and kill them like animals."

22

DAY 10 (MIKE'S JOURNEY)

The "Welcome to Ohio" sign dripped with water from the storm that blew through earlier. Once Mike saw that sign, he knew they were at the halfway mark. The caravan of people behind him was spaced out along the highway, huddled in their own separate groups.

The To family walked directly behind Mike. Fay, Nelson, and Sean were to his left. Tom and Clarence brought up the rear.

They hadn't run into another person for almost three hours, and Mike was glad. The people they ran into were interested in either one of two things: following them or hurting them. So far they'd been lucky enough to avoid the latter, but Mike knew it was only a matter of time. If they ran into a group large enough with the guns and manpower to take them, they'd be in trouble.

Everyone but Mike seemed to think that the road was safer than staying at the airport, but they hadn't experienced true desperation yet. They hadn't felt it put its hands around their necks, trying to squeeze the life out of them, draining their energy and resources until there was nothing left.

Mike feared that the people he was helping now would soon turn out to be his enemies. He desperately wanted to believe that the people walking behind him were good, decent people, but he also knew what a man could do when he was hungry enough. And what happened to the man who was foolish enough to feed him.

Jung walked up beside Mike, carrying his daughter, Claire, on his back, her head resting there, her thick black hair clinging to her forehead from the sweat collecting on her face.

"How far along are we?" Jung asked.

"We're halfway. If we keep us this pace, we should be there in less than forty-eight hours."

"That's great news."

Mike glanced down at Jung's belt. He held no knives, pistols, or weapons of any kind.

"Jung, you should carry the extra pistol. If something happens or if we get separated, you'll need to protect your family."

"I am protecting my family, Mike. Men fool themselves into thinking that the justification of violence for protection safeguards them from it. All it does is paint a target on your back signaling to those who share your views that you will have to face each other and fight until one of you dies."

"You think that because I carry a gun that it invites, rather than deters, danger?"

"No. It's the mentality of how you carry the gun and why you have it. If someone came out of those bushes with a knife in his hand and saw that you had a gun, he'd know the only way to get what he wants is to kill you. If he doesn't kill you, then you'd kill him. If a man pops out of those bushes and pulls a gun on me and I have nothing to counter him, he'll be less likely to pull the trigger."

"Only if you give him what he wants."

"What I want is my life and the lives of my family to be safe. That's what I want. I want to be able to ensure that my family has the chance to survive and go on."

"Well, your family won't survive for very long without the supplies those people with guns take from you. You can only go three days without water and a week without food. If what you have on your back is it, then that is your life. You keep that, then you'll have a chance at survival. You don't get to keep it, well, then you're better off having the robber shoot you then and there."

"Don't lose your faith in people, Mike."

"I haven't lost my faith in people. I've just lost caring about them."

The thunder from the storm clouds in front of them rumbled through the sky. The storm was moving away, but in the same direction they were heading.

Sean and Jung Jr. splashed in the puddles left in the road when the storm passed through earlier. Claire frowned, but Jung and

Nelson both gave their boys a good-natured smile. With all of the things that were going on in the world, seeing their boys laugh and act like kids was worth the cost of their shoes and clothes getting muddy.

Sean kept pretending that there was something in one of the larger puddles, trying to pull him in. Fay kept egging him on with her laughter.

"Your boy's quite the comedian," she said, looking at Nelson.

"His mother's the funny one. I've been told I have the sense of humor of paint thinner."

"Well, depending on how much paint thinner you sniff, you could have one hell of a time."

Fay held the other rifle in her hands that Mike and Clarence had grabbed from the weapons cache at the airport. She kept the barrel leaned up against her shoulder as she walked.

"What happened?" Fay asked.

"To what?" Nelson said.

"Your wife."

"She's a vice president for an engineering company in Pittsburgh. She was in the city when everything stopped working. We stayed at the house for almost a week, waiting for her to come home, but after what happened in our neighborhood, we left with Mike."

"What happened to your neighborhood?"

"The same thing that happens to people who give up."

"Which is?"

"We forget how to be human."

"Maybe it's just how we really are."

"You really think that? You think that we're such a depraved species that at the first sign of trouble we all turn on each other like animals?"

"Nelson, we've both seen what people can do when they're desperate. They don't have any rules. They don't have any principles. They just go by what they need at the moment. With everything that's happened people aren't planning for the future; they're not showing restraint. They're only worried about what they're going to get for their next meal, and they don't care how they get it."

"I don't think so. I think we can still get out of this."

Fay raised her arm, her gesture encompassing the scene around them: the scattered abandoned cars with their windows smashed, the rising of fires in the distance sending smoke into the sky.

"Look around, Nelson."

"I am."

Fay noticed that Nelson wasn't looking at her when he said that. His eyes were focused on Mike, up ahead.

Fay remembered her conversation with Mike the night before they left the airport. She wanted to believe what Nelson was saying was true. She wanted to believe that Mike could get them out of harm's way and keep them safe. She wasn't sure what was more frightening though: the fact that she was actually able to believe it, or that she was resisting it so much.

* * *

WITH THE SUN fading in the sky, Mike decided to call it a day. The sighs of relief immediately followed.

A forest ran parallel along the highway. Mike picked out a spot on the tree line where they'd be concealed from view by anyone on the road, but still close enough to jump back on it quickly if they needed to get out in a hurry.

Just as in the airport, the group set up shifts to keep watch. Tom had the first shift and posted up against a tree with the rifle across his lap.

"Just don't shoot me in my sleep," Clarence said as he lay down on his sleeping bag.

"'White businessman shoots black male in the woods.' That sounds like a CNN headline if I've ever heard one."

"Good thing I'm more of an NPR man," Clarence said.

The group settled in for the night, and Tom drummed the rifle in his lap lightly. He'd never really fired a gun before, except on a business trip to Kentucky once. The clients there had been hunting fanatics and insisted on taking him out. He didn't kill anything, but he did show a few trees a thing or two.

Tom absentmindedly checked his watch. He'd kept doing that since the first day when everything turned off. He always checked his watch. He was always in a hurry to go to a meeting, have lunch with a new client, look over his emails, check his voicemails, or review the earnings report that had just come out.

Clarence had asked him the day before why he hadn't thrown the watch away once he realized it wasn't working. After the explanation that it was an Omega failed to justify his reason for not throwing it out, he simply turned to the one reason that made the most sense to him.

It represented what his life had been, and God willing, would be again. The craftsmanship of the watch, the efficiency, the quality of detail that set it apart from its peers—his whole life he'd strived to be the man who earned that watch, and he had worn it every day for the past three years since he bought it as a symbol of what he had achieved.

The clouds drifted in the sky above, obscuring the stars from view. The leaves in the trees rustled from a breeze drifting past. Tom adjusted his back against the trunk of the oak where he had propped himself.

After the first hour, he got up to stretch. His back popped from being crouched on the ground for so long. He walked away from the group deeper into the woods to go to the bathroom, rifle in hand.

He found a spot behind a tree and unzipped his pants. Afterward, as he turned back to rejoin the group, he heard a twig snap.

Tom froze. The gun stayed at his side. The only things he allowed to move were his eyes. He slowly turned his neck and then allowed his body to turn with it.

He brought the rifle up to his shoulder. He rocked it awkwardly in his arms. His footsteps were clumsy, stepping on branches and making more noise than whatever had caused the sound from earlier.

Tom squinted into the darkness, looking for the source of the noise. The lack of light from the moon and stars made it harder to see through the trees in the forest. He kept the rifle pointed outwards, trying to scan the area and find whatever was out there.

After a few more minutes of not hearing anything but the sound of his breathing and a few owls, he turned around and headed back over to the rest of the group. He stepped over a fallen tree limb, and when his foot came down on the other side, he slipped and smacked hard against the ground.

"Goddammit," Tom said, spreading his hands into the dirt, steadying himself to get up. Then a scent hit his nose. It smelled rotten.

He fumbled around, looking for the rifle he dropped, and pulled out one of the glow sticks he had in his pocket. He snapped it in half, triggering the phosphorescent light.

The green light spread across the ground, and Tom moved the stick in large sweeping motions. He knelt down next to the limb where he had slipped. He shone the light onto the ground, where he saw bits and pieces of guts that he stepped in.

"Christ," he said.

Tom kept scanning the ground, looking for the rifle. He wandered around, combing the forest floor on his hands and knees until he felt his hand fall on something stiff, yet organic. The smell was stronger here, and when he turned around, he saw the lifeless eyes of a corpse staring back at him.

"SHIT!" he screamed.

Tom jumped up and took off running, dropping the light. He tore through the camp, waking everyone up.

Mike jolted from his sleeping bag and had his pistol out, scanning the depths of the forest that Tom just ran from. The rest of the camp awoke, rubbing their eyes.

"What happened?" Mike asked.

Tom doubled over with his hands on his knees, gasping for breath. He kept pointing in the forest repeatedly.

"Saw… body… in… there," Tom spit out.

Mike kept his weapon pointed into the trees.

"How many?" Mike asked.

"Just one," Tom said.

"Where's your rifle?" Clarence asked.

Tom threw his hands up in the air. Mike frowned.

"Nelson, Clarence, come with me. Tom, you lead us. We need to find that rifle," Mike said.

Tom led the other three back the best way he could remember. The green glow stick he had dropped made it a little easier to pinpoint where to start looking. Clarence picked up the glow stick and held it out to see if he could get a better look at the surroundings.

"The body was over there, I think," Tom said.

Mike stepped over the guts by the tree limb. It didn't take him long to spot the boulder-size mass next to the tree. When he saw the body, he tucked the pistol back into his waistband.

"Clarence, toss me that light," Mike said.

The corpse was completely mangled. Animals had ripped the stomach open, most likely, but what caused Mike to grimace was what had happened to the man below his waist.

The body didn't have any pants on and had been castrated. Nelson and Clarence timidly came over, covering their mouths with their shirts, trying to shield themselves from the smell.

"Oh my God," Nelson said.

"Who would do that to someone?" Clarence asked.

"The question is what did he do, to make someone do that to him?" Mike asked.

23

DAY 10 (THE BIKERS)

*H*alf the crew was outside the motel. After Garrett's wake, most people slept where they fell. Jake, at least, had made it into his room.

Open pill bottles littered the floor. Cigarette butts overflowed out of an ashtray. Jake lay passed out on the bed, still wearing all of his clothes. A pistol was on the pillow next to him.

He moaned when he woke up. He cracked his neck as he stood up. The room was hot, musty, and filthy. He flung the door open to let some air in and stumbled over to the mirror above the kitchen sink.

Jake rubbed his hands across the growing stubble on his chin. His eyes were bloodshot red. He picked up some of the pills lying on the floor and washed them down with a swig of beer from a bottle left unfinished.

He sat on the carpet, leaning his head back against the bed, taking sips of beer. His long hair, dirty and matted, stuck to his face. He ran his hands through it a few times trying to tame it, but was unsuccessful.

His mind was still gone from the night before. He hoped the oxy he just took would cause the jackhammer in his brain to shut off, at least for a few minutes. He waited for the drugs to take over so he could go to sleep.

Jake looked at the room. The sheets were torn off the other bed. Dirt, pill bottles, beer cans, and half-smoked cigarettes lined the floor. He dug into his pocket and pulled a pack of smokes out.

When he flipped the lid of the pack open, he saw that he only had two left. He pulled one out, flicked the lighter, and lit the tip. The first drag was always the best. He let the smoke and heat fill his lungs, then released it in one long exhale.

"Like a fucking dragon," Jake said.

Once the nicotine and oxy started to fill his bloodstream, the headache subsided. He tucked the cigarette into the side of his mouth and stepped outside.

Whatever food they were able to salvage from the grocery they'd piled up in the main lobby behind the front desk. There were boxes of food packed with canned goods. He grabbed a Hostess cake and ripped the bag open. He stuffed the pie into his mouth, and in two bites it was gone.

He ripped a Gatorade out of its plastic ring holder and chugged half the bottle. The yellow liquid dribbled down his chin. He gave a few throaty coughs and then headed back out to the courtyard where most of his crew was still passed out.

Jake saw Frankie sprawled out on the edge of the fountain in the middle of the courtyard. Jake kicked Frankie's boot. Frankie didn't move. Jake sent his toe harder in the side of Frankie's leg, shaking his whole body.

"Wake up, asshole," Jake said.

Frankie moaned. He jerked his head up. He squinted his eyes open and put his hand up to shield them from the sun.

"What?" Frankie asked.

"Where's the girl?"

It took Frankie a minute to process what Jake had told him. Jake kicked him again, impatiently.

"I don't know, man. I think she's still in my room," Frankie said.

"Wake up the rest of the boys and have them meet us in your room then."

Jake and his boys killed everyone in town they could find. The only souls that got away from them were the three girls that Frankie let escape. Jake had thought about who could have killed Garrett, and he still wanted justice. He would find the people that murdered his brother and make them pay.

He didn't think the girls had any weapons on them to kill Garrett with, and Jake had also considered that it could have been a drifter passing through, but he wanted to narrow the field of who to hunt down, and he had a good idea to determine if it was the girls who did it.

Jake allowed his boys to keep the mother around. It was a good... stress-reliever for them. They needed to let off some steam from time to time, and she reluctantly provided the services to do so.

Jake pushed the door to Frankie's room open, and she lay naked on the bed. Her wrists were tied to the headrest. Black and blue bruises spotted her legs and neck. Her eyes had opened at the sound of the door.

The bed next to the one she was lying on had some crumpled sheets. Jake tore one off and placed it over her body, covering her up. Unlike the rest of his crew, he hadn't touched her.

The cigarette Jake had was down to a nub, so he dropped it to the carpet, putting it out with the toe of his boot. He pulled out the cigarette from his pack and lit it. He took a drag and sat down on the bed across from her. He just sat there, smoking and staring at her.

Her lower lip was cut and swollen, and her mangled hair half-fell over her face, partly hiding her eyes from view. She tried to shift her body under the sheets, and in doing so, the top part of the sheet fell away, exposing one of her breasts.

Jake leaned forward, reaching his hand out. Her body shuddered as she recoiled, trying to escape his touch, but he pulled the sheet back up, covering her.

She started breathing heavily. Jake took another drag from the smoke, watching her examine him. Trying to understand why he was there.

"Let me go," she said.

Jake tapped the end of his cigarette. The bits of gray ash fell to the carpet and on top of his boot.

"What's your name?" Jake asked.

Her voice was barely above a whisper when she spoke. The name came out in hushed breaths.

"Hannah," she said.

"Hannah. A beautiful name," Jake said.

Jake took another drag on the cigarette. The smoke began to cloud his face from her view. It became thick and heavy in the room. She coughed a little.

"Have you had anything to drink or eat?" Jake asked.

"No."

Jake rose from the bed and left the room, just as Frankie and a few of the others were stumbling in.

"The rest wouldn't budge, Jake. Everybody's passed out stone-cold. It got wild last night," Frankie said.

"Search the rooms. Look for any women's clothing and bring it to me. Nobody touches her this morning. Just drop the stuff off."

"Yeah, sure, no problem, Jake," Frankie said.

Jake headed back up to the motel lobby, grabbed a box of peanut butter crackers, two bottles of water, and a Gatorade. When he returned to the room, he saw that the men were waiting outside.

"Everybody leave," Jake said, pushing past them and entering the room.

His crew scattered, most of them stumbling back to bed. When Jake entered, he saw a line of pants, blouses, and shirts on the dresser. He set the crackers and Gatorade next to them and walked over to the side of the bed. He bent down intimately close to her. He placed his hand gently on her face and brushed the hair out of her eyes. He held her small chin in his hand.

"I'm going to untie you. If you do anything stupid, I'll bring everyone in here and every single one of my men will fuck you. Do you understand me?" Jake asked.

She nodded her head. Jake reached up and untied the rope binding her to the bed. Red lines marked her wrists made by the rope she desperately struggled against to free herself. Jake tossed her the clothes.

"Once you change I have some food for you," Jake said, pointing to the peanut butter crackers on the dresser.

"The bathroom's over there. Come out when you're done," he said.

Hannah clutched the sheet to her chest and picked up the clothes Jake had thrown her. She walked to the bathroom and shut the door. A few minutes later she came out wearing a shirt that was a few sizes too large and a pair of baggy jeans. She pulled her hair back into a ponytail and walked to the dresser. Her hands shook when she picked up the box of crackers. She tried opening one of the packs, but was too weak to do it.

Jake grabbed the pack from her hand and ripped one end of the plastic open. He extended his hand, offering it to her. His hand lingered in the air for a moment before she took it. The first cracker went to her lips slowly, but she brought the rest to her mouth greedily. She grabbed the bottle of water and chugged it down, coughing a bit from drinking too fast.

Once she was finished with one pack, she tore open another one and devoured it, continuously sipping water while she did.

Jake sat on the bed across from her, patiently waiting for her to finish. Once she was done he leaned forward, his hands folded together.

"What were you and your family doing here?" Jake asked.

"Vacation," she said.

"Where are you from?"

"California."

Hannah's eyes watered. The swollen lip started to quiver. Her head dropped, and then she started nodding.

"What did your husband do?" Jake asked.

Hannah wiped her eyes on the shirtsleeves and rubbed her nose clean of any snot dribbling down.

"H-he was a financial investor."

"And what were you guys doing in Ohio on your vacation?"

"We were doing a cross-country trip. My h-husband and I wanted o-our girls to see the country."

Jake could see her barely holding it together. Her whole body was shaking. She was tired and afraid. She had no idea where her girls were and no husband. Jake knew, just as she did, that her life was over.

"What you did to save your girls was courageous, Hannah. You're a very brave woman. Frankie would have raped all of them," Jake said.

Jake stood up and paced the room. He ran his hands through his matted hair.

"You see, Frankie's different than I am. He lacks a certain amount of control. He's more animal than man. He's vicious, dangerous, manipulative, and angry. Whatever he wants, he takes. He doesn't care who gets hurt along the way. Now, you add him to this type of climate where everything is chaos? Where there's no law, no rules, no decency? Well… this is a world he was made for, and he'll live for a very, very long time."

Hannah had pulled her legs and arms in and formed herself into a ball sitting on the bed. Jake looked at her curled up, retreating into herself.

"With the way things are now, people like you and your husband will die. People like your daughters will die. You and your family don't have what it takes to survive in this type of world. You don't know how to flip that switch on that transforms you into someone like Frankie."

Jake joined her on the bed. Hannah jumped back, recoiling when he sat next to her. A few stray strands of hair had escaped her ponytail. He smoothed them out with his hand. Hannah flinched, her eyes closing when he touched her.

"One of my men was killed yesterday. Now, the only people that made it out of here alive when we showed up were your girls. Do you think their survival switch flipped on? Do you think that seeing their mother raped in front of them and the fear of knowing they would be next finally caused them to see the world for what it really is? What it's always been?"

"They wouldn't hurt anyone," Hannah said.

Her voice was shaking as she said it. Jake could hear the effort put forth in being strong, but she was betrayed by her emotions.

"And that's why you won't make it, Hannah. Just like your husband, you don't understand what people are really capable of," Jake said

* * *

"HOW'S HE DOING?" Ulysses asked. Thanks to the meds, Ray had been dozing for a while.

Anne tossed the bloody bandages into the trash. She pumped a few sprays of hand sanitizer onto her hands and rubbed them together.

"His fever's down. The antibiotics seem to be working," Anne said.

Ulysses rubbed his knee. It was still sore from the previous day. He could walk on his own still, but he couldn't move very fast, and he wasn't able to put a lot of pressure on the left leg.

"How about the girls?" Ulysses asked.

"The only one that's said anything has been Mary. The other two haven't said a word," Anne answered.

"Did they tell you what happened?"

Anne turned to Ulysses. She had the face of a worried mother. Someone who feared for the safety of the people put in her care.

"Mary did. Ulysses, if those people find out we're here, they'll—"

"Nobody saw me, Anne. We're safe. Trust me. The only way you could find this cabin is if you knew where you were going," Ulysses said.

Nancy sat crouched in the hall, eavesdropping on their conversation.

"But what if someone else stumbles across us? What if someone else finds us by accident? By now people have started roaming around looking for shelter, food, safety. That's what people are looking for and will kill to get it," Anne said.

"Anne, we'll be okay."

Nancy could hear footsteps coming from the kitchen, and she took off back down the hallway into Freddy's room where she and her sisters were sleeping. Freddy was staying in Ulysses's room to make space.

Mary was brushing Erin's hair when Nancy burst in.

"What are you in a hurry about?" Mary asked.

"They're going to give us up," Nancy said.

"Who?"

"These people."

"Nancy, they're trying to help us."

"Mom wouldn't want us to be with strangers."

"Mom would want us to be safe, and right now we're safe with them."

"But Mom—"

Mary slammed the brush on the bed. Erin hopped down and backed away from her. Mary's voice was exasperated when she spoke, the stress from the last few days finally boiling over.

"Dammit, Nancy, Mom's not here!" Mary said.

Nancy stood there quietly. Erin crouched in the corner of the room. Nancy walked to Erin and put her arm around her. Mary exhaled.

"I'm sorry," Mary said.

"You're sorry? You're sorry for what? For scaring Erin? For yelling at me? For giving up on Mom?"

"I didn't give up on Mom, Nancy."

Mary picked up the brush from the bed. She ran her fingers over individual prongs. She felt the tiny balls of plastic move over her palm.

"If you haven't given up on her, then why is it that every time I talk about her you change the subject?" Nancy asked.

"Because I'm scared."

"You're scared?" Erin asked.

Mary and Nancy stared at Erin. It was the first time she'd spoken since they left the motel. Mary got off the bed and joined her sisters.

"Yes, but it's okay," Mary said.

"Is Mommy really dead?" Erin asked.

"No, she's not dead. She'll never be gone from us. She loved you very much, Erin. She loved the both of you more than you could ever know."

Mary threw her arms around both of her sisters, and the three of them rocked back and forth with each other in silence.

* * *

KALEN HAD her ear pressed against the other side of the door, listening to Mary, Nancy, and Erin. Both Anne and Ulysses heard the commotion from inside their room and lingered at the end of the hallway. Kalen walked down to meet them.

"It's going to be hard for them," Kalen said when she joined her mom in the kitchen.

"It's been hard for everyone, sweetheart," Anne said.

"Maybe, but me and Freddy only lost Dad. We still have you and Grandpa. They lost both their parents."

Kalen realized that they hadn't spoken about her dad since they arrived. No one had mentioned him. None of them had taken the time to slow down and talk about it.

"We didn't get to say goodbye," Kalen said.

"No, we didn't," Anne said.

Ulysses moved uncomfortably in his chair. He pushed himself up off the armrests and hobbled to the door. He limped down the front steps and onto the pine-needle ground of the forest floor. The pain shooting up his leg became too much, and he stopped to lean against the Jeep, propping himself up for support.

Anne and Kalen came running outside after him.

"Ulysses," Anne said.

Kalen wrapped her arms around her grandfather and buried her face into his chest. Ulysses wrapped her up. His body was shaking. Anne walked up to him and wrapped her arms around him.

24

DAY 11 (MIKE'S JOURNEY)

"*I* don't have anything else!" Fay screamed.

"That's bullshit and you know it!" he said.

"Guys, knock it off," Mike said.

It was the third time they had stopped like this today. Fay and Tom had been building up some animosity toward one another since yesterday.

Fay had her rifle gripped a little too tightly. The barrel was next to Tom's head. He shoved the barrel down. Mike jumped in before Fay swung at him.

"Enough!" Mike said.

Jung and Jenna held Jung Jr. and Claire in their arms. Sean hid behind Nelson's legs. Clarence came over with Mike to help defuse the situation.

"Break it up, you two," Clarence said.

"Look, I'm not the one who decided to remember to bring their stupid watch instead of enough food to last them the trip!" Fay shouted.

"The only reason I didn't have enough food was because I was helping you get your supplies," Tom said.

"Take it easy, Tom," Mike said.

Mike turned, took Fay by the shoulders, and pointed her down the road.

"And you keep walking," he said.

Fay stomped off and headed down the pavement. The To family,

Nelson and Sean, and Clarence followed after her. Mike hung back with Tom.

"She knows I'm right," Tom said.

"You don't have anything left?" Mike asked.

When Tom exhaled, the fight went out of him. He swung his pack around and unzipped the main pouch. He opened it up, and Mike glanced inside. It was completely empty.

"I told you that it would be at least a two-day trip, Tom," Mike said.

"I know! It's just... I haven't been rationing like you told us to."

Mike dropped his pack to the ground and pulled out a can of peaches. He handed it to Tom.

"I only have one of those left, so that has to last you until tonight. We should be at the cabin by then," Mike said.

"Thanks."

* * *

THE ROAD WAS TAKING its toll on everyone, especially the kids. Sean had been such a good sport the entire time, but he was starting to wear down. Nelson could see it on his face.

"Dad?" Sean asked.

"Yeah, buddy?"

"How much longer do we have to go?"

"We're almost there. Just a little while longer."

The lump on the side of Nelson's face had gone down. The headaches were also starting to subside. He hadn't mentioned anything to anyone, but he was still having nightmares from when they were mugged on their first day out.

He was so embarrassed about what happened. If Mike hadn't been there, then he could have died. Sean could have been hurt, kidnapped, or killed.

He was also struggling with what he'd done back in the neighborhood when Mike's house was burning down. Nelson tried to justify it in his mind that if he hadn't killed Ted, then Mike would have been the one to die. The justification of killing was never a choice he thought he'd have to make.

"Hey, Dad?" Sean asked.

"Yeah?"

"How long do you think it'll take Mom to catch up with us once she gets home?"

That was a topic Nelson had evaded desperately. He hadn't spoken about his wife with Sean since they'd left. He knew it was going to be hard for Sean to understand that they wouldn't see her again, and he didn't want to see his son suffer anymore.

"I don't know, bud," Nelson said.

"I just hope we left her enough food to make it. I know that we don't have much left, and I think we took more than we left for her."

"Well, you know Mom could never finish her meals anyway. We always had to help her with dessert, remember?"

"That's true."

Sean stayed quiet a moment before he spoke up again.

"Is Mom dead?" Sean asked.

"What? Why would you say that?" Nelson asked.

"I don't know. We don't talk about her, and I thought she'd be here by now. I keep thinking that any minute she's going to appear behind us on the road, shouting our names, and we'll see her running to catch up with us, but every time I turn around to check, nobody's there."

Nelson could feel his legs growing weak. He knelt down in front of his son. He smoothed Sean's wavy blond hair. He had his mother's nose and her eyes. When he looked into his son's face, he could see her as clear as day.

"Well, then let's talk about her more, okay? That way we can remember all the good stuff," Nelson answered.

"Okay."

"Do you remember her favorite ice cream?"

"Mint chocolate chip."

"That's right. And do you remember what she did when you were in the school play last year as Peter Pan and you lost your costume the day before opening night?"

"She made me a new one," Sean said, smiling.

As they walked, Nelson continued to talk about his wife with his son. Its purpose had been to make Sean feel better, but the more they spoke about her, the lighter the burden of remembering her felt.

"She made the best macaroni and cheese," Sean added.

"Do you remember when you were in first grade and Mom wasn't feeling well and you tried to cook some of the spaghetti art you made for her?"

"Yeah, I remember you finding me and asking me what I was

doing and then we had to throw away all of the spaghetti art in the house because I got mad at you for not letting me cook for her."

"I actually don't think I'd mind having some of that spaghetti art right about now."

"Me either."

Sean giggled, and Nelson threw his arm around his son. He turned around and saw Mike making his way toward them with Tom in tow.

"Looks like Tom and Fay sorted out whatever was wrong," Nelson said.

Mike pulled Nelson aside. He kept his voice low so nobody within earshot could hear.

"Everyone's running low on food. Watch yourself," Mike said.

Nelson watched Mike head to the front of the group, but saw him slow down once he made it. The whole group stopped, but nobody understood why. Nelson squinted in the distance to see what Mike was looking at, but it was too far to see. It wasn't until the gunshots rang out that he realized what Mike was looking at.

* * *

"Jenna!" Jung yelled.

He rushed over to her. Claire and Jung Jr. were both crying. Jung Jr. had his mother's blood on his face, shirt, and hands. He stared down at her lying on the ground with a hole in her shoulder, oozing blood.

Everyone hit the ground once the gunshots were fired. Mike had waited for more shots to ring out, but nothing came. He looked through the sight of his rifle, trying to locate the source of the shot. He scanned the roadside, along the trees, around the abandoned cars, but he couldn't see anyone.

He could only hear the screams coming from Jung, who was hunched over his wife, keeping pressure on the wound.

"Jung! Get your family off the road and into the trees. Tom, help Jung carry Jenna," Mike said.

Tom rushed over and hoisted Jenna up, lifting under her armpits. Mike looked up at Fay, who was also flat on her belly looking through her scope, scanning to see where the gunfire had come from.

"Anything, Fay?" Mike asked.

Her right eye was squinted shut while the other peered through the scope. Her mouth hung open as she tried to locate the shooter.

"Not yet." She continued looking. "Wait, I think I have something. Red sedan about one hundred yards out," Fay said.

Mike swung his rifle to the sedan. She was right. Mike could see the top half of a head through the shattered back windows.

"Do you have a shot?" Mike asked.

"No."

"Keep an eye on him until we get Jenna over to the trees."

The tree line was thirty yards from the highway. Mike watched Jung and Tom carry Jenna through the open field of grass. He glanced back into his sight, relocating the shooter, whose rifle was positioned on the trunk of the car, pointed in the direction where Jenna was being taken.

Mike exhaled. He lined up his shot and squeezed the trigger on his rifle. The opposing shooter ducked back behind the vehicle. Mike's eyes searched the rest of the car. He went up and down, trying to see if he could get another clean shot off, but found none. He looked back over and saw that the group had made it safely to the tree line.

"Fay, head for the forest. I'll cover you. When you get in position, keep an eye on the shooter for my run over, got it?" Mike asked.

"Okay," she answered.

Mike stared down the road at the sedan. He could hear Fay's footsteps hit the pavement and then disappear onto the grass. He felt the gravel of the road digging through his shirt into his stomach. His elbows rested on the hard asphalt, causing pain to shoot up through his arms. He waited a few more seconds before he looked over and saw Fay in the tree line with her rifle pointed toward the sedan.

Mike pushed himself off the pavement and sprinted toward the forest to meet with the rest of the group. His feet were heavy and slow. After days of walking with little to no sleep, his body wasn't holding together very well.

When he made it to the forest, he smacked against a tree trunk for support. He could feel the sharp pain in his lungs with each breath. He tried to gain his composure, but he was feeling light-headed.

Jung gripped Mike's shoulder. Jenna's blood covered Jung's hands.

"Mike, help Jenna," Jung said.

"Fay, make sure you keep an eye out," Mike said.

"Got it," Fay answered.

The bloodstain around Jenna's shoulder covered most of her arm and the top half of her shirt. Mike ripped the shirt around the source of the wound to get a better look. The blood poured out of her like a river. He checked the back of her shoulder for an exit wound.

"The bullet's still inside," Mike said.

Mike grabbed Tom's hands and placed them over Jenna's shoulder. She cried out in pain from the pressure.

"Keep firm, even pressure on it," Mike explained. "It's going to hurt for her either way, so we need to keep as much blood in her as possible."

Mike swung his backpack around. He unzipped the main pack and flung out extra clothes, water, and food until he pulled out a small medical kit he found at the airport. He popped the hatches off the top and pushed the bandages aside until he reached a pair of tweezers.

"Clarence, hold her down," Mike said.

Clarence brought the weight of his body down on Jenna's arms and legs.

"Jenna, this is going to hurt, but I need to get the bullet out so it doesn't get infected, okay?" Mike said.

"G-give me some medicine," Jenna said.

"I don't have anything to give you. I'll try and make it quick," Mike said.

Mike dug the tweezers into the open gash on Fay's shoulder, and she let out a scream. Her good arm and legs swung wildly as she tried to push them off of her.

"Keep her still!" Mike said.

Clarence pressed down harder, but Fay was going wild. Each time Mike dug deeper into Fay's shoulder, more blood poured out, followed by writhing and screams. Mike probed through the jagged pieces of flesh until he reached the tip of the bullet.

"I think it got it," Mike said.

Mike pulled out a .224 round and dumped it on the ground. The leaves, grass, and twigs around them were stained red. He grabbed the bandages from the medical kit. He handed a few to Tom and placed the bulk of the bandages on the wound itself. Mike wrapped it tightly.

"I've done what I can," Mike said.

Jung dropped to his wife's side. He held her hand in his. Mike crept over to Fay, who was still watching the red sedan in the distance.

"Whoever shot her is still there. I didn't see anyone come or go," Fay said.

"Just the one?" Mike asked.

"As far as I can tell. Unless there's another person down the road, or back behind the tree lines."

"Let me see your scope," Mike said.

The red sedan came into view, but he couldn't see anyone. He moved the barrel a bit to the right to get a different view and then saw the shooter with his gun over the hood of the car, aimed right at him.

The bullet flew into the tree next to Mike, sending pieces of wood splintering into the air.

"So I guess he's still there," Fay said.

"Move everyone deeper into the trees," Mike said.

Nelson grabbed Jung Jr. and Claire and led them deeper into the forest. Jung and Tom carried Jenna, and Clarence came up to join Mike and Fay by the tree line.

"What are we going to do?" Clarence asked.

Mike poked his head out just a bit to get another look at the sedan, then glanced up into the sky. It was only mid-afternoon, and it would be another six hours before it became dark.

"If we don't get Jenna some serious medical attention, she could get an infection, blood poisoning, anything," Mike said.

"But you took the bullet out," Clarence said.

"That doesn't mean she's in the clear just yet," Mike answered.

"We can move through the trees, deep enough to where he wouldn't be able to hit us, but close enough for us to still see the road," Fay said.

"I don't want to risk this guy following us," Mike said. "Clarence, you still have the pistol I gave you?"

"Yeah, why?"

"Trade me."

Clarence pulled the pistol from his waistband and handed it to Mike, who gave him the rifle.

"Listen, I'm going to move down the edge of the forest until I get parallel with the car. I'm going to make a sprint for the sedan and try to force him out. When I start firing, that's when you guys give me cover," Mike said.

"Mike, that's a terrible idea," Fay said.

"Yeah, what if we miss, or what if he shoots you before you get to the car?" Clarence added.

"You two are the best shots in the group beside myself, and neither of you have had any training in close combat situations, so I'm making the run. It'll force his hand. He'll either fire back, or he'll run."

"Mike, think about what you're doing," Fay said.

"Keep a bead on him. We'll hit from both angles. Confuse him," Mike said.

Before Fay could stop him, Mike rushed off. He weaved in and out of the trees, keeping an eye on the sedan in the distance. Once he was parallel to the car on the road, he crouched down.

Mike ejected the magazine from the pistol, checking the number of shots he had. *Thirteen.*

He shoved the magazine back into the pistol and racked the bullet from the magazine into the chamber. His thumb flipped the safety off. He took a deep breath and exhaled, letting the nerves melt out of him. He closed his eyes, slowly controlling his breathing through his nose.

When Mike opened his eyes, he aimed the pistol and sprinted for the sedan twenty yards away. Dirt flew up from the ground as he tore off into the field separating the highway from the forest. He squeezed the trigger, sending bullets into the trunk of the car, then another barrage of bullets went flying into the side of the sedan coming from Fay and Clarence.

Mike was ten yards away now, and he could see the boots of a man underneath the front of the car by the hood. The clank of bullets from Fay and Clarence smacked against the side of the car.

Mike could see the shooter's head now, and the hail of bullets from Fay and Clarence hitting the car stopped when Mike reached the trunk. He dashed along the backside, his finger on the trigger, when the shooter came into full view.

He must have been no older than seventeen. The boy's rifle was on the ground next to him, and his hands were in the air. Mike's finger left the trigger as he kicked the boy's rifle away from him on the ground.

"Please," the boy said.

"What are you doing out here? Why'd you shoot at us?" Mike asked.

"I thought you were with the people in town. I thought you were coming to hurt my family."

"People in town? What town?"

"Carrollton. It's just a few miles west of here. We had a group of bikers ride through, and they killed everyone. They killed my grandfather. I just didn't want anyone else to hurt my family."

Mike picked the boy up by the scruff of his neck and threw him onto the hood of the car.

"So you thought you'd shoot at a group of people traveling with children?" Mike asked, keeping the gun pointed at him.

The young man's arms were out wide, his palms still up in surrender.

"I didn't even mean to hit anyone. I was just trying to scare you. I swear," the boy said.

"Your family still in town?"

"No, we have a farm just outside of it. It runs right along this road a few miles west. That's why I was out here, to keep watch."

Mike glanced down the road where the boy's farm would be then grabbed the collar of his shirt, pulling him toward him.

"You have anyone else keeping watch?" Mike asked.

"No, it's just me. It's just me."

Mike backed up, leaving the boy on the hood of the car. Mike picked up the rifle the boy dropped and slung it over his shoulder. With his pistol, Mike gestured toward the tree line.

"Walk," Mike said.

The boy rolled off the hood of the car and started marching toward the forest. He kept glancing back at Mike, his eyes red and wet.

"Please, don't kill me. I didn't mean to hurt anyone. I swear," the boy said.

Mike walked up behind him, bringing both of the boy's arms to his head.

"Keep your hands up where I can see them," Mike said.

Clarence and Fay came out from behind their cover and started walking toward them.

"Mike, what are you doing?" Fay asked.

"Stop," Mike said.

The boy froze, his hands still tucked behind the back of his head. Mike kicked the boy's legs from under him, collapsing him to the ground. Mike tossed the boy's rifle to Fay.

Tom and Nelson came rushing out.

"He's just a kid," Tom said.

"I keep telling him that it was just an accident. I wasn't trying to hurt any of you. I was just trying to scare you off. I just wanted to protect my family," the boy said.

"What do we do with him?" Clarence asked.

"You're going to let him go, right, Mike?" Nelson asked.

"No, he's going to take us to his barn, and then we're going to drop him off there and make sure he doesn't follow us," Mike said.

The boy's expression eased. The color flushed back into his face, and his body lost some of its tension.

"Thank you. Thank you, so much," the boy said.

Jung came out from behind the trees. The boy caught sight of the blood stained over his clothes. Jung had a dazed look on his face. He walked like a zombie; jagged, limping steps propelled him forward. He stared at the boy sitting at the base of the tree.

"It was him?" Jung asked, still looking at the boy.

"Yes," Mike said.

The look Mike saw in Jung's eye was a look he'd seen before. As much as Jung spoke about taking the nonviolent road, he could see the struggle in the man's face. It was the first time someone had hurt a member of his family like that. It was the first time Jung had a taste of real violence in his life.

"You shot my wife," Jung said.

"It was an accident," the boy said.

"You could have hit my kids."

"Take it easy, Jung," Mike said, inching closer to Jung, who had his eyes glued on the boy.

Before Mike had to intervene, Jung turned away and headed back to his wife.

"Did she die?" the boy whispered.

"Not yet," Mike answered.

* * *

JENNA WAS TOO weak to move, and everyone was too weak to carry her for a distance longer than twenty feet. Mike and Tom tried to carry her through the trees to the highway but couldn't even make it that far.

The boy, who told them his name was Billy Murth, said the farm he was from was a mile down the road.

"The farm has a cart we could wheel her back in," Billy said.

"Fine. Me, Tom, and Nelson will go with Billy and grab the cart," Mike said.

"I should come with you," Jung said.

"No, you should stay here and make sure your wife and kids are okay," Mike said. "That's the best thing that you can do right now, Jung."

Mike gave Nelson Billy's rifle, and Mike took one of the rifles from their own stash and gave the handgun he was carrying to Tom. Mike pulled Fay to the side out of earshot from the rest of the group.

"If we don't make it back, there might be a good chance that his family will come back here looking for you guys. Have somebody posted on watch at all times. The kid could be playing us," Mike said.

"What am I supposed to do if you guys don't make it back?" Fay asked.

"If we're not back by nightfall and if Jenna gets some of her strength back, follow the tree line down the highway. There's a dirt road that's hidden with some brush about four miles west. It'll be on the left side. You won't be able to see the entrance from the highway, so when you guys are walking make sure you stay to the left."

"Where does the road lead?"

"My cabin. My family will recognize Sean, so make sure you keep him safe."

"No, Mike, this is insane. You don't know what you're walking into."

"If we don't get Jenna somewhere where we can sterilize that wound, she's going to die of infection. The only place that I know of is my cabin, and the only way I can get her there right now is to find something to carry her with."

"Be careful."

Mike kept his hand on Billy's shoulder, and the four of them took off down the road. He made sure to keep his eyes peeled for anything suspicious.

"How many people do you have at the farm?" Mike asked.

"Four," Billy said.

"Who?"

"Me, my dad, my mom, and my younger brother."

"Do they have any weapons, other than the rifle you had?"

"Yeah, my dad's got a lot of guns. He's a hunter. He takes tourists out on hunting trips for deer. Or he used to."

"Great," Tom said. "So we're walking into a situation where we're holding the son of a hunter and gun enthusiast hostage."

"Will he be home when we get there?" Mike asked.

"I don't know. He sent me to cover the east road while he went out hunting. He usually doesn't come back till closer to sundown."

"What about your mom and brother?"

"They'll be home."

"Can your mom shoot?" Tom asked.

"Yeah," Billy answered.

"So much for catching a break," Tom said.

It took them twenty minutes to reach the farm. The house sat in a clearing off the highway. An open pasture cut through the middle of the forest, and cattle, horses, and other livestock roamed the fields grazing.

A large steel gate surrounded the property, fencing the cattle in. The gate creaked when Mike undid the lock and swung it open.

They kicked up dust from the dirt road as they walked closer to the house. Mike could see a barn in the back. Bells from the cattle dinged in the fields around them. Suddenly the front door of the house flew open, and a woman wielding a shotgun marched onto the front porch.

"Let my son go, or so help me God, I will pump you full of lead," Beth said.

Beth was a skinny woman. Her body looked far too frail for the 12-gauge she was holding, but the barrel of the gun stood rock steady.

Mike kept his grip on Billy's shoulder but made sure his gun wasn't pointing anywhere near the boy.

"We don't want any trouble, ma'am," Mike said.

"If you don't want any trouble, then why did you come onto my property, holding my son hostage, and armed to the teeth?"

"Your boy shot one of the people in our party. The girl he shot needs help. All we need is a cart to carry her, and we'll be on our way."

"Tell them to put their guns down."

Mike nodded to Tom and Nelson, and they placed their rifles on the ground in front of them.

"Kick them away from you," Beth said.

Tom and Nelson complied, sending the guns sliding across the gravel. Mike placed his gun down last, but kept Billy close.

"You all right, Billy?" Beth asked.

"I'm fine."

"Did they hurt you?"

"No."

Beth walked toward them, keeping the barrel of the gun pointed at the three of them. The sun reflected off the steel of the shotgun. When she got close enough, Mike let Billy go, and he ran for his mom.

"Mom, it's okay. They're not going to hurt us," Billy said.

Beth kept the shotgun pointed at them. She paused for a moment taking all of them in, their hands in the air, waiting for her judgment.

The barrel of the gun finally dropped, and Tom and Nelson let out a sigh.

"Thank God," Tom said.

"The cart's around back. How bad is she hurt?" Beth asked.

"She took a bullet to the shoulder, but she lost a lot of blood. She's not strong enough to walk yet, and we need to move her quickly," Mike said.

Mike followed Beth around the side of the house, and his eye fell on an old wooden cart. It was six feet long and stood four feet high. The wood was cracked and splintered along the bed. Two long handles jutted out from the front, where it looked like it would normally be pulled by a horse or ox.

"That thing looks like it's about to fall apart," Tom said.

"It's sturdy. We still use it to push around some of the livestock feed," Billy said.

Mike grabbed the front handles and turned it around.

"We don't have a lot of options. Nelson, grab the other handle and help me pull. Tom, grab the guns on the way out," Mike said.

Tom tossed Billy his rifle back and collected their guns from the ground and put them on the bed of the cart, shielding his mouth from the dust kicked up by the wheels.

* * *

JUNG HELD his wife's hand. Her eyes were half-open. He had pulled out his sleeping bag and laid her down on it. The white bandages covering her shoulder were soaked red. Sean kept their two children preoccupied by playing a game with them. Jung watched from a distance as their two small children tried knocking an empty can from a tree trunk with a rock.

"Jung," Jenna whispered.

"Shh, it's okay. You're going to be okay," Jung said. "Mike went to get us something to carry you in, and then we'll go to his cabin. Mike said he'd be able to help you more once we get there."

Jung tilted her head up and pressed a bottle of water to her lips.

"Do you remember that vacation we took to Sea World last year? I kept complaining about flying all the way to California for a week filled with nothing but sea animals?" Jung said.

"You tried to convince the kids to just take a weekend trip to the coast."

"And they wouldn't even budge because of all of the pictures you showed them. They were so excited, and when we finally left for the trip and we made it there, they wanted to leave right away, but you couldn't peel me away from it."

"You kept wanting to get your picture taken with penguins."

"They were so cool, but they smelled awful."

Jung's face broke into a smile, reflecting Jenna's. The creases of his eyes wrinkled up, while the dark circles underneath seemed to be under more stress.

"You were right about that trip. It was a good idea. We should do it again," Jung said.

"I'm glad you liked it."

His smile faded. The circles under his eyes darkened. Tears began running down his cheeks.

"Jung," Fay said. "Mike's back."

Mike and Nelson dragged the cart all the way through the field to the edge of the trees.

"Tom, come help me get Jenna on here," Mike said.

Mike and Tom scooped her up while Jung grabbed the bags underneath her. Jung spread the sleeping bags on the bed of the cart. Mike and Tom laid her down. Jenna winced as the guys set her in the cart.

Jung managed to put Claire and Jung Jr. in the cart with their mother. Jung and Nelson pulled while Fay, Tom, and Mike kept watch on the sides and front of the group. Sean kept close to his father while Clarence brought up the rear.

The rickety cart's wheels clattered against the pavement, the handles vibrating in Jung and Nelson's hands.

Mike knew they'd be slower now, and he wasn't sure how the group was going to get the cart up the dirt path to the cabin, but for now they were moving, and that was priority number one. Fay came up behind him.

"So, what happened back there? How did you get the cart?" Fay asked.

"I asked for it," Mike answered.

"Are you going to bring it back to her?"

"If it survives the trip."

With their rifles loaded and the dirt path to the cabin only a few more miles up the road, Mike let himself hope. He hoped that his family was there. He hoped that they were all okay. He hoped that Jenna would make it.

It was a feeling he hadn't let himself experience since they left the neighborhood. He didn't want to let false expectations get in the way of having to do what needed to be done. He knew the trip would be hard. He knew there wouldn't be any guarantee that he would make it to the cabin and that there wouldn't be any guarantee that his family was there when he did arrive, but being so close to the finish line caused the hope that he kept at bay for so long to creep in.

"We're close, right?" Fay asked.

"Yeah, we're close," Mike answered.

25

DAY 11 (CABIN)

"I don't want you going outside by yourself," Anne said.

"Mom, I'll be fine," Freddy answered.

Freddy hadn't been outside since his grandfather brought the three girls back from town. He was kicked out of his room, so they could have his space, and moved in with his grandfather. He heard his mom arguing with his grandfather about it the other night. She was still worried about what happened in the town nearby.

The three toys Freddy brought with him were starting to bore him and he wanted to explore outside, but his mom refused to let him go alone.

"I have to get lunch ready. If you want to go outside then ask your sister if she'll go with you," Anne said.

"But she *never* wants to go outside. She just sits in her room all day."

"Well, maybe she'll change her mind today."

Freddy threw his head back in exasperation and marched over to his sister's room. The door was shut. He gave it three knocks.

"Kalen, will you come outside with me for a little while?" Freddy asked.

The room was silent. Freddy knocked again.

"Kalen, open up. Pleeeeease, Mom won't let me go outside unless you come with. I'm dying in here."

Freddy slumped his whole body against the door. He pathetically clawed the wood and jiggled the handle. He almost fell over when Kalen jerked the door open.

"What do you want?" Kalen asked.

Freddy caught himself from falling face-first onto the floor when Kalen swung the door open.

"Please, please, please, please, please come outside with meeeeeee?" Freddy asked.

He dropped to his knees and clenched his hands together, begging her. Kalen rolled her eyes and walked over to her bed. He saw her reach for her shoes and slide them on.

"Yes!" Freddy said.

Mary, Erin, and Nancy joined them outside. There was a storm in the distance and the sun was hidden by clouds, but Freddy didn't care. He ran around the cabin, exploring everything he hadn't been able to see since they arrived.

After doing a lap of the cabin he circled back around to Mary and Kalen sitting on the front steps. Freddy held his arms out, closed his eyes, looked up into the sky, and spun around.

"Happy?" Kalen asked.

"You have no idea," Freddy answered.

Freddy opened his eyes back up, and they widened with excitement as a thought occurred to him. He gasped.

"Do you guys want to play Agent Match and Dr. Doomsday?" he asked.

Erin and Nancy looked at him questioningly.

"What's that?" Erin asked.

"It's a comic book that I read. Agent Match works for a super-top-secret agency, and his nemesis, Dr. Doomsday, tries to destroy the world," Freddy said.

"That sounds dumb," Nancy said.

"It's not dumb, it's fun!" Freddy exclaimed.

Erin was the only one smiling.

"I'll play," she said.

"Okay, I'll be Dr. Doomsday, and you can be Agent Match. You have to stop me from building my Doom Ray and destroying the world."

Freddy grabbed Erin's hand and pulled her to a cluster of bushes in front of the cabin. She giggled. Nancy joined Mary and Kalen on the front door steps of the cabin.

"Okay, so this is your headquarters. Now you stay here and count to ten, and I'll go to my base where you try and find me, okay?"

"Okay."

Freddy took off and headed around the back of the cabin. There stood a cluster of trees in the back with a few low-hanging branches. He rushed over to them, climbed up along the trees, and perched himself as high as he could go.

He heard Erin yell ten and watched her run around looking for him. He could see the top of the cabin, all around the house, and deep into the forest. Beyond the trees he could see the town that Erin came from. It didn't look dangerous from where he sat. He wondered what his mom was so worried about.

Erin checked around the cabin, peering into bushes, looking around trees, but she never looked up. Freddy smiled at her running around searching for him. After about ten minutes he climbed down the tree and decided to sneak up on her and scare her. She was to the left of him as he quietly descended the tree.

Freddy stepped lightly on the ground. Erin was crouched down looking through a bush when he snuck up behind her and poked her in the back and screamed.

"AHHHHHHH," Erin yelped.

Freddy fell onto his back laughing. Mary, Kalen, and Nancy came running around toward them, their eyes frantic.

"Freddy!" Kalen yelled.

Freddy looked up from the leaves, dirt, and grass he'd fallen in and saw Erin crying. Nancy came over and wrapped Erin in her arms. She tossed a nasty look at Freddy.

"What did you do?" Nancy asked.

Freddy's mouth hung open. He pushed himself up off the ground, wiping the dirt from his pants.

"We were just playing. She couldn't find me, so I snuck up behind her. That's all. I didn't mean to make her cry like that," Freddy said.

Anne came marching toward them, upset. Her hands were stained with bits of berries from some of the surrounding bushes.

"What is going on?" Anne said.

"Mom, I'm sorry. I didn't mean to scare her," Freddy said.

"Frederick, get in the house now."

"But, Mom."

"Now!"

Freddy kept his head down. He lumbered to the front of the cabin. Before he reached the door, he gave one last look at the trees around him. He figured he wouldn't be allowed outside for a while.

Anne marched him inside and took him to his grandfather's room. Freddy sat on his bed, and his mother towered over him.

"What is wrong with you? Don't you know what those girls have been through? You can't sneak up on them like that," Anne said.

"Mom, I didn't mean to scare her. I swear. It wasn't supposed to be a big deal. We were just playing."

"You stay in this room, and you are not to go outside. Do you understand me?"

"But it's not fair!"

Freddy slammed his fist into the bed. His face turned red, and his eyes were getting wet. He jumped off the bed and stomped to the window.

"Do *not* take that tone of voice with me, young man," Anne said.

"I don't care! Everyone's worried about other people. You helped Ray, Grandpa helped those girls, but nobody went back after Dad! Nobody cared about Dad!"

Anne's face softened as Freddy collapsed to the ground. She walked toward her son and knelt down. She lifted his head up. Tears streamed down his cheeks, and he buried his face in her shoulder. Anne stroked his hair.

"It's okay, sweetheart. It's okay," Anne said.

"I miss him."

"Me, too."

* * *

FREDDY AND ERIN made up by dinner, although Nancy was still flashing Freddy dirty looks.

Ray was finally feeling better enough to join them at the table. He'd been on his back for most of the past few days from the fever after his leg became infected. He still needed help moving around, but he was eating again.

Once dinner was over, Kalen was the first to get up and head toward her room. Anne stopped her.

"Honey, wait. Why don't we all play a game? I think there are some old board games downstairs."

"Mom, do we have to?" Kalen asked.

"I think it'll be good for everyone. Freddy, go downstairs with your sister and bring us something up. We'll play it in the living room," Anne said.

Freddy smiled. He shoved his hands against the table, his chair squeaking as he pushed back. Kalen followed less enthusiastically.

Freddy swung the lantern past the shelves to the box in the corner where the games were stashed. He tore the lid off and started sifting through the choices.

"What about Monopoly?" Freddy asked.

"Well, that would be a good way to pass the time for the next three months."

"Okay, how about Life?"

"You want to play that one because the one we're in is so great?"

Freddy dropped the game back into the box.

"Fine, Kalen, you pick," he said.

Freddy moved away from the box, and his sister walked over and looked inside. Freddy stood back, lantern in hand, when something caught his eye on one of the shelves next to him. The light from the lantern reflected off a metallic box on the bottom shelf. He moved over to get a better look and then set the lantern down.

The box wasn't large or heavy when Freddy pulled it from its place on the shelf. It had tinfoil tightly wrapped around the outside of it. He ran his fingers along the sides, feeling the smooth, slick metal.

"Kalen, what's this?"

Freddy held out the box, and Kalen stopped her search of games to examine it.

"Probably something you're not supposed to touch," she said.

Freddy snatched the box back from his sister and rushed upstairs. Everyone was gathered in the living room. Ray lay stretched across the couch, Ulysses sat in the armchair, Anne was stoking the fireplace, and Mary, Nancy, and Erin were sitting on the floor.

"What'd you get?" Anne asked.

"I don't know. Whatever this is," Freddy said.

"Wait, I know what that is. It's a Faraday cage," Ulysses said.

"A what?" Freddy asked.

"It's a homemade Faraday cage. It protects electronics from EMP blasts," Ulysses said.

Freddy brought the box over to his grandfather and sat it in his lap. Every eye in the room turned to Ulysses.

"What's in it?" Mary asked.

"Is it a phone?" Nancy asked.

"A computer?" Kalen asked.

Ulysses peeled the top off the box, and his jaw dropped.

"What is it?" Freddy asked.

"It's a pair of radios," Ulysses said.

Ulysses pulled them out of the box. They were medium sized, black, and each with a long antenna.

"They look like they're used for long-range communication," Ray said.

"Do they work?" Anne asked.

Ulysses turned the knob on top, and the radio squealed on. The room was completely silent except for the static of the radio. Ulysses scanned the frequencies, slowly.

Everyone leaned forward. Each of them prayed that something would come through the speaker other than the clicks and pops of static. After ten minutes of silence, Ray finally spoke up.

"You should turn the battery off, Ulysses. We don't want to waste it," he said.

"You're right."

Ulysses clicked it off. He put the radios back in the box and handed it to Freddy.

"Go put them back downstairs, Fred."

Before Freddy could grab them, Nancy cut in between the two of them and snatched the box out of their hands. She clutched the box to her chest, protecting it.

"No! We need to keep it on. We need to call for help!"

"Nancy, put it down," Mary said.

"We can use it to call help for Mom. She doesn't have to be with those people anymore. We can save her."

"Nancy, put it down now!"

Nancy handed the box back to Freddy and collapsed into a pile of tears.

"It's not fair," Nancy said.

"I know," Mary said.

Freddy walked back down into the basement. He set the box back on the shelf but stared at it for a moment. The tinfoil shone in the lantern light like a star in the darkness. He set the lantern back down and pulled one of the radios out. He turned the knob on, and the same hum of static blew through the speakers. He squeezed the talk button on the side. He brought the radio close to his mouth.

"Dad? If you're out there, we need your help. Everyone's sad. We're all scared and we need you. I miss you a lot."

Freddy let go of the talk button, and more static blew through.

He waited, listening, hoping that he would hear his father's voice come through to tell him it would be all right, but it never came. Freddy turned the radio off and put it back in the box.

* * *

THE REST of the cabin was sleeping, but Kalen was wide-awake. She lay on her bed staring out the window. Most of the cluster of trees around them blocked out the night sky, but there was one patch of space open where she could see the stars in the cloudless night. She was on top of her sheets, drumming her hands on her stomach.

She thought about the men down there in the town. She thought about what they did to Mary, Nancy, and Erin's family. She thought about how someone like them hurt her, made her afraid.

Silently, she slid out of bed. The bedroom door creaked when she opened it, sounding loud in the quiet of the cabin. She stood frozen, making sure no one had heard her. After a few moments of waiting she didn't see anyone come out, so she headed for the basement.

She kept the door shut and almost slipped down the stairs in the darkness. She didn't want to turn the lantern on until she was all the way at the bottom, afraid that someone would see the light through the crack in the door.

She took the lids off the boxes in the far corner of the room. She rummaged through them, looking for a spare key she knew was somewhere amidst the junk.

"C'mon, where are you?"

The floor of the basement was lined with sheets, gauze, and winter clothes from pulling the materials out of their containers. She kicked one of the coats across the floor in frustration.

She let out a sigh and started packing up what she'd torn apart until a small black box caught her eye. She snatched it up. The insides were lined with spare batteries, ammo, and a ring of keys.

She took the keys, and they jingled in a lock on a safe against the wall. Kalen pulled the safe door open, and a row of guns lined the inside. Rifles, shotguns, and handguns organized neatly together. She picked up a 9mm Glock. She felt the plastic composite around her hand. She gripped the pistol in her hand, remembering what her dad had told her when shooting.

Keep your right hand high on the handle. Thumbs over thumbs. Don't put your finger on the trigger until you're ready to squeeze.

She brought the pistol up to her eye and pointed it at different objects around the basement. She kept her finger hovering over the trigger, never letting it touch. She ejected the magazine. It was fully loaded. She shoved it back in and racked a bullet into the chamber. She tucked the pistol behind her back and headed upstairs.

She was sneaking back to her room down the hallway when a whisper caused her to turn around. Mary was leaning out of her room into the hallway, watching her.

"What are you doing?" Mary asked.

"Nothing. Go back to bed."

Mary stepped out into the hallway, closing the door behind her. She tiptoed to Kalen, who kept waving her to go back into her room. When Kalen finally determined that Mary wouldn't go, she pulled her into her room and shut the door.

"Why are you up this late?" Mary asked.

"I could ask you the same thing."

"I couldn't sleep."

Kalen wasn't sure how Mary would react to the gun, so she kept it tucked behind her back. Mary walked over to the bed and sat herself on the edge.

"I don't sleep much anymore," Mary said.

Should she tell her? Should she let her in on what she was planning to do? Kalen figured that Mary had just as much right as she did to hurt the people in town, but she wasn't sure if she would go through with it.

"It's because of them, isn't it?" Kalen said, gesturing in the direction of the town.

"Yeah. I keep seeing my mom's face, or my dad's lifeless eyes just staring back at me. It doesn't scare me anymore, it's just... I don't know."

"You want to do something about it."

It was the way Kalen said it that made Mary look up at her. The faint moonlight coming through the window cast pale shadows along Kalen's figure.

"Do what?" Mary asked.

"Make them feel what you felt. Make them suffer like you suffered."

Kalen watched Mary's face carefully.

"How? They have guns. They have more people. They don't care what they do. They have no conscience. They're—"

"Animals."

Kalen wasn't sure if that was the word that Mary was going to use, but looking at Mary's face, she knew it was the right one.

"You have to hate them as much as they hated you, because that's what made them do it. They didn't do it because they were bored. They didn't do it because they were forced to. They did it because they liked it," Kalen said.

Mary's answer came out like a whisper. A realization of what Kalen spoke of.

"Yes," Mary said.

Kalen pulled the pistol from behind her back. The black metal glowed from the reflection of the moonlight. Mary took the pistol from Kalen's hand. She laid it across her palm, flat.

"I can get you one," Kalen said.

Mary looked up at her. She placed the gun down next to her on the bed and got up quickly. She started shaking her head and moved toward the door.

"No, I can't do this," Mary said.

Kalen rushed up behind her and grabbed Mary's arm. She spun her around. Her fingers dug into Mary's arm, hard.

"Stop it. Let me go," Mary whispered.

"You want to just hide out here for the rest of your life? If you don't do something now, you'll die here. Those bikers in town may not be the ones who do it, but someone like them will. They'll come through here and rape your sisters, then kill them in front of you, and just before they put a bullet in your head, they'll have their way with you too."

Kalen had Mary's face less than an inch from her own. Kalen's teeth gritted together. She could feel the harshness of her words. The sting they sent with each syllable.

Mary stopped resisting, but it wasn't from Kalen's words, it was from something she was looking at past her. Kalen could see a faint orange light in the reflection of Mary's eyes, and she turned around.

Through the trees out of the window, there was the small twinkling of a fire. Kalen moved closer to the window to get a better look. The flames were in the distance, dancing into the night air.

26

DAY 11 (THE BIKERS)

*J*ake walked along the line of his men standing in front of him. The sun was sinking in the west, sending a golden glow across the town that gave it a false beauty with the pile of bodies circled around a post where Hannah was tied and bound.

A red metal container of gasoline sat on the ground next to Frankie, who looked up at Hannah, blew a kiss, and smiled.

The blood from Hannah's lip dripped onto the pile of bodies below her. She looked at the faces of, not the bikers around her, but of the blank stares of the rotting corpses. Some eyes were closed; some were open, while flies and maggots picked at the flesh on their faces. She could taste the stench of the bodies.

"Our club has been around for over fifty years. In those fifty years, we have never let anyone walk over us. Not the cops, other clubs, no one," Jake said.

The rope wrapped around her wrists and ankles was rough and tight. Her hands and feet had gone numb. She listened to Jake's calm, even tone.

"We never let anyone walk on us because the only thing that matters in this world is strength, and we are strong."

As the bikers clapped and nodded, she could feel her muscles tightening.

"The Diablos have never lost a fight. We beat the Warriors, the Rebels, the Suns—anyone who's come up against us has lost, and I'll be damned if I let anyone beat us now. Those bitches that killed

Garrett will come back. They'll come back for her," Jake said, pointing at Hannah.

Hannah felt her body start to shake when the cheers from the bikers exploded. Strands of her hair covered her face, but she could see Jake pick up the red container of gasoline.

When the gas made contact with the open cuts along her body, she cried out. Her skin burned. The taste of the dead below her was replaced by the taste of gas. It burned her mouth, her eyes, everything.

Jake pulled out a box of matches in his pocket and lit one. He pinched the match in between his fingers. The sun had disappeared below the horizon, and the glow of the fire in his hands accentuated the encroaching night sky.

Hannah thought of her children. She thought of her husband. She could see each of them as clear as if they were in front of her now. Their smiling faces looking up at her, letting her know that she would see them soon.

"Everything we touch. Burns," Jake said.

He dropped the match onto the pile of bodies, and the massive flame spread upwards into the sky. The flames swallowed the flesh, and when the heat reached Hannah, she began to scream. The fire crawled up her legs, consuming her body. She thrashed on the pole, her screams piercing through the cheers of the bikers. She could feel the fire tearing at her flesh. Finally, her body went limp, engulfed in the orange flames dancing along her charred body.

Jake watched the bodies burn. The fire danced in the reflection of his eyes. He'd always loved fire. It had ferocity, beauty, and power. He closed his eyes, letting him feel the heat from the flames, his cheeks reddening from the burning flesh. He pulled Frankie away from the group, and the two of them headed toward the lobby.

"You think they'll come back?" Frankie asked.

"They will. They'll want to know what happened to their mother, and when they do come back, they and whoever they bring with them to help will burn."

27

DAY 12 (MIKE'S JOURNEY)

*T*he sun rose above the horizon. Mike had pulled the cart carrying Jenna the entire night. It took them twice as long with the cart as it would have without it. The path up to the cabin was meant for a vehicle with four-wheel-drive capabilities, not two men dragging an injured woman in a cart from the early twentieth century.

Everyone begged to stop, but Mike wouldn't let them rest. He was so close to his family. Every time he slipped on the trail, or he felt the pain in his hands, legs, and back, he thought of them.

Jung was the only one as motivated as he was to get there. He pulled the other side of the cart along with Mike when everyone else was giving up. They were less than a hundred yards from the cabin now. It wouldn't be much longer.

The wheels of the car bumped along the roots and rocks of the beaten path. With the sun coming up, he searched the ground for tire tracks that he hadn't been able to see in the dead of night. They approached a stretch of mud, and Mike saw the familiar tread of his Jeep's tires in the soil.

Mike's heart leapt. *They made it.* His family was there. Mike could feel his legs losing their fatigue. His eyes lost their weariness. His hands gripped the wooden handles harder.

"We're almost there," Mike said.

He could see the cabin now. The Jeep was parked on the side. Everything seemed to be intact. There wasn't any damage that Mike noticed. His feet trudged faster through the mud and dirt.

When he finally reached the cabin and stood in front of the door, he felt like he was in a dream. None of it seemed real.

"Tom, Jung, grab Jenna and we'll get her inside," Mike said, setting the cart down.

Mike rushed to the door, flinging it open. The first person he saw was Ray lying on the couch in the living room. Ray opened his eyes, and his jaw dropped.

"Mike?" Ray asked.

"Anne? Freddy? Kalen? Dad?" Mike called out.

Mike didn't acknowledge Ray's presence. He could only think of his family. He heard the creak of doors opening. The first person out was Anne. Mike stood at the end of the hallway when she stepped out of their room. She gasped as her hands covered her mouth in shock.

The next door that opened was Freddy, then Kalen. The hallway was silent as the four of them stared at each other.

"Dad?" Freddy asked.

A tear rolled down Mike's face. His son, his daughter, his wife, they were here. They were safe. They were alive.

"Dad!" Freddy yelled.

Mike dropped to his knee as Freddy rushed toward him. He threw his arms around Freddy and wrapped him in a tight hug. Kalen came in next to her brother, and Mike pulled her in. He clutched his children, kissing the tops of their heads. Each of them squeezing back as hard as he was.

Anne walked slowly toward him. The sight of her children with their father was better than seeing Mike alone. She wanted to join, but she didn't want to miss what she was seeing. She finally made it to the three of them. Mike opened his arms, and she stepped inside the circle. The four of them just sat, huddled on the floor, holding onto each other.

When Tom and Jung carried Jenna inside, Mike finally got up, still holding his family close. Everyone stared at each other for a moment. Anne was the first to speak when she saw that Jenna was hurt.

"What happened?" Anne asked.

"She was shot. I'll grab the spare cot downstairs and bring it up," Mike said.

Mike rummaged through the basement, searching for the cot, and found it lying on its side against some of the medical supplies. On his way back, he glanced at the gun cabinet. It was unlocked.

Mike set the cot up in the living room, and Tom and Jung set Jenna down on it to rest. Anne felt Jenna's forehead with the back of her hand.

"She's burning up. I'll grab some Ibuprofen and some new bandages to dress her wounds," Anne said.

"Dad, I can't believe you're here," Freddy said, looking up at his father.

Mike scooped him up and gave him a kiss on the cheek.

"I missed you, bud," Mike said.

"I missed you too."

When Ulysses opened the door of his room, he noticed that he was drying his eyes on the corner of his shirt. He didn't say anything but walked up to Mike and gave him a hug, squishing Freddy in between the two of them.

"It's good to have you home, son," Ulysses said.

"Thanks, Pop."

* * *

JENNA LAY PASSED out on the cot. She had fresh bandages on her shoulder, and Anne had given her some of the antibiotics that Ray was taking. Everyone was crowded around the kitchen table.

After introductions, the group caught up on what happened. Ulysses and Anne explained about the storm and the tree falling, which hurt Ray's leg, and the trip to town where Ulysses found Mary and her sisters. She purposefully left out the situation with Kalen. She would fill Mike in about that later in private.

"The bikers killed everyone," Mary said.

Mike noticed that her voice was emotionless. She stood there not with a face of pain, but of solace. He couldn't imagine what those three girls had gone through, but he found it odd how put together she seemed after what happened. Maybe it was her way of coping.

Mike explained what Nelson had done and how he saved him after the house caught fire. He told them about the trip and the detour to the airport, the boy who shot Jenna, and the trip to the farm.

After the explanations, Anne, Mary, and Tom, who claimed to be an excellent cook, started breakfast for everyone. Powdered eggs, dried fruit, and nuts were on the menu. Tom explained that he didn't have access to his normal ingredients and he did the best he could, but nobody cared. It was the first hot meal any of them had in days.

When breakfast was over, they did some rearranging. The cabin was built to only hold five, and there were now eighteen of them. Mary, Nancy, Erin, Kalen, and Fay would crash in Kalen's room. Nelson, Sean, Ulysses, and Freddy would stay in Ulysses's room. Jung, Jenna, Jung Jr. and Claire would get Freddy's room. Clarence, Tom, and Ray would be in the living room. Mike and Anne would stay in their room, which they tried to give up, but nobody would take.

It took most of the morning to get everyone situated, and by the time they did, it was lunchtime. They cracked open the canned food and had lunch outside. Mike noticed that Mary kept glancing at the smoke rising from the town. She caught him looking at her once and didn't look back at the town again.

There were chores to get done, but Mike put them all off. He did nothing except be with his family. Everything that needed to be done he would put off until tomorrow. That was his gift to himself for making it this far.

The day went by fast. Everyone got along well enough. There were some awkward moments with everyone coming in and out of the outhouse, but for the most part it went smoothly.

That night Mike walked into his father's room to tuck Freddy in. His son was in his sleeping bag on the ground. He watched Freddy's smile as he ran his fingers through his son's hair. He kissed his son's forehead.

"I love you," Mike said.

"I love you, too."

Mike pulled the pocket watch out and set it down in Freddy's hands. Freddy picked it up by its chain and it spun, sparkling in the candlelight.

"That was your grandfather's. I want you to have it," Mike said.

Freddy flipped the watch open. The hands ticked steadily forward. The time was in roman numerals.

"Thanks, Dad," Freddy said.

When Mike walked to Kalen's room, the girls were settling in. Kalen had tried giving up the bed, but no one would take it. Mike looked at her like when she was a little girl, her hair messy and curly, looking up at him with her big brown eyes. He weaved in and out of the girls on the floor and made it to the side of her bed where he sat.

"I missed you, kiddo," Mike said.

"I missed you too, Dad."

Mike placed his hand over hers, which lay across her stomach. He rubbed her fingers in his rough hands and bent down and kissed her on the cheek.

"I'm glad you're safe," Mike said.

Ray, Tom, and Clarence were sprawled out in the living room. Ray on the couch, and Tom and Clarence on the floor.

"Night, guys," Mike said, walking down the hallway to his room.

"Night," they said together.

Mike pushed the door to his room open. Candles flickered, and Anne was lying across the bed, waiting for him. He lingered in the doorway for a moment looking at her. She wore an old T-shirt of his, and her hair fell down to her shoulders. It was the most beautiful sight he'd ever laid eyes on. He shut the door behind him and crawled into bed next to her.

"Hey," Mike said

"Hey."

The light from the candles danced across their faces. They lay there holding each other until their lips met. Mike breathed deep the moment his lips hit hers. He pulled her closer, her body running the length of his.

Anne pulled herself back after a moment.

"What is it?" Mike asked.

"Mike, something happened on our way to the cabin."

He noticed that her voice sounded scared.

"What?" Mike asked.

"We stopped halfway here. Freddy needed to go to the bathroom and couldn't hold it, so your dad pulled over next to a wooded area."

Mike's heart pounded through his chest. His mind flashed back to the corpse he saw just beyond the Ohio borderline where they camped a few nights ago.

"She went into the woods, and there was someone there," Anne said.

Mike got out of bed. His adrenaline coursed through his veins.

"Your dad was able to get there before anything happened, but she got beat up a little."

"Someone tried to rape my daughter?"

"Honey, she's okay. Your dad got to her in time."

Mike fell back against the wall. He slid down to the floor across from the bed. He buried his face in his hands. He played the scenario over in his head: the man grabbing her from behind, tossing her to the ground, pulling a knife to her throat, ripping her clothes off.

Anne crawled out of bed and bent down to her husband. She took his hands off his face and held them in hers.

"My baby girl," Mike said, his eyes watering with tears.

Anne cradled his head in her chest. He let himself go. His shoulders shook as the sobs left his body.

* * *

MIKE SLEPT WELL past sunrise into the next day. When he woke he stretched his neck and cracked his knuckles, wincing at the stiffness and pain throughout his body. He looked over and saw that Anne was already out of bed.

THE LIVING ROOM and kitchen were buzzing with kids laughing and chasing each other, Ulysses and Ray debating baseball statistics, Fay showing Mary and Kalen her tattoos, Jung and his children still yawning from waking up, Freddy eating a bowl of cereal complaining about the powdered milk with his hair sticking straight up, and Anne trying to put it down.

MIKE THOUGHT of all of the implications of having this group here. The shortage of food, water, medical supplies, the danger of being seen and heard, protecting them from danger, all of these things ran through his mind. He thought of the biker gang in the town a mile away who already murdered several people. As he glanced around the room and looked to each of them individually. He wasn't sure he could keep them alive until his eyes found his wife. She stood straight, her head held back with a smile in her eyes. He saw how strong she was, how she had held everyone together while he was gone. He could make it through this. They could all survive.

WHEN THE GROUP noticed him standing quietly in the hallway, they all stopped what they were doing and watched him. They looked to him with the hope that he could keep them alive.

DAY 8 (KATIE)

*W*hen Katie turned onto 24th Street, her jaw dropped. The cars along the streets were trashed with bullet holes and broken windows. The houses were violated by looters breaking in and stealing whatever they could find. A few trashcans smoldered from the remains of fires started then left alone to burn out.

Sam walked behind her, his pistol at the ready, on alert for any signs of danger. When they walked past Mike's house, she covered her mouth. It was nothing more than a burnt pile of wreckage.

Katie looked at the two crosses sitting in the Beachums' yard. The two mounds of dirt rising from the earth caused her heart to sink in her stomach.

"Your house?" Sam asked.

"No."

Katie pulled the front door to her own house open. The door creaked as it swung open. She lingered there in the doorframe, afraid of what she'd find inside. When she finally crossed the threshold, she tiptoed gently.

Most of the house was intact. When Katie walked past the living room, she stopped. All of the furniture was rearranged.

Sam stood patiently in the foyer, watching her examine the living room. He could see pictures of her family along the walls leading up the staircase.

The couch legs squeaked against the wooden floorboards when

she pushed it aside, allowing herself into the circle of furniture. The empty space in the middle suggested there was something there before, but whatever Nelson and Sean had left her was gone.

Katie sat down on one of the chairs. She looked up at their family portrait hanging above the fireplace. The photo was taken last fall. On their way to the studio that day, she remembered the leaves falling from the trees and gathering on the road. The faded browns and oranges of fall decorated the black pavement. She could hear Sean laughing in the back seat from Nelson's singing, begging for him to stop.

Katie forgot Sam's presence until he spoke very quietly.

"Mrs. Miller," Sam said.

Katie continued to look at the family portrait. That day she was thinking of in her mind seemed so far away.

"I'm never going to see them again, Sam," Katie said.

"You don't know that."

"I do. Look at the rest of the neighborhood. They either died when everything collapsed on them, or they ran off. Either way, I won't be able to find them."

"Maybe they headed back into the city looking for you."

"I hope not. I hope they got as far away from this place as they could."

Katie leaned forward, burying her face in her hands. She didn't cry, and she didn't feel angry. She was just tired. She was foolish to think she could find them, to think that they were still here. Of course they left, just as she should have left the city the first day the blast hit.

"I'm going to look around, make sure the rest of the house is secure," Sam said.

Katie nodded her head. She leaned back into the chair, sliding down against the burgundy velvet seat. Her eyes focused lazily on the fireplace. She could feel her eyelids drooping down, the exhaustion from the day of traveling hitting her all at once. She tilted her head down, and that's when she saw the crumpled-up ball under the couch.

Her head perked up. She dropped to her hands and knees and reached under the couch, grasping the ball of paper in her hands. She smoothed the crumpled sheet out on the couch. After reading it, a few tears fell and stained the edges.

Sam came back downstairs and stopped when he saw her crying.

"Mrs. Miller?" he asked.

Katie looked up at him. She was laughing through her sobs.

"I know where they are."

Broken Ties

DAY 1 (FIRST DAY OF BLACKOUT)

*T*he trucks burst through the security gates and peeled out onto the highway. The military MPs were hot on their tails. Gunshots blasted back and forth from both sides. The driver of the lead truck, trying to escape, clicked his radio mic on.

"When do we blow it? Well, how much farther do we have to go? They'll have air support on our asses in less than two minutes! Roger that."

The driver clicked his mic off angrily. His passenger next to him, dressed in army fatigues, reloaded his rifle. The name McGuire was pasted on across the uniform.

"What'd he say, Blake?" McGuire asked.

Blake shifted into sixth gear as the speedometer pushed to ninety.

"We can't blow it until we're twenty miles out," Blake said.

"Shit, are you serious?"

"Yeah."

Blake checked the side rearview mirror and saw an RPG flying into the rear truck. The blast almost shook them off the road, and fire and metal flew through the air.

"We're not gonna make it!" McGuire screamed.

"Tell Team Two to hop on the fifty-caliber," Blake said.

"Copy that."

McGuire flipped on the radio and gave the instructions to the truck behind them. A few minutes later, they could hear the thunderous shots of the gun blasting away at the MPs chasing them.

"You sure they won't be able to crack the code before we launch?" McGuire asked.

"They won't be able to get through the fire wall."

"How much further?"

"Fifteen miles."

"Slow down."

"What?"

"I'll have Team Two catch up with us, and then we'll concentrate fire."

"Copy that."

McGuire moved to the back seat of the truck and jumped through the opening in the roof to man the .50-caliber on their armored truck.

He racked the chamber, and when the second truck moved into position, he squeezed the trigger. Between the two guns, they lit up the cars behind them like fireworks.

Blake had the gas pedal almost all the way to the floor. The speedometer was over one hundred miles per hour. He did his best to keep the wheel steady, but with the increased speed, any sort of adjustments were jerky.

Only twelve more miles.

"How we looking back there?" Blake asked.

"They're starting to drop back, but we've got choppers coming inbound fast," McGuire replied.

Blake knew that once air support made it their way, they'd be toast. He didn't have an option.

"McGuire! Come down and take the wheel," Blake said.

McGuire descended back into the truck, and he grabbed hold of the wheel while Blake kept his foot on the gas. He pulled the laptop from his bag and flipped it open.

His fingers flew across the keyboard, opening files and entering passcodes until a screen finally popped up that read, "Launch Code Sequence."

"I thought we had to be twenty miles out?" McGuire asked.

"We do."

"Then what are you doing?"

"Keeping us alive."

Blake finished typing in the last piece of code and hit enter. Behind them, they could hear the blastoff of the missile launching into the atmosphere.

30

DAY 13 (THE CABIN)

*M*ike's hand twitched on the clipboard, and the pen dropped to the floor. He winced, forming a fist, fighting through the pain. He paused, letting his will gather to force his hand open again. Once the shaking subsided, he bent down to pick up the pen.

The shelves in the basement of the cabin were still lined with rations, but Mike knew it wouldn't last them much longer. He'd planned for a six-month supply of food, but that was for five people. Now he had seventeen mouths to feed. If they kept consuming at the rate they were going, the shelves would be barren in a matter of weeks.

With the inventory done, Mike picked up the lantern with one hand and the basket with the morning's breakfast in the other and headed upstairs.

Anne was pulling some of the pots and pans out of the cabinet when Mike set the basket on the counter.

"How's it looking down there?" Anne asked.

Mike handed her the clipboard. She ran her finger down the list, shaking her head as she flipped through the pages.

"How long do we have?" Anne asked.

"Best case, six weeks. Worst case, three."

When Mike reached for the clipboard, his hand shook from another tremor.

"Mike," Anne said.

She grabbed his hand and rubbed gently.

"They're fine," Mike said.

"Take some of the medicine downstairs."

"No, I don't want to waste it. They don't hurt that bad yet."

Mike focused all of his will to keep his hands steady when Anne reached down to kiss them. He didn't want to tell her that it took him twenty minutes in the morning, working through the pain, to perform the simple task of curling his fingers into a fist.

"I'll start getting everyone up. We need to have a house meeting," Mike said.

Mike's dad, Ulysses, was already up when he stepped into his room. Nelson, his son Sean, and Freddy were still asleep on the floor.

"I tried giving the boys the bed, but they wouldn't take it," Ulysses said, stepping in between the bodies lying on the floor.

"Don't give them a hard time about it. They just want to make sure you're comfortable."

"No, they just want to give it to me because I'm old."

Mike waited to roll his eyes until Ulysses brushed past him. He watched his son for a moment before he woke him. He always enjoyed watching him sleep. Before the EMP blast, every day before work, Mike would walk into each of his kids' rooms and kiss them on the forehead before heading to work. It was his ritual, and it helped make the five a.m. wake-up time a little easier.

"Hey, bud. Time to get up," Mike said.

Freddy groaned and rolled onto his back. His Spiderman shirt was pulled up, exposing his belly. Mike tickled him. Freddy squirmed and giggled.

"Dad! Stop!"

"It's time for breakfast. Get Sean up, will you?"

Nelson woke up, looking groggy, and reached for his glasses.

"Breakfast in ten, Nelson."

"Right," Nelson said, yawning.

Mike headed down the hallway to his daughter's room. Before he reached the handle, the door swung open.

"Hey, Dad," Kalen said.

"Hey, Kay."

It threw Mike off, her being awake. It wasn't like her. On the weekends when they had to be somewhere in the morning, he would have to use a crowbar to pry her out of bed, but then again, things had changed since then.

"Breakfast ready?" Kalen asked.

"Your mom's getting everything ready. You sleep okay?"

"Yeah, it was fine."

The bruising around her neck had mostly faded with the exception of a few blotches of faint purple on the sides. When Mike arrived at the cabin yesterday, his wife told him what happened while he was gone. She waited to tell him until last night, and it hadn't left Mike's mind since. It festered like a disease. His daughter was almost raped, and he was powerless to do anything about it.

Mike watched Kalen head down to the kitchen. He was worried about her. She seemed too put together for what happened. Something didn't feel right.

"You've got quite a girl, Mike," Fay said, walking up behind him.

Fay pulled her hair back and flipped it through a band, giving herself a ponytail. Mike's eye went to the pistol strapped to her hip.

"Did you sleep with that thing?" Mike asked.

Fay laughed.

"Mike, who the hell sleeps anymore?"

She slapped his arm and went to join everyone at breakfast.

"Hi, Mr. Grant," Mary said.

Mike hadn't noticed her until she spoke. Behind Mary were her two younger sisters starting to wake, both of them dressed in some of Freddy's and Kalen's old clothes that were left at the cabin a few years back.

The three girls had been in the town, Carrollton, a mile west of the cabin with their parents on vacation when the EMP blast crippled the country. Then, a few days ago, a biker gang came through and wiped almost everyone out. Mary's father was part of the body count. Her mother fared much worse.

Ulysses found them hiding in the tall grass fields on the edge of town. The girls hid there for almost two days without any food or water.

"You girls head for the kitchen. Breakfast will be ready soon," Mike said.

The last door on the hallway was Freddy's room. Inside were Jung, his wife Jenna, and their two children, Claire and Jung Jr. Mike brought the To family with him on his way from Pittsburgh to the cabin. He found them in an airport, and when Jung found out about the cabin and where Mike was going, he begged to bring his family along.

Mike knew the dangers of bringing the family with him. He wasn't sure if they'd even make the journey. On their way here,

Jenna was shot in the shoulder. It wasn't a fatal hit, and Mike was able to get the bullet out. But she lost a lot of blood, and without professional medical attention, there was always the risk of complications.

Jung hadn't stopped shaking since his wife was hit. Before Mike knocked on the door, he could hear whispering on the other side.

"Jung?" Mike asked.

Mike pushed the door open. Jung was kneeling on the side of the bed, Jenna lying motionless on top of the sheets. His head was bowed, and his hands clutched a string of beads wrapped around his knuckles.

The youngest, Claire, was cuddled up to Jenna on the bed, while Jung Jr. sat in the corner reading an old picture book that belonged to Freddy when he was a kid.

Jenna looked bad. Her face dripped with sweat. Her skin was pale.

"Jung?" Mike repeated.

The whispering stopped. Jung looked back at Mike. His eyes were red and strained from either crying or a sleepless night.

"Whenever you're done, everyone's in the kitchen," Mike said.

Jung inclined his head and went back to his whispers. Mike shut the door gently behind him. He knew what Jung was going through right now. It's what Mike went through during his four-day journey trying to get back to his own family.

When Mike's family escaped the neighborhood after everyone turned on him, he wasn't sure if he'd ever see them again. He knew that he'd give everything he had to find them, but in the back of his mind stood the looming presence of reality. It was a reality he faced with every step of the eighty miles he walked to get there.

Ray, Tom, and Clarence were up after all the commotion and traffic from people passing the living room where they slept.

The cabin was loud with chatter about what was for breakfast. Stomachs growled, and Anne started handing out a few cans of pears. People passed them around as Tom came in to help Anne fire up the skillet.

Mike waited until after breakfast to speak with everyone. He thought it best to tell people difficult news on a full stomach rather than an empty one.

"Hey, everyone, listen up," Mike said.

The kitchen and living room fell silent. Every eye in the cabin was staring at him. It was an odd feeling for Mike, the air of authority he now possessed; it was an unspoken agreement from everyone he'd helped stay alive. They wouldn't be here without him.

"With the amount of people we have here now, the cabin is beyond its intended capacity. I built this place with the idea that there'd only be five occupants. Now, there's more than triple that. I stashed enough food rations and water to last five people six months. With the rate we've been going through food and the number of mouths we now have to feed, our food rations will be gone much sooner."

"So what's the call?" Clarence asked.

"The husband of the woman who let us borrow the cart to bring Jenna up here is a hunter. He knows the area well. I'm going back there today to see if we can work out an arrangement. See if there is anything we can trade," Mike said.

"The family of the boy who shot my wife?" Jung asked.

Mike hadn't noticed Jung join them. The beads were still wrapped tight around Jung's hand, swinging back and forth.

"Jung, it was an accident," Mike said.

"I don't know, Mike. The family wasn't exactly thrilled to see us when we went there the first time," Tom said.

"We're going to need food. It's better if we're able to work something out now before things get too scarce. I don't know how long we'll be here, but if we end up staying through the winter, we're going to need to know the game in the area," Mike replied.

"Winter?" Fay asked. "You don't think everything will get figured out by then?"

"We can't count on the power coming back on. While I hope things will get better, we have to prepare for the worst. We have to think long term," Mike answered.

"Mike's right," Nelson said. "We don't know what's going to happen. It's better to be overprepared than underprepared."

"I want everybody moving in pairs when you're outside the cabin. Anne and Ulysses will give everyone a breakdown of chores. Everyone pulls their own weight. No exceptions," Mike said.

He wasn't sure how the group was going to handle being here. Seventeen people living under the roof of one four-bedroom cabin for an extended period of time was going to be rough. Throwing in the fact that half of them had only known each other for a few days wasn't going to help.

Mike pushed it out of his mind. *One thing at a time*. Right now he just needed to focus on setting up a sustainable food channel.

"Fay, you're with me," Mike said.

Anne raised her eyebrow and pulled Mike aside once Fay had turned her back.

"Why don't you take your dad?" Anne asked.

"I want him here. Ulysses already knows where everything is, and you'll need his help to pick up the slack from Ray and Jenna being down."

Anne grabbed his shirt collar and pulled him close for a kiss.

"Just make sure blondie doesn't get any porridge."

Mike smiled.

"Yes, ma'am."

Once breakfast was over, Mike and Fay headed out for the Murths' farm. The trip there would only take a few hours, but Mike packed a day's worth of rations for him and Fay.

"I'm not too sure of the welcome we're going to get, so if things go bad, don't hesitate. Either shoot or run," Mike said.

"You really think they're going to just give us food?"

"No, the family didn't strike me as the type to give handouts, but we might be able to work out a bartering deal. I'm willing to bet I've got some things they don't."

Mike kept to the east on his way down to the highway. He wanted to avoid getting close to the town. After hearing the stories from Mary and Ulysses about the biker gang, he didn't want to take any unnecessary risks.

Once they made it to the highway, the farm was only a few miles down the road. Mike could see it in the distance.

The farm was modest, roughly twenty acres or so from what he could tell, although he wasn't sure how much land the family owned beyond the fences. They could have come through the back way, but Mike didn't want to risk spooking them. The last time he saw them he *did* have their son at gunpoint.

"You have your safety off?" Mike asked.

"Always."

Mike swung the gate open, and the two of them headed down the dirt road toward the house, the cart kicking up dust behind them. The house was sixty yards away when Mike heard the click of a hammer behind him.

"Drop it," Ken said.

Mike kept his hands in the air.

"Easy. We're not here to cause trouble," Mike said.

"You always keep your rifles on you when you're not looking for trouble?" Ken asked.

"Put it down, Fay. It's all right," Mike said.

Fay placed her rifle on the ground. Mike could feel the barrel of the pistol pressing hard against the back of his skull.

"You have sixty seconds to explain what you're doing here, and if I don't like the answer, I'll be staining my driveway red," Ken said.

"Are you Mr. Murth?" Mike asked.

"Who wants to know?"

"My name is Mike. I came here yesterday with your son. Your wife let me borrow your cart to wheel a woman in our group who was injured up to my cabin."

Mike felt the pressure of the barrel on his head ease. He turned slowly, keeping his hands in the air.

"You're the guy who shot at Billy?" Ken asked.

Ken Murth looked as rough as he sounded. White and gray scruff covered his face. What little hair he had was messy and tussled. His lower lip puffed out, concealing the dip in his mouth. His face and hands were dark and worn from working outdoors.

"He opened fire first," Mike answered.

Ken spit a brown wad onto the ground. The juices from the dip dribbled down his chin.

"I know," Ken said.

It was a father's order to his son to protect his family at all costs. There wasn't any remorse in Ken's eyes, and with the barrel of the gun still aimed at Mike, he wasn't sure how willing Ken was to broker a mutual agreement.

"I was hoping we could talk," Mike said.

The brown and yellow of Ken's teeth flashed in a crooked smile.

"Your boyfriend sure has some balls on him," Ken said, giving Fay a look up and down. "All right. Let's talk."

Beth and Billy were walking from the barn to the house when Mike, Ken, and Fay reached the front porch.

Ken insisted on keeping the rifles if they wanted to chat. Mike complied, hoping the show of good faith would build him some trust.

The inside of the house was simple, clean, and neat. The living room was absent of any television, computer, or any electronic device that he could see. A wooden cross with a figure of Jesus crucified was fixed as the centerpiece above the dining room table.

The back door swung open as Mike and Fay sat on the couch in the living room.

"Ken? Who's in there with you?" Beth asked.

"They're from the party that Billy shot at," Ken answered.

"They bring back our cart?"

Ken sent another wad of brown spit into an empty soup can. He wiped his mouth with his sleeve and kept his eyes on Mike.

"Yeah," Ken said.

Billy froze when he saw Mike, then when his eyes landed on Fay he blushed.

Beth set a basket of eggs on the counter and wiped her hands on the front of her apron as she walked into the living room.

"I'm sure you know what's happened, or at least have an idea of what's happened. The whole country's gone down. There's no power, no water, no transportation, nothing," Mike said.

Ken laughed.

"Boy, you just described my childhood. What are you getting at?"

"Your son mentioned to me that you're a hunter, been doing it a long time. I'm sure you know these woods better than anyone. I was hoping we could set up a trade."

Ken's head slowly turned to his son. Billy kept his head down. His fingers fumbled with the front of his shirt nervously.

"What else did you tell him?" Ken asked.

"I didn't tell him anything else," Billy said.

"I have medical supplies, clothes, ammunition. I was hoping we could work something out," Mike said.

"What kind of ammunition?" Ken asked.

"Every kind."

"I see," Ken said, rubbing his chin. He walked over to Mike slowly. The wooden floors creaked under his boots.

"We can help you hunt," Fay added. "It's been a while, but my dad used to take me all the time. Deer, boar, turkeys, I've tracked them all."

Mike tried to hide his surprise at the statement, but he turned his head a little too quickly. She never mentioned anything like that. When he showed Fay how to shoot the rifle at the airport, he just thought she was a natural. Now he knew why.

"You provide the ammo for the hunts, along with an extra five boxes each of nine millimeter, two twenty-three, and forty-five shells each month," Ken said.

Mike extended his hand.

"Done."

Ken flashed another yellow-stained smile. He squeezed Mike's hand and laughed.

"Well, okay then. I'll take this month's supply up front," Ken said.

"What?" Fay asked.

"Hey, you came here looking for my help, remember? Unless you think you'll be able to find the game around here by yourself?" Ken asked.

All of those extra mouths handicapped Mike. It was like he was wearing a pair of cement shoes and then was asked to run a marathon. He didn't have a choice but to give Ken what he wanted.

"It's fine. We'll bring the ammo back first thing in the morning," Mike said.

"No, I'll come and collect the ammo now," Ken said. "Besides, it'll be nice to know where you are in case we need to stop by for some… sugar."

Ken looked at Fay when he said it. She took a step forward, but Mike stepped in between them.

"The cabin's a few hours away. We better get going," Mike said.

Ken brought Billy with him to help carry the gear back. On the way back Mike didn't want to show him the entrance from the main road, so he just cut through the forest.

Mike and Ken were up front, while Fay and Billy walked behind them. There wasn't much talk on the way up. Fay kept her eyes on Ken, while Billy kept his eyes on Fay.

"Your dad always like that?" Fay finally asked.

"Yeah, most of the time. It's been worse over the past couple weeks. He pretends that what's happened doesn't affect us, but it does, especially since the town's been taken over by those bikers."

"I heard your grandfather was there when they came in. I'm sorry."

"Thanks."

"Were you guys close?"

"Not really. My dad and he never really saw eye to eye. They always butted heads. The only time I got to see him was when I went into town alone. I don't know why my dad always hated him."

"Well, you know what they say; you can't choose your family."

Fay noticed that Billy kept looking away when she would look at him. She smiled.

"So, you have a girlfriend, Bill?"

"Um, no, I… uh… well, not that I haven't wanted one, it's just, I, um… you know helping out with the farm, and… hey, how much longer till we get to the cabin?"

* * *

MIKE SPENT most of the walk trying to figure out who Ken was, but the man was a closed book. He wouldn't budge on anything. He wouldn't say how long he'd lived here or who he knew in town, and when Mike brought up the fact that it'd be good to get to know each other a bit, Ken simply popped another piece of chew in his mouth and laughed.

So Mike focused most of his brainpower on how much food they'd need to ration moving forward. Just because he'd set the agreement up with Ken didn't mean they'd get food whenever they wanted. They still had to hunt for it.

The only game Mike had seen were a few birds. If they could get a deer, they'd be able to cure it and it could last them a few weeks. If he could pull down a deer every other week, they'd be in good shape.

"When's the next time you're heading out hunting?" Mike asked.

"Mornin'."

"What time?"

"I'll let you know when I get my ammo."

"Look, Ken, if this is going to work, we're going to need a little trust. It's not like I'm asking for your social security number."

"You wanna know why the rest of the country's gone to shit and I'm still alive? It's because of that trust. Except my trust isn't with other people, it's with me. I know how to stay alive. I know how to keep moving forward. It's no skin off my back if no one else knows how to do that."

There wasn't any doubt in Mike's mind that Ken was right about being able to survive, about not needing to depend on others to make it through, but Mike wondered if that's what he would have to become. Would he have to push everything out of him except his own stubborn will to survive? And if he did, then what did that mean for his family?

"You're pretty cynical for a man with all those crosses in your house," Mike said.

"Ha! That's all of the wife's shit. She's the one who dragged our boys to church every Sunday. The only thing I miss from before the power went out was having those Sunday mornings to myself while the rest of them were gone. What about you? Have you found solace in the fact that God will save us?"

The last sentence came out in a sarcastic plea. Mike listened to the stillness of the forest. It was midafternoon now, and there wasn't even the rustle of leaves, just the sound of their boots crunching on the forest floor and the periodic spit of the man next to him.

"No. Whatever saving happens comes from us."

31

DAY 13 (BIKER GANG)

*T*he bags under Jake's eyes told the story of his night. It told the story for most of his nights over the past few weeks. The cold concrete of the fountain he leaned against was uncomfortable, but he was too numb to move. The sky was gray, struggling to turn blue with the morning's rising sun.

Jake took another swig of the nearly empty bottle of Jack Daniels and finally succumbed to the heaviness of his eyelids.

Find the bitches. Make them suffer. Kill them. Burn them.

He opened his eyes and saw the charred corpses on the ground and the woman tied to the pole. She was the mother of the three girls he believed killed one of his brothers. He ran his hand over the president's patch on his cut, feeling the outline of the raised letters against the leather.

That patch was his life. The club was his life. Everything he did was for the prosperity of his brothers, the advancement of the club… the amelioration of his own survival.

He walked back to his room at the motel. He passed the open doors of his brothers asleep in their beds, snoring, slumbering from restless dreams.

When he made it to his room, he felt his body collapse onto the dirty sheets of his bed. They were stained with sweat and dirt from the past week. The room was starting to smell. He was starting to smell. The whole goddamn town reeked of death. It was a death that he brought, a death that he would always bring.

Jake tore the sheets off the bed, balled them up, and threw them in the trash. He picked up the pieces of garbage, collecting the empty wrappers and half-eaten sandwiches from the floor. As he bent over, he felt dizzy and collapsed.

The room was spinning. He looked at the whiskey still clutched in his hand. The brown liquid sloshed back and forth. He smiled, laughed.

Jake steadied himself, rose, then began chugging the rest of the bottle in defiance. He wouldn't let anything stand in the way of him finishing the things he wanted, no matter what the cost.

The last few drops were drained from the bottle, and he threw it against the wall violently. The bottle burst into jagged shards that rained to the carpet.

Jake fell onto the nightstand behind him. The lamp crashed to the bed, and the blank clock slid into the space between the wall and the stand.

The edges of the smashed glass were sharp when he picked them up. The pieces dug into his skin, drawing blood as he pinched them between his fingers.

When the bottle was whole, the glass was harmless. He could run his fingers along the edges without hurting himself. The bottle only became a weapon when he made it one. The bottle only became dangerous because of him.

Jake liked that. He liked the violence in him. That violence propelled him to lead the storied Diablo Motorcycle Club. Everyone knew who he was back in Cleveland. Everyone feared him there, just as he had made everyone fear him here in Carrollton.

That fear gave him strength. It gave him purpose.

* * *

KALEN WAITED for her mother to head outside with the rest of the group to start work on the garden. They'd taken what they needed from the basement, but Kalen wanted to make sure she could get the other pistol out of the safe quickly, so she did a few practice runs.

The safe downstairs had been relocked. Kalen searched the boxes for the key but couldn't find it. She figured her dad must have it. She knew he had a spare, but she wasn't sure where he kept it.

When she came back up from the basement, her mom was coming back inside.

"Mom," Kalen said.

"Yeah."

"Do you know where the key to the gun safe is?"

"What?"

"I wanted to show Mary how to handle a weapon."

"Kalen, I don't think it's a good idea."

"We won't be shooting. I just want to make sure she feels comfortable with it. She's still pretty spooked about what happened to her parents. I think having some knowledge of how to protect herself will help her feel safer."

There was some truth to that. Mary *was* still having trouble dealing with her parents. Kalen just chose to leave out her own motives.

"Okay," Anne said.

Kalen followed her mom down to her bedroom. Anne pulled the key out of the top dresser drawer and dropped it into Kalen's hand.

"Just put everything back when you're done. And make sure the pistols aren't loaded."

"Thanks, Mom."

Kalen rushed back downstairs to the basement. Some of the rifles were gone, since her dad left this morning, but there was still a large assortment to choose from.

The .223 Remington with a lever action, the 12-gauge shotguns, and a number of AR-15s were all organized in the safe. There were also 9mm and .45, .22, and .40-caliber pistols lining the inside of the safe.

Kalen grabbed two AR-15 rifles along with several boxes of ammunition and four spare magazines. She placed the rifles, ammunition, and magazines into a duffle bag. She also grabbed one of the 9mm Smith and Wesson pistols and tucked it behind her waistband.

When Kalen found Mary, she was outside helping with the garden. She brought her around to the front of the house and pulled out the 9mm.

"It's not loaded," Kalen said. "See how it feels. You want it to be comfortable."

"It's heavy."

Mary aimed at one of the trees, peering through the three-white-dot alignment sight. After a few moments, the gun began to shake in her hands. Mary's face twitched, and the corners of her mouth folded downward. Finally she lowered the gun.

"I can't do this," Mary said.

"What?"

"Whatever it is you think we can do, Kalen. We're not soldiers. I don't know how to fight."

Mary extended the pistol back to Kalen. It lingered in the air between the two of them. Kalen finally placed her hands on top of Mary's, stepped directly behind her, and guided the pistol's sight back up to eye level.

"Those men down there will come for you again. They'll make you hurt long before they decide to put a bullet in your brain and end you," Kalen said.

Kalen kept Mary's hand steady. She continued to whisper in her ear.

"They won't care about the type of person you are. They'll only care what they can do to you, every terrible thing imaginable and worse. All of your fears, whatever they are, won't be as bad as their reality."

Kalen guided Mary's finger to the trigger.

"Remember what they did to your parents?" Kalen asked.

Mary's body tensed up. She could see her father lying on the ground, blood pouring from his stomach, and the biker with the smile across his face. She saw her mother lying on the bed naked with the biker on top of her. She could feel the rocking of the bed as her mother was being raped.

"Once they kill you they'll find your sisters, then they'll hurt them," Kalen said.

She could see her sisters crying, begging for help. When she saw their faces in her mind, she could feel a shift.

"Pull the trigger, Mary," Kalen said.

Whatever fear she was feeling had to be put aside. She couldn't let her sisters suffer the same fate as their parents.

"Pull it!" Kalen said.

The click of the firing pin went off. Kalen let Mary go, and the pistol dropped to the ground. Kalen picked the pistol up, dusting some of the dirt and leaves from the side. She tucked it back into her waistband.

Mary looked down at her hand. It was shaking. She closed her eyes, focusing her energy on forming a fist, trying to squeeze the adrenaline out of her body.

"Are we going to die?" Mary asked.

"Only if we want to."

* * *

Frankie pulled a state map of Ohio from behind the lobby counter. He spread it out on the desk, and his finger ran along the paper creases from Cleveland to Carrollton. He snatched a pen from a jar and picked up a ruler from the desk.

He placed the end of the ruler on the center of Carrollton and marked a small line a few inches out. He made similar marks of equal length around the entire town. Then he drew a circle, connecting each mark on the map, which encompassed an area around Carrollton.

Frankie tossed the pen and ruler back behind the counter and stormed out of the lobby, grabbing a bag of chips from the food pile on his way out.

When Frankie made it to Jake's room, he was on the bed, cleaning his pistol. Frankie stopped at the doorway before he entered. Scanning the room, he saw that the bed was made and the trash from their week's stay had been picked from the floor.

"Housekeeping come by?" Frankie asked.

"What'd you find?" Jake asked.
Frankie spread the map out on the bed adjacent from where Jake was sitting.

"Carrollton's the only town for at least twenty miles in any direction. It's just highways and woods until you get anywhere," Frankie said.

"What'd Spence find with tracks?"

"Nothing. We think they went through the grass fields."

Jake slid the rag along the barrel of the gun. He dropped a few bits of lubricant on the barrel's rim then wiped the excess clean.

"If they had transportation, we would have heard them. They must have gone on foot," Jake said.

"Jake, whoever killed Garrett isn't coming back. They're long gone. The chances of us finding them are... aren't there."

Jake set the barrel of the gun down next to the other pieces on the bed. He tossed the dirty rag in the trash and picked up the different pieces of the pistol, examining each of them individually in his hand.

"Each part of this gun serves a purpose. They all work in an understanding that each element will do its job. The gun needs all of its parts to work properly, and when they do, the outcome is exactly what the shooter intends it to be... deadly," Jake said.

The pieces of the gun clicked into place as Jake reassembled the weapon. When he put the slide back on and slid the magazine inside, he racked a bullet into the chamber, clicking the safety off.

"This club works the same way. If we don't follow through with our commitment of avenging our brother's death, then we become as useless as a gun with no trigger. We lose our direction and our bond," Jake said.

Jake pointed the pistol at Frankie. Frankie took a step back, folding the map in his hands.

"I'll check the public records. See if there's any property registered in the woods around the town."

JAKE HOLSTERED HIS PISTOL.

"Good."

* * *

THE TWO AR-15s were on Kalen's bed. She shoved the last bullet the spare magazine would hold, and threw it in the duffle bag. The rest of the magazines were full with thirty bullets apiece. Counting the bullets already loaded into both rifles, it gave her a total of one hundred eighty shots.

From Mary's and Ulysses's description, there were no more than twenty bikers in town. Nine bullets apiece, she figured that would be enough.

Kalen stuffed the empty bullet boxes in the bag she brought up from the basement and shoved it under her bed to hide it. The door to her room opened, and Mary entered, holding the pistol at her side.

"When do we leave?"

Kalen smiled. She picked up one of the AR-15s and handed it to Mary.

"Now."

Mary slipped the rifle strap over her shoulder, and Kalen did the same. The two headed outside, and before they reached the forest, Ulysses stopped them.

"Where are you two going?" Ulysses asked.

"We're heading to the rifle stand," Kalen answered.

"Those things loaded?"

"No, but we have some extra magazines… just in case."

"You should let me come with you."

"No offense, Grandpa, but we were hoping for some girl time."

Ulysses threw his hands up.

"Okay. Don't go far."

Kalen led them through the forest. They walked for fifteen minutes before she changed course and headed for Carrollton.

"So, what happens when we get there?" Mary asked.

"We'll be outnumbered, but we'll have the element of surprise on our side. If we can funnel them into a central location, we can pin them down. We'll be able to take a lot of them out that way, especially since they don't know we're coming."

"What if they stay spread out?"

"Then we pick off as many as we can and keep moving. The moment they know where we are we'll be in trouble. It won't matter how many bullets we have at that point."

Kalen acted as if she were going on a hunt with her dad. It wasn't any different in her mind. She'd killed before. The only difference this time was the animals could shoot back.

Her mind went back to the man in the forest. The one who tried to rape her on their trip from Pittsburgh to the cabin. She could still feel his hands around her neck. She still remembered the weight of his body on top of hers, the helplessness she felt, and the greedy lust in the man's eyes. The curling lip that formed a smile was fresh in her mind.

That man didn't care who she was, what she wanted from life, or how it made her feel. The man had no regard for the nightmares she'd had since that day or the number of pills she took to stop making her feel anything than the hate she filled her mind and heart with to replace the fear. He didn't care about any of that. All he cared about was taking what he wanted.

Kalen knew the bikers in town were the same way. They rode in, killed who they wanted, and had zero regard for what it meant to own something, to work for something, to truly value something.

All of them were the same in Kalen's mind. There was no difference between the face of the man in the forest and the faces of the bikers in town.

"Kalen, are you okay?" Mary asked.

Kalen was squeezing the rifle's handle so hard that her arms were shaking. She suddenly became aware of the sweat on her face. Her knuckles had turned white, and when she removed her hand from the pistol grip on the front of the rifle, she felt her skin peel off like Velcro.

"I'm fine," Kalen said.

She wasn't sure how much time she was going to get before her family realized she was gone. She knew that once her dad came home he'd come looking for them at the shooting stand, and when he saw they weren't there he'd be worried.

That was the only thing weighing on her. She knew not coming back alive would hurt her family. She understood what it would do to her father, how it would change him, but this was her choice, and it was a choice she had the right to make.

* * *

THE RIFLE still felt awkward for Mary. She wasn't used to the weight or the feel of it. Kalen had explained as much to her about shooting as she could. She did her best to pay attention, to try and focus on the task at hand, but her mind wandered.

Thoughts of her mother, her father, and her sisters flashed like lightning strikes in her mind. Her imagination ran wild with the horrors the biker gang was committing on her mother.

At night she lay awake, still feeling the rocking of the bed she was on as her mom lay next to her with that biker on top of her. She could still hear his grunts, heavy breaths, the violent commands he barked at her, each syllable sending a tremor through her body.

The longer they walked, the more she questioned what she was doing. She knew it was fear that was fogging her mind. She tried focusing on the thought of protecting her sisters, but it didn't seem strong enough to keep the fear at bay.

Mary kept a few steps behind Kalen the entire journey through the woods. She watched Kalen, observed how she moved, how she carried herself. The girl she saw the first day she arrived at the cabin was gone.

Mary remembered seeing how out of touch Kalen was. When she took Kalen back to her room where she passed out on the bed, she figured she was on some type of drug. Then when Mary found the bottle of pills in the nightstand, which was almost empty, it confirmed her suspicions.

When Mary told Kalen what happened to her family, she saw something change in Kalen. A switch flipped. Kalen's resolve hardened. That's what made Mary follow her. Mary was leaning on Kalen's strength to help find her own.

"How do you do it?" Mary asked.

"Do what?"

"Act like you're not afraid."

"I don't."

"Well, you're doing a good job of hiding it."

"That's just it. You can't hide it. You can't shove something that big into a corner without it being seen. So you expose it to the light for everyone to see, then instead of you being afraid of the fear, the fear becomes afraid of what you've done to unmask it. The fear yields to you."

"What if you can't control it?"

"Then it kills you. Either way, your struggle's over."

Was that her fate if she accepted her fear? She'd never been in any position like that her entire life. She'd never experienced the type of fear and pain that she'd felt over the past two weeks.

There was a time when the only things she was scared of were the final exams at school and seeing what she got on her report card.

But the lump in her throat wouldn't give way, and the pit in her stomach wouldn't fill up. What she was feeling was endless, and she couldn't see a way out.

* * *

FRANKIE DUMPED the rest of the red fuel cans on the concrete next to the bikes. He managed to pull a total of twelve five-gallon cans from the mechanic's shop.

"We can try and siphon some gas out of the cars, but aside from that, this is it, Jake," Frankie said.

Jake counted the bikes in the row. Most of them still had some fuel left in the tank, but the majority of them were low. The ride from Cleveland drained a lot of the gas they had. The old bikes they rode here managed to survive the EMP blast because they didn't have any microprocessors in them, but they also had terrible gas mileage.

"Any bike that's below a quarter of a tank, fill it up. I want everyone able to ride," Jake said.

Frankie grabbed two other members, and the three of them started checking the bikes' fuel gauges.

Jake pulled out the map with the radius of how far the girls could have traveled. He figured they stayed close. There were a handful of cabins Frankie was able to find in the county office. He wanted to start hitting those first. If they traveled through the woods, it would be a good place to start.

Tank, Jake's vice president of the club, came up behind him. Tank's eyes were hidden behind his shades. His long gray beard was greased with grime and clumped together from weeks without a shower. His belly poked through the space between his cut, the buttons barely holding back the weight behind them.

"Jake, we need to talk," Tank said.

The two men walked out of earshot of the rest of the club.

"I don't know if this is the best time for us to be doing this," Tank said.

"One of our brothers is dead. You don't want to make sure whoever did this pays for that?"

"You really think those girls killed Garrett? C'mon, Jake. They're long gone and starving somewhere in the woods."

"Well, if they're close by just sitting under the trees in the shade, they'll be easy to find."

Jake slammed his shoulder into Tank when he moved past him. Tank put his hand on Jake's shoulder to spin him around, but Jake twisted the old man's hand. Tank winced.

"We are going to find whoever did this. I don't care what it costs us, you understand me? Diablos don't let one of their own die without the bastards who killed them answering for their crime," Jake said.

Jake let Tank's hand go. Tank backed away slowly, both hands in the air, surrendering.

"Okay, brother. Okay," Tank said.

"And you make sure the rest of the club knows that too," Jake finished.

Keep the club together. That's what Jake needed to do. He couldn't let his club waver now, not with what they had in front of them. He knew his men would need a distraction. If the group wasn't heading somewhere, anywhere, with a goal in mind, they would fall apart.

Jake passed the pile of burnt bodies on the way to his room. For better or worse, he was their leader, and no matter what hell he brought on them, they'd follow him to the end. That was their brotherhood, a family of death.

* * *

The perimeter of the town was deserted. Kalen couldn't see anyone on patrol. From what Mary had told her, the biker gang had men on watch around the clock.

When she double-checked the east end of the town, she figured they were either gone or focused on something important. Either way, they had a clear entrance.

When Kalen came back from scouting, Mary looked like she hadn't breathed since she left.

"You ready?" Kalen asked.

Mary nodded her head quickly, avoiding Kalen's eyes. Kalen grabbed Mary's chin and pulled her face toward hers.

"We can't have any doubts once we cross this line. I need to know now if you're ready for this," Kalen said.

"I'm ready."

"All right then. Stay close behind me. I'll find you a good spot with cover, and then I'll position myself. I think they must be gathered together since there aren't any patrols. Let's go."

The two girls left the cover of the tall grass and headed for the first building on the right side. They inched their way up the street, ducking behind cars, doors, anything large enough to hide behind.

Kalen kept glancing back at Mary, who was still behind her. Every time she checked to see if Mary was there, she expected her to be gone or frozen in the last spot she saw her. Kalen was having second thoughts about bringing her along. She needed someone who was willing to do what it took. She needed to have confidence in her partner.

A team was only as strong as the weakest link, and Mary wasn't looking very strong. If Kalen's life came down to Mary's ability to keep her alive, it wasn't going to end well. But it was a fate she'd come to terms with.

It was an odd feeling though, thinking about death with such indifference. Kalen never considered it before. It seemed so far away, like a dream you couldn't remember.

The days of boys, parties, and going to college just weren't a part of her reality anymore. The only thing that felt real was the rifle in her hands and the extra magazines loaded in her bag, smacking against her back as she pressed forward.

The motel sign was just ahead. Kalen recognized it from Mary's description. When she saw the group of a dozen bikers starting their bikes, she whipped around to grab Mary's attention.

"They're leaving!"

But Mary's eyes were focused on something in the courtyard of the motel. Kalen followed her line of sight to the pile of black and brown figures stacked around a pole. There was something tied to the pole, but she couldn't tell what it was.

Mary stood up, oblivious of being seen. Kalen yanked her back down.

"What are you doing?" Kalen asked.
"That's... a person... on the pole."

Kalen peered through the scope on her rifle. When the object on the pole came into view, her stomach turned.

It wasn't a person anymore. It was a charred piece of meat slumped over a pile of another dozen burnt bodies.

"Jesus," Kalen said.

She wanted to look for a building with a second-story window to give them the advantage of higher ground, but she wasn't sure if they'd have time now.

A few bikers had already started to weave through the parking lot and onto the street. When three of the bikers disappeared heading toward the west side of town, Kalen checked to see if the others would be joining them, but no one else showed.

"Must be a scout party," Kalen said.

"What did they do to those people?" Mary asked.

"Mary, listen to me. I'm going to the other side of the motel. I'll fire a few shots in the air to draw them out. When they do, you open fire, understand? If it gets bad, head back for the tall grass."

"It was a woman tied up there."

"Once you open fire, I'll start taking them out on my side. We'll bottleneck them. They'll think there are more than two of us in the beginning, but that'll only last for a little while."

"There's a reason she's up there. Why is she up there?"

"Mary!"

Kalen shook Mary's shoulders, trying to bring her back to the moment.

"You want to help that woman on the pole? The one they burned? The one they hurt? Shoot them, and don't let up. Here,"

Kalen said, giving her two of the loaded magazines. "If you need to reload, you shove the magazine in like this, and rack the chamber. You'll only need to do it once."

Mary nodded.

"Remember, bring the rifle to your eyes, squeeze the trigger, don't pull it, and be prepared for some recoil. It'll hurt the first couple times," Kalen said.

Kalen took off, leaving Mary behind one of the cars. She kept low, sprinting toward the other side. Once she was clear and caught her breath, she closed her eyes.

Focus. This is why you're here. You can do this. You can do this. Just do it.

She aimed her pistol in the air, poised to fire the opening shots that would draw the bikers out, but just before she squeezed the trigger, she stopped herself. She peeked back around the corner of the building she was hiding behind and saw the row of motorcycles that were still parked in the lot. She smiled.

"Might as well make an entrance."

She brought the Harleys into her crosshairs and squeezed the trigger. The bullets blasted through two of the bikes closest to her, knocking them over.

Shouts from inside the rooms immediately followed. The bikers had their guns drawn, rushing outside. When Kalen heard the shots from Mary's rifle, she ran for a parked car that had a better vantage point in front of the motel.

One of the bikers must have seen her because as soon as she ducked behind the car's engine, she could hear the thud of bullets hitting the metal.

Be patient. Wait for your shot. Draw them out.

There was a break in the firing. Kalen jumped up from her cover. There were five of them she could see. The closest was out in the open, exposed. He tried to make a run for it, but Kalen had a bead on him.

Squeeze it.

The sound of the bullet leaving the barrel and the spray of blood from the biker's chest was simultaneous. When he hit the ground, she moved on to the next.

One of the bikers ducked behind the fountain in the courtyard. He was crouched low, but the top of his head was still exposed. She squeezed the trigger, and a bullet nicked the concrete fountain. She missed.

Kalen ducked behind the car again. Another round of bullets volleyed back at her. She could hear Mary's shots coming from her right.

Kalen jumped back up on the hood, hoping the biker behind the fountain would give her a better shot.

"Gotcha."

The bullet sliced the biker's head in two. Kalen swung the rifle up to the second floor where some of the bikers were coming out of their rooms.

Bullets ricocheted off the iron posts from the guardrail on the second floor. She hit one of the bikers in the leg, and he crumpled to the ground. Kalen sent several rounds of bullets into him to finish the job.

More bikers were filling the courtyard now, each of them with pistols, rifles, and shotguns. The cars Kalen and Mary were hiding behind were starting to look like Swiss cheese. The time frame between the bikers reloading was getting smaller.

The side mirror exploded over Mary, sending a rain of glass on top of her. She ducked lower, shielding herself from the endless firing of gunshots.

"Mary! Head to the other side of the street! I'll cover you!" Kalen said.

Mary nodded. Kalen inched toward the trunk of the car, keeping herself low so the bikers couldn't see her. When she made it to the rear of the car, the tires exploded, dropping the car lower.

Kalen ducked with it, keeping her head down as more bullets rained upon her. She jumped up and gave Mary the cover fire she needed to sprint across the street.

A few of the bikers had grown bold and left themselves exposed. Kalen killed three more before they could find cover.

As Kalen dropped back behind the car, she could hear the shouts of one of the bikers.

"Send some around back. We'll cut them off."

"Jake wants them alive!"

Kalen sprinted back toward the corner of the building where she was earlier. Her feet smacked against the pavement as she fired a few more shots into the biker's direction, then heard the click of the firing pen.

Empty.

Once she made it to the building's corner, clear from the exposed road, the empty magazine hit the sidewalk. She loaded a new magazine in and racked the chamber.

She wanted to cut the bikers off before they made it to the other side of town. If the bikers sandwiched them in one of the buildings, they'd be goners.

Kalen ran past the storefronts toward the west side of town, trying to beat the bikers there. She skidded to a stop just before the buildings ended.

Four of the bikers pursued her. They inched their way toward her, moving from car to car up the side of the street and using some of the doors to the shops for cover.

"Shit," Kalen said.

She looked around, trying to think of a way out. When the bikers came around from the back, she'd be cornered.

It was a good thirty yards from her location to safety on the other side of the street, thirty yards without any cover. She could make a run for it, but it would expose her.

The bikers were getting closer. Kalen could feel her heart pounding in her chest. Her hands gripped the rifle harder. Was this it? Was this how it was going to end?

No.

She still had more left. The dirt flew up from the ground as she dug her heels and dashed for the other side of Main Street. She aimed the rifle back blindly, shooting at random, trying to provide her own cover for the run.

When she made it to the other side, she kept running. She didn't stop until she made it to the back of the building.

Kalen couldn't remember how many stores down Mary was or which one she ran inside. The first store she ran inside was the old gun shop. Most of it was cleaned out, but there were still some cases and a few rifles and pistols lying around.

Kalen found two 9mm pistols and a box of ammo. She shoved them both in her bag and did one last scan for any .223 shells for her rifle.

She scanned the barren shelves, desperately searching for more bullets. She shoved a few cases of shotgun shells out of the way and found an entire case of .223 ammo.

She stuffed five boxes into her bag, with the pistols and other ammo she had remaining, and hurried out the back door.

The gunshots coming from the front of the store were becoming more frequent, which was a good thing in Kalen's mind. As long as the guns kept firing, then Mary was still alive.

Kalen checked a few more back doors before she finally found Mary in what was left of the hardware store. She was still by the front, holding her ground. Two empty magazines were at her feet.

"Mary!" Kalen shouted.

When Mary turned around, a hail of bullets came down on them, sending both of them to the floor.

Kalen crawled forward, dragging the bag with her, shelves of hardware supplies exploding above her from the gunshots.

A box of nails exploded from a gunshot and sent one of the four-inch nails flying into Kalen's leg. She screamed in pain. Half the nail dug into her flesh. She reached her hand down, her body shaking, and when she yanked it out, a spurt of blood followed.

She let out a relieved gasp and continued her progression forward toward the front of the store.

Mary covered her ears, her arms around the top of her head, attempting to protect herself from harm. Kalen ripped Mary's hands off her head and handed her one of the empty magazines and a box of shells.

"Load the magazines," Kalen ordered.

The first few bullets Mary grabbed slipped out of her shaking hands. She finally managed to pick one up and pressed it down into the magazine. She loaded them as fast as her nerves would let her.

Kalen poked her head over the windowpane. There were a half-dozen bikers advancing at them. She knew it wouldn't be long before the others in the gang would be behind them. She had to get the gun loaded and have one of them guard the back. It was the only way they'd still have a chance.

Mary held up one of the finished magazines, and Kalen snatched it from her. The bullets were still screaming into the hardware store. Both of them were crouched low, avoiding the blasts.

"Watch the back. They'll most likely be coming from the left. There's no cover back there, so they'll have to duck in between the buildings," Kalen said.

"What about you?" Mary asked.

Kalen dumped the boxes of ammo onto the floor.

"I'm watching the front," Kalen said.

Mary grabbed her rifle, a box of shells, and the other empty magazine and crawled to the back.

The bikers' gunshots were relentless. Kalen knew they'd have to go back and get more ammo soon. They had to reload at some point.

Kalen took the time to reload the magazines she had and made sure the two pistols were loaded as well. A few moments later the gunfire lightened and she jumped up, rifle in hand, and squeezed the trigger. She was able to hit two of the bikers, killing one while the other dragged himself behind a car.

Then, before she could duck back down, she felt the sharp pain of steel and metal slice through her arm. The force of the bullet pushed her back, and the rifle fell from her hand.

Kalen hit the floor, pressing her hand against her arm. The blood was warm, sticking to her fingers and shirt as she tried to stop the bleeding. She tried moving, but each time she did, it sent stabbing pain through the left side of her body.

Kalen could see one of the pistols on the ground. She stretched out her good arm, her fingertips almost touching the composite of the handle, when a boot pressed down on her hand.

When she looked up, Frankie had his pistol aimed at her head.

"Game's up, sweetheart," Frankie said.

The rest of the bikers converged on them and dragged both girls to the motel. Neither of them screamed or resisted. Kalen simply kept pressure on her arm, trying to staunch the bleeding.

All of the tortures she was about to experience raced through her mind. When she made the decision to do this, she knew this could be one of the outcomes.

No matter what happened though, she wouldn't scream. She wouldn't cry for help. They wouldn't get the satisfaction of hearing her beg.

DAY 13 (THE CABIN)

*W*hatever doubts Ken had about Mike in regards to their deal dissipated when he saw the amount of ammo he had stockpiled.

There were enough rounds to keep them hunting for the next decade. Mike agreed to give Ken the boxes up front, but he made Ken agree to take them hunting tomorrow.

"I need fresh game, and I need it soon," Mike said.

"Okay. Meet me at the trailhead that leads down to the road in the morning."

Mike looked at him, surprised. He specifically took Ken the way he did to avoid the trailhead entrance at the highway.

"I've been hunting this land for more than forty years; you really think I didn't know about the road entrance to your cabin, did you?" Ken asked.

"I guess not."

"Six a.m. We'll need to get started before the sun comes up."

Before the two men could shake on it, Freddy came running into the basement. He almost tripped over himself coming down the stairs.

"Dad! You have to hear this! Come upstairs!" Freddy said.

"What is it?" Mike asked.

"There's someone on the radio!"

Upstairs the entire household was gathered in the living room, circled around one of the radios Freddy had found the day before, protected from the EMP by the faraday box Mike made to store them in.

It was a woman's voice coming over the radio. Mike couldn't tell if it was a recording. The sound kept breaking in and out.

"We have food, water, shelter, medical attention, and protection. We have our operations up and running, and we are restoring power to our area. If you have the ability to arrive, please know that we can help. We can offer assistance. We can keep you safe."

"She's not saying where it is. Where is it?" Jung said.

The rest of the group hushed him. The tension cut through the air as the group waited to hear more.

"Cincinnati has been chosen as the starting point for relief efforts in Ohio. Similar cities have been chosen in other states to act as rallying points in bringing power back online along with other basic utilities. Again, if you are in the area and can make it to Cincinnati, we have food, water, shelter, medical assistance, and protection."

The signal went dead, and the woman's voice was replaced by static. It filled the room as everyone looked at each other, letting what they'd just heard sink in.

"What are we waiting for? We need to get there now!" Jung said.

"Jung, we don't even know who that was. It could be a recording from weeks ago," Mike said.

"But shouldn't we at least try? What if it's true? What if the power is on in Cincinnati? We have the Jeep. We can send a few people," Tom said.

"The only highway around here that leads to the interstate has to go through Carrollton. That means dealing with the biker gang that's down there. A gang that's killed most of the townspeople," Mike said.

"We have to try something!" Jung screamed.

The group members around Jung separated themselves from him. His body was shaking. His eyes were desperate, pleading to the group. He had the look of a man who was willing to do anything to save his wife.

Mike understood. It was a feeling he had the entire walk from Pittsburgh to here. He was willing to do whatever he needed to get to his family, but just because Mike understood Jung's pain didn't mean he could let him take the Jeep.

"We'll keep the radio on, Jung. See if anything else comes through. Okay?" Mike said.

He placed his hand on Jung's shoulder, trying to comfort him. Jung jerked Mike's hand off him and headed back to his room.

"Okay, everyone. Sitting around won't make the radio magically work again. Back to work," Ulysses said.

As the crowd dispersed, Ken let out a whistle.

"Looks like not everyone's happy to have your hospitality," Ken said.

"I'll see you in the morning," Mike said.

The two men shook hands, and Ken headed out the door. Once Ken was gone, Anne came and wrapped her arms around Mike.

"I didn't think you wanted to bring him back here," Anne said.

"I didn't, but it was part of his agreement."

"You think we can trust him?"

"I'm not sure yet, but we're going to need the food, so I don't have much of a choice."

"What are we going to do about the radio? You think it's real?"

Mike found it hard to believe the power would come back up that fast, especially after what he saw in Pittsburgh. He figured by next spring the country would be in a better position to rebuild, but maybe it was happening faster than he thought.

"We can't worry about that right now. We have supplies here that will last us a while, and with Ken helping me hunt, we'll have a fresh supply of food coming in. How's the garden coming?" Mike asked.

"Good. We've got peas, squash, and corn in the ground," Anne said.

Mike gave her a kiss on the forehead.

"I'm gonna keep the radio in our room. We don't need it being a distraction for anyone. Where's Kalen?"

"She went out to the old shooting stand with Mary."

Mike raised his eyebrows.

"Did she say why?" Mike asked.

"Mary's been having some trouble dealing with what happened to her mom. Kalen thought that if she showed her how to handle a weapon, it'd make her feel… safer."

Mike didn't like that the girls had gone out alone, but he felt a surge of pride about his daughter helping Mary.

"Okay, I'm going to get things ready for the morning. I'll be in the basement if you need me."

* * *

It was getting dark, and Kalen and Mary still hadn't returned. Mike was getting worried. He grabbed his rifle and decided to head out to the hunting stand where the girls said they were going.

Mike kept his ears open, but the closer he moved to the stand, the more concerned he became. He'd been walking for almost fifteen minutes, and he hadn't heard a single shot go off. He quickened his pace, his boots smashing the forest dirt underneath.

The stand was only forty yards away, and from what he could see, it was empty. He brought his rifle up and flicked the safety off.

"Kalen?" Mike said.

He circled the stand. There weren't any shell casings on the ground, no foot tracks in the dirt, no sign the girls were ever there at all.

Mike's pulse quickened. His breathing accelerated. The irrational panic of his daughter not being there rushed over him.

"Kalen! Mary!"

They're not here. They never came here, but why? Why would they need rifles if they weren't—

"The bikers," Mike said.

Mike sprinted back to the cabin. It was a two-mile hike and usually took close to forty minutes on foot for a one-way trip. He made it back in less than twenty-five minutes.

Ulysses was the first to see Mike burst through the trees into the cabin's front yard.

"Michael?" Ulysses asked.

"Mary and Kalen? Did I miss them?"

"No, I thought you were going to get them."

"They never went to the stand."

Mike could see Ulysses's eyes make the connection. He was the one who brought Mary and her sisters back to the cabin after he found them in town. Mary's mother was raped in front of them, and they watched their father die.

Mike gathered Erin and Nancy, Mary's sisters, in the living room. The rest of the group lingered in the kitchen and hallway, letting Mike speak to them in semiprivacy.

"I just need to know where they went, Nancy. I'm not mad; I just want to know where we can find them. I want to make sure they're safe," Mike said.

Nancy looked up at him, her eyes wide and wet.

"I don't know. She never told me anything," Nancy said.

Mike lowered his head. He believed her.

"Why did she leave us? She promised me she wouldn't leave us," Nancy said.

Nancy broke down crying. Mike scooped her up in his arms. The little girl buried her face into Mike's shirt, wrapping her arms around his neck.

Anne came over and peeled the girl off of him, rocking her back and forth. The younger sister, Erin, didn't say anything. She kept her head down, twisting the edge of her shirt. Mike gently rested his hand on the top of her head.

Mike didn't make eye contact with anyone as he headed for the basement. Ulysses followed. The two of them started gathering as much ammo and weapons as they could carry.

They said nothing to each other as they collected bullets, loaded magazines, attached scopes, and threw holsters around their waist and shoulders. It was an unspoken agreement between a father and grandfather. Their offspring were in trouble, and they were going to get them out.

Fay, Tom, and Clarence crept down the steps. They watched Ulysses and Mike in the glow of the candlelight. Each of them had bullets and guns strapped around their waists and shoulders. They didn't look like normal men anymore; they were soldiers preparing for war.

"So you're just going to go in there guns blazing?" Tom asked.

Mike shoved a magazine into his Smith and Wesson .45, holstered it, and looked up at the two of them on the stairway.

"I don't expect you three to come. It's going to get bad," Mike said.

Fay grabbed one of the rifles and started loading shells into one of the empty magazines. She said nothing. She didn't look at Mike until he put his hand on her shoulder.

"Thank you," Mike said.

Fay gave a half smile. Clarence was the next to join. He picked up one of the shotguns and found a case of twelve-guage shells and started loading.

Tom let out a sigh at the top of the staircase.

"Fine, but I want the biggest guns you have. With my aim, I'll need all the help I can get," Tom said.

It took them thirty minutes to gather everything they needed. At least everything Mike thought they would need.

They were loaded to the teeth with weapons and ammo. Mike also thought to pack some medical supplies, which he hoped he wouldn't need.

Anne didn't say much. When she walked up to Mike, she placed her hands on his shirt, twisting his collar.

"You bring our girl home."

Mike led Ulysses, Fay, Clarence, and Tom down the trail. Dusk had settled outside, with the night growing darker.

Anne's words rang through Mike's mind like a chorus, repeating over and over. He wasn't going to let his daughter suffer a cruel fate like those he'd seen over the past two weeks. *Bring her home.*

DAY 13 (BIKER GANG)

*T*he cots from the prison cell were removed. It was nothing but concrete and steel. Mary sat in the corner, huddled in a ball, listening to the bikers inside the interrogation room scream at Kalen.

Every once in a while she would hear something hard hit the ground, but she never heard Kalen scream. Mary didn't know what was happening in there, but she was able to imagine a few scenarios.

She wondered why she chose to come with Kalen. She didn't want to die. Her mind wandered to her sisters. Their faces were burning in her thoughts.

Mary promised she wouldn't leave them, let them be alone, and now that promise was broken. She broke it to fulfill the selfish need of revenge.

Frankie recognized her immediately when they finally captured her and Kalen. He didn't say anything to her as he threw her in the cell. He just smiled and laughed.

The laugh wasn't human. It was senseless, malicious. It was the same laugh he had when he killed her dad and the same smile when he raped her mother.

What would they do to her? Would she be passed around to the other bikers? Used only for their pleasure at the expense of her suffering?

Stop it.

Mary pushed it out of her mind. She couldn't go to pieces now. As dire as everything was, she couldn't let her imagination get the better of her. She had to think about what she could control, and right now the only thing that she could control was how she would react to whatever came next.

The door to the interrogation room flung open. Mary rushed to the front of the cell, grasping her hands around the old flaky iron bars.

Two of the bikers dragged Kalen past her cell. Her head was down, her hair covering her face, but Mary could see the drops of blood falling from her body.

Kalen's body was limp. The bikers were carrying her by her arms. Once Kalen was out of sight, Mary could hear the thud of Kalen's body hit the cell floor next to hers, followed by the door slamming shut.

Mary let go of the bars and backed to the rear wall of the cell as Frankie rested his forehead in between the cell bars.

"Your turn, sweetheart," Frankie said.

When Frankie brought her into the interrogation room, the first thing she noticed was the bloodstains on the floor. The next thing she saw was the smeared red on Jake's knuckles.

There were only two chairs and one small table. Frankie pushed her down into the chair across from Jake. The two of them were only two feet apart. She didn't like it. The setting felt too intimate.

"Whatever you're going to do to me, just get it over with," Mary said.

Jake leaned back, wiping his knuckles clean of Kalen's blood with a rag, which he tossed to the floor when he was done.

"What do you want us to do to you?" Jake asked.

"I'm not giving you anything," Mary said.

"You don't even know what we want," Jake said.

"You want to hurt us."

"I do."

The simple answer frightened her. There was a vicious truth in those words. He didn't just have the ability to hurt her, but the desire.

"I want to see my mom," Mary said.

Frankie let out a chuckle, but she kept her eyes on Jake.

"I'm not sure you do," Jake answered.

"I need to see her."

"No. You want to see her. You want to see her the way you used to see her. You want to see her before what happened here. Trust me, girl. It's better that you keep the image of what your mother used to be. It's much better than the image she is now."

"The last image I have of my mother was her being raped in front of me. The last image I have of my father was his blood pouring out of his stomach and him gasping for breath."

"I'm going to ask you some questions. It will be better if you give me the truth the first time around."

"I guess Kalen didn't tell you the truth? That's why she's unconscious in her cell right now?"

"She didn't lie."

Mary's mouth went dry. Jake leaned forward on the table. Mary caught herself staring at Jake's hands. The only bits of blood that remained covered the rings he wore.

Jake twisted one of the rings off his hand and extended it to Mary.

"I was going to clean them off, but I liked the new color too much. What do you think?" Jake asked.

"You're a coward."

Jake slid the ring back on his finger. He formed his hand into a fist, his joints cracking the harder he squeezed.

"A coward is afraid. I'm not afraid, and that's what makes it so bad for you. I'm not afraid to hit a woman. I'm not afraid to make a little girl cry. I'm not afraid to hear them scream."

Mary felt Frankie place his hands on her shoulders. She could feel the calluses on his hands running up along the side of her neck.

"Did you kill any of my men before today?" Jake asked.

"No."

Frankie grabbed a handful of her hair and yanked her head back, exposing her neck. He brought the edge of a blade to her flesh.

"Did you kill any of my men before today?" Jake repeated.

"No," Mary answered.

Frankie slammed her head down on the table. She was able to brace herself with her hands, but she felt the trickle of blood run from her nose over her lips.

"Two days ago, one of my men was killed. Who did it?" Jake asked.

Mary wiped her hand under her nose. A streak of blood smeared across her finger.

"I don't know," Mary answered.

"The cabin you're staying at. Where is it?"

Her sisters. She couldn't give them up. She wasn't going to give them anything.

"I know you're staying with a family. I know someone helped you escape. I will find it eventually. The only difference you can make now is how I treat your sisters when I find them."

They're bluffing. They couldn't know where the cabin was.

Jake rose from the table at her silence. He kicked her chair leg, knocking her over and sending her to the floor. He grabbed her arm and flung her against the wall. He slapped her across the face.

When his hand made contact with her cheek, it was like being dumped in cold water. The pain was overwhelming and shocking all at once.

Jake's hand came across the other side of her face, harder than before. Mary could feel her face reddening. The stings from each hit lingered then swelled.

"Where's the cabin?" Jake asked.

His voice was calm. Mary felt his hand closing around her windpipe. The grip tightened. She gasped for breath. She tried to peel his hand off her but struggled against his size and strength.

Life was being choked from her. Mary started to panic. Her head felt light. Her vision started to blur. Just before she thought she'd pass out, he let go.

Mary dropped to the floor, coughing, hacking, and gasping for air. Jake kicked her stomach. The shot sent pain rippling through her body.

"Give me the knife," Jake said.

Frankie handed him the blade. He grabbed Mary's hand, stepping on her wrist to keep her arm pinned down. He dug the tip of the blade into the flesh of her exposed palm, slowly.

Mary screamed. She reached for the knife with her free hand, but Frankie held her down. She writhed and twisted on the ground, crying and screaming as Jake dug the blade's tip deeper into her hand, cutting away flesh, scraping against the bones.

"Where's the cabin?" Jake shouted.

"Stop! P-p-please stop!" Mary cried.

Jake pulled the knife out and lifted his boot off Mary's wrist. Each time she tried to move a finger, a sharp pain shot up through her arm.

"Stand her up," Jake said.

Mary pulled the injured hand to her, pressing it against her chest to stop the bleeding. Frankie lifted her from the ground.

"You wanted to see your mom? Let's go see her," Jake said.

Frankie pulled her through the sheriff's office. She looked back at Kalen still lying on the floor of her cell, passed out. Maybe she *was* dead. No one could take that kind of pain. They had to have killed her. That's why Kalen never screamed.

Now, they were going to kill her, probably in front of her mother. More torture. Or maybe they'd rape her in front of her mom, make the both of them suffer more before she died.

They were closer to the motel now. The pain in Mary's hand was replaced by the adrenaline coursing through her veins.

When they turned the corner, Mary's stomach started to sink. They weren't leading her to one of the rooms. They were taking her to the center of the courtyard. They were taking her to the burnt bodies.

"No," Mary said.

She didn't want to see them. She didn't want to hear the truth that was sinking in right now.

"God, no, please don't, no," Mary said.

Mary pushed and pulled against Frankie's grip, but she couldn't break free.

"You wanted to see her?" Jake asked.

Frankie tossed her to the ground in front of the charred bodies, which formed an altar of death. Mary could smell the remnants of flesh no longer covering their bones.

"There she is," Jake said.

Mary looked up at the corpse, shriveled and still tied with her hands behind her back to the pole. Her mother's body was rigid, holding her in place.

The woman she knew was gone. She was always told by people that she looked like her mother. They had the same hair, the same eyes. She always wore that compliment like a badge of pride.

Those similarities were gone now. Mary couldn't prove that she was the daughter of the woman on the pole. She was gone. Completely wiped clean by fire.

Mary fell to her side, sobbing hysterically.

"Mom," Mary said.

She mouthed the words more than she said them. The spit and tears coming from her face mixed together. Whatever pain they caused her before, whatever pain they would bring her next wouldn't hurt like this. This was the type of pain that you never came back from. It was the type of pain that you carried forever.

* * *

THE ROOM WAS SPINNING. Kalen's vision was blurred. The concrete floor felt cool against her skin. She lay there, motionless.

Kalen gently lifted her shirt up. Black and blue bruises were blotched along her rib cage. She managed to roll onto her back. Her hands found her face, and she ran her fingertips across the lumps and welts, wincing with each touch.

The last thing she remembered before she blacked out was a fist slamming into her cheek and her body hitting the ground. She lasted a long time, and she didn't break. She didn't give them anything.

It was hard though. The hardest thing she'd ever done. There were times where she wanted to give them all the answers to the questions they asked.

When she raised her head from the ground to get a better look at her surroundings, she saw the door to the interrogation room was open and the room empty. The only thing in there was her blood staining the floor.

Kalen flipped to her belly and crawled to the front of the cell. Her neck strained as she looked down the halls, trying to see where they took Mary.

"Mary?" Kalen said.

Her voice came out in a hoarse whisper. The exertion of speaking was painful. Her ribs felt razor-sharp, stabbing her insides with each breath, word, and movement. She squinted her eyes shut, trying to block the pain out.

Kalen focused on figuring out where she saw Mary last. Did she see her when she came out? No. Her last memories before her blackout were still in the room.

The hardware store? No, they were dragged to the sheriff's office together. The cells. She remembered Mary being thrown into one of the cells as she was taken to the interrogation room.

"Mary?" Kalen repeated.

Another shot of pain went through Kalen's stomach; guilt. She was the one who convinced Mary to come. She was the one who gave her the gun. Whatever fate Mary had run into was because of her actions.

Kalen rested her back against the wall. She placed her right hand on the cell bars and gripped the metal tight. Her arm started to shake.

Don't break. Don't give in. Fight it. Fight it!

She held the tears back. She wasn't going to cry. She wasn't going to show weakness. If the bikers came back in, they wouldn't find a self-pitying girl wallowing in tears. All they would see was her resolve and the lumps across her face.

34

NIGHT OF DAY 13 (THE CABIN)

*N*elson pulled the sheets over Sean. He bent down to kiss his forehead, brushing the hair out of his eyes. He dimmed the candlelight in the lantern and shut the door.

He walked down the hall quietly. When he reached the living room, Ray was on the couch, his leg propped up on a few pillows as he flipped through the pages of a hunting magazine Freddy had brought up for him from the basement.

Nelson leaned back in the armchair across from the couch slowly and let out a sigh. He closed his eyes and rested his head back on the cushion behind him.

"Crazy day," Ray said.

"Yeah," Nelson answered.

"Any reason you didn't go with Mike?"

Nelson opened his eyes. Ray had set the magazine down and was looking at him.

"What are you getting at?" Nelson asked.

"Well, I know why I didn't go," Ray said, gesturing to his leg.

"We couldn't send everyone," Nelson answered.

Ray turned back to his magazine.

"I'm not a coward, Ray."

The magazine fell to Ray's lap. He turned on his side, making sure he was looking Nelson full in the face.

"No, I know you're not a coward, Nelson. But you're also not a man of action. You let things happen to you. You let things happen to your family. You're no better than the people who burned down Mike's house in our neighborhood."

Nelson shot up out of his chair. He marched over to Ray, his temper rising.

"I don't know where you were when Mike's house was getting burned to the ground, but I'm the one who pulled him out of the fire. If I hadn't been there to pull him out, he would have died."

The words came out in stinging, harsh whispers. Nelson was right in Ray's face, and Ray grabbed hold of his collar.

"The only reason you were able to pull him out was because you were tucked away in your house. I saw you out there on the lawn. I saw you walk away," Ray said.

Nelson grabbed hold of Ray's shirt. The two men locked together. Ray's body hit the floor as Nelson pulled him from the couch. The commotion caused Anne to run from the hall into the living room.

"Enough! Stop it, you two!" Anne said.

She peeled them off each other. Ray sat propped up against the couch, his leg lying at an awkward angle.

"Now is not the time to start this. Am I clear?" Anne said.

The two men nodded, looking at one another, each breathing heavily.

"Sorry," Ray said.

"It's all right," Nelson answered.

Then when the door to the cabin opened and Nelson looked up, he didn't think it was real.

Katie's face was smeared with dirt, and her tattered business clothes were filthy. She almost looked like a stranger, but her green eyes staring back at him were familiar territory.

"Katie?" Nelson asked.

Her name left his lips like a whisper. He wasn't sure how long he sat there before he jumped to his feet and rushed to her. He held her, kissed her, afraid letting go would stop making the moment real, as if she would dissipate into the night air like she had in so many of his dreams.

"Sean? Is he okay?" Katie asked.

"Yes, he's fine. I just put him to bed."

Nelson noticed Sam standing there in the doorway behind her, looking unsure of whether he should say anything.

"Sam?" Nelson asked.

"Hi, Nelson," Sam answered.

"He helped get me out. I wouldn't have made it without him," Katie said.

Sam extended his hand, but Nelson embraced him in a hug.

"Thank you," Nelson said.

Sam patted him on the back.

"Can I see him?" Katie asked.

"Of course."

Nelson led her to the bedroom where Sean was sleeping. When he opened the door to let her in, she took a moment just watching him sleep. He was still, peaceful.

She walked to him and knelt down by his side. She ran her hands softly along the length of his small arms and legs—a feather's touch.

Nelson saw the smile spread across Sean's face when he opened his eyes. Sean jumped up and threw his arms around Katie.

"Mom!"

"Hey, baby," Katie said.

Nelson left them alone. There would be time for words later. For now, seeing his wife with his son was all that he needed.

* * *

SEAN FELL asleep in Katie's lap in the living room. She didn't want to move him; she just let him sleep and brushed his hair with her fingers.

Jung had joined Anne, Ray, Sam, Nelson, and Katie in the living room. The six of them were sitting around, trying not to speak too loudly to wake Sean.

"We thought the relief center would be safe, but it didn't last very long. All of the hospitals, Red Cross locations, or public welfare stations giving out food rations were looted. It was chaos everywhere," Sam said.

"Did you guys hear anything about the rest of the country? Is there any spot that's safe?" Anne asked.

"No, none of the authorities we spoke with had any information," Katie answered.

"Nobody mentioned anything about Cincinnati?" Jung asked.

"Cincinnati?" Katie asked.

"We have a radio. It works, and we heard a broadcast come through," Anne said.

"It said that Cincinnati was the rallying point for the power coming back on in Ohio. A woman's voice came through and said that there was food, shelter, protection," Nelson said.

"Sounds too good to be true," Sam said.

"That's what I said," Ray said.

"I don't think they'd be able to set something up that fast. And even if they did, there's no way of knowing if the place is already overrun. I'm sure whatever was set up had good intentions, but people are desperate now. Good intentions will get you killed," Sam said.

"Where's Mike? What did he say about all this?" Katie asked.

Katie watched everyone's eyes shift around awkwardly. Everyone seemed to look at Anne, but Anne focused on Katie.

"Kalen disappeared this morning. Mike went to go find her," Anne said.

"Oh my God. Anne, I'm sorry," Katie said.

"Mike wanted us to stay put. We have enough supplies to last us a while, and we just set up an agreement with a local hunter for fresh game. Leaving now would be too much of a risk. We'd lose more than we'd gain," Anne said.

Jung stormed out of the living room, heading to his room at the end of the hallway.

"It's a bit of a sore subject with him," Ray said.

"His wife was shot on the way here. The antibiotics we have aren't helping with her infection. She's not doing very well," Anne explained.

Anne got up from the chair she brought in from the kitchen.

"I'll sleep in Kalen's room. You and Nelson should take my and Mike's room," Anne said.

"No, Anne, we can't do that," Katie said.

"It's fine. It's going to be a long night for me anyway, and I probably won't get much sleep. You two take it. You need the time alone," Anne said.

"Thanks, Anne," Nelson said.

The rest of the group headed to bed as Katie scooped Sean up in her arms and let him down in Freddy's room. She kissed him on the forehead and slowly shut the door behind her.

Nelson took Katie's hand, and they walked side by side down the hall into Mike and Anne's room.

There was a small glow of a candle lighting the bedroom. Katie walked in and sat on the edge of the bed. Nelson hung back at the door.

"I missed you," Nelson said.

"I missed you too."

Nelson walked to her. Each step slow, savoring the anticipation of being with her again.

"I thought I'd lost you," Nelson said.

"I tried getting out sooner, but by the time we realized what was going on, the city was locked down. Sam tried getting a group of us out, but we were picked up by an army reserve patrol. We went with them, but after six days at the relief center, everything just collapsed. There wasn't enough food for the number of people who were there. People just... turned on each other."

"That's what happened to the neighborhood."

"I saw the two grave markers at the Beachums'. Is that what happened to them?"

"Bessie was the one who started it."

"What?"

"She organized half the neighborhood to turn on Mike and his family."

"Mike killed them?"

"No, Ray killed Bessie and—"

Nelson cut himself short. He hadn't spoken out loud about what happened that day, what he did. He found himself ashamed to tell his wife, afraid of what she'd think. Would she judge him? Would she think less of him knowing that he took someone's life?

"What is it?" Katie asked.

"I killed Ted."

Nelson wasn't sure how long the silence between them lasted. Each second that ticked by sent a stab into his stomach, which turned over and over again.

Then Katie took his hand and brought it to her lips. She pressed it to the side of her face, her cheek running along the back of his hand.

"You kept our family safe. You did what you had to do. There's no shame in that," Katie said.

Nelson exhaled. Of all the answers he thought he'd hear, that was the one he wanted most. He sought affirmation, and she gave it to him. Nelson reached for the candle on the nightstand and pinched the wick, extinguishing the light, letting the room fall into darkness.

* * *

JENNA'S BREATHING WAS LABORED. Her face was dripping with sweat. Jung placed the cloth into the bowl of water, rewetting it, and patted her forehead. She was whispering nonsense, delirious from the fever.

When Jung lifted the bandage off her shoulder to look at the bullet wound, he could see the flesh blackening around the bullet's entrance point. Red dots lined her arm and crept up her neck. He could feel the heat coming off her body.

Jung didn't know what to do. The medication Anne gave him wasn't helping. The only hope he had was to get her to the relief center in Cincinnati, but he couldn't persuade anyone else to come with him.

They didn't care. None of them were in the position he was. He was the one with the sick wife. He was the one who had to do something now. Nobody was going to save his family. He had to do it.

All he had to do was find the key to the Jeep. With the car, he could make the trip in an hour. Even if they did want to follow him, it'd take them days to catch up by foot. He wouldn't even need to take any supplies with him, just his family.

He just wasn't sure how to sneak his wife and kids outside without waking up the rest of the house. There was the window, but it was small, and Jenna could barely stay awake, let alone gather the strength to pull herself from bed.

Jenna started coughing. She hacked and convulsed on the bed. Jung tried to steady her, giving her the cloth to cover her mouth.

She fell back against the bed, trying to catch her breath as the cloth fell from her hand. Jung grabbed it and noticed the red, pinkish stains covering the white cloth. He had to do something. He had to get her help. He couldn't let her die here. He couldn't let their children grow up without their mother.

* * *

ANNE PACED THE BACKYARD, looking up through the branches of the trees into the night sky. Whatever hell she thought she'd been through before didn't feel like this. Her daughter was in danger. Her husband was about to run headfirst into that danger, and she had no idea if she'd see either of them again.

The cigarette in her hand stayed unlit. She just felt better holding it. It'd been more than fifteen years since she smoked, but tonight she desperately wanted to light it.

It remained pinched between her fingers. Every once in a while she'd bring it to her lips, a motion that felt seamless. She'd let it hang there, dangling from her lower lip, begging to be lit. Then she'd rip it out of her mouth and clutch the cigarette in her hand tightly.

Mike would bring Kalen home. Anne knew that. He wouldn't let their daughter stay in the hands of whatever creatures were in that town.

A SHUDDER RAN through her thinking of what they would do to her if they caught her, of what they'd do to Mary.

Anne just couldn't wrap her head around why her daughter would leave. Why would she put herself in that type of danger? She knew Kalen had been through a lot, but she seemed like she was getting better.

She shoved the cigarette back into the package. She crushed the packet in her hands and tossed it angrily into the depths of the forest.

35

NIGHT OF DAY 13 (CARROLLTON)

*T*he town was dark. The only light provided was the reflection of the moon. Mike, Ulysses, Tom, Clarence, and Fay all moved in unison. Mike and Ulysses were up front, while Tom, Clarence, and Fay brought up the rear.

Mike could tell his father was still limping from twisting his knee a few days ago, but he didn't have the brainpower to concentrate on anything but getting Kalen back.

He knew Fay would be able to keep up, and Clarence was a decent enough shot, but the weakest link of the group was Tom. This wasn't an elite group of fighters, but it was what Mike had to work with.

"You said there were twenty bikers?" Mike asked.

"Yeah, could be more though. I only got a look at a handful of them, but there were a lot of bikes parked out front at the motel," Ulysses answered.

The five of them took time to scan the streets on the edge of the town, hiding in the tall grass. If Mike could swing it, he'd like to get his daughter back without having to fire a shot, but the doubt of that happening was growing in the back of his mind.

If the bikers saw or heard him before they were able to get Kalen out, they'd hurt her. Mike couldn't take that chance.

"Okay, here's the plan. Fay, Clarence, and Ulysses, you go and set yourselves up on the second story of one of the buildings across from the motel. You have enough ammo to provide a lot of cover fire. I only want you to shoot if you hear someone else shooting first, understand?" Mike asked.

"Of course," Clarence said.

"Got it," Fay replied.

"I should be coming with you," Ulysses said.

"Dad, you're still limping from the other day. Whoever goes in to get the girls will have to be mobile, and right now you're not."

"I'm on the ground with you?" Tom asked.

"You stay on my tail the whole way in. You have the silencer I gave you?" Mike asked.

"I got it," Tom said.

"If the girls are dead," Mike said, pausing after the last word left his mouth. "Then I'm going to draw the bikers out. And I want to bury all of them. If you have a problem with that, then tell me now."

The others didn't say anything.

"Let's go," Mike said.

The group took off. Ulysses, Clarence, and Fay headed toward the other side of the street, keeping low until they found a good spot across from the motel.

While Mike tried to be as quiet as possible, Tom marched behind him like an elephant stampeding through a field.

"Try and keep it quiet," Mike said.

"I am."

Mike counted the bikes out front. Ulysses was right; there were at least twenty of them. If they doubled up when they rode here, then there could be even more.

"We'll check the first floor and work our way around. I'll check the windows. You just make sure no one sees us," Mike said.

"And if someone does?"

"Kill them fast."

The first few rooms were empty. When they got to the end of the hall and started making their way to the other side, one of the doors opened. Mike and Tom jumped behind a staircase to hide.

The biker never looked their way as he headed through the courtyard. Mike stayed put, making sure he didn't come back, then made his way to the room he just left.

Mike kept the barrel of the rifle buried in the crack of the door and slowly turned the handle. The inside was dark. After his eyes adjusted to the darkness, he could see the room was empty.

They left and continued checking the other rooms as they passed them. A few of them had bikers inside, making Mike and Tom crawl for a few feet below the window, but Kalen and Mary weren't anywhere on the first floor.

The second floor wasn't any better. All of those rooms were empty. Wherever the girls were, the bikers weren't keeping them at the motel.

Mike sat on the edge of the bed in the last empty room they checked. The dim light of hope that his daughter was still alive was fading.

Then he heard two voices coming up the stairs outside. Mike raised his rifle, poised to shoot, aiming at the door.

Tom's head was on a swivel as he kept glancing between the window and Mike. He slowly moved to the back of the room.

Mike positioned himself in the right front corner next to the window so he could get a clear shot.

"I wish Jake hadn't beaten them up so bad."

"Yeah, they would've been a good lay if their faces weren't all fucked up."

"Did he say what he wanted to do with them?"

"They're supposed to stay alive for now. Jake thinks they got help from people staying in a cabin nearby. We're going to check in the morning."

Mike watched the patches on the backs of the bikers' cuts fade out of view along with the sound of their voices.

The girls were hurt, but they were still alive. The bikers were coming from somewhere. Now he just had to find out where they were coming from.

Mike cracked the door and saw one of the bikers turn into a room a few doors down while the other kept walking. He waited until the other biker disappeared into his own room.

"Mike," Tom said.

"We'll go down and ambush him. But we have to keep him quiet. I'll hold him down while you gag him."

"Mike, listen."

"What?"

"If we know they're alive and it looks like most of the bikers will be heading out for a search party in the morning, why don't we just wait until then to look for them? There'll be less chance of us getting caught."

"Because they might not be alive in the morning."

Tom didn't have kids. He wasn't a father. If he could do something to get his daughter out, then he was going to explore every opportunity that presented itself, and right now one of them was less than a hundred feet away from them.

Mike counted the rooms off quietly in his head. *One. Two. Three.* He could feel his pulse quicken. He checked the window. The room was empty, but the bathroom door was open.

Mike opened the door quietly, keeping the handle turned when he shut it to avoid the door clicking when he closed it.

He set the rifle on the bed and motioned for Tom to do the same. The sound of the urine hitting the toilet was followed by the groan of relief. Mike put his back to the wall just outside the door, and when the biker came out, Mike covered his mouth and held him in a headlock.

"Grab the zip ties out of my bag," Mike said.

Tom pulled two zip ties and grabbed the biker's legs, taking a boot to the face in the process but eventually tying him up.

Mike replaced his hand with the biker's bandana, shoved it in his mouth, then zip-tied his hands behind his back.

The biker squirmed on the bed, struggling to free himself. Sweat dripped from the tip of Mike's nose as he pulled a blade from his belt. He could see the whites of the biker's eyes stare at the sharp edge of steel in his hand.

Mike brought the knife to the biker's throat. The edge dug into his skin, drawing blood that trickled beneath his shirt and onto the bed.

"The girls you were talking to your friend about earlier. Where are they?" Mike asked.

What came out of the biker's mouth was "duck you," but Mike figured that wasn't what he meant.

He slammed the knife into the biker's calf. The blood oozed from the gash as Mike kept pressure on the blade, digging it deeper into the flesh. The biker thrashed on the bed, screaming into the bandana.

"Where is she?" Mike asked.

The gurgling sound of blood and the cutting of meat followed every twist of the knife Mike gave. He could feel the blade scrape along the bone. The biker's body jerked and convulsed.

"Harrifs ahffice. Harrifs ahffice," the biker said.

Mike slammed the butt of his rifle into the biker's forehead, knocking him unconscious.

"Let's go," Mike said.

Mike hurried down the steps and crouched behind a car on the street. He looked up at the second floor of the laundromat and waved his arms, trying to get Fay's, Clarence's, and Ulysses's attention.

He saw Fay wave back, and he pointed down the street toward the sheriff's office. She gave a thumbs-up in response.

"They'll have guards inside. We're not detaining this time. You shoot to kill, got it?" Mike said.

"Got it," Tom said.

Mike was alert. Adrenaline pumped through his veins. His daughter was alive, and he was less than sixty feet away from getting her out.

Then, when Frankie came out of his room and saw Mike and Tom running across the courtyard, everything started to move in slow motion.

"Hey!" Frankie shouted.

Frankie started screaming for everyone to get out of bed. Mike pulled the pistol from his side and fired in Frankie's direction. When he did, he could hear his sniper team open fire from their position.

Mike kicked down the sheriff's door, poised to shoot with his finger on the trigger.

Through his sights, he could see Jake with a knife to Kalen's throat, using her as a human shield. His daughter's face was bruised and cut. Her right eye was completely swollen shut.

"I knew someone would come for them," Jake said.

Mike kept his finger on the trigger. He might be able to get a shot off, but it would be risky. Jake had Kalen close. There wasn't a lot of room for error.

"Let her go," Mike said.

"I don't think so. You put your gun down, or I slit her throat right here."

Mike took a step forward, and Jake dug the blade deeper into Kalen's skin, making her tense up.

"I'm not bluffing. I killed everyone in this town. One more dead bitch is no skin off my back," Jake said. "Put the gun down."

It would only be a matter of time before more bikers came rushing in and put a bullet in Mike's back, which did Kalen zero good. If he was captured, at least he could be here with her. That was something... for now.

Mike took his finger off the trigger. He lowered the rifle and disarmed himself of all guns, knives, and ammunition.

"Your friend too," Jake said.

Tom lowered his rifle and put his hands in the air.

"Let's take a walk," Jake said.

* * *

ULYSSES TOOK THE FIRST SHOT, aiming for Frankie, who was running after Mike. He missed only by a few inches, but it was enough to give Frankie time to duck for cover. The next biker who came into Ulysses's crosshairs wasn't as lucky.

Fay opened fire on a group running into the courtyard, ducking behind a cluster of stone statues, which she redecorated with some .223 ammo.

Clarence concentrated on the top floor, for any bikers rushing out. He managed to pick one off before the other realized where the shooting was coming from.

They were in a good position. Any biker who came out of his room was met with a hail of gunfire.

Ulysses was the first to stop firing when he saw Mike with his hands in the air. Kalen was being dragged behind him with a knife to her throat.

"Fay," Ulysses said.

She stopped shooting. Clarence did as well. Fay glanced through the sights. Jake's shoulder was in her crosshairs.

"I think I have a shot," Fay said.

"No, it's too close," Clarence said.

Fay took the rifle off the windowpane and ducked behind the wall.

"Hello, friends," Jake said.

His voice echoed in the street, hanging in the night air.

"What do you want?" Ulysses asked.

"I want you to come down here, guns and hands in the air, and join us," Jake said.

"We've got a good bead on you from up here, so why don't we do this? You let our people go, we leave, and no one else dies," Ulysses said.

"No," Jake said.

Jake pulled a pistol from the back of his shirt and aimed at Tom's head. A shot rang out, and bits of blood, bone, and brain matter exploded out the side of Tom's temple. Tom's body hit the floor, and Jake pointed the pistol at Kalen's head.

"You come down now, or I continue my new paint job of Main Street with your people's blood," Jake said.

Ulysses motioned for Fay to creep back from the windows where they couldn't be seen. Clarence did the same. His voice was a whisper when he spoke.

"I'm going down. You two head back to the cabin and warn the others. Take them to that farm if you have to, but don't let any of them come into town."

"Ulysses, if you go down there, they'll kill you, Mike, *and* Kalen," Fay said.

"I can't let you go down there alone, Ulysses," Clarence said.

"They'll kill them anyway if I don't go down there. If they think one of us got away, that means they still might keep us for leverage. They don't know how many people we have."

"Ulysses, I don't like this," Fay said.

"Just go. Hurry!"

Fay disappeared behind the stores and kept low in the tall grass until Ulysses couldn't see her anymore.

"I'm with you. Us old guys have to stick together," Clarence said.

When the two came out front, they both kept their hands in the air. Two bikers patted them down then threw their arms behind their backs.

Frankie had Kalen, and another biker had Mike. Jake walked up to Ulysses and Clarence, smiling.

"Where's your other friend?" Jake asked.

"It was just the two of us up there," Clarence said.

Jake brought his pistol up to Clarence's forehead.

"Never play poker, old timer. You'd lose every hand," Jake said.

Jake squeezed the trigger, and Clarence's body collapsed to the ground.

"Who wants to play next?" Jake asked.

36

NIGHT OF DAY 13 (THE CABIN)

*O*nce Fay had put some distance between herself and the town, she jumped out of the tall grass and started the jog back up to the cabin. She had all three rifles slung over her shoulder, which slammed into her back with every step.

When she heard the other gunshot go off in the distance while she was running through the fields, she stopped to look back. She wanted to turn back, help them, but she knew Ulysses was right. She couldn't do it by herself.

She never let up, even with her muscles cramping and burning; she told herself she wouldn't stop until she reached the cabin. When she finally arrived, she opened the door and collapsed.

Ray jolted up from the couch at the sound of her entrance, and when he saw Fay on the ground, he yelled for help. Sam was lying on the floor and was the first person by Fay's side.

Anne came in through the back kitchen door. She rushed toward Fay on the ground and helped sit her up against the wall as she took gasps of air, trying to catch her breath.

"What happened? Where's Mike?" Anne asked.

"They… have him… and Ulysses."

"Just breathe," Sam said.

"Did you see Kalen? Is she all right?" Anne asked.

"She's… fine… Tom's dead… and someone else… I couldn't see who though."

"Jesus."

"Slow, deep breaths. In through your nose and out through your mouth," Sam said, coaching her to try to get her heart rate down.

"We need to get out of here now," Fay answered.

"What?" Ray asked, still propping himself up by his arms, trying to listen to the conversation.

"Ulysses said we should head to the farm," Fay said.

"The farm with the hunter we're trading with?" Anne asked.

"Yeah, he said that would be a good place to fall back to."

Jung came running into the living room, hearing the commotion that was going on.

"What's happening? Fay, are you okay?" Jung asked.

"I'm fine, but we need to get going," Fay replied.

"We're going to Cincinnati?" Jung asked, his eyes wide with relief.

"No, we need to get to the farm," Fay answered.

Jung shook his head. He stepped in between Anne and Fay, pleading with them.

"If something's happened, then our best chance is to drive to Cincinnati. We can't stay here anymore. It's not safe."

"That's why we're going to the farm, Jung," Fay said.

"*No!*"

Jung's voice thundered through the cabin. His body went rigid, his hands clenched into fists at his side.

Sam's hand instinctively went to his sidearm. Anne saw the motion, and she shook her head. Sam let go of the pistol's handle.

"We need to get to Cincinnati. It's our only chance to be safe. We can't stay here. I need to get Jenna to a hospital."

"Jung, we ca—"

"We have to! She's going to die if we don't. I can't let her die. I won't let her die!" Jung said.

"Take it easy, pal," Sam said.

Fay had never seen Jung like this before. When they were at the airport together, he was always so calm, so collected. He was always the first to help, to volunteer.

"Jung, I know what you're feeling," Fay said.

"No, you don't. None of you have a wife who is dying in the room down the hall!"

Jung pushed Nelson and Katie aside, who heard him screaming, and then slammed the door to his room shut.

"Someone needs to keep an eye on him. He's going to do something reckless," Sam said.

"He'll be fine. He's not dangerous, and… who are you again?" Fay asked.

"Sam," he said, extending his hand.

"My wife's bodyguard," Nelson said, smiling.

"Hi," Katie said.

"Katie, this is Fay. She's one of the people who are staying here with us," Nelson said.

"Nice to meet you," Katie said, and the two women shook hands.

"We don't have a lot of time. The gang's going to find out where we are. They'll use Kalen against Mike to make him talk. We need to move," Fay said.

"Did your husband leave any weapons when he left?" Sam asked.

"Yes, I think so," Anne answered.

"Sam, what are you doing?" Katie asked.

"I can help. I might be able to get your family back, but I'll have to move quickly. Show me where the guns are."

Only one rifle was left. Sam grabbed magazines, ammo, holsters, anything that would allow him to bring as much weaponry as possible without slowing him down.

"You've done this kind of thing before?" Anne asked.

"Before I got into private security, I was part of the Seventy-fifth Ranger Regiment for more than ten years."

Sam clicked the magazine into the bushmaster and started loading some shotgun shells into the pump-action 12-gauge.

Anne placed her hand on Sam's arm, and his rhythmic motions ceased. He looked down at her.

"Thank you for doing this," Anne said.

"Yes, ma'am."

Anne let go of his arm, and Sam continued getting everything together. He grabbed one of the hunting knives off the table and slid it into his belt. Two 9mm pistols were at his sides, with four backup magazines, and he had a Bushmaster M4 in his hands and the 12-gauge strapped to his back.

"If I don't make it back, then that means nobody made it," Sam said, standing in the doorway.

"Well, then come back," Anne said.

"Katie, Nelson. Tell Sean I said hi," Sam said.

"Sam, I can't thank you enough for bringing Katie here, for keeping her safe. I owe you my life," Nelson said.

Nelson shook his hand, and then Sam was gone. He trotted off into the forest, leaving the rest of them at the cabin.

* * *

Jung paced the room. Both of his kids were awake now from the shouting from earlier. His daughter was sobbing from being tired and scared, and his son tried to comfort her.

Jenna was still passed out on the bed. She hadn't moved for hours. She was still breathing, but her body was burning up. He tried giving her more ibuprofen to help bring the fever down, but it wasn't working.

He needed to move her now. He wouldn't get another chance. The only people left here who could try and stop him were Fay and Anne. He knew Nelson wouldn't be a problem, and Ray's broken leg put him out of commission.

Jung knelt down to his children. He kissed them both on the forehead, and he tried to speak as calmly as he could.

"Daddy needs to get us out of here, okay? Now, I need the two of you to be brave for Mommy. She needs our help because she doesn't feel well," Jung said.
"Is Mommy going to be okay, Daddy?" Jung Jr. asked.

His son still had some tears streaked down his cheeks. Jung gently took his thumb and wiped them away.

"Yes. Now when I say it's safe, I want you to come out and follow me, okay? I love you."

When he checked the hallway, Anne and Fay were still in the living room. He couldn't hear what they were saying, but both of their backs were turned to him. He slid out the door and tiptoed to the basement.

The gun safe was still open. Almost everything was gone. The only thing left was a small revolver at the bottom shelf. Jung picked it up and tried searching through the boxes of ammo. He had to check three different types of boxes before he got the right size that fit in the gun.

It was a six-shooter, so he took the rest of the bullets and dumped them in his pocket. Before he headed back upstairs, he saw a box of zip ties. He grabbed a handful of them, clicked the hammer back on the pistol, and headed upstairs.

Jung kept the pistol pointed in front of him. Anne and Fay didn't see him until he finally spoke.

"Give me the keys to the Jeep, Anne."

"Jung… what are you doing?"

"I'm saving my family. Where are the keys?"
Fay started to get up, but Jung swung the pistol at her.

"Sit down!" he screamed.

"Jung, don't do this," Fay said.

"I don't have a choice. Keys, Anne. Now."

Nelson came out of the room down the hall again.

"What is going on out he—"

Nelson froze when Jung swung the pistol at him.

"Get in the living room, Nelson," Jung said.

Nelson kept his hands in the air, moving slowly down the hall. Jung made him sit down next to Anne at the kitchen table.

"So what are you going to do now, Jung?" Ray asked, propping himself up from the couch.

Jung tossed Nelson some zip ties.
"Tie Ray up, then Fay."

Nelson tied Ray's hands and legs together then fastened Fay to the solid oak table. Once they were secure, Jung tossed one of the zip ties to Anne.

"Now, tie Nelson up," Jung said.

Anne looped the zip tie around Nelson's wrists, then another one at his ankles.

"Good. Now, where are the keys?" Jung asked.

"They're in my room," Anne said.

"Katie's still in there," Nelson said.

"As long as I get the keys, then nobody gets hurt. I just want to get my family out of here. That's all."

Jung walked behind Anne, staying close enough to where he could easily shoot her, but far enough away to make sure she didn't try anything stupid.

Katie got out of the bed when Anne entered, but when she saw Jung follow her in with the pistol in his hand, she sat back down.

"Don't move," Jung said.

Anne opened one of the drawers to the dresser and pulled the keys out.

"Now, you two, help me get Jenna into the Jeep."

The two women carried Jenna from her bed down the hallway. Jung gathered his kids and led them down the hallway, making sure they kept their eyes closed as he guided them.

Anne and Katie propped Jenna up in the passenger seat of the car. They strapped her in and closed the door. Jung put Claire and Jung Jr. in the back seat.

He marched the two women back into the house. He had Anne zip-tie Katie, then Jung tied Anne's hands up.

"Jung, listen to me. You don't know what you're doing," Anne said.

"I know exactly what I'm doing. I'm doing what your husband taught me to do. Keep my family safe."

"Not like this, Jung. You're making a mistake."

Jung turned to leave, but before he made it to the door, he stopped, turning back to the people behind him.

All of them were restrained. These people helped him. Each of their faces looked betrayed.

"I'm sorry," Jung said.

"Coward," Ray replied.

Jung looked at the pistol in his hand. It was shaking. He placed it on the windowsill next to the front door before he left.

When he got in the Jeep, he cranked the engine to life and told his kids they could open their eyes.

"Where are we going, Daddy?" Jung Jr. asked.

"To get Mommy some help."

DAY 13 (THE FARM)

*K*en stashed the bullets in one of the kitchen cabinets. Beth was getting lunch ready and yelled for the boys to come inside.

Billy and Joey came running in from the front yard, chasing after one another and laughing.

"Enough, you two. Sit down," Beth said.

The two boys pulled their chairs out from the kitchen table and sat down. Ken sat at the head of the table while Beth set their plates down.

"What'd those people say?" Beth asked.

The soup dribbled down Ken's chin as he slurped it up. He spoke with his mouth still half full.

"They want food," Ken answered.

Ken continued to shovel the food into his mouth as he spoke. Joey mimicked his father, taking down big gulps. Billy didn't eat.

"They have enough ammo stashed in that cabin to last for years," Ken said.

"So they made good on the deal?" Billy asked.

"Yeah," Ken replied.

"I think they're good people," Billy said.

Ken laughed as he brought the bowl to his mouth and downed the last of the soup. When he was done, he slammed it on the table.

"They're naïve," Ken said.

"You think we can take them?" Beth asked.

Ken shook his head, wiping his mouth with the sleeve of his shirt.

"No, there're too many of them right now. The only way we're going to beat them is to pick them off one at a time. We can use the bikers in town to our advantage. When I take Mike out tomorrow for the hunt, I'll take care of him then blame the gang. I'll say they came after us," Ken said.

"You can't do that," Billy said.

Ken cocked his head to the side. His son had never spoken to him in that tone before, never questioned him.

"I'll do whatever I want, boy," Ken said.

"You can't just go back on your deal like that. It's not right. They're good people. They could have killed me when I shot that guy's wife, but they didn't. They brought me back here. They kept me alive."

"And what do you think I'm doing? You don't think I'm keeping you alive?"

Ken rose from the table. He walked over to his son. He glanced down in his soup bowl, still half full. Billy recoiled into his chair, with his father towering over him.

"Or maybe you think you'd be better off on your own? Getting your own food, protecting yourself, living out in the woods with no bed, no water, nothing. You think people just get things? That they just happen? No, if you want something in this world, you have to take it. And you have to be strong enough to be able to make sure nobody takes it from you once you have it. If you don't, then you die. End of story."

"Dad, they're not trying to hurt us. They're trying to help."

Ken looked back at his wife.

"You see the crap that preacher filled his head with? You see what it's doing now? It's made him weak."

"I'm not weak," Billy said.

Ken slapped his son across the face, sending him out of his chair and onto the floor. Billy crawled away from his father advancing on him.

"You are weak because you trust people. You can't trust anybody, you understand? If you do, they'll take advantage of you. That's how the world works, boy. Even your God knows it. That's how he controls you. That's how he makes sure you stay weak."

Ken raised his hand again, and Billy braced himself for another blow. Ken didn't hit him. He smiled.

"Hard to believe you're any son of mine. Finish your lunch. You've got work to do."

* * *

JOEY HELPED BILLY PULL the cart through the pasture. They'd walk for a while then dump some of the hay in a pile for the cows and horses to circle around.

"Why'd you have to go and make Dad so mad earlier?" Joey asked.

Joey was five years younger than Billy. He'd always looked up to their father in a way that Billy never did. There was always a disconnect between Billy and his dad. Billy was afraid of him. Joey wasn't.

"It's not something I do on purpose, Joe," Billy said.

"He gets angry at you a lot."

"I know."

Both Billy and Joey were homeschooled. The town had a school, but it was small. Their mother made the decision to keep the boys out of public school. It allowed her to teach what she wanted them to learn, and it opened up more time for the boys to help with the farm work.

"You think Dad will let me go hunting with him tomorrow?" Joey asked.

"Probably not. There's too much work to do around here."

Billy tossed the last of the hay into the pile and then set the cart down for a break. Joey hopped up into the back of the empty cart, and Billy handed him some of the water he had.

"I could do it," Joey said.

"Do what?"

"I could kill them."

"What?"

"Those people at the cabin. If I needed to, I could do it. To keep us safe."

Billy grabbed the water from Joey's hand. He placed the other on his younger brother's shoulder. He knew his brother always wanted to please their father and that the two of them shared a similar frame of mind, but he refused to believe that his brother was the same man as their father.

"Joey, you don't mean that."

"I do. I could do it. It's like Dad said—you can't be weak. And I'm not weak."

"There's a difference between being weak and doing the right thing."

Joey shoved Billy's hands off him and jumped off the edge of the cart.

"Dad's right. You are weak. You're not strong enough to do what needs to be done."

Joey started walking back to the barn. Billy tried calling out to him, but Joey ignored him.

Maybe Joey and his father were right. Maybe he didn't have what it took to keep his family safe. But what did that mean? Did that mean he would have to change who he was? What he believed in?

Whatever Billy did now, he would have to live with for the rest of his life, and he wasn't sure if living in what the world was now was even worth it.

* * *

Ken spread the parts of the rifle along his workbench. He ran the cleaning rags along the creases of the inner workings of the gun.

It was completely torn apart. Ken oiled the firing pin around the edges of the barrel and placed little drops along any surface where metal grinded together.

He'd had that rifle for more than ten years. It brought down more deer, boar, and turkeys than any other gun he'd ever owned. That rifle was his prized possession.

It wasn't because the rifle was expensive. He purchased it for five hundred dollars. He made a few modifications on it, upgrading to a better scope, switching out the stock for one that fit against his shoulder better, but the dollar amount wasn't what made the gun so special to him.

When Ken was out hunting, tracking game, he felt alive. Out of all the things he'd ever done in his life, hunting was what he loved. There wasn't anything else like it.

He never understood how people could just sit behind a desk or push paper for a living. He couldn't grasp the concept of working at a bank or a store. He had to be outside. He had to be in the woods. He had to hunt.

The first time he went was when he was nine. He remembered his father getting him his first rifle. It was just a little .22-caliber, but when his hands felt the wood and steel and the power it gave him, he was never the same.

The moment he had his hands on the gun, he was out the door and running for the woods. He had to try it out, see how it felt to finally go shooting.

Ken had been hunting with his father before but was never allowed to actually shoot anything. His father told him he had to earn that right. Once he did, he would be given his own gun.

He learned everything he could in those lessons with his father. He watched how he walked through the forest, the way he carried his gun, his alertness, and the way he noticed even the smallest detail.

As much as Ken hated his father, he did give the old man one piece of credit. He wouldn't have become the hunter he was without him.

Ken's dad taught him how to track anything and everything. He always told Ken that any fool could aim a gun and shoot an animal, but it took a hunter to find them.

Hunting wasn't luck. It was a skill, one which Ken had been mastering for the last forty years.

That first day when he was in the woods by himself, he ran across a pair of deer tracks. As soon as he saw them, his face lit up. He kept himself upwind, maneuvering through the forest, tracking the animal.

It was almost an hour before he finally came across them. A mother and her baby were grazing between the trees. The fawn must have only been a few weeks old. Its legs wobbled underneath it.

He knew the .22 wouldn't be able to bring the mother down, but he knew he'd be able to take the fawn.

Then he remembered what his father told him about the hunting laws, how you could only shoot a deer that was a certain size. He was conflicted. He knew what he wanted to do, but he also knew what he wanted was wrong.

The fawn pranced around its mother aimlessly. Ken could feel the itch of the trigger, just waiting to be pulled. He wanted to do it. He wanted to show his father that he was just as good as he was. He wanted to prove that he could do it, that he was worthy.

When he finally squeezed the trigger, the mother ran and the fawn collapsed to the ground.

It took him nearly twice as long to get back to the farm, dragging the deer carcass with him. He left the deer outside by the gutting station and rushed inside to find his father.

When Ken brought his dad outside, the look on his father's face was one he never forgot. His father was disgusted. He snatched the rifle from Ken's hands and told him that he wouldn't get it back until he learned that hunting was a privilege, not a right, and that he had to learn and understand the laws and abide by them.

The surge of pride he felt from killing the deer deflated out of him and was replaced with anger.

His father taught him something very valuable that day. No matter what you do or how you do it, there is someone out there who can always take away the thing you want the most. And at that moment, he vowed to never let anyone take away the things he wanted ever again.

* * *

WITH ALL OF the chores done for the day, Billy came back into the house. His mother was in the kitchen, getting dinner ready.

"Mom, have you seen Joe?" Billy asked.

"I think he's with your father."

Billy lingered in the kitchen. He wanted to speak with his mother, try and get some perspective on everything that was happening, but he knew she would always side with his father.

"Mom," Billy said.

The knife sliced through the carrots, each time a thud hitting the cutting board in a melodic rhythm.

"What?" Beth asked.

"I think Dad's wrong."

The chopping ceased. Beth wiped the blade clean on her apron and set it on the counter.

"They haven't done anything to us. Hurting them could hurt us in the long run," Billy said.

"Billy, your father made his decision. Now, drop it."

She went back to preparing dinner and dumped the carrots into a boiling pot of water.

"And you agree with him?" Billy asked.

Beth was a small woman, but when she was mad about something, she looked larger than her size suggested.

"Listen to me. The decisions your father makes are to keep us alive. That's what he does. You may not like it or agree with it, but it's something that has to be done. All you have to do is have the backbone to go through with it, because if you don't, then it could be your brother who dies. Is that what you want? To place other people above your own family?"

"No... I... that's not what I want, but there has to be a better way."

"What makes you think they won't try and steal from us? You think they're better than us? Is that it?"

"Mom, no, that's not what I'm saying."

"That's because you don't know what you're talking about. Listen to me, son. If you don't wipe that idealistic bullshit from your mind, then the only thing that you'll get in return is a bullet from somebody who knows how the world works. How it *really* works."

Billy didn't have a rebuttal, no counterpunch. He was stuck in a world that he didn't understand. Whatever he thought was bad before all of this happened wouldn't hold a candle to what was going to happen moving forward.

38

NIGHT OF DAY 13 (THE TOWN)

*T*he Jeep bounced back and forth as Jung maneuvered the dirt road. He was going faster than what was safe, but he didn't care. He wanted to put as much distance between himself and the cabin as possible.

The headlights on the Jeep illuminated the path through the winding trees. It was pitch-black, with the trees blocking the light from the moon. The headlights were the only guidance that Jung had.

Jenna's head bobbed back and forth from the dips and curves of the road. Her whole body was limp.

"Hang on, honey," Jung said.

When Jung finally saw the road ahead, his heart lightened. All he had to do now was follow the road, and the signs would take him to Cincinnati. He turned west onto the highway. He was going to make it. His wife was going to live.

* * *

MIKE COULD TASTE the metallic fluid filling his mouth. He spit the blood on the ground and forced himself to stand up. The biker gang circled him. He could see his daughter, his father, and Mary tied up on the ground, watching the beating.

Frankie and Jake had taken turns with him. Whenever one got tired, he would tag his partner in to take his place.

Mike landed a few blows in the beginning, but the arthritis in his hands was starting to get the better of him. He could barely form a fist, and each time he did, it felt like jagged glass digging into his joints.

Frankie danced around him, throwing a few jabs, causing Mike to back up. A sharp pain shot through his left side any time he took a deep breath. He figured one of his ribs punctured his lung.

Mike wasn't sure how much longer he was going to last. This was a fight he was going to lose, but he needed to make it last. Every punch he took was one his daughter didn't have to take.

"C'mon, daddio," Frankie said. "You're not getting tired on me, are you?"

Mike forced his hands up. He saw three of Frankie, so he aimed for the one in the middle. He moved in and threw a right cross. Frankie dodged and countered with his own right across Mike's chin.

More blood and a tooth flew from Mike's mouth. Mike shook it off. He hit Frankie with a three-punch combo, knocking him to the ground.

"Oh-*ho*! Looks like the old man's got some spunk left in him, Frankie," Jake said.

Frankie wiped the blood from his nose and jumped back up. He slapped Jake's hand and retreated from the ring.

Jake walked in with a swagger, taking his cut and shirt off and tossing it to one of his guys. He was a lot faster than Frankie was, and he worked Mike's face like a punching bag.

Mike's stance started to waver. He was losing his balance. Everything was starting to fade in and out of darkness. The more he tried to fight it, the harder it became.

"C'mon, Jake! Finish it already!" Frankie shouted.

Jake moved in, and with one massive haymaker, Mike hit the ground.

Mike's whole body was numb. He couldn't move. This was it. He couldn't go on any longer.

"Pick him up," Jake said.

When they moved Mike, he felt like he was floating. He looked down at his feet and saw himself standing, but he couldn't feel the ground.

Jake walked up and patted Mike's cheek.

"Hey, fun time's over. Wake up," Jake said.

Mike's head swayed back and forth, looking left, then right, until his eyes finally focused on one thing; his daughter. When he saw her, a surge of strength ran through him.

Keep going. Keep going for her.

"As much as I've enjoyed beating the shit out of you, it's time to take care of business. Since neither of the girls confessed to murdering our brother, and since the two of you have killed some of our club members tonight, you'll be facing the death penalty," Jake said.

The bikers grunted in agreement.

"Now, since there are ten of us and only four of you, we can't all kill you, so I thought it would be better to watch you kill each other," Jake said.

"What?" Mike asked.

"You're going to duel."

"No."

"Then you watch me kill her."

Jake pointed to Kalen tied up on the ground. Mike struggled against the bikers holding him but couldn't break free. Jake moved in close. His voice dropped to a whisper.

"Or maybe I have some fun with her first. How does that sound, Dad?"

Mike's mind wandered to when Kalen was a little girl. She was riding her bike for the first time. She kept screaming for him to let go, but he didn't want to. He wanted to keep her safe, protect her. It was the same instinct guiding him now. After all these years, he still hadn't let go.

"Okay," Mike said.

"Bring the old man and the girl," Jake said.

Kalen was tossed over to Jake while Ulysses was shoved into the circle with Mike.

Two pistols were emptied with the exception of one bullet. They spaced Mike and Ulysses ten feet apart.

"The first person to shoot wins, then dies, so take your time," Jake said.

The gang laughed.

"Oh, and if either of you get any ideas about who you're going to shoot, let me present to you my insurance," Jake said.

Jake took out his pistol, cocked it, and put the barrel to Kalen's temple.

One of the bikers shoved the pistol into Mike's hand. He gripped it loosely, keeping it at his side; Ulysses had one as well.

"You only get one shot, so make it count!" Frankie said.

All of the bikers placed bets on who would shoot first, laughing, egging both of them on to get it over with.

"Don't be a pussy!"

"C'mon, pull the trigger!"

"Kill him!"

Mike couldn't lift the pistol. It was deadweight in his hand. Across from him was the man who raised him. His father was the one who taught him wrong from right. He was the one who made him the man he was today—a good man.

There were times when Ulysses was harder than the steel that poured from Pittsburgh's mills, but he could say one word to make everything all right.

If Mike didn't shoot his father or his father shoot him, then his daughter would die. He struggled, trying to bring the pistol up from his waist. His entire arm was shaking.

"I'm getting bored, boys," Jake said.

Mike finally forced the gun up. His index finger went to the trigger, barely touching the small sliver of steel. Ulysses's head was lined up in the sights. Tears started to well up in Mike's eyes. They streamed down his face. He couldn't keep the gun steady.

"Dad," Mike said.

"It's okay, son."

Mike's knuckles turned white against the black composite of the handle. He squeezed the grip so hard he thought it would crush in his hand. He knew what he had to do, but he couldn't bring himself to do it, and as the gun dropped to his side, he stood there crying, shaking his head.

"I'm sorry. I can't do it. Dad, I can't do it," Mike said.

His father's figure was blurred through the tears pouring from his eyes. Mike looked to Kalen, who was sobbing. His family was falling apart. He couldn't save them. Everything he'd done, all he had sacrificed, was for naught.

"Michael," Ulysses said.

His father looked calm. A faint smile grew on his face. It wasn't a smile of happiness, but one of pain.

"I love you," Ulysses said.

Mike couldn't hear his own screams above the sound of the gun when Ulysses put the pistol to his temple and squeezed the trigger.

* * *

Ulysses lay collapsed on the ground. He was nothing more than a pile of flesh, lifeless and motionless. Everything was silent with the exception of the high-pitched hum of the ringing in his ears from the sound of the pistol.

Frankie ripped the pistol from Mike's hand and put the barrel to the back of his head.

"Congratulations. You've moved on to the next round. Too bad it's sudden death," Frankie said.

Mike saw Kalen, who was crying hysterically, crumpling to a heaped mess on the floor. This was the world now. This was what happened to people when they had something of value; it was taken from them.

"Goodbye, asshole," Frankie said.

Before Frankie could squeeze the trigger, the ringing in Mike's ears was replaced by another sound. He turned his head to the east, and he could see lights in the distance, moving quickly toward the town.

Mike felt the barrel of the gun removed from his head.

"What the hell?" Frankie said.

"Move some of the cars, block the road!" Jake shouted.

Frankie started to run off, but Jake called him back.

"Secure them first," Jake yelled.

A few of the bikers helped Frankie drag them back to the sheriff's office, tossing them in separate cells.

Jake's crew managed to move four cars, staggering them across Main Street.

"When it slows down, aim for the tires," Jake ordered.

"It's a Jeep!" Frankie shouted.

When the Jeep came within shooting range, it didn't slow down. It sped up.

"Fire!" Jake said.

The Jeep smashed through the first car, the front crumpling, but still moved forward. It swerved to try and miss the second, but was met by the gang's gunfire.

The bullets blew out the driver's side tire, and the Jeep lost control, flipping onto its side, and skidded into another one of the parked cars.

Tank was the first person who made it to the Jeep. When he looked inside, he saw the kids crying in the back seat. Jung was stirring awake, and Jenna was motionless.

"There're kids in here!" Tank shouted.

Tank unbuckled Claire first and then grabbed Jung Jr. Both of them were screaming for their parents as Tank set them on the sidewalk, making sure they were okay.

He pressed his finger to Jenna's neck, trying to feel a pulse, but there was nothing. The side of her head was covered in blood. He unbuckled her and pulled her from the Jeep, laying her away from the kids.

Jung was starting to regain consciousness when Tank got to him.

"W-where's Jenna?" he asked.

"Just hold on, pal," Tank said.

Jung was bleeding from his forehead, and a shard of glass stuck out of his arm.

"What are you doing?" Jake asked.

"They're hurt," Tank answered.

"I know. Now finish the job. Let's get this Jeep flipped over and see if it'll still run. It could come in handy."

Tank pushed Jake in the back, sending him to the ground. When Jake got up, he pulled his gun on Tank.

"You gonna make them duel too?" Tank shouted.

"You're way out of line, brother," Jake said.

"We can't keep going down this path, Jake. We don't kill kids."

"We'll go down whatever path I take us."

"We've killed a lot of people since this shit went down, Jake, but we've never hurt kids before. It's not something I'm going to start doing now."

Jake lowered the pistol and holstered it.

"The kids are on you. Do what you want with them. Take the other two to the sheriff's cells. Let's see if they know our friends in there."

"The woman's dead. She doesn't have a pulse."

"Fine, then take the man."

* * *

MIKE TRIED to make sense of everything that just happened, but he couldn't. He just watched his father kill himself, sacrifice his life so Mike wouldn't have the burden of pulling the trigger.

When Frankie came in and tossed Jung inside the cell with him, Mike was brought back to reality. His wife and son were still at the cabin, and his daughter was still alive; he was still alive. There was still a chance.

"Looks like you're getting a little company," Frankie said.

Jung was unconscious when he hit the floor. Mike crawled to him, checked his pulse, and made sure he was still breathing.

"Jung," Mike said. "Jung, what happened?"

Jung's reply was nothing but mumbles and groans. Mike couldn't understand what he was babbling on about.

"Cincinnati… Jenna… I'm sorry," Jung said.

"Cincinnati? Jung, where's Anne? Where's Freddy?"

Mike brought his hand to the side of Jung's head, and blood stuck to his fingers.

"Jesus, Jung, what happened?"

Jung started to cry. Mike wasn't sure if it was from the pain or something else. He just kept shaking his head and weeping. The sobs were silent, but every once in a while a gasp would escape.

He rocked back and forth on the ground, curled in a ball, until he didn't have any tears left. Finally, he spoke.

"I took the Jeep," Jung said.

"What?"

"Jenna was getting worse. The antibiotics weren't working. The only way she was going to live was if I got her to Cincinnati."

"Where's my family, Jung?"

"They're at the cabin. I… I tied them up and stole the car and got out of there as fast as I could."

Jung didn't look Mike in the eye. He kept his face down, ashamed.

The pain Mike felt was fading away. His father was dead, his daughter was beaten to a pulp, and now a man who he let into his home, protected, fed, and made sure his family was safe, betrayed him.

"Did you hurt them?" Mike asked.

"No, no, they're okay."

Mike wanted to smash what was left of Jung's life into oblivion. There were a lot of things that Mike could forgive, but attempting to hurt his family by stealing from him wasn't one of them.

"Daddy!" Jung Jr. said.

"See? Daddy's okay. He's just in here," Tank said.

Jung crawled to the front of the cell, pushing his arms through the bars, grasping his children.

"Are you guys okay?" Jung asked.

Jung Jr. and Claire nodded. Tank unlocked the cell.

"C'mon, I'm taking you to one of the motel rooms. You can stay with your kids there," Tank said.

"Thank you. Thank you so much," Jung said. "Wait. What about the rest of them?"

"You know these people?"

"Yes."

"Listen, it's better if you act like you don't know them. Trust me."

Jung didn't bother to turn around. He just left with his kids, and Tank locked the cell. If he had turned around, he would have seen a face that haunted him for the rest of his life. Mike never felt more disgusted in his entire life.

* * *

WHEN SAM SAW the Jeep heading down the dirt road to the highway, he double-timed it. Whatever made them leave must have been bad.

He still had his business shoes on, which made it awkward to run, especially through the uneven forest floor. Sam pushed through it though. The moment he left the cabin, he went into operation mode.

Every mission he went on as an Army Ranger, he would get into a single mind-set. *Complete the objective.*

It was all just a job, a task given to him and carried out as quickly and efficiently as he and his team could do it.

When he was done, he felt no remorse for anything that happened on the mission. It wasn't because he was heartless but because it was the only way for him to keep on living once the mission was over.

Once he made it out of the forest and onto the highway, he was able to pick up his pace. The flat, level road was easier to run on than the divots and tree roots of the forest.

Sam kept his rifle up at all times, scanning the perimeter of the town. When he made it to Main Street, he saw the Jeep flipped on its side.

He could hear some commotion down the street. It was the sound of a child crying. Sam advanced, each step hitting the sidewalk quickly, quietly.

Tank was taking Jung and his two kids up the stairs to the second floor of the motel. Sam watched them go into one of the rooms a few doors down.

Sam peered through the scope. Room 24. He sat there for a

261

moment, taking in the surroundings. The motel had forty-two rooms, twenty-one rooms on each floor. From what he heard at the cabin, there were no more than twenty bikers, probably fewer if Mike was a good shot.

It wasn't likely the bikers would have bunked up, so they were probably in their own rooms. Sam didn't see anyone on watch, so they either didn't have enough men for that, were too tired, or thought they weren't in danger anymore. Either way, he had the advantage.

Sam wanted to keep this as covert as possible. It wouldn't do any good to let the gang know he was here by running in guns blazing. He climbed the staircase then pressed his ear to the door of Room 24.

There was nothing but mumbles, but he recognized Jung's voice. He never saw the biker who went in there with him come out, so he'd have to act fast the moment he opened the door. He strapped the rifle over his shoulder and pulled the knife from his belt.

One. Two. Three.

He swung the door open and immediately went for Tank, who had his back to him. Sam made it to him in two steps, and in less than three seconds, he had his hand over Tank's mouth and the knife slicing his throat.

Jung gasped and jumped back, covering his children. Tank let out a few gargled chokes of breath before he finally passed out.

"Shh, Jung, it's me, Sam. I'm here to help. Are you all right?"

Jung just stared at Sam, then his face twisted into grief and he started to cry.

"She's d-dead. I-I killed h-her," Jung said.

"What? Who's dead?"

"J-jenna. My w-wife. Oh, G-god."

Jung collapsed on the ground; both his children were starting to cry now. The louder they became, the more attention they'd bring, and that was something Sam wanted to avoid.

"Jung, listen to me. I know you're hurting, but we have to get out of here now. We can't stay. I need you to pull it together for me. Do you know where the others are?"

Jung tried to compose himself.

"There… in the sheriff's office. They have them locked up in the cells."

"Who has the keys?"

Jung motioned over to Tank, collapsed on the bed.

He patted Tank down and found the keys on the inside pocket of his cut. Then he could hear a voice coming up the stairs.

"Tank, everything all right in there?"

Sam stuffed the keys into his pocket and brought his knife at the ready. He put his back against the wall, hiding himself behind the door. When the biker came in and saw Tank dead with Jung on the bed next to him, he pulled his gun.

"You son of a bit—"

One swift snap of the neck and the biker folded to the floor like a stack of cards.

"C'mon," Sam said. "We've got to get out of here."

Sam checked the hallway to see if anyone else heard the scuffle, but no one came. He wasn't sure what he was going to do with Jung and his family. The man was obviously in no shape to fight, and it was too dangerous to move forward with the kids around.

The best bet was to stash them somewhere then come back for them once he had everyone accounted for.

"Head for the hardware store, then go out the back and hide in the tall grass. I'll come back for you once this is over. If I don't come back in the next twenty minutes, then get out of here. Head back to the cabin."

Jung didn't say anything. No thank-you, no handshake, nothing. He just took his kids and headed across the street, and Sam watched him disappear in the shadows of the store.

Sam made his way down to the sheriff's office. When he entered, there weren't any guards, no one on patrol, nothing.

He saw Mary and Kalen first, then Mike in the last cell down the hall. All of them were beaten badly. Kalen had the worst of it.

"You guys all right? Just hang on, I'll get you out of here."

Sam went for Mary's cell first, then Kalen's, then Mike's. The moment Mike was out, he rushed to his daughter, who collapsed in his arms. Sam didn't want to break up the moment, but he knew they had to move.

Mike didn't know the man who just let him out, but he didn't care. He had his daughter again. It was a small victory for the high cost he paid today.

"Are you Mike or Ulysses?" Sam asked.

"Mike."

"I'm Sam. Your wife sent me. I came in with Nelson's wife, Katie. We need to get out of here. I don't know how many of these guys are left, but I've already taken out two."

"Give me one of your pistols."

Sam tossed Mike one of his 9mms.

"Any extra magazines?" Mike asked.

Sam handed him two of the magazines he had on him. Mike tucked them into his pocket then clicked the gun's safety off.

"Take them back to the cabin," Mike said.

"Whoa, you're not in any condition to do what I think you're going to do," Sam said.

"This isn't any of your business."

"Maybe, but I do know that rule number one of war is you only start one if there's a chance of winning."

"I didn't start this."

Mike disappeared out of the sheriff's office, leaving Sam with Kalen and Mary.

"Shit."

Sam grabbed the girls and gave them the same instructions he did to Jung. He handed Kalen the other pistol he had.

"You shoot anyone you don't know."

Kalen grabbed Mary, and the two of them leaned on each other, with Kalen gripping the pistol in her right hand as they walked out the door.

Mike was already out of sight when Sam made it to the motel. Sam scanned the top floor when he heard the first shots go off in a room down the hall.

"Here we go," Sam said.

Once the gunfire went off, the remaining bikers flew out of their rooms, guns loaded, looking to shoot anything that moved.

Sam picked off the first one easy. The other six were smarter than their friends. Whoever Mike was looking for must not have been anyone who came out on the first floor because he went straight for the back of the motel.

Sam didn't let up. His training kicked in, and he advanced, moving closer to engage, funneling the bikers into a corner.

It was like shooting fish in a barrel. Each shot Sam squeezed off either killed someone or exposed them from their cover. The only exit the bikers had was to retreat back into the rooms, and from there they wouldn't have anywhere to go.

One biker made a run for it in the opposite direction, thinking he could outrun the bead Sam had on him. He was wrong.

The biker's jaw exploded off his face, and he dropped to the ground. There were only three of them left now; that's when the bargaining started.

"All right. We don't want any more trouble."

"Getting tired?" Sam shouted back.

"We just want to get out of here in one piece."

Sam reloaded the rifle with his last magazine.

"So did those girls," Sam said.

He knew he had them on the ropes now. He jumped up from behind the stone fountain he positioned himself against and fired into the corner, where the bikers tried to hide behind the staircase.

Sam sent two shots through the space in the steps and sent each bullet through an eye of the gang members.

Frankie was the only one left. He jumped from behind the staircase and aimed his pistol at Sam, but when he squeezed the trigger, all that came out was the click of the firing pin. Sam lowered his rifle.

"Empty," Sam said.

The biker tossed his gun on the ground and threw his hands in the air.

"You think we'll be the last? There will be more people like me. You won't be able to kill us all."

Sam pulled the knife out. Tank's blood was still stained on the blade.

"Maybe not, but you'll do for now."

* * *

MIKE KNEW he was out there. He saw him run around back, trying to escape. All of his rage was focused on one point: kill Jake.

The pain shooting through his body didn't faze him. He wheezed with every breath, a knife-like pain stabbed his lung, his hands felt like they were going to break off, but he pushed through it.

He limped along the backside of the stores. When he made it to the edge, he could see Jake running back up Main Street by the storefronts. He was trying to flank Sam.

Mike sprinted as fast as he could. Every movement and breath was like swallowing glass, feeling it scrape along his insides as it slid down his throat and into his stomach.

When Mike heard the gunshot go off, his pace quickened, then when he turned the corner onto Main Street, he saw Jake lying on the road with Kalen towering over him.

"No," he whispered.

Killing was something you never came back from. It changed you, turned you into something else. That was what it did to him. You couldn't unpull the trigger. You couldn't rechamber that bullet once it had been fired.

Jake's blood pooled on the street, oozing from his neck where Kalen had shot him. Whatever childhood she had left in her was gone forever.

39

NIGHT OF DAY 13 (THE CABIN)

*F*reddy waited until he couldn't hear the Jeep's engine anymore before he opened the door to his room. He and Sean had stayed hidden inside when Jung was tying everyone up.

Freddy wanted to do something. He wanted to help, but Sean was too scared to move, so Freddy stayed with him. They hid under the bed until Freddy was sure Jung was long gone.

When Freddy came out, his mother let out a sigh of relief.

"Freddy, thank God," Anne said.

"Mom, are you okay?" Freddy asked.

"I'm fine, sweetheart. See if you can find some scissors in the kitchen."

Sean ran to his mom, burying his face into her stomach.

"I'm sorry I didn't help. I was scared."

"It's okay," Katie said. "I'm glad you're safe. That's all that matters."

Freddy found the scissors in one of the kitchen drawers and started cutting everyone loose. Anne and Fay were the first ones out the door but came back in quickly.

"He's long gone now," Fay said.

"Why would he do that? I know his wife's sick, but did he really think this was his best option?" Katie asked.

"Desperate people do desperate things," Fay said, picking up the revolver Jung had left behind.

Ray propped himself up in a sitting position after Freddy took the zip ties off him. He had his leg on the coffee table and was gently adjusting the splint around it.

"So, what's the call, Anne?" Ray asked.

"What?"

"Well, right now we know three things: Mike, Ulysses, and Tom are in trouble, Jung took the Jeep, and Sam went to go help Mike. Assuming Sam doesn't come back and the bikers come looking for us, our one chance of escape is now gone."

"You think we should leave?"

"That's your call, Anne. This is your place, and it's your family down there."

Anne knew he was right. She had to be the one who made the call. What did Mike always tell her? *Hope for the best, prepare for the worst.*

"We'll head to the farm. If things turn that bad, then we'll have a better place to defend ourselves. We'll be able to see them coming. If we stay here, we're sitting ducks, especially if they come back tonight," Anne said.

"What if Mike comes back?" Fay asked.

"If he comes back, then he'll know where we went. The farm will be the first place he checks. Better to cause him a little worry now and keep everyone safe than try and be stubborn and stay here," Anne answered.

There was only one problem with the plan they had, and everyone knew it. They just didn't say it out loud.

Ray couldn't make the journey to the farm, and if the bikers came back tonight, he wouldn't survive.

"I'll be fine, Anne," Ray said, responding to the look on her face.

"I don't know how we're going to move you, Ray, but we will."

"You leave me a twelve-gauge and a box of shells, and I'll give anyone who comes through that door a nice surprise."

"They still have the cart. If we bring it back, we can wheel him out of here," Fay said. "Just like we did with Jung's wife."

"Let's get started," Anne said.

Anne had everyone grab a few things. There was the potential of them never coming back, so whatever they didn't want to lose she told them to bring with them.

Fay still had her rifle. Anne picked up the pistol that Jung left behind and grabbed a new box of ammo, along with some rations, water, first aid kit, and a few spare articles of clothing. She packed enough for both her and Freddy.

They gave Ray one of the rifles Fay brought back and some ammo. They moved him over to a chair in the living room where he had a better angle at the door and was hidden from the view of the window.

"We'll be back, Ray," Anne said.

"I'll be here when you do."

Once everything was packed up, Fay led the group through the trees to Ken's farm. Anne looked back at the cabin as they departed. This was the second time she was forced to leave her home. It was easier this time, leaving, and that sense of detachment worried her. She wasn't sure if her family would really ever have a home again.

* * *

FAY WAS GREETED with the barrel of a shotgun sticking in her face when Ken opened the door to their house. It must have been close to midnight by the time they arrived, and the late-night call did nothing to improve Ken's already less than cordial manner in regards to visitors.

"What in the hell are you people doing here at this time of night?" Ken asked.

"We have a reservation," Fay answered.

"Don't get smart with me, woman."

Anne pushed her way to the front of the group. From Mike's description of Ken, she knew what she was walking into. Even with the agreement he had set up with Mike, there wasn't a guarantee that he'd help them, but he was their last hope.

"Mr. Murth, my name's Anne Grant. You spoke with my husband earlier today," Anne said.

"What does that have to do with your visit?"

"I know you're aware of the biker gang in town?"

"Yeah."

"I think they may be on their way to the cabin. I was hoping we would be able to stay with you until my husband comes back."

"If your husband went down to face that gang, then he's as good as dead. And so is our agreement."

Ken went to slam the door shut, but Anne grabbed it before it closed. She could only see a sliver of his profile through the crack of the door.

"The agreement will still be honored. We can help you bring the ammo back here. One of the members in our group has a broken leg. If we can use the cart to bring him back, we can load the rest of the ammo in with him," Anne said.

The door neither opened nor closed any further.

"All of it?" Ken asked.

"Yes."

Anne took her hand off the door. Ken slammed it quickly. The one thing she tried to do to save her family didn't work. They had nowhere else to go, and without the cart to wheel Ray to safety, there was no telling what kind of fate would befall him.

When the front door swung open, Anne jumped back as Ken stepped out with his rifle slung over his shoulder.

"The cart's around back. I'll need someone to come with me to help carry it back," Ken said.

"I'll come with you," Anne said.

"No, him," Ken said, pointing at Nelson. "I'll need somebody who can pull the weight we'll have to deal with."

Anne started to protest, but Nelson assured her it was fine. Before he took off, Anne slipped him the revolver. He didn't say anything when he felt it fall into his hand. He simply nodded and hid the gun in his pants pocket.

Nelson kissed Katie and Sean and headed off with the cart in tow back toward the cabin.

* * *

FREDDY AND SEAN shared the couch in the living room while Anne, Katie, Fay, and Beth sat in the kitchen. Beth grabbed a kettle of tea from the stove and poured them each a cup.

"We can't thank you enough, Mrs. Murth," Katie said.

"I should thank you. With that ammo we'll be able to hunt until Ken and I are in the dirt."

The steam rose from the cup. Katie put it to her lips and sipped slowly. The warm blast of liquid scorched her tongue and lips.

"If that isn't warm enough for you…" Beth said, pulling a flask from her pocket. "This might help."

Katie smiled and extended her cup, then winced when she took a sip.

"That's… strong," Katie said.

Beth poured some in Fay's, but Anne declined. Beth took a swig straight from the flask and tucked it back into her pocket.

"Hard day calls for a hard drink," Beth said.

"How long have you and Ken been married?" Katie asked.

"Going on thirty years now."

"Nelson and I just hit our fifteenth this past year. Anne, you and Mike have been married for twenty years?"

"Twenty-five next spring."

Katie glanced at Fay, who held up her barren left hand.

"Divorced," Fay said.

"I'm sorry," Katie said.

"I'm not."

Katie glanced around the house. She admired the rustic look of the home. She wasn't sure if it was a look by design or of purpose. Judging from the look of Beth and her husband, she figured it was the latter.

Then Katie's eyes landed on the crucifix hanging high on the wall in the kitchen. It was an old piece, but kept in good condition. The polish of the metal shone and reflected the candlelight.

"That's beautiful," Katie said, pointing to the crucifix.

"That's been in my family for five generations," Beth answered. "It's always been passed down to the eldest daughter in the family."

"Do you have any daughters?" Katie asked.

"No, just Billy and Joey."

"I'm sure it'll be hard giving it away to one of their wives once they're married."

"No, I won't be giving it to their wives."

"Why?"

"That crucifix doesn't just represent the blood of Christ, it has the blood of my family. It's been with us through wars, droughts, depressions, and no matter what has come our way, we've always survived. My family has always found a way. It's never easy pushing through hell, but we did it, and we'll keep doing it. Some woman from the outside wouldn't understand that. They wouldn't appreciate what that pain means."

Beth pulled the flask back out and took another swig. Katie thought it was an odd statement to make but agreed that the pain you went through to push forward couldn't truly be appreciated unless experienced firsthand.

There was an exultation that came from conquering that pain, but when Beth spoke, her tone had no hope, no redemption. It was as if the pain was there not to make you stronger, but make you callous.

"I'll run and grab you ladies some sheets. I'm sure the boys will be back soon. It's been a long day," Beth said.

Beth pushed her chair back, and it squeaked along the wooden floorboards. Anne reached for her arm before she left, and Beth whipped around to her.

"Thank you for helping us," Anne said.

When Beth was sure she was out of sight from the kitchen, she leaned up against the wall. In the dark hallway, she felt the guilt wrestling in her conscience. She knew what she had to do, but the conflict raging inside her intensified.

She pounded her fist into the cushioned back of the chair next to her. She punched it over and over again. Each hit, submitting to her guilt.

She brushed the loose strands of her hair out of her face and regained her composure. She walked to the end of the hall and pulled open a closet. The shelves were lined with blankets, pillows, and sewing supplies. She reached into the corner and pulled out a shotgun.

Beth made sure the gun was loaded, then tucked the shotgun under the crook of her arm and walked back to the kitchen.

* * *

KEN DIDN'T SAY anything on the way up to the cabin. The only noise the two of them created was the creak of the cart's wheels as they hauled it through the forest.

Nelson kept touching the side of his pant leg, feeling the outline of the pistol. He wasn't sure why Anne had given it to him. Was she worried about what Ken might do? Could he be trusted?

He shook the notion out of his mind. Of course he could trust Ken. Mike wouldn't have cooperated with him if he didn't believe it. He was overthinking. His imagination was getting the better of him.

Nelson hadn't done much exploring since he'd been at the cabin, but the times he did go for a walk he couldn't help but see the beauty around him. Aside from the circumstances that brought him here, he felt like he could be on vacation.

The forest was different at night. During the day he could see all of the details, the small nests in the trees, the bushels of fresh berries, the squirrels and birds traveling from branch to branch. Everything was so green, lush, and full of life.

The walk during the night was cooler though. There was a crisp lightness in the air. But in the darkness Nelson couldn't see the green leaves or the bushes bearing fruit. Everything was lumped together in shadows.

Nelson felt the cart jerk to a stop, and he stumbled forward a bit. He hadn't realized they were already at the cabin.

"C'mon," Ken said.

Nelson made sure to let Ray know who it was before he approached the door. He didn't want to get a belly full of lead.

"Ray?" Nelson asked, walking through the front door.

"You alone?" Ray asked.

"No, Ken's with me. We're here to grab you."

Ken pushed his way inside. Ray sat in the dark corner of the living room, aiming the rifle at the two of them.

"We load the ammo first, then we grab him," Ken instructed.

Ken didn't wait for permission, or for Nelson, as he made his way to the basement door. Between Nelson and Ken, it only took them twenty minutes to load all of the ammunition into the cart, but Ken insisted on gathering as much of the other supplies as they could.

Boxes and cases of different caliber rounds weighed the cart down. Nelson couldn't believe how much Mike was able to stockpile. It was enough bullets to supply a small army. The rest of the space in the cart was occupied by first aid kits, a few tools, and food rations.

"That's the last of it," Nelson said.

Ken followed Nelson back inside. When Nelson grabbed the rifle from Ray and threw his arm around his shoulders to steady him, Ken aimed his rifle at the two of them.

"What are you doing?" Nelson asked.

"Slide the rifle over to me," Ken said.

"You son of a bitch," Ray said.

"No hard feelings, boys, but I couldn't just let all of these supplies go to waste, not after the bikers finish off the rest of your group."

"We don't even know if they're dead or not. They could still be alive," Nelson said.

"The gang wiped out the whole town. They killed everyone. Your people walked into a meat grinder. They're not coming back," Ken said.

"What about your deal with Mike?" Nelson asked.

"I was going to kill him tomorrow, but it looks like the bikers saved me some trouble."

"You can't do this."

"I can."

If Ken was going to kill them, then what would happen to Nelson's family? He just got his wife back, and now he was going to lose her. His son would probably suffer the same fate as him.

He couldn't let that happen, not after everything they'd been through, not after they were finally together again.

"Well, get it over with then," Ray said.

Nelson looked down. The rifle rested at his feet. The butt of the gun faced him and was slightly elevated off the ground. By the time Ken realized what Nelson was thinking, it was too late.

Nelson kicked the rifle up and sent it flying toward Ken, who dodged out of the way and fired in their direction, hitting Ray in the shoulder. Nelson pushed both of them to the floor and reached for the revolver in his pocket.

When Ken got up, Nelson fired a few rounds, missing Ken completely, but it caused Ken to retreat down the hall, looking for cover. It gave Nelson and Ray enough time to crawl and drag their way through the kitchen.

If Nelson could get to the back door and make it in the woods, then they might have a chance. Nelson gave Ray the pistol.

"I'll pull, you shoot," Nelson said.

Nelson grabbed Ray by his shoulders and pulled him through the dirt toward the trees. Ken appeared in the doorway, and Ray squeezed a few rounds off.

The kitchen window's glass shattered, and Ken shoved his rifle through the opening, firing shots in their direction.

Nelson gave one last heave and pulled both him and Ray behind a tree, shielding themselves from the barrage of bullets splintering the oak's trunk.

Ray kept reaching for his leg, wincing. When Nelson tried to adjust the splint, Ray screamed and smacked his hand away.

"Sorry," Nelson said.

Ray's breath was labored. Nelson didn't know what to do. There was no way he could drag Ray through the woods, not in the condition he was in.

"Just go," Ray said.

"What?"

"I'll hold him off as long as I can."

"Ray, I'm not going to leave you here."

"If you don't go and warn Mike, then his family's going to die, if they haven't killed them already."

Ray pushed Nelson backwards, pointing for him to run. Another spray of bullets peppered the tree behind them.

"You're not being a coward for leaving me here, Nelson. This is my choice. Now, go," Ray said.

Nelson grabbed Ray's hand and squeezed tight.

"Good luck," Nelson said.

"You, too."

Ray gave Nelson some cover fire as he disappeared deeper into the woods, then checked the revolver, seeing how many bullets he had left.

Two.

He knew his fate the moment he chose to stay behind. Ken had an unlimited supply of ammo within an arm's reach, and Ray couldn't hobble more than a few feet without crashing to the ground. He was a sitting duck.

"Hey!" Ray shouted.

The firing ceased. Ray pushed himself off the ground with his good leg, using the tree trunk to help give him leverage. His leg felt like it was going to explode.

"You go back on your deals that quick?" Ray asked.

Gunfire blasted the tree again. Ray ducked, trying to shield himself from the ricochet.

"Guess so," Ray mumbled.

After a moment, everything was silent. Ray aimed the pistol at the cabin, switching targets between the door and the kitchen window, but he couldn't see Ken.

"Drop it," Ken said.

Ray froze. The pistol hit the ground, and he put his hands in the air.

"Where'd he go?" Ken asked.

Ray said nothing. He wouldn't let his last breaths in life betray the people who helped him.

"You think I'm a bad man, don't you?" Ken asked.

"I think you're a coward."

Ken laughed.

"You people. In all of your self-righteous bullshit you think that the act of sacrifice is so noble, that we should all elevate ourselves to your level. Well, this is what you get for your noble deeds."

The barrel of the gun pressed firmly against Ray's forehead. It was hot, burning a circle into his skin. Ray didn't move. Whatever pain Ken would put him through, he wasn't going to give him any satisfaction of showing that he was hurting.

"Surviving without a soul isn't living," Ray said.

"Neither is having a bullet in your brain."

Ken squeezed the trigger, and Ray's body hit the ground.

40

NIGHT OF DAY 13 (THE TOWN)

*M*ike wheezed; the pain in his side was sharp. He stood above his father's body. There were bits of bone and splashes of blood strewn around Ulysses's head where the bullet entered and left.

The gun Ulysses used on himself lay by his side. His eyes were still open, staring up into the night sky.

Nothing seemed real at that moment. This town Mike was in couldn't exist. That wasn't his father dead on the ground. This wasn't his broken body he was trapped in. That wasn't his daughter who was almost beaten to death. This wasn't his life.

"Mike?" Sam asked.

The graveyard where his mother was buried had an empty spot right next to her. That's where his father should be right now. He wanted to take him home, away from this hell he died in.

"Mike, we need to get you checked out. Your daughter's over at the pharmacy," Sam said.

"What?"

"Your daughter."

"Right."

He couldn't dwell on the pain he was feeling now. His daughter was still alive. He still had a family to protect. He still had a job to do.

The town felt quiet after the gunfight. There wasn't any motion in the town now. At one point in time, this place was filled with people enjoying their lives, people with a purpose.

When the biker gang came through, all of that was replaced with fear and death. Now that the bikers were gone, the town was filled with neither fear nor purpose. It was just there, a shell of what it used to be, frozen in time.

Mike's Jeep was still flipped on its side. On the sidewalk next to it, Jung rocked Jenna back and forth in his arms. Mike could see the pain on his face, and when he thought to himself that whatever pain Jung received was justified, he felt no guilt.

Most of the pharmacy was barren. The bikers had come through like locusts, pillaging the stores, stealing supplies, destroying what they wanted.

Kalen sifted through the bottles and supplies thrown on the ground. When Mike walked in, she turned around.

The only thing worse than seeing his daughter beaten and bloody was the knowledge of what she had seen. He knew the bruises would fade, the bones would mend, and the wounds would close, but the violence she'd been exposed to, witnessing evil in its most terrible forms and letting it become a part of her... that was a scar that would leave its mark for a very, very long time.

Mike picked up a bottle of hydrogen peroxide and a bag of cotton balls. He led Kalen over to the counter. She hopped on top of it. Mike dumped some of the peroxide onto the cotton ball.

Kalen winced when the peroxide made contact. Mike ran the cotton ball gently along the cuts on her face.

"I'm sorry, Dad," Kalen said.

"It's okay."

"No, it's not. Grandpa's dead, you're hurt, everyone is hurt. I shouldn't have come here. It was stupid."

Mike knew whatever words left his mouth now would have a deciding factor in the type of life his daughter would have moving forward. He knew the guilt she was feeling. It was a guilt that could consume her life, send her into a spiral that she wouldn't be able to come out of.

"You came here because of what these people did. You stood up to those who tried to hurt you and the people you care about," Mike said.

"Your dad's right," Mary said.

Mike hadn't seen her when he entered. He couldn't make out the features on her face, but the tone of her voice made her sound older than she was.

"Whatever we lost today, we gained more by not having that gang here anymore. All of them deserved to die," Mary said.

"When someone pushes you to the brink of killing, when it comes down to your survival or the survival of your family, then you do what you have to do," Mike said. "No repentance."

Kalen nodded and leaned into his chest. He hoped the words reached her. It would take time—he knew that—for her to accept it, but he wanted it to be sooner rather than later.

Sam helped patch them up as best he could. Most of the injuries would heal over time. When Sam checked Mike out, he agreed that one of the ribs punctured a lung, but only time would tell how bad it really was.

Jung was still on the sidewalk, his children on either side of him. His kids were crying, but he wasn't.

Mike wanted to hurt him, even more than the pain he was going through right now. All of those talks Mike had with Jung about trusting people, about having faith, were all erased by what he did.

Ulysses always taught Mike that he needed to have something to stand for; he needed a line in the sand. Every man did. That value was your guiding path, and no matter what, you never went back on it.

And that was exactly what Jung did. The line in the sand he so proudly toed, all of it was a lie.

"Mike," Jung said, "I'm sorry. I'm so sorry."

Mike said nothing. He simply turned his back and started the long walk back to the cabin.

"You're just going to leave them here?" Sam asked.

"Yes."

"What about the kids?"

Mike knew what type of fate he would be leaving them to, but that was his line in the sand. He wouldn't sacrifice the safety of his family for the well-being of others.

"It's a father's job to protect his children. That's his responsibility. Not mine," Mike said.

Before Mike left, he wanted to bury Ulysses. He grabbed some shovels from the hardware store and picked a spot on the edge of town by the tall grass. Sam helped him dig the grave, and once they were six feet down, he wrapped his father's body in a tarp and carried him to the spot. This was as close to a funeral as there was going to be.

"My father was a good man. He loved his family, his work, and the Pittsburgh Pirates," Mike said.

Everyone gave a slight smile.

"He was a man who always stood up for what he believed in, no matter the cost. He couldn't be bribed, threatened, or beaten into anything he didn't want to do. In his last moments on Earth, he held true to that belief that he was in control of everything he did. He had a choice, and he made the choice to keep his family safe," Mike said.

The tears started to flow now. All of the memories of his childhood, being with his father, collided with the reality that he'd never see his dad again. He would no longer be able to ask him for advice, to hear his words of comfort and wisdom when he needed them most. A pillar in Mike's life was struck down, and for the first time he wondered whether he would be able to go on.

"I never knew, or will ever know, a better man, husband, or father than my dad," Mike said.

The first tear that hit the dirt was followed by a rain that Mike couldn't stop. He'd never cried like this before. Each sob was a stab digging into his heart.

Kalen came over and wrapped her arms around him. Mike clutched his daughter and held her tight. Just as he had held her earlier, she was holding him now.

Sam began shoveling the dirt back into the hole. After Mike composed himself, he picked up the other shovel and helped.

They packed the dirt tight. Mary picked some flowers she found along the side of the road and arranged a small bouquet. She laid them down on the fresh mound of dirt.

"Okay," Mike said. "Let's gather up any weapons and ammo we can find. Grab anything that's high quality or in good condition. Sam, do you know how to ride a motorcycle?"

"I had one when I was in the Rangers."

"Good. If we can't get the Jeep running, we'll take the bikes back to the cabin."

"Nelson?" Sam asked.

Mike turned around and saw a man running down the highway toward them. His arms flailed wildly at his sides, and his legs wobbled.

Nelson collapsed in Mike's arms when he made it to him and brought the two of them to the ground. Nelson could barely speak he was so out of breath.

"Ken... took... supplies," Nelson said.

"What?"

"Katie... Anne... Sean, Freddy... they're in trouble."

Mike closed his eyes. Jung wasn't the only one going back on his word.

41

NIGHT OF DAY 13 (THE FARM)

*I*t took Ken twice as long to bring the supplies back to the farm than when he left. Beth was still awake when he got home. She helped him unload the supplies and bring them in the house.

"What happened to him?" Beth asked.

"He got away," Ken said.

"You didn't kill him?"

"No, but I killed the friend they had at the cabin."

"He's going to come back, Ken."

"Only if Mike's still alive, which I doubt. Besides, even if he does come back, we have his guns, ammo, and supplies."

"And his family."

Ken stopped. He set the case of 9mm bullets on the kitchen counter and turned to his wife.

"You didn't kill them?" Ken asked.

Beth said nothing. When she turned to pick up the rest of the supplies, Ken grabbed her arm.

"Where are they?" Ken asked.

"I put them in the storm cellar."

"Goddamn it, Beth, we talked about this. You weren't supposed to keep them alive."

"And you weren't supposed to let one of them get away, but it happened."

There was viciousness in her words as she jerked her arm out of Ken's grip and stormed outside to the cart. Ken followed her.

"What happened?" Ken asked.

"I know why we're doing this, Ken. I do," Beth said, turning around to face him. "You've been responsible for keeping this family safe, but... what if we don't have to hurt people like we have? What if there's another way?"

"Did they talk to you? Get in your head?"

"No, but we can't keep going on like this forever, can we?"

"Of course we can! The moment we let guilt slip into our minds is the moment we start digging our own graves."

Ken grabbed one of the rifles out of the back of his cart along with a box of ammo. He started loading bullets into the rifle's magazine.

"What are you doing?" Beth asked.

"Your job."

"Ken, the boys, they're no older than Joey. You ca—"

"It's them or us, Beth. There can't be both."

"What if they come back? What if they managed to kill the bikers? We'll need a bargaining chip."

Ken stopped. On the slim chance that Mike *did* manage to kill the bikers, he would come looking for his family. Mike didn't strike him as someone who forgave easily, and with the knowledge of how prepared he was, Ken figured that Mike knew how to handle himself in a fight. He set the rifle back down on the cart and grabbed a box with first aid supplies.

"We give it one day," Ken said.

* * *

THE ONLY LIGHT in the storm cellar was a single candle. It was a small, cramped space, not meant for an extended stay, and Anne had no idea how long they'd be there.

The boys finally fell asleep, but she, Fay, and Katie couldn't. Anne twirled her wedding ring on her hand, watching Freddy's slow breaths.

"Mike will come back," Fay said.

"I know," Anne replied.

That's what she kept telling herself. He would come back. He wouldn't let them suffer a fate like this when he had the ability to save them. She knew her husband better than any soul on Earth, and the one thing she learned about him a long time ago was he never

283

quit, no matter what. As long as Mike had air in his lungs, then they had a chance of getting out.

"I'm sure Nelson will be back too," Anne added.

Katie hadn't said much after they were put in the cellar. Anne was worried about her. She knew what it was like to have your family back and then immediately be ripped away from you, not knowing if you'd ever see them again.

"Why are they doing this to us?" Katie asked.

"Because they're assholes," Fay replied.

"They think this is the best way to survive. They think it's the only way to survive," Anne said.

"What is wrong with people?" Katie asked.

"They're assholes," Fay answered.

"Fay," Anne said. "Please."

Fay crossed her arms and leaned back against the wall. Anne sat and watched the flame flicker. The orange-and-yellow light danced in the darkness, causing shadows to drift over their faces.

"What do you think they'll do?" Katie asked.

"I don't know," Anne said.

Anne had been trying to answer that question since Beth threw all of them in here. She just couldn't make sense of it. The family didn't seem desperate or in need of anything. In fact, it was Mike who came to them for help in the first place.

Whatever fate would fall upon them, Anne only hoped Freddy would be okay. Maybe she could bargain with them, strike a deal to keep him alive.

"You know, I never thought I'd see him again," Katie said.

Katie was looking at her son, Sean.

"A part of me wishes I never did," Katie added.

"You don't mean that," Anne said.

"I know, and I feel ashamed for saying it, but there's a part of me that does mean it. When I first came back to the house after Sam and I finally made it out of the city, I thought, 'This is it. They're gone,' but when I finally saw the letter there was a hope that burned inside of me. The hope that I could see them again, and it raged within me, propelling me to keep moving forward, to keep pushing, no matter how hard it was."

"That's a good thing."

"Is it? It did keep me going forward, and yes, I did find my family again, but how many of us let that hope burn and consume them?

How many never find what they're looking for? It can lead you on an endless quest of pain."

Maybe Katie was right. Letting a false hope fuel you could be more dangerous than the alternative, but that meant taking away every chance, and Anne couldn't do that. She had to believe. She had to take every chance she could.

* * *

Billy's parents didn't see him watching them argue from the second-floor bedroom window. He knew they were bickering about his mother letting the family live.

When his mother came and woke him up to ask him for his help, he dreaded what she would make him do, but then when she told him her plan of keeping them alive, he felt a burst of pride rush through him.

He might have actually gotten through to her. Maybe she was starting to understand what he was telling her.

They couldn't keep going on like this. Sooner or later, everything they'd done would come back to haunt them, he was sure of that. But he also knew it wasn't too late for them to change. He could still save his parents from the violent fates they were heading toward.

Billy thought of his brother and how much he idolized their father. If he could change his dad, then his brother would change too. It could be done. He could do it.

DAWN OF DAY 14 (THE FARM)

*T*he sky was lightening. The sun would be coming up soon. Mike wanted to use the darkness to his advantage, so he'd have to move in quickly.

He knew if Ken was going hunting, he'd be up by now, getting things ready, but if he had to haul the supplies back by himself, it would have taken him most of the night, so there was the chance he was still asleep.

Even in the physical state Mike was in, between himself, Sam, and Nelson, he was confident they'd be able to take Ken out. Sam could probably do it singlehandedly, but Mike wasn't going to let one man be the deciding factor in his family's fate.

Mike made sure everyone was loaded down with weapons. He gave a pistol to Mary and Kalen but told them they had to stay hidden.

Kalen didn't argue. Mary simply nodded. After everything that happened, now wasn't the time to question him.

"Where do you think they're keeping them?" Nelson asked.

"Wouldn't they just be in the house?" Sam asked.

"No, I've been inside. There isn't any space for them to hide in the house. They'll have to be somewhere else on the property. Nelson, did you see anything when you left? Anywhere they would keep them?" Mike asked.

"No, I didn't see anything."

"Most farms around here would have a storm cellar, I would

think. It'd be out of sight, no windows, one door. It'd be a good place to hide them," Sam said.

"That's as good a place to start looking as any," Mike answered.

Mike followed the forest line that faced the side of the house. He wanted to approach from there because it had the fewest windows and areas to spot them coming.

"Okay, Sam, you look for the storm cellar. If you find it before we do, then take everyone to Kalen and Mary's location. We'll catch up with you. Nelson and I will handle the house," Mike said.

"Roger that," Sam said.

"Okay," Nelson replied.

Fatigue was starting to catch up with Mike. He had to force his hands closed over his rifle. The pain in his side still hadn't let up, and it was getting harder to breathe. He closed his eyes and counted to three.

One.

They're alive. You have to keep moving. They're going to be okay.

Two.

Push the pain out of your mind. You only have to go a little bit further.

Three.

Done.

Mike led the three of them as they jogged across the field toward the house. They had to weave around some of the cows in the pasture, but it was an easy jog for the most part.

Sam separated himself from the rest of the group and headed around back while Mike and Nelson moved to the front of the house.

As much as Mike wanted to go in and shoot first, he couldn't risk them hurting his family. He had no idea what he could potentially be walking into, so he kept it quiet.

The wind blew the chimes hanging from the front porch and also rocked a chair that creaked back and forth on the splintered wooden panels.

Each step Mike took was slow, deliberate. He reached his hand for the screen door and gently pulled it open. He placed his hand on the brass knob to the front door and jiggled the handle. It was open.

Mike looked back at Nelson and raised his hand to count down when they'd enter. Five. Four. Three. Two. One.

Mike pushed the door open, rifle at the ready, and stepped inside. The living room was empty. He listened for any sign of struggle, mumbles for help, but heard nothing.

"I don't think they're here," Mike whispered.

The two of them entered the kitchen, their eyes never leaving the sights of their rifles. A thud from upstairs caused the nose of their guns to point upward.

Mike motioned toward the staircase. The old steps creaked with each step up. His hands were aching badly. He could barely control the tremors. If someone came out, he wasn't even sure if he could keep the gun steady enough to get a shot off.

At the top of the stairs, Mike could see someone walking back and forth through a crack in the door that was opened slightly. He figured that was where the noise came from, but he wasn't sure who it was.

Nelson was right behind him, matching him step for step. When Mike pointed toward the door, Nelson nodded in understanding. They both lined up on either side, waiting for the person to come out.

Mike couldn't hear anyone speaking, so he figured whoever was in there was alone. He peeked through the crack. As soon as he did, the door opened and Mike subdued Billy, dragging him back into the room, keeping his hand over his mouth.

Nelson followed quickly, shutting the three of them in the room. Billy was struggling against Mike but stopped once Nelson put the barrel of his rifle to his face.

"Is my family still alive?" Mike asked.

Billy nodded his head.

"Listen to me, Billy. I know you're not a bad person. I know you wouldn't try and hurt anyone. I just want my family. Nothing else. I spared your life once. Now I'm asking you to spare my family's," Mike said.

Billy's eyes darted back and forth between Mike and Nelson. His breathing was quick.

"I'm going to let you go, and when I do you're going to take me to my family. Do you understand?" Mike asked.

Mike slowly moved his hand from Billy's mouth. Billy didn't scream.

"Where are they?" Mike asked.

"My mom put them in the storm shelter," Billy said.

"Show me."

The three of them snuck back down the stairs quietly. On their way out, Billy opened one of the drawers, grabbing the spare key to the shelter.

Billy led them out the back door into the fields. Mike looked around for Sam but didn't see him anywhere.

"Over here," Billy said.

The storm cellar was underground, covered by overgrown grass and bushes; it was meant to be hidden. Billy unlocked the latch and pulled the door open.

When Mike looked inside, it was completely empty.

"Where are they?" Nelson asked.

Mike grabbed Billy by the throat and slammed him to the ground.

"Is this some kind of joke?"

Billy struggled for breath.

"No! They were here! I helped my mother put them here!"

Mike let go. Billy coughed, catching his breath. Mike paced around the shelter, looking in all directions, searching for any sign of his family, but there were none to be seen. Was this how he was going to lose them? Was this how it would end for him?

"Mike," Nelson said.

Nelson was staring at the ground to the left of the shelter. When Mike went over, he could see several footprints in the dirt.

"They're still alive," Mike said.

"Oh God," Billy said.

"What?" Mike asked.

"My dad. He must have come and got them after we went to bed."

"Do you know where he's taking them?" Nelson asked.

"Hunting," Billy said.

* * *

KALEN LEANED up against the trunk of a tree. Her mind wandered. Everything felt like a haze. She could see, but she couldn't understand. She couldn't comprehend what happened. It was too much. All of it was too much.

She could still see Jake's face, his blood pouring from the bullet hole in his head. When she squeezed the trigger, she felt nothing. She saw him. She was angry. She killed him.

The progression of her thoughts that led her to that point was fast, unmerciful. Whatever satisfaction she thought she'd receive never came. It was nothing more than an illusion.

That emptiness she felt inside her, the fear and void that she replaced with anger, didn't fade away. It simply grew.

She traded all of her pain for more pain, but this was different than before. There wasn't a numbness. This had more clarity to it. She had an unexplainable need for more.

"Kalen," Mary said.

"What?"

Mary moved to her quickly. She pointed behind Kalen, her eyes fixed on something in the distance.

When Kalen turned around, she could see her mother and brother walking through the forest. Behind them were Mary's sisters and Fay.

Mary started to run to them, but Kalen pulled her back down.

"Look," Kalen said.

Just behind their family members, Ken watched them with his rifle aimed at the back of their heads, marching them forward.

Kalen could feel that burning inside her grow. Her hand went to the pistol her dad left her. When she pulled it out of her pocket, Mary grabbed her wrist.

"No. If you miss, he might hurt them," Mary said.

"If we hesitate, he'll kill them before we have a chance to do anything," Kalen replied.

"We need to go and get your dad."

Kalen tossed Mary's arm off her.

"We don't have time."

Before Mary could stop her, Kalen was chasing after them. Kalen knew from what her father had said that Ken was a skilled hunter. She felt a slight thrill run through her. The void was filling up again. This is what she needed. She needed to hunt.

* * *

KEN SNUCK out of bed and headed downstairs. It was still dark out, so he knew he had time but needed to act fast.

The promise of waiting to kill those people was a lie. He knew that even if Mike made it back, there wouldn't be any bargaining, not after this.

If the rest of his family was kept alive, then his family would be outnumbered, and he knew it would only be a matter of time before they were killed. He didn't care what type of good intentions Mike would spit out. In the end it would be either him or Mike, and Ken wasn't about to lie down.

The looks on their faces when Ken opened that cellar were tired. They hadn't slept all night, and when they saw him with the rifle, he could tell they knew what was coming.

"Please," Anne said. "Don't do this."

"Everyone out," Ken replied.

He marched them off to the woods. There was a place he would take them, his hunting spot deep within the forest. It was far enough away from the farm and town that Mike would never find their bodies. It was a spot that you couldn't get to unless you knew where it was.

Ken found his eyes falling onto Freddy and Sean. His mind went back to the fawn he killed as a boy and the scolding his father gave him.

It wouldn't be any different than anyone else he'd killed. All he had to do was pull the trigger.

None of them cried or begged on their march. He was impressed by it actually. He could never understand the sniveling characteristics of a beggar. All anyone had to do in life was figure out what they wanted and then take it. It was that simple. It was exactly what he was doing now.

He had enough bullets for all of them, but for some reason, he felt exposed. It was a feeling he couldn't shake. Something was off, but he couldn't put his finger on it.

Then when the first shot rang out, he realized that it wasn't the dread of killing these people that he was feeling, but that he was being followed.

* * *

WHEN MIKE HEARD THE SHOTS, Billy and Nelson had a hard time keeping up with him. It was a burst of energy that came out of nowhere, a primal surge that coursed through his veins.

The firing was going back and forth. It grew louder the closer he moved. Screams echoed in between the shots. He just couldn't tell whose screams it was.

Mike finally saw Sam up ahead, firing and ducking behind a tree. Bullets whizzed past. Mike dropped behind a log next to Sam.

"I thought I had a clear shot. I tripped on a goddamn rock," Sam said, reloading a magazine into his rifle.

"Who were you shooting at?" Mike asked.

"The guy who had the rifle pointing at your family."

Mike glanced over the log, and he could see people running toward him. Katie had Sean with her, but he couldn't see Fay, Anne, or Freddy.

"Where'd they go?" Mike asked.

"He ran north," Sam said.

"He's heading to his hunting spot," Billy said. "It's where he takes his game to gut and clean before he brings it home."

"Show me," Mike said.

They were on foot for a few more minutes before they came across Fay, scanning the woods.

"Mike?" Fay asked.

"You all right?"

"I'm sorry, Mike. I'm so sorry."

"Where's Ann? Where's Freddy?"

"Ken grabbed Freddy, and Anne and I started chasing after him, but I got turned around. I don't know where they went."

"It's not much farther," Billy said. "C'mon."

As Billy brought them closer to Ken's spot, they came across Anne's body. She was unconscious on the ground, but still alive.

"Fay, Nelson, you two make sure she's okay. Billy, Sam, you two with me," Mike said.

Billy slowed down once they were close. He gathered Mike and Sam around him.

"It's just beyond those trees. My dad can smell an ambush coming, and right now we're downwind. He'll know we're coming, so we have to be careful," Billy said.

Mike shoved Billy out of the way, marching forward in stubborn persistence.

"Mike!" Billy said.

"Ken!" Mike shouted. "Let my boy go! If you want to hurt someone, hurt me."

Ken's face appeared from behind a tree. He kept his hand over Freddy's mouth, keeping him quiet. Ken had a gun to his head with his finger on the trigger.

"Funny, ain't it, Mike? You had my son as a hostage, and now I've got yours. I just don't know if I'm going to be as willing to let him go as you were for mine."

"Ken, you don't have to do this. Please, let him go."

"Tell whoever you've got back there with you to come out, or I kill your boy right now."

Mike didn't have to ask Sam or Billy to come out; they did it on their own. When Mike saw Ken's reaction to Billy being there, he was surprised.

There was no look of shock on Ken's face. He just started to laugh.

"Just couldn't let it go, could you, boy?" Ken asked.

"Dad, let him go. This isn't right," Billy said.

"Right?" Ken shouted. "What's right isn't for my own son to betray me! It isn't right for my own blood to turn against me!"

"I'm not turning against you, Dad, but I can't let you do this."

Freddy squirmed against Ken, trying to free himself, but Ken's grip was too strong. He couldn't get loose. Then Ken felt the tip of Kalen's pistol on the back of his head.

"Put the gun down," Kalen said. "And let my brother go."

"Kalen?" Mike asked.

Ken slowly raised his hands in the air, letting Freddy go and setting the pistol on the ground. Kalen walked around to face him, the gun aimed at his face. Freddy ran to his father, and Mike scooped him up.

"Well done, girl," Ken said.

"Kalen, it's okay. It's over," Mike said.

Kalen only took her eyes off Ken for a second, but it was enough for him to get the drop on her. He knocked the gun from her hands and went for his pistol on the ground.

The moment Ken had his hand on the gun and jumped up to aim at Kalen, a shot rang out and Ken flew backwards, a bullet tearing through his chest.

The smoke from Billy's rifle rose into the morning air. As quickly as he fired the shot, he ran to his father.

"Dad!"

Ken coughed up blood. He grabbed Billy's collar and pulled him toward him.

"Dad, I'm sorry. I'm so sorry," Billy said, tears streaming down his face. "Somebody help him!"

Sam rushed over, putting pressure on the wound, but there was too much blood.

Ken's fingers slowly lost their grip on Billy's shirt, and his hand went limp. Sam checked his pulse, listened for his breathing, but there was nothing. Ken was gone.

Billy screamed. He shook his father, but nothing brought back the life in Ken's eyes. Billy just sat there, hunched over his dad, crying.

Mike wasn't sure what would happen next. Billy was emotional. He could turn on the rest of the group. He walked up and picked up the rifle so Billy couldn't do anything rash.

"Billy, he's gone," Mike said.

Mike placed his hand on the boy's back, and Billy shoved him off him. He kept shoving Mike's chest, pushing him back.

"You made me do this! This is your fault!" Billy said.

"Billy, I know what you're going through. I do."

"No, you don't!"

The adrenaline finally left him, and Billy fell to the ground. Mike and Sam picked him up and carried him back to the farm.

43

DAY 16 (THE CABIN)

*T*he reports coming in from Cincinnati had been constant for the past forty-eight hours. It was something Mike couldn't ignore anymore.

He decided to give himself and the rest of his family a few more days before they would head out. He and Kalen had been sleeping during most of the days and nights. He'd never been so exhausted in his life. The days were more for him than anyone else.

The breathing was getting a little easier, but he still couldn't move around a lot. His body felt like concrete, heavy and rigid. He was resting in his room when Anne came and knocked on the door.

"Honey, Fay's here," Anne said.

"Send her in."

Fay had her daily basket of provisions that she came in from town to get.

"I suppose you still haven't changed your mind?" Fay asked.

"No."

"There has to be a way to fix this, Mike."

"There isn't."

"If you could just talk to him. Hear him out."

"It's good to see you, Fay."

Mike didn't have anything else to add on the subject. He closed his eyes and went back to sleep.

He knew what she wanted. She wanted him to let Jung back in the cabin, into their circle. But it was something he just couldn't do. Jung crossed a line that he never should have tried. He put Mike's family in danger, and it almost got them killed. It wasn't something that he took lightly.

Fay had chosen to stay with Jung and his kids at the motel in town. He knew she felt that he was being too hard on him, but Mike didn't care. He'd given enough already. He didn't have any more charity to offer.

* * *

The cabin was gathered around the dinner table. It was the first time Mike and Kalen decided to join everyone and eat in the kitchen.

There was a sense of relief when everyone saw Mike and Kalen walk in. For them it was a sign of things getting back to normal. For Mike and Kalen, it was them ready to face the people around them.

There wasn't much talk. A few comments here and there, but Mike was thankful he didn't have to say anything.

He knew everyone was already aware of the trip to Cincinnati. There wasn't much objection when it was brought up. Everyone seemed to be glad to go. It gave everyone a sense of hope that once they made it to Cincinnati they'd be safe and that soon they'd be able to go home.

Mike wasn't sure what home meant to him anymore. He wanted to believe that it was still a place where his family was, and that was true, but if his family wasn't safe, then how could they enjoy their time together? How was someone supposed to grow and love and feel joy when the constant threat of violence was hanging over their heads?

He couldn't answer that question now. All he was focusing on were the faces around the table. These were the people he could trust. This was his family.

44

SIX MONTHS AFTER BLACKOUT

*B*en Sullivan took his glasses off and rubbed his eyes. He'd been staring at data and spreadsheets for the past three hours. His eyes were dry and bloodshot. He needed to take a break.

He walked over to the snack machine and swiped his card. He pressed A7, and a Snickers dropped to the slot at the bottom.

His partner, Mitch, walked in with another file just as Ben was about to take a bite.

"C'mon, Mitch. I need a break," Ben said.

"Trust me, you'll want to take a look at this one. It's Cincinnati."

Ben raised his eyebrows. He stuffed the rest of the candy bar in his mouth and snatched the file from Mitch's hands.

He flipped through the manila folder, studying the notes, pictures, and interviews that had already taken place.

"When did he get here?" Ben asked, not looking up from the file.

"About an hour ago. We have him in a holding cell. Should I bring him in?"

"I'll meet you there in five minutes."

Ben couldn't believe it. Since the power came back on, he must have questioned more than one hundred people who were indicted with crimes during the power outage.

He was put in charge with investigating all major crimes in the Northeast that were committed during the time the EMP blast took out power for the entire country.

Most of the stuff he ran across were murder charges, but this guy, he was a big fish. The allegations coming out of Cincinnati were huge. People were still scrambling to figure out what happened, and if this guy was everything the file was telling him, then Ben could have just found the biggest break of his career.

Ben took a seat behind the two-way glass as Mitch brought in the suspect. His face was bearded, and he looked nothing like the picture in his file.

The violence on this guy's record was incredible. Ben was surprised they didn't bring him in with a straitjacket on.

Once the prisoner was secure with his hands and feet shackled, Ben walked in and sat down across from him. He slapped the file on the clean steel table between them, folded his hands together, and leaned forward.

"That file doesn't paint a very flattering picture," Ben said.

The prisoner said nothing.

"We're going to be spending quite a lot of time together, and I can tell you that it will make both our lives a lot easier if you cooperate," Ben said.

The prisoner wouldn't look at Ben. He kept his face down, staring at his hands. That's when Ben noticed the rigidness of the man's fingers. They were swollen and crooked.

"If you give me something now, I might be able to do something about your hands. Maybe a little extra pain reliever? Hmm? How does that sound?" Ben asked.

"Pain?"

"Pain reliever. For your hands. It looks like pretty bad arthritis."

The prisoner looked up, his eyes shielded from the ragged strands of hair. He leaned forward.

"There is nothing on this planet that can numb me after the things I've done," the prisoner said.

Ben leaned back into his chair. He pulled the Snickers bar from his pocket and took a bite.

"Well," Ben said, trying to talk and chew at the same time. "It could be a long night for the both of us, Mike."

45

SIX MONTHS BEFORE THE EMP
BLAST

*D*r. Wyatt's knee bounced nervously under the desk. The Senate committee would be entering any minute. He kept glancing around, his gaze never staying on one item for too long. The building itself was simple, yet grandiose. It had the stale scent of wood, but the overwhelming sense of power.

His mouth felt dry. He reached for the glass of water, and the condensation rolled down the glass and onto his tie. He drank too fast and coughed, spilling some of the water on the files on the desk.

"Damn it," he said.

The senators entered and took their places while Dr. Wyatt brushed the water off the file with a napkin. Once the senators had taken their seats, the sergeant at arms called everyone to attention.

"Ladies and gentlemen, the Vice President of the United States of America," he said.

Dr. Wyatt shot out of his chair quicker than the rest of the building. The vice president took his spot at the center of the table, and once he was seated, everyone else sat down.

The vice president smacked the gavel on the desk, calling everyone to order.

"Today's hearing will be discussing the budgetary needs of the nation's main utility functions. We will hear from one of the EPA's representatives and the results of his research. Dr. Wyatt, you have the floor," the vice president said.

Dr. Wyatt took a breath and leaned into the microphone. Feedback squealed, and the entire room covered their ears. Dr. Wyatt flushed red.

"Thank you, Mr. Vice President," Wyatt said. "Senators and guests, I have spent the past eight months reviewing our nation's security measures for our basic utility functions, and the results that I've found are disturbing."

Dr. Wyatt was able to save his notes from the water spill, and he flipped to the first page.

"We'll start with our water utilities for the eastern hub of the country. As you can see on page two ther—"

"Dr. Wyatt, this committee has not received a copy of your research," the vice president said.

"Oh, I uh… I thought I had my assistant—"

"Your assistant did not provide us with any of the information prior to this meeting."

Dr. Wyatt loosened the collar around his neck. He felt hot, uncomfortable. All eyes were on him, waiting for an explanation. When it didn't come, the vice president let out a sigh, looking frustrated.

"Dr. Wyatt, the purpose of this committee is to assess our nation's utility needs, not to waste the time and resources of our taxpayers by coming unprepared."

"Of course, Mr. Vice President. That's not what I was attempting to do."

"I move we adjourn here and reconvene at a later time when Dr. Wyatt has the courtesy to provide us with the data he allegedly collected over the past eight months."

Just before the vice president reached for his gavel, Dr. Wyatt grabbed the microphone.

"Mr. Vice President, putting this meeting off would be detrimental to national security."

The room went into a quiet murmur. Senators, political aids, and members of the press whispered to their neighbors.

"Dr. Wyatt, it's unwise to casually mention the threat of national security in today's climate in a forum such as this," the vice president said.

Dr. Wyatt closed the report in front of him. He knew whatever he said next wouldn't just have an effect on his career but on the entire country as well.

"Our entire national utility infrastructure is at risk. Power and water utilities are completely exposed, and if we don't invest in the resources necessary to protect them, then this country will be sent back to the Stone Age," Dr. Wyatt said.

"Congress has passed laws to help strengthen our national security and assess all threats to utilities and develop countermeasures to ensure the safety of our nation's people," the vice president responded.

"If you're referring to the Homeland Security Presidential Directives, then I'm sorry to say those measures are nowhere near the level of preparedness that we need. It will only take the demolition of nine power substations around the country and we would be without power for months, possibly over a year, and that's not even taking into consideration the probability of an EMP attack."

"There isn't a known EMP device powerful enough to take out our nation's power grid, Dr. Wyatt."

"It doesn't just have to do with the size or range of the device; you also have to take into consideration the placement of detonation. If an EMP bomb was detonated in the atmosphere over the Midwest, the effects of the blast would be felt around the entire country."

The vice president started to laugh.

"Doctor, what you're proposing is a missile launch over US soil. If such a missile was launched, our air defense systems would be able to handle it."

"Not if the launch happened internally."

The vice president's expression turned from dismissive to impatient. He gripped the microphone on the desk and moved in close.

"Dr. Wyatt, your tone is neither amusing nor welcome. The idea of a missile launching on US soil against its own citizens isn't just preposterous, it's treasonous," the vice president said.

"If we don't prepare for all possible scenarios, then this country will be sent back to the days of horse-drawn carriages and steam engines."

Dr. Wyatt's chest was heaving as he tried to catch his breath from the anger welling up inside. The press snapped a few pictures before the vice president finally spoke.

"This hearing is in recess until Dr. Wyatt can give us the documented facts of his allegations and present them in a more professional manner."

The vice president slammed the gavel on the table, ending the session. Dr. Wyatt's eyes closed when he heard that sound. However long this "recess" was going to last was time he knew the country couldn't afford. Every minute that ticked by was one less to help prepare.

A few of the reporters came up to him, barking questions, but he didn't hear what they said. The only sound left was the ringing of the gavel still lingering in his ears.

When the cleaning crew came in, he was asked to leave. He didn't want to, though. He knew the world outside would call him eccentric, or a fearmonger, trying to panic the American people.

Outside, the Capitol building was buzzing with tourists running around snapping pictures on the Capitol steps. He walked around to the National Mall, and he could see the Washington Monument protruding into the sky. Just beyond that, the lights were turning on in the Lincoln Memorial.

The construction of those buildings was a testament to the human spirit, the will to go on; it renewed his strength to keep pushing. The men who made those monuments were the embodiment of this nation's endurance, of its reason.

It was hard for him to imagine a world where that voice of reason was snuffed out by the fear and hypocrisy of politicians. Whatever fate awaited him after today's events wouldn't be as bad as that to come if men like the vice president remained in power.

"I was wondering when you'd come out of there."

Dr. Wyatt turned around. Walking toward him was a tall, well-dressed man. The cut of his suit suggested wealth, but the manner in which he wore it gave him an air of power.

"I'm sorry. Can I help you?" Dr. Wyatt asked.

"I hope so. My name's Bram Thorn."

"What can I do for you, Mr. Thorn?"

"Please, call me Bram."

"Okay, what can I do for you, Bram?"

"Those comments you made in the Senate hearing today were bold, but I don't think you got your point across."

"Those hearings were closed to the general public. The only people allowed to attend were government officials and the press, so which one are you?"

"I'm like you, Dr. Wyatt. A kindred spirit in trying to bring awareness to our nation's weaknesses."

"Well, in that case it looks like you're the only friend I have right now."

"Then perhaps you could give your friend a few minutes of your time."

* * *

Bram's office had the same opulence as the car that drove Dr. Wyatt there. The office was small, but whatever it lacked in size it made up for in location. It was on the top floor of a high-rise in downtown Washington, DC. The view was spectacular. You could see some of DC's most notable sites: the Capitol building, Washington Monument, Lincoln Memorial, and the White House.

"One of the reasons I bought the place," Bram said.

"Did you know they stopped construction on the Washington Monument for over two decades? When they went to finish it, they had to use another type of marble. It's one of my favorite monuments," Dr. Wyatt said.

"*The storms of winter must blow and beat upon it... the lightnings of Heaven may scar and blacken it. An earthquake may shake its foundations... but the character which it commemorates and illustrates is secure.*"

"Who wrote that?"

"It was a speech written by Robert Winthrop at the dedication ceremony of the Washington Monument. Please, have a seat."

A group of chairs surrounded a small coffee table in the center of the office. As he set his bag down, a young man entered.

"Can I get you anything, Dr. Wyatt? Something to eat or drink?" the young man asked.

"No, I'm fine. Thank you."

"I'll take an iced tea, Trent," Bram said.

Trent left, leaving Bram and Dr. Wyatt alone.

"I'm glad you could make time for me today," Bram said.

"Well, you were a hard man to say no to, what with the phone calls, and e-mails, and the car that you sent to come and pick me up."

"I know what I want, Dr. Wyatt."

Trent came back with the iced tea, set it on a coaster on the table, then left.

"What is it that you do, Mr. Thorn, I-I mean, Bram?" Dr. Wyatt asked.

"A few years ago, I engineered a new piece of software that protected financial information. That success led me to expand into the development of hardware. Today my company is the fifth-largest microprocessor manufacturer in the country, and we continue to grow."

"I can see that."

Dr. Wyatt took another glance around the office. The place had a simple elegance to it. The office was neither intimidating nor excessive; it was powerfully quiet.

There were a few pictures on the walls. Most of them looked as though they were from the company's first few days. There were also a couple of ribbon-cutting ceremonies for factories, personal vacations around the world, and one with him in military fatigues surrounded by military personnel.

"What branch?" Dr. Wyatt asked.

"Marines."

"How long did you serve?"

Bram's mouth curved into a taut smile.

"Too long," Bram answered and then broke the tension with a small chuckle. "My back still isn't the same from lugging that pack around."

"Bram, I have to be honest with you. I'm not sure you want to be associated with me after yesterday's events. Aggravating the vice president like I did isn't the best career advancer. If you're looking for someone to help with producing funds, or getting an inside scoop on any appropriations in the technology industry, I'm afraid I won't be of much use."

"Dr. Wyatt, I didn't bring you here because of your tenure with working in government. Your talents far exceed any politician's. I read your research. It was very thorough."

"So, you're looking for a consultant?"

"A partner."

"I'm afraid I don't understand."

"The hardware my company produces is useless without the utilities to power it. If the country's grid goes down, so does my business."

"Mr. Thorn, I feel I must tell you that even with the small chance that the results of my research do get approved, it'll take years before the security measures are put into place, and by the time that happens there could be new threats that arise. Our legislative process is just too slow."

"And that's why I need your help. Our elected officials have done nothing but prolong the inevitable."

"And what is that?"

"Our fall from being a world power."

"Mr. Thorn, I'm afraid I can't help you with that."

Bram set the iced tea down on the table and reached for his

inside jacket pocket. He pulled out a card and handed it to Dr. Wyatt.

"If you change your mind," Bram said.

Dr. Wyatt took the card hesitantly. He shook Bram's hand and headed for the door.

"We could do a lot, Dr. Wyatt," Bram said.

Dr. Wyatt gave him a nod, and Trent escorted him out.

* * *

WHEN HE ARRIVED HOME, Dr. Wyatt flicked on the living room light and set his bag on the couch. His apartment was modest. The living room was filled to the brim with books and papers spread across every surface.

The research from his work on the national utilities was in the same spot he left it when he arrived home yesterday: the trash.

He rescued it from under an empty soup can and set the wrinkled and bound papers on his desk. He pressed the pages down, trying to smooth them out, then flipped through his work, remembering the countless hours spent collecting the data, analyzing it, and coming up with solutions that could solve the problems found.

"All for nothing," Dr. Wyatt said, dropping them back on the desk.

Maybe Bram was right. The politicians were the root of the problem. There wasn't any place for knowledge or facts, not when favors and political pull overrode everything.

His fingers ran along the edges of Bram's business card in his pocket. He touched the corners, letting the paper dig into his skin. Finally, he pulled the card out and held it under the lamp on his desk, the gold letters shining in the light.

Dr. Wyatt's eyes kept moving from the card to his phone. The conflict was burning inside him. He wanted to call but was afraid of what that meant. He'd spent his entire life working for the government in the belief that he was making a difference, but now, there seemed to be no difference at all.

His fingers found the keypad on the phone, and when he heard the ringing on the other line, he felt his pulse quicken. Within three rings he heard not the voice of Trent but Bram himself. It wasn't something he expected.

"Mr. Thorn? Yes, right, Bram... I was wondering if your offer was still on the table?... Great. When can we get started?"

46

DAY 20 AFTER THE BLACKOUT (THE CABIN)

*M*ike opened Freddy's door. His son was sound asleep, just as he'd been every morning when he checked on him. Mike liked watching him rest. Whatever peace Freddy had in those moments Mike felt a part of.

"Dad."

Kalen stood behind him in the hallway. He gave her a nod and closed Freddy's door. His daughter was up with him every morning for the past week. The scars and bruises on her face were almost healed. Aside from a few lumps and a little discoloring, you couldn't tell she was almost beaten to death.

"Nelson up?" Mike asked.

"Yeah, he's outside. You think Sam was able to fix the Jeep?"

"We'll find out soon enough."

This new bond the two of them shared was one he wished had never formed. Both of them were veterans of bloody conflicts. Each of them had inflicted pain, and they had received it in kind.

Nelson looked half asleep when they walked outside, but he was standing. The three of them headed down the dirt path that would take them to the highway. Once they were on the road, they'd follow it to the small town of Carrollton.

None of them made any unnecessary trips there over the past week. It was a place consumed with death. The biker gang responsible for his daughter's injuries was the same group that laid waste to everyone in the town that they came into contact with.

The grass fields that surrounded the town were filled with the people that used to live inside it. The bodies were too burned and charred to be identified by any records, so an unmarked stone was placed for each body. The stones formed a circle around the mass grave Mike and his group had dug.

The casualties of the gang's violence were made personal when they killed Mike's father, Ulysses, and two other members of his group. Ulysses sacrificed himself to save Mike and Kalen.

When they were digging the graves, Ulysses's body wasn't placed with the townspeople. Mike dug his father his own grave along with four others. Two were for the mother and father of three girls that Ulysses had saved from the brutality of the bikers' violence, one was for Tom, and the other was for Jung's wife.

Mike hadn't visited the grave since he put his father in the ground. He didn't need to. He saw his father every time he fell asleep. In his nightmares he relived the pain of watching his dad put a gun to his own head and squeeze the trigger.

Kalen was up front taking point, gun at the ready. Mike noticed that she still hadn't let her guard down. She always had a firearm within arm's reach, even when she was at the cabin.

Despite all of the pain Kalen went through, a part of Mike was glad she experienced it. She was sharper, more aware of everything she did.

That's how you had to be now. In a split second, everything could change, and your life, or the lives of the people you love, could be over.

Nelson hadn't said much since the events. Out of the whole group, his family suffered the least. Mike figured Nelson felt guilty about it. His wife had been kept safe by Sam, who was her security escort for her vice president position at the engineering firm she worked at, and Mike had managed to keep Nelson and his son safe on their travels from Pittsburgh to the cabin.

"How are you holding up?" Mike asked.

"I should be asking you that," Nelson said.

"Everything seems to be healing all right."

"What about Kalen? How's she doing?"

"As good as she can be."

"Mike, I don't know if this is a good time to bring it up, but when we get into town, you know that Sam's not the only person that's going to be there, right?"

"I know."

"We all know what Jung did was terrible, and we're with you on your decision, but if you jus—"

"I'm not changing my mind. And I shouldn't have to remind you that he didn't just put my family in danger, Nelson, he put yours as well. He let desperation and fear guide his choices, and I don't want that anywhere near my family. I wouldn't think you would either."

"What about Fay?"

Mike paused. He didn't agree with Fay staying with Jung. She was a valuable member of their group. He didn't want to lose her, but he wasn't going to budge on their disagreement with Jung's fate.

"It's her decision. She's still welcome to come with us, but I won't allow her to bring Jung," Mike said. "It's not up for discussion."

Mike continued down the path, catching up to Kalen, who'd stopped to wait for them. Nelson was quiet the rest of the way down.

* * *

SAM DROPPED the wrench to the ground, and it clanged against the concrete. The barrage of bullets that flew into the engine damaged the battery and the coolant tank of the Jeep. The tank was easy enough to repair, and luckily the mechanic's garage in town had some spare batteries.

After a few other adjustments with getting new tires and knocking out the cracked, bullet-ridden windshield, the Jeep was as good as it was going to get. The only test now was to see if it'd run.

It had been a lot of trial and error over the past week, trying to figure out which parts were working and which weren't. Sam grabbed the keys, hopped into the driver's seat, and put the key in the ignition. He waited a few moments before finally turning the engine over.

The Jeep cranked to life, and Sam leaned back and smiled. He threw the shifter in reverse to take it for a spin.

Sam pulled onto the road and shifted the Jeep into second gear. The clutch was a little touchy, but everything seemed to be working fine. He did a few laps up and down Main Street.

The sound of the engine caused Fay to come out of her motel room. Sam gave her a wave when he saw her, and she threw her hands up in the air and started clapping. Sam parked in one of the motel's spaces, and she came out to greet him.

"Feel like going for a ride?" Sam asked.

"Only if you can take me to a place with a shower."

"I hear Cincinnati is nice this time of year."

Fay's smile faded.

"You haven't talked to Mike about it, have you?" Sam said.

"He hasn't been in the talking mood lately."

"Well, he's on his way down this morning. You'll get your chance."

"Yeah."

Sam patted the seat, and Fay's smile came back. She hopped up in the passenger's side, and Sam tore off.

The two of them rode through the fields. Sam spun the tires and did a few donuts. Fay screamed and held on tight to the roll bar as the dirt and dust flew up around them. Sam finally brought the Jeep to a stop, and the two of them started to laugh.

"I think she'll run just fine," Sam said.

When Sam came back into town from the fields, he could see Mike, Nelson, and Kalen walking down Main Street toward the garage. Nelson and Kalen spun around and sprinted toward him when they heard the Jeep's engine.

"You got it running!" Nelson shouted.

"You say that like it's a surprise," Sam said.

"Good work, Sam," Mike said. "How's the fuel situation looking?"

"We should be okay. The garage had enough fuel left in spare tanks to fill up the bikes and the Jeep."

"We should be able to fit the girls in the Jeep along with Sean and Freddy. The rest of us will have to ride the bikes. Nelson, I suggest you start practicing now."

"Right," Nelson said.

"C'mon, I'll give you a few pointers," Sam said.

Nelson and Sam headed off to one of the old Harleys at the end of the row. Kalen followed.

"Where are you going?" Mike asked.

"If I ride, there'll be more room for supplies in the Jeep," Kalen said.

Mike and Fay were left alone.

"How are you healing up?" Fay asked.

"I'm good."

Mike answered quickly. His tone came out harsher than he intended it to be. He knew Fay's heart was in the right place staying with Jung, but that wasn't going to change what happened.

"You should come with us," Mike said.

"What about Jung?"

"What about him?"

"He's not doing very well."

"He's not my responsibility."

"The man I met at the airport wouldn't have thought that. If he had the ability to save someone, he did."

"I don't want that anymore."

Mike joined Sam, Nelson, and Kalen by the Harleys, leaving Fay alone.

* * *

THE SHADES WERE BARELY CRACKED, letting in a few rays of light. Jung sat on the edge of the bed, staring into the corner. His kids were still asleep.

He liked it when they slept. He didn't have to think about them or worry about them needing anything. They were so still. A part of him wished they could sleep forever. He didn't want them to see the world they lived in anymore.

Jung reached into his pocket, pulling out his prayer beads. He rolled them between his fingertips, feeling the smooth wood on his skin. He wasn't sure why he still had them. Whatever God he prayed to stopped listening.

He shoved the beads back into his pocket and paced the room. He was always restless. He hadn't slept or eaten anything in days; that need had vanished. The only thing he wanted to do now was waste away. He wanted to drift off as his children did every night, but he never wanted to wake up.

Those terrifying moments when he did drift off to sleep, he would be holding his wife's lifeless body in his hands, begging for her to come back.

There was no escaping what happened. It haunted him while he dreamed, and it tortured him while he was awake.

Jung bent down slowly, picking up a nearly empty bottle of liquor. That was the one thing he couldn't get enough of. Whatever he could do to numb himself he indulged in.

He did have some pills he managed to steal from the pharmacy, but Fay found them and tossed them down the drain. She'd come by every day to check on him and the kids.

The thought of someone else taking care of his children used to be such a ludicrous idea, but now he was glad someone was there to make sure his children were safe, although he wasn't sure how much longer that was going to last.

He knew that Mike and the rest of the group were planning to head to Cincinnati soon. A week ago he would have been going with them, but not now.

Jung thought back to their first meeting at the airport. He remembered the talks the two of them had about family, and keeping faith.

Mike didn't have to help him, but he did. Mike opened up his home, his supplies, and his protection to Jung's family, and he repaid Mike by spitting in his face.

The need to protect his own family blinded him to everything else. The moment he tied Mike's family up at gunpoint, along with the rest of the group, leaving them to die at the hands of the bikers, was the point of no return.

There wasn't a doubt in Jung's mind that Mike wanted to kill him. He wasn't sure what was stopping him, but he wished Mike would come and finish the job. Maybe that was his punishment though, a fate worse than death: to live with the guilt and shame of losing his faith.

The sound of the Jeep's engine outside snapped him out of the stupor. He kept the bottle of liquor in his hand as he walked to the window. He pulled back the curtain slightly and peeked down into the motel's parking lot. He could see Sam, Nelson, and Kalen by the bikes. Fay and Mike were talking by the Jeep.

If the Jeep was working, they'd be leaving any day now. He drew the curtain back and set the liquor bottle on the carpet.

* * *

THE GRAVE MARKER rose from the earth like a lump, nestled between two trees. The branches provided good shade. Billy and his family decided to lay Ken to rest here, next to his hunting spot, where he started his day every morning.

Billy had visited the grave every day since his father was buried. He never set out to start his morning hunts there, but each time he began walking into the forest, his feet led him there with a mind of their own.

His mother and younger brother still hadn't forgiven him for what he did. Every time he tried to explain himself, he would be greeted with the same disgusted look. He just stopped trying after a few days.

He couldn't force them to listen to him. Deep down he knew they knew what kind of man his father was. If Billy hadn't done something to stop him, more people would have been hurt.

The sound of a gunshot would wake him each night. It was never real, but he couldn't stop the dreams from coming. Each time he closed his eyes and laid his head to rest, he would see the bullet he fired from his own gun flying through his father's chest.

The dreams never ended with his father dying though. Screams of betrayal and hate flew from the mouths of his mother and brother. Then he would wake up with a cold sweat covering his body, shaking.

Billy wasn't sure how long the nightmares would last. Maybe it was something that would always be there, hanging over his head.

The rest of the morning was spent hunting game. He enjoyed being out in the woods now, more than he did before his father died. Whenever he went hunting with his dad, it felt malicious, void of anything good.

Now, he felt a purpose to it. The skills he learned were put into practice to provide food for his family. He no longer felt the pang of guilt every time he sent a bullet through a bird, squirrel, or deer.

After nabbing two turkeys, Billy called it a day. He was on his way back to the farm when he bumped into Joey, who had a string of squirrels and rabbits on his belt.

Joey hadn't said a word to him since they buried their father. In fact, the two had barely seen each other. Neither of them wanted to discuss what their minds were begging to say.

"Nice haul," Billy said.

Joey had his gun over his shoulder. He said nothing. He brushed past Billy and kept walking.

That's how their relationship was now. Whatever brotherly bonds the two of them had had ended with their father's last breaths.

"Hey, we need to talk," Billy said.

"No, we don't."

Billy grabbed Joey's shoulder and spun him around.

"Yes, we do," Billy said.

"What's there to talk about? You want to tell me what it was like to kill Dad? You want me to forgive you? I'll never forgive you. I hate you. I HATE YOU!"

Joey squirmed free from Billy's grip and ran. Joey wove in and out of the trees until Billy couldn't see him anymore.

The last bit of hope started to dissipate out of him. His brother wasn't going to forgive him. That hate would burn in him for a long time. The only thing Billy wasn't sure of was if he'd still be alive when his brother's hate finally burned out.

* * *

THE FRONT DOOR was open when Billy made it back to the farm, and the house was empty. He walked out back and could see his mother coming from the barn with the pelts from the rabbits and squirrels Joey brought back.

Beth's hands and apron were bloody. She looked older than she did before, rougher. The small hunch she had seemed more prominent. It was as if she was retreating within herself.

"Joey still back there?" Billy asked.

His mom didn't answer. She didn't even look at him. A few minutes later Joey appeared, heading in his direction with the meat from his game, following their mother's example in silence.

Billy spent the next hour cleaning the turkeys. When he walked back into the kitchen, his mother was canning the squirrel meat. He dropped the cuts on the counter. Beth picked them up and threw them in the garbage.

"Hey!" Billy said.

Beth slammed the knife into the counter. The force of the blow caused Billy to pause before reaching for the meat.

"It's a waste if we don't eat it," Billy said.

"We don't eat anything you bring in this house," Beth said.

Billy stood frozen, half bent reaching for the turkey in the trash, half watching the knife gripped tightly in his mother's hand. Her tone was low. It wasn't a statement. It was a threat.

"Mom, I—"

"Don't."

There wasn't anything he could say, or do, to get his family back. The trust was broken.

"I'm sorry," Billy said.

Billy left his mother in the kitchen and walked upstairs to his room. He passed his brother's room, and the door was cracked. Quiet sobs escaped through the sliver of an opening, and Billy stopped. He leaned in close to listen and peer inside.

Joey was on the edge of his bed, his face in his hands. He looked up when Billy entered, his face red.

"Get out!" Joey screamed.

"Joey."

"Get OUT!"

Joey jumped off the bed and shoved Billy out of his room, slamming the door in his face. Billy stood in the hallway, the door inches from his nose. He gently rested his forehead on the cool wood of the door panel and let out a slow breath.

Billy went back to his room and collapsed onto his bed. The pain of his family was weighing on him.

Under those layers of hate, he knew there was still a foundation of love. If he could hold onto that, he might be able to get his family back.

* * *

ANNE THREW the last of the medical supplies into the bag. She wanted to bring as many of the modern amenities they had with them as possible. As optimistic as she was about Cincinnati having everything they hoped it would, she still wanted to be ready if it didn't.

She lugged the bag up the basement stairs and stacked it on the growing pile of supplies everyone had packed for the journey.

"Anything else we need to grab?" Katie asked, walking down the hallway toward the living room.

"No, I think we're all set," Anne said.

"The boys are ready."

"Good."

Katie sat down on one of the chairs in the living room. Anne repositioned some of the gear.

"Do you think it'll be today?" Katie asked.

"Well, Sam said he'd be done with the Jeep by today, so I guess we'll know when Mike gets back."

"What if Cincinnati isn't what we think it is? What if it's just as bad as everywhere else? The broadcasts we heard could just be loops of old recordings."

"That's a lot of trouble to go through for a prank."

"But what if—"

"Katie, we'll be fine."

"You're right. I'm sorry."

"Why don't you get breakfast ready for the boys. I'll go and grab them."

Katie nodded and headed for the kitchen. Anne noticed that she had been hesitant about going to Cincinnati. She figured it was because of what happened in Pittsburgh. The "relief" center Katie was stuck in didn't hold up to its name.

Anne had her doubts too though, after hearing the stories of what went on in Pittsburgh and seeing firsthand what happened here. A part of her thought it was too good to be true, but there was another part that desperately wanted to believe. Both were dangerous.

Freddy and Sean were playing on the floor when she entered Freddy's room. She knocked on the door and the two boys looked up, realizing she was watching them.

"You boys hungry?" Anne asked.

"Yes!" both of them answered at the same time.

"Sean, your mom is getting breakfast started. Why don't you two go and help her?"

Freddy and Sean tore out of the room past her and down the hallway. Anne stayed in the doorway of Freddy's room, listening to the sounds coming from the kitchen.

It'd been a long week, and it was starting to wear her down. She'd exhausted a lot of energy nursing Mike and Kalen back to health, and it wasn't just the physical demands but the emotional stressors too.

Her husband and daughter had been beaten bloody, within an inch of their lives; it wasn't an easy thing to see. She made sure Freddy didn't have to be witness to it. She kept him out of their rooms for the first few days, giving them time to rest.

Anne wasn't worried about Mike, but she was concerned about Kalen. Her daughter had been through a lot, and it changed her. The girl she'd known was gone. The person that worried about boys and school and getting her own car had vanished, hardened by the harsh realities of the world around her.

"Mrs. Grant?"

"Mary, you scared me," Anne said, laughing a bit. "What is it, sweetheart?"

"I know we're leaving tomorrow, and everyone's busy getting ready, but I wanted to take my sisters down to visit our parents' graves. Give us one last chance to say goodbye."

"Of course. Let me finish up here, and we'll head down together."

"Thank you."

Mary disappeared into Kalen's room, and Anne listened to the boys' laughter coming from the kitchen. That sound kept her going. Whatever burdens she felt lifted with the voices echoing through the cabin.

* * *

ERIN SEEMED oblivious to the whole thing. Nancy wouldn't stop crying, but Mary felt an eerie calm about her.

The two headstones were close together. Kalen helped Mary carve her parents' names in with a knife. It looked crude, but Mary refused to let the graves go unmarked.

"Nance, go and pick some flowers. Take Erin with you," Mary said.

Nancy wiped her eyes and nose with her forearm and grabbed Erin's hand. There was a patch of wildflowers a little deeper into the fields, and the two girls trotted off together.

Mary was left alone with her parents, or at least what was left of them. She couldn't pick her father's body out of the other burned victims, so the grave next to her mother's was empty.

Her mother had been alone her last days on this earth. She was beaten and raped with the knowledge that her husband was dead and no information as to whether her daughters were still alive.

Mary thought back to all of the times she bickered with her mom, arguing over petty things like what she wore, or not getting the new phone she wanted. She could remember every hurtful thing she screamed at her.

Now the one thing she wanted more than anything, she would never get. Her father would never tell her he loved her again. Her mother wouldn't be there to hold her and stroke her hair when she was having a bad day. All of that was buried now.

"I love you," Mary said.

The words left her reflexively. She tried saying the phrase as she used to say it before she would go to bed at night, when her parents would come and tuck her in. But when she said the words now, they sounded different. There wouldn't be another time in her life where she would be in this position again, to say goodbye. There was a finality underlined in the weight of those words.

Erin came back, struggling to push her way through the tall grass with Nancy guiding her to ensure that she made it through okay.

She had a bundle of flowers in her arms and held them up for Mary to see.

"They're very pretty, Erin," Mary said.

Erin smiled and placed some of them on their father's grave, while the rest were left on their mother's.

Nancy's eyes were still red, but she wasn't crying anymore. Mary wrapped her up in her arms, and Nancy reciprocated. The two of them watched Erin bounce around the two pieces of stone, running her small, chubby fingers over the names of their parents carved on the rocks.

* * *

It took a few tries, but Nelson and Kalen finally managed to ride the length of Main Street back and forth twice on the motorcycles. They pulled into the parking lot and shut the engines off.

"How'd it feel?" Mike asked.

"I don't know why I ever thought of asking for a car. You can get me a motorcycle for Christmas this year," Kalen said.

"Pretty soon you'll have to get your first ink," Fay said.

"Um, no," Anne replied.

"I ate a few bugs, but other than that it was all right," Nelson added.

"It's good protein," Sam said.

Mary laughed, and Erin giggled. Even Nancy cracked a smile.

"Dad," Kalen said.

Jung was standing in the courtyard of the motel behind them, next to the fountain, half looking at them and half looking at the ground.

The whole group tensed up. Almost every person Jung tied up and left for dead was standing in front of him. None of them had seen him since that day, and none of them wanted to. Mike started to walk toward him, but Anne grabbed his arm, stopping him.

"I won't kill him," Mike said.

Jung didn't make eye contact with Mike until he was right in front of him, and even then it was minimal.

"What do you want?" Mike asked.

Jung fidgeted nervously. His hands kept wandering over his body, unsure of what to do. His eyes stayed aimed at the ground.

"Mike, I... I..."

Jung's voice was trembling. The words came out jumbled and

quiet. Jung was swaying back and forth. Mike could smell the booze on him.

"I'm sorry, Mike," Jung said.

"You remember what you told me on the road from the airport to the cabin?" Mike asked.

"I was only trying to keep my family safe."

"And what about my family? What about Nelson's family? Did you keep them safe? Did you think about that when you pointed a gun at my wife and children?"

Mike's forehead was almost touching Jung's, whose head was still bowed in submission. Mike wanted to break him. He wanted to reach for the pistol at his side and put that man out of his misery for good. It wouldn't be a loss. If anything the world would have one less nuisance.

The group behind Mike crept closer, trying to hear what was being said and who was speaking. Finally they were right behind him. The only one of them that separated from the group was Fay.

"Whatever you think you're entitled to, whatever rights you think you have, they don't exist anymore. Not for you," Mike said.

"It doesn't have to be this way," Fay said.

"Yes, it does."

Mike was done. He wasn't going to waste any more time on the subject. He turned to go, and the rest of the group followed. One by one they all turned their backs on Jung, just as he did to them, but Kalen stayed behind. When Mike looked back, she was visibly shaking. He could see her hands tighten around the rifle.

"Kalen," Mike said.

"You're not a man," Kalen said, her eyes locked on Jung. "You think you can just try and hurt our family and then we forgive you? Is that what you pray to your God about? Forgiveness?"

"Kalen, c'mon," Mike said.

"You don't get forgiveness. You'll never get it," Kalen said.

When Kalen walked away, Jung broke down. The dam of tears he held back gave way. Whatever resolve he had left was gone. He collapsed in a heaped mess, and only Fay was left to help him up.

Mike didn't want her to stay. Fay wasn't just a valuable member of their group, she had become a member of his family. She made her choice though, and Mike wasn't going to be able to change her mind. Each of them had to live with the repercussions of their actions.

47

SIX MONTHS AFTER THE EMP BLAST

$\mathcal{A}$ gent Ben Sullivan flipped through the file in his hands. The evidence, the confession, it was all there, wrapped up in a bow.

"It doesn't fit," Ben said.

His partner, Mitch Hamon, leaned back in his chair, his large hands resting on his equally large stomach. Mitch had just been paired with Ben for the investigation, but the old man wasn't much help.

"You're overthinking it, Sullivan," Mitch said. "People went nuts when the lights went out, and this guy was at the center of everything. It's all there."

"So this guy organizes an EMP missile launch, a coup against the government, and then decides to blow everything up? It doesn't make sense."

"Like I said, people went nuts."

"He had enough supplies and manpower to pretty much do whatever he wanted. You really think he'd just give it all up like that?"

"People. Went. Nuts."

Ben brushed Mitch off. Of all the things they heard about from across the country during the blackout, this one took the cake.

"Agent Sullivan?"

Ben looked up from the file. One of the office assistants had opened the door to their office.

"Yes?" Ben asked.

"I have a man out here asking to speak with you."

"Tell him I'm busy."

"He says he has information about the Cincinnati case."

Ben shot a glance at Mitch.

"People went nuts, huh?" Ben asked.

The agency was packed. There were people from all around the country. Allegations and reports of what people did to each other ranged from murder to theft. The dust was still clearing, but the majority of the country was back on its feet.

Power started to come back on in most major cities two months ago. Once that happened and communication channels opened back up, people started to calm down.

Ben was selected to head the task force to ensure that all claims of serious illegal activity during the time of the blackout were heard.

It wasn't a job anyone wanted. It was a slew of hearsay and "he said, she said." People just kept passing the blame and pointing fingers elsewhere for misdirection.

Ben hadn't run across a single solid case until this guy walked in and turned himself in voluntarily. He said he was responsible for everything. The planning of the EMP missile launch, the organized coup in Cincinnati, murder, treason—all were admitted by him in a written statement.

The guy even had knowledge about the detailed inner workings of how it went on. He gave them names, locations, anything and everything that would tie him to the crime. The only thing that didn't match up was the guy's profile before the lights went out.

Ben requested this information a few days ago, and it finally arrived today. The guy had no priors, no criminal history of any kind. The two pieces of the guy's life were total contradictions.

The assistant brought Ben and Mitch into a private room set aside for one-on-ones that required a quiet place to talk, away from the chaos of the main floor.

Inside was an older man dressed in an old tweed jacket and a bow tie. The assistant left, and Ben extended his hand, which the old man took hesitantly.

"I'm Agent Sullivan. This is my partner, Agent Hamon. You told one of our assistants that you had information on a suspect we're holding?"

"Yes, I believe I can help."

"Well, what can you tell us?"

The old man's fingers fumbled nervously over each other. His eyes roamed the floor, as if there were words written down there that could help him speak. He paced the office for a moment, not saying anything.

"Listen, pal," Mitch said. "If you've got something that can help us, let's get on with it. We have other things we need to get done."

"I'm sure you think you have an open-and-shut case."

"Yeah, the guy confessed to everything," Mitch said.

"What do you know?" Ben asked.

"I know that whatever facts you heard were based on half-truths."

"Do you know the man in custody?" Ben asked.

"Yes."

"What do you know that he's not telling us?"

"Everything."

Ben rubbed his eyes. The long nights and cryptic messages of what was true and what was false were starting to weigh on him.

"Then why don't you tell us, Dr. Wyatt, exactly what you know," Ben said.

Dr. Wyatt took a seat in the corner of the room, where the lights were low and his face was cast in shadows.

"I want to see him first," Dr. Wyatt said.

* * *

BEN AND MITCH went back to their office, leaving Dr. Wyatt alone in the waiting room.

"The guy's lying," Mitch said.

Ben pulled open a drawer of one of the filing cabinets. He flipped through the files, searching for a document he remembered seeing a while back.

"Ben, you can't let that guy see our suspect," Mitch said.

"Where's the file on utilities hearing?" Ben asked.

"What?"

"We had the minutes to a utilities hearing in Congress that happened over a year ago. We received the file from a senator when we first started getting things up and running. I know we have it somewhere."

Ben went through every drawer and file but couldn't find it. He slammed the last drawer shut and fell back into his chair.

Mitch walked over to his desk and opened the bottom drawer.

He pulled out a stack of papers and dropped it in front of Ben. Ben flipped through the pages, making sure they were from the meeting he was looking for.

"I still don't think we should let him see him," Mitch said.

Ben ran his finger along the text on the pieces of paper. He started reading aloud.

"Dr. Wyatt suggested that the United States was susceptible to an open attack on its power and water facilities."

"You think the doctor was in on it?" Mitch asked.

"No photos of our guy are going to be sent out to the public until tomorrow. The only people that know we're holding him are here in this building. Let's show the doctor a lineup. See if he can point our guy out. That'll at least tell us if he has a connection with him."

* * *

DR. WYATT SAT on the other side of the one-way glass, waiting for the suspects to walk in. Ben told him to identify the man he believed they had in custody.

A group of ten individuals walked in, all similar in height, ethnicity, and appearance, each with a number in front of them. Dr. Wyatt took a few moments examining the group before speaking.

"Number eight," Dr. Wyatt said.

Ben shot Mitch a look and then sent everyone except the man Wyatt identified out the door.

"You sure?" Ben asked.

"Yes. It took me a minute because of the facial hair, but that's him."

"Okay, then. You know him. Now you're going to tell us about him."

"I was a part of the original planning of the attack. I'm sure you've read the articles that were written in regards to my meeting with the Senate committee before the blast happened. I was approached by a man afterwards who was looking for a partner."

"This partner was the man that planned the attacks? And was responsible for what happened in Cincinnati?" Ben asked.

"Yes, he was the man who tried to purge the country of everyone who wasn't prepared. That's what he wanted, for people to hurt," Dr. Wyatt said.

Mitch threw his arms up in the air.

"I told you, Sullivan. Put a bow on it. This is done. We've got his partner in custody," Mitch said.

"No, I'm afraid it's not," Dr. Wyatt said.

Mitch's arms fell to his side, deflated.

"What do you mean?" Ben asked.

"The man I identified just now had nothing to do with the EMP attack, or the coup to overthrow the government," Dr. Wyatt said.

"Then why would he confess? Why would he turn himself in and say he did all of these things that he had nothing to do with?" Ben asked.

"Penance, I suppose."

"So why are you here?"

"To help him, as he helped me."

"Do you have any proof? Anything that can back up what you're telling me? Because you're going to have to give us something to overturn the written confession we have."

"No, I'm afraid I don't, but if you could just let me speak to him, have a few minutes alone—"

"Oh, no," Mitch said. "There's no way in hell you're seeing our guy alone."

The blinds to the waiting room were closed, blocking them from the rest of the office. Ben could still hear the bustle of people outside, their voices talking about the weekend, what they were going to do that night.

All of it was still pretty surreal to him. He couldn't imagine what some of the people in this very office did to stay alive during the outage. The worst of human nature seemed to turn on when the power went off.

Whatever really happened between people during the blackout was between them. He knew that most cases would get thrown out because there just wasn't enough evidence.

Ben had to pull something tangible out of this mayhem. He needed to prove to himself and the rest of the country that what people did wasn't okay. He wanted to show that the line of right and wrong was a very clear one, and those that tried to cross it would be brought to justice.

"There might be one piece of evidence that I could give you, but I'm not sure if it still exists," Dr. Wyatt said.

"What is it?" Ben asked.

"I kept a journal, detailing the plans of the attack and the rebuilding process we wanted to go through."

"Who has it?"

Dr. Wyatt looked back through the one-way glass at the suspect standing alone in the room.

"Mike Grant," Dr. Wyatt said.

48

DAY 21 (CINCINNATI)

*T*he vibrations from the bike made Mike think his still-healing ribs would crack back in half.

After they passed through Carrollton, he found himself struggling not to turn around. Fay wasn't outside when they drove through. He even made a point to slow down, scanning every piece of sidewalk up and down the street, but she was nowhere to be seen.

A shot of guilt ran through him, but it was only for a moment. Once it passed, it felt as though it had never happened at all.

Mike led the caravan of vintage Harleys and the Jeep. Sam, Nelson, and Kalen were on their own motorcycles, while Anne, Katie, Sam, Sean, Mary, Nancy, and Erin were packed in the Jeep along with whatever supplies and weapons they could fit with them.

Mike's hands felt as if they had pieces of steel wedged into them, and each time he tried bending them, the steel would crack. He had to pull over a few times, turning the four-hour drive into six hours.

Most of the time when he pulled over, he would say it was for bathroom breaks, but Anne knew what was happening. She gave him some pain reliever between stops. Everyone else just figured it was for his injuries. No one knew about his hands except Anne.

The abandoned cars became more frequent the closer they moved to the city. When Mike saw the massive green signs telling them Cincinnati was ten miles out, Mike pulled everyone over.

He took a few seconds on the bike, focusing on stopping his hands from trembling before he approached the group.

Nelson walked with a slight waddle after getting off the bike. Katie laughed at him.

"Hey, I've been on that thing for almost six hours. Cut me some slack," Nelson said.

"How is everyone on fuel?" Mike asked.

"Jeep's looking okay. We have about a quarter tank," Anne said.

"I'm running low," Sam said.

"Me too," Kalen replied.

"Same," Nelson answered.

"I don't have much left either," Mike said. "We should still have enough to make it into the city, but if things go bad, I want Kalen to jump in the Jeep with Sam, and you guys head as fast and far as you can in the opposite direction. Nelson and I will hang back, try and buy you all some time."

"Whoa, what?" Katie asked.

"As much as we all want to believe this is the real deal, I want us to have an escape plan if things go south," Mike answered.

"But the radio signals. They kept coming in. This place wouldn't keep sending them if it wasn't safe, right?" Nelson asked.

"Hopefully, but we won't be the only ones that came across the signal, and we won't be the only ones who have wandered into Cincinnati," Mike said. "Everyone keep your eyes open."

Mike climbed back onto the Harley. The seat was a hard composite, and the metal grips didn't offer much comfort for his hands. In another time he would have loved to have a bike like this. He remembered when he was younger watching "Easy Rider" how much he wanted to ride across the country, going on adventures. Now, all he wanted to do was dump the bike he was riding in a scrap heap and watch it burn.

The group turned off onto the first exit they saw for Cincinnati and made their way into the city's streets.

Most of it was what Mike had expected. Storefront windows were smashed. Trash was everywhere. The road was so cluttered with cars Anne had to take the Jeep onto the sidewalk for a bit.

There was something off about the way the cars were left in the street. They were abandoned after the EMP blast, which he was sure of, but the cars seemed too organized. It was as though they were roadblocks.

Mike glanced down a few side streets on their way and could see that every road heading toward the center of the city had similar clusters of cars, but the crossroads were completely clear.

There also weren't any signs of people. They'd been riding for almost ten minutes, and Mike hadn't seen a single soul. The deeper they went into the city, the less disheveled it appeared to be.

Then Sam caught Mike's attention, pulling up right next to him and gesturing up to some of the windows in buildings above them.

It took Mike a minute to see them because they were fairly well hidden, but he noticed the slight movement in the windows.

Men with rifles were stationed in different buildings on the fifth floor, keeping a bead on them.

The road finally cleared out, and just before Mike could accelerate, four armored trucks converged around them, blocking any escape.

Soldiers got out of the vehicles with their guns pointed at Mike and the rest of his group. They moved in close. Mike put his hands in the air. The rest of the group followed suit.

One by one, the soldiers removed everyone's weapons. They were forced to get out of the Jeep and line up on the sidewalk, keeping their hands behind their heads.

One of the soldiers pulled Mike aside and patted him down.

"How'd you find us?" the soldier asked.

"We heard your message over the radio," Mike said.

The soldiers piled the guns and supplies they found in the Jeep into one of their trucks.

"I'll want those back," Mike said.

"Where'd you get the vehicles?" the soldier asked.

Mike didn't answer. He wasn't going to play twenty questions with someone who just had a gun to his head.

"What is this place?" Mike asked.

The soldier flashed a smile.

"Shelter from the storm," he said. "We'll collect your vehicles and any rations you have. All of your personal effects will be returned to you after the interview process."

"Interview?" Mike asked.

"Just to make sure you're... safe," the soldier said.

One of the armored trucks stayed with Mike's group, and they were escorted deeper into the city. The longer they walked, the further Mike's jaw dropped.

People were driving around in cars. Every person Mike saw walking on the streets looked clean and healthy and had the attitude of someone heading to work.

They finally stopped at a bank high-rise that was guarded by two soldiers. When the doors to the building opened, the first thing Mike felt was the cool rush of air hitting his face as he walked through the entrance.

"Oh my God," Kalen said.

All of the kids rushed to the large industrial fan sitting in the lobby, pushing each other out of the way, letting the air blow past their faces.

Mike stared up at the ceiling bulbs illuminating the depths of the offices and down the winding hallways.

"The power's on for the entire building?" Mike asked.

"We have everything functional in this building on the first floor except the A/C. We only have the capacity to run that at the hospital and living quarters. That's why we have the industrial fans here," the soldier answered.

"The hospital is up and running? With doctors?" Nelson asked.

"Yes."

Mike knew what everyone was thinking, because that's where his mind went despite trying to block it out. The doctors here could have saved Jung's wife.

"The interviews will happen on a one-on-one basis. Every person will be evaluated, and their value will be determined based on the interviewer's assessment," the soldier said.

"Their value?" Nelson asked.

"We have everyone keeping this place running based on their previous occupation. If you want to stay, you have to work. We don't have the luxury to keep loafers," the soldier explained.

"And what happens to those people that aren't useful?" Katie asked.

"They don't stay."

"What about kids?" Anne asked.

"Their value is based on their potential. If the interviewer determines that they could be of use once they turn sixteen, then they stay."

Mike watched Freddy smiling in front of the fan. His hair was blown back, and then he moved out of the way to make room for Sean and Kalen. Freddy just wouldn't stop giggling.

The soldier led them down the hall of the first floor and sent them into separate rooms, with the exception of the kids, whom Anne insisted on having one of the adults stay with.

The soldier brought Mike into a small office where a young man, barely into his twenties, sat behind a desk with a few sheets of paper. He gestured to the seat across from him.

"Please," the young man said.

Mike pulled the chair out and sat down, keeping his hands in his lap under the cover of the desk.

"My name is Paul," he said, extending his hand.

"Mike," he answered, not accepting the handshake.

Paul withdrew his hand, a sad smile spreading across his face. He leaned forward on the desk, attempting to draw Mike in.

"I can imagine it's been difficult out there. No power, no food, no water. But you don't have to be afraid anymore. The power is coming back on. We already have most of the city on our side. It's just a matter of time before we take all of it back," Paul said.

"On your side?" Mike asked. "What does that mean?"

"I'm just going to ask you a few questions, and we'll see how it goes, okay? So, where are you from?"

"Pittsburgh."

"Go Steelers!"

Paul's attempted enthusiasm didn't change Mike's expression. Paul brought his fist down from the air and rested his hand back on the table, returning to his list of questions.

"What's your birth date?"

"January 12, 1971."

"Married?"

"Yes."

"How long?"

"Twenty-five years."

"Has your spouse survived the blackout?"

Mike paused before answering.

"Yes."

Each time Mike responded, Paul would jot down notes and mark little checks along the sheets in his hands. Mike tried getting a look at what Paul was writing, but the print was too small for him to see.

"What was your occupation before the blackout?" Paul asked.

"Welder."

"And how long were you in that occupation?"

"Twenty-five years."

"You chose the girl, huh?"

"What?"

"You said you've been married for twenty-five years, and you've been a welder for the same amount of time. Based on your birthday, it sounds like you met your wife either in college or right after and then decided to stick around. You're from Pittsburgh, so you grabbed the first good-paying, steady job you could find to support you and your new wife."

"How many of these questions do I have to answer?"

Paul glanced down at his sheets of paper. He flipped through them, mouthing the numbers to himself.

"Looks like we have quite a bit more to get through," Paul said.

"What is this for?"

Paul set the pencil and clipboard on the desk. The pleasantry act dropped, and Mike saw the focus in Paul's eyes drilling into him.

"Do you know what this place is, Mike?" Paul asked.

"No."

"This is a chance for us to start over. A place for this country to rebuild, make us great again. You've seen what it's like out there. People are losing their minds. They're starving, dying, and killing each other over cans of food. We can bring them back from that."

Paul picked the clipboard and pencil back up. He flipped back to the page where he left off, and the smile returned to his face.

"So, what have you been doing since the blackout?" Paul asked.

* * *

THE QUESTIONS TOOK OVER AN HOUR. After they were done, Mike was shoved out the back door of the building and left in a fenced-in lot by himself.

One by one, the rest of his group joined him. Kalen was the next person out, followed by Nelson, Sam, Anne, Freddy, Mary, Erin, Nancy, and Katie.

"That was different," Nelson said.

Freddy ran up to Mike and wrapped his arms around his legs. Mike patted the top of his head.

"You okay, bud?" Mike asked.

"I didn't like it," Freddy answered.

"What happened in there?" Anne asked.

"They kept asking questions about you guys. Where we lived, my birthday, what I liked to do for fun."

"That doesn't sound too bad," Nelson said.

The rear door opened, and a man they hadn't seen before dressed in army fatigues entered. Judging by the way the men behind him were following, Mike guessed that he was someone important.

"Who's in charge?" he asked.

Everyone's eyes turned to Mike.

"You're with me. The rest of you will stay here."

The soldier's men grabbed Mike and pulled him back into the building.

Mike was dragged through the winding hallways, deeper into the building. He wasn't sure he'd be able to remember his way out. The journey finally ended outside a small office door.

One of the soldiers entered while the rest stayed with Mike in the hallway. Whoever was inside, Mike figured was important. The soldier stepped out and kept the door open.

"The colonel will see you now."

"Colonel?" Mike asked.

The office was completely empty with the exception of a desk, one filing cabinet, and a folded American flag in a case that sat on top of it. The colonel, clean-cut and shaven, sat behind the desk. Mike could see the finely pressed creases of the uniform.

"Have a seat," the colonel said without looking up from his work on the desk. "I'll be with you in a moment. You're dismissed, Blake."

"Yes, sir!"

Blake saluted, turned on his heel, and closed the door when he left. There was only one other chair in the room. Mike sat down and noticed the name "Col. Cadogan" embroidered on the front of his uniform. The colonel was scanning pages of a file.

"Those our answers?" Mike asked.

"Just yours."

Cadogan waited a few more minutes before finally snapping the file shut and stacking the papers neatly on the corner of the desk.

"You've been through it, Mr. Grant," Cadogan finally said.

"What do you want?"

"You know what all those questions told us?"

"What?"

"That you're dangerous."

Mike felt his body tense up. He caught himself reaching for the gun at his hip that he knew wasn't there.

"Dangerous to who?" Mike asked.

"To whoever you don't like, Mr. Grant."

"No, I'm only dangerous to anyone that threatens my family, Colonel."

"I can see that," Cadogan said. "During your questioning you said you heard our radio broadcasts, and that's how you knew where to find us."

"Yes."

"Other members of your group made a similar statement. Tell me, how did the radio survive the EMP blast?"

"A Faraday cage."

"And you came here on four motorcycles and a Jeep, correct?"

"That's right."

"Resourceful. Luckily for you, there are two things I admire in a man: honesty and ingenuity. You have both."

Cadogan rose from his chair and grabbed the case with the American flag folded tightly inside its triangular box. The colonel carried it gently.

"I received this flag when my youngest was brought back in a box from Iraq," Cadogan said.

"I'm sorry."

"I'm not. It was one of the proudest moments of my life. I wasn't going to get my son back, but I knew what he died for, and the way he died was honorable."

Cadogan set the flag down gingerly on his desk. His hands lingered on it for a moment before finally letting it be.

"People don't have that anymore, Mr. Grant," Cadogan said. "I'm hoping we can bring that back."

"And you think it can happen here?"

"Yes."

Mike shifted in his seat. He could still feel the pain in his ribs, the broken bones trying to mend, the punctured lung trying to heal. This place was uncomfortable to him, but then again, everything seemed uncomfortable these days.

"So what does that mean for my family?" Mike asked.

Cadogan gave a smile. He walked back behind his desk to the filing cabinet.

"You'll each have your own quarters, and will be assigned to a specific job that you will report to each day," Cadogan said.

"What are these jobs going to have us doing?"

"Each assignment for the members of your group is based on the evaluation of our interviewers and the answers to the questions that were asked of you. Sergeant Blake?"

The door to Cadogan's office opened, and Blake stepped back inside.

"Yes, sir?"

"Escort Mr. Grant back to his group and have them all report to their quarters for the evening. They'll begin their training in the morning."

Cadogan handed Blake the orders. When Mike turned to leave, Cadogan called out to him.

"Mr. Grant," Cadogan said. "Don't make me regret keeping you here."

* * *

WHEN MIKE MADE it back to his group, everyone had questions, but there wasn't much time for him to answer. The soldiers led them out of the fenced lot and back around to the front of the building.

They were brought to a hotel high-rise a few blocks from where they were interrogated. On the way there Mike noticed that not all of the buildings had guards, only the ones that looked occupied.

The guard at the hotel's entrance reviewed the papers, nodded, and then opened the doors for them.

The collective sigh of everyone that entered the building was followed by laughter and giggles from the kids.

"Air-conditioning!" Freddy yelled.

"Here are your room keys and numbers," Blake said.

Kalen snatched the card out of Blake's hand and made a beeline toward the stairs.

"I call first shower!" Kalen said.

Kalen ended up stopping herself before she got to the door and looked over at the elevator. She glanced back at Blake, who nodded.

"Those work, too," he said.

Freddy and Sean ran after her as the elevator doors opened, and the three of them disappeared behind closed doors with smiles still on their faces.

"Well, hopefully she'll leave enough hot water for the rest of us," Anne said.

"I wouldn't count on it," Mike replied.

"We'll be back here at zero six hundred to begin training. Meet me in the lobby," Blake said.

The hallways of the apartment complex were mostly empty. There was only one other individual Mike saw when walking to their room, and it was a guard.

Mike slid the key card in the door and pushed it open. It was a simple single-bed hotel room. He walked over to the window and looked outside. He could see a fire escape on the side of the building, but the stairs below the fourth floor were destroyed.

There was a light switch on the wall next to the entrance. Mike sat there for a moment, looking at it. He reached his hand out slowly and flipped the switch on. The lights from the lamps instantly brightened the room. Anne started laughing.

"Weren't sure if they'd work?" Anne asked.

"I'm still not sure if I believe it."

Anne grabbed his hand and started pulling him toward the bathroom.

"C'mon. Let's test the shower," she said.

* * *

It took a second for Mike to realize the buzzing was the alarm. That first moment when he turned it off, he thought he was back in Pittsburgh. Then reality set in as he rested his feet on the carpet of the hotel floor. He wasn't in Pittsburgh. He was in Cincinnati, and the stiffness in his hands brought back the wall he'd been keeping up for the last three weeks.

He gave Anne a kiss before waking her, and she climbed out of bed and opened the curtains. The sun had yet to join them.

Mike walked down the hall to Freddy and Kalen's room. He was given a key to their room, so he cracked the door open, checking to see if they were awake.

Kalen was up, already dressed, lacing her shoes.

"Hey, Dad," Kalen said.

"How'd you sleep?"

"Not as well as him."

She gave a half smile and nodded back to Freddy.

"Good luck getting him out of bed today," Kalen said.

"Thanks."

"I'll see you downstairs."

It took Mike twenty minutes just to get Freddy to sit upright, and another twenty minutes to finally remove him from the bed. By the time he made it downstairs, he was ten minutes late. There wasn't anyone else left except Blake, tapping his boot.

"I'm sorry. My son, he—"

"Save it," Blake said.

He pulled the two of them outside, and they headed deeper into the city. They stopped at a smaller building with a playground on the side.

"The boy will stay here. You can pick him up after your training is over," Blake said.

"What is this?" Mike asked.

Freddy hid behind Mike's legs.

"This is our school," Blake said.

"I want to go inside before I leave my son anywhere."

"We're already late."

"Then it won't make much of a difference if I take a few more minutes."

Mike grabbed Freddy's hand, and the two of them headed inside. It was a simple one-story building, a little older, but kept in good condition.

The "School of Young Minds" sign out front suggested it was some kind of gifted school before the blackout. Judging by the brick walls and intricate garden beds, Mike imagined it wouldn't have been something he could have afforded to send his son to.

Inside were the typical school hallways. Lockers and classroom doors were shut. Mike walked past a few of them, checking inside the windows.

Each room Mike passed was filled with kids. It looked as though the rooms were broken up by age groups. The farther Mike walked down the hallway, the younger the kids looked.

Finally, Mike saw Sean. The teacher inside noticed Mike and greeted him at the door.

"You must be new," she said.

"Yeah. This is my son Freddy," Mike said.

"Nice to meet you, Freddy. I'm Ms. Franklin."

Freddy took her hand timidly and then jumped behind Mike. He tugged on his dad's pants, and Mike bent down so Freddy could whisper in his ear.

"Do I have to stay here?" Freddy asked.

"Afraid so, bud."

Mike kissed Freddy's forehead and watched his son walk into the classroom and grab a seat next to Sean.

"He'll be fine," Ms. Franklin said.

"What time do they get out?"

"Today's your first day?"

"Yes."

"You'll be able to pick him up before the day's over. Good luck."

"Thanks."

When Mike walked back outside, he and Blake two-timed it through the streets until they made it to a city park. He could hear the gunshots beyond the trees.

"Where are we going?" Mike asked.

"To train."

When they made it through the walkway and past the trees, the park opened up into a massive field. Targets were set up with men and women practicing their marksmanship. Demonstrations of field-cleaning a rifle, hand-to-hand combat, and how to handle heavy artillery were set up along the edges of the field.

"Welcome to boot camp," Blake said.

"I don't understand."

"You were selected for security duty based on your evaluation with your interviewer. A couple other people from your group made this list too."

"Who else?"

"Sam and Kalen."

Mike's heart dropped. He brought his family here so they could be safe, not to put them in the line of fire.

"My daughter does something else," Mike said.

"No can do. All assignments are final. Here, your first stop is the range to assess your accuracy."

Mike was handed an AR-15 with a full clip of ammo. Blake kept a close watch on him the entire time. The targets were spread out in ten-yard intervals. The closest was ten yards, and the farthest was one hundred.

"You get three shots per target," Blake instructed.

Mike brought the scope up to his eyes. The round bull's-eye target fell between the crosshairs. He flipped the lever from spray to single shot.

He moved through each target fairly quickly. When he made it to the one-hundred-yard marker, he had a little trouble, but managed to hit one bull's-eye and got the other two close to the center.

"What's next?" Mike asked.

Blake made a few marks on his clipboard and nodded over to the hand-to-hand combat area.

The trainer was a tall, lean man with sweatpants and a shirt on. He was demonstrating a few disarming techniques during a knife fight.

After watching the instructor walk through the motions a few more times, they broke off into pairs. Mike's eyes kept finding Kalen, who was practicing with another woman. His lack of focus was causing his opponent to kill him every time.

"You two. Stop," the instructor said.

It took Mike a moment to realize who the instructor was talking to, until the instructor started walking over.

"You need to be more decisive. Any hesitation and your opponent kills you," he said, grabbing the knife from Mike's sparring partner.

The instructor poised himself for attack, and before Mike could do anything, he was on his back with the instructor's blade to his throat.

"You're slow, old man," the instructor said.

Mike brought his knee up to the instructor's stomach and rolled him over, struggling to get the knife from him.

Before Mike could grab the blade, the instructor answered with a right cross against Mike's jaw, almost knocking him out.

"You've still got spirit though," the instructor said, extending his hand and helping Mike up.

Kalen rushed over to help steady him, but Mike waved her off.

"I'm fine," Mike said.

"Dad, you're not fine. You need to rest."

"I said I'm fine."

He didn't mean for his tone to come out as harsh as it did, but he didn't want to appear weak. Not here.

"All right, everyone. Back to your partners," the instructor ordered.

The rest of the day seemed to go smoothly enough. There weren't any more combat or shooting exercises. Everything was about strategy and ensuring the unit of men and women you were with understood each other's roles.

They were dismissed shortly after lunch, and Mike, Sam, and Kalen all walked back together. It was the first time they'd really been able to talk since this morning.

"Where'd your mom go?" Mike asked.

"Hospital," Kalen said.

"What about everyone else?" Mike asked.

"Katie's doing administrative work at some office, Nelson's with maintenance, and Mary's at the hospital. The rest were under sixteen, so they're at the school," Sam replied.

"Let's grab Freddy on our way back," Mike said.

When they arrived at the school, the timid boy who didn't want to be left this morning was replaced by a disheartened boy who didn't want to leave.

"Can't we stay a little bit longer? Ms. Franklin is so cool!" Freddy shouted.

"Yeah, Mr. Grant. When my dad comes to get us, he can make sure he picks Freddy up too," Sean added.

"All right. You two be careful," Mike said.

"Yes! Thanks, Dad!" Freddy yelled, running back onto the playground with Sean.

"He seems to be adjusting well," Kalen said.

"Yeah," Mike replied.

"If they have any beginner combat lessons here, you might be able to find someone more your speed," Kalen said.

Kalen laughed, and Mike chased after her playfully. It was nice seeing his daughter smiling again. He hadn't heard her laugh in weeks. He almost forgot what it sounded like.

The three of them headed back to the hotel for a quick shower and ran into Katie on the way over.

"How was the office?" Sam asked.

"A lot different than the way I would run things," Katie answered.

"Have you seen Anne?" Mike asked.

"No, not since this morning," Katie replied.

"Did Mary and her sisters get set up in a room?" Kalen asked.

"Yeah, they're on our floor. Don't worry. We'll keep an eye on them," Katie said.

The guards were still stationed at the hotel entrance when they arrived. Mike hoped that after Kalen was done with training she would get something simple like what these soldiers were doing. Overall, aside from the sessions today, he hadn't really seen the guards around the city do a whole lot.

He kept wondering, why all the training? Why have such a military presence? Mike understood wanting to protect what they were trying to rebuild, but he couldn't figure out who they were protecting it from.

Anne was coming out of the bathroom when Mike entered. She gave him a kiss as she walked over to the dresser where her clothes were.

"I'm pretty sure I still smell like hospital food," Anne said.

"Is that what they have you doing?"

"It's not glamorous, but everyone was nice. How was your day?"

Mike rubbed his jaw. It was still sore.

"A little rough," Mike said.

He sat on the edge of the bed as Anne dressed. They still had only the clothes they brought with them. He wasn't sure if they were going to get any others while they were here, but that was the least of his worries.

"They put Kalen with the soldiers," Mike said.

"What?"

Anne dropped on the bed next to Mike. She gripped his arm.

"Why?" Anne asked.

"It was based on the interviewer's evaluation."

"They can't do that."

"We don't have a choice right now."

"No!"

It was the involuntary scream that shocked Mike. His wife was visibly upset. He hadn't seen her like this in a long time.

"I'll make sure she's okay," Mike said.

"She's not okay, Mike. She's different. The things she's been through, they've... changed her. Putting her in this 'militia' isn't going to help."

"Have you seen what the guards do here? They stand in front of buildings and patrol the streets. There isn't any fighting here. Her being in the guard is probably the safest she'll be."

"We've only been here for a day. We don't know what they'll do. We don't know anything about these people."

"Isn't this what we were searching for? A safe place for our family? The cabin was always supposed to be temporary anyway. If these people have the power back on for an entire city, then it won't be long before it spreads."

She knelt down, grabbing his hands. He forgot how strong her hands were. When she held them, his hands didn't ache. He drew vitality from them; the tremors faded.

"I don't want to lose her," Anne said.

"We won't."

* * *

COLONEL CADOGAN HIT the elevator button, sending him to the top floor. Files were tucked under his arm. He was alone, as requested.

When the elevator doors opened, he stepped out into the penthouse suite that took up the entire fiftieth floor. It was simply furnished, with only the necessities one would need for a single-person apartment, but had the open space only luxury could afford.

On the south end of the apartment the entire wall was made of glass, giving a spectacular view of the city, which Bram was enjoying when Cadogan walked up behind him.

"The files?" Bram asked.

"Yes, sir," Cadogan replied.

Bram flipped through the pages.

"They arrived in vehicles?" Bram asked.

"Yes, their vehicles predated the use of microprocessors in engines."

"Smart. Weapons?"

"A few automatic rifles, handguns, and shotguns. No heavy artillery."

Bram snapped the file shut and handed it back to Cadogan.

"Any troublemakers?" Bram asked.

"Not yet, but we're keeping a close eye on them, per protocol with new citizens."

"Where are we at with recruitment?"

"The only recruiter we're still waiting to check in is Cain, but he shouldn't be much longer. Our other scouts have been scouring the north, and we've already received word that units from Indianapolis and Columbus are trained and ready to join us."

"Good."

"Anything else, sir?"

"This Mike Grant that came in today. I'd like to meet him. Set up a meeting for us sometime this week."

"Yes, sir."

"That will be all. Thank you, Colonel."

49

DAY 23 (CARROLLTON)

*T*he stacked cans of food and water seemed to be shrinking. It was all Fay could stare at. She knew she was thinking about it too much, but it was something she couldn't get out of her mind.

There wasn't another town for miles. She spent all day yesterday gathering as many supplies as she could and storing them in her and Jung's rooms, but the bikers had picked over pretty much everything when they arrived, and what they hadn't eaten was already spoiled.

The stress creeping into her mind was intensified by the knowledge that she wasn't just responsible for herself anymore. Jung was useless. If she was going to keep him and his children alive, she was going to have to do it herself.

They still had enough food to last them for some time, but there was no guarantee of it lasting until the power came back on.

She would catch herself looking down the road at night, toward Cincinnati, hoping to see some light in the distance letting her know that help would be coming, but she knew it was ridiculous.

If they ran out of food before the power came back on, there was only one place left for her to go, but she refused to go back there. The last time she saw the Murth family, they tried to kill her.

Still, she had to face the reality of what could happen, and she needed to start preparing for it now.

Fay picked up her rifle and walked outside. It was already midafternoon, and she knew the kids were probably hungry. She made her way down to Jung's room and knocked on the door.

She didn't know why she knocked. There was never an answer from Jung. She was just waiting for the day she walked in and found Jung dead with his kids crying over his body.

Jung was lying on the bed with his back turned to the door when Fay entered. Jung Jr. and Claire were sitting on the floor, playing with some toys that Fay managed to find to keep them entertained while their father was… nonresponsive.

"Hey, guys!" Fay said.

Both of them looked up at her and smiled. They were both young enough not to grasp the gravity of what was happening around them, but old enough to recognize that their mother wasn't there anymore, and that something was wrong with their dad.

"Hi," Jung Jr. said.

Fay was always amazed at how much Jung Jr. looked like his dad. Claire still couldn't speak, at least not in terms of anything that Fay could understand. She put her arms out, wanting Fay to pick her up. Fay reached down and grabbed her, swinging the rifle out of the way and positioning Claire on her hip.

"You guys hungry?" Fay asked.

She tickled Claire, and Jung Jr. threw his arms up in the air, waving.

"Let's get something to eat. Do you guys like Brussels sprouts?" Fay asked.

"EEEWWWWWWW!" Jung Jr. said, sticking his tongue out and scrunching his nose up.

Fay laughed, and Jung Jr. grabbed her hand.

"Jung, you want anything?" Fay asked.

She always asked, and there was never a response. He hadn't said a word since Mike and everyone else left.

"I'll be downstairs in the kitchen if you change your mind," Fay said.

Both kids squinted into the sun. Jung kept the blinds drawn to their room all the time, so it always took some time for their eyes to adjust.

When they made it down into the courtyard, Jung Jr. wrestled out of Fay's grip and sprinted around the courtyard, jumping up and down, enjoying being outside.

Fay wanted to pull him back, but there wasn't anything left in the town that could hurt him, and she hadn't seen him this happy since they were at the airport. She didn't want to be the reason the smile from his face faded.

Claire squirmed in her arms, letting her know that she wanted down too. Fay set her on the ground and she chased after her brother, her chubby legs unable to keep up with him, squealing in the delight of trying.

Whatever obstacles she'd have to face in the future seemed less strenuous. The sight of those kids running after each other and the smiles on their faces hardened her resolve. She wasn't going to quit. She wasn't going to fail.

It was the sudden sound of silence that snapped Fay out of her daze. Both Claire and Jung Jr. were standing frozen by the fountain in the courtyard. Fay turned around, rifle aimed with her finger on the trigger, and the figure she saw through the scope was Billy with his hands in the air.

Fay lowered the weapon slowly. Of all the people she thought she'd see standing behind her, he was the last she'd expect.

"What are you doing here?" Fay asked.

"I could ask you the same thing. I thought your group went to Cincinnati?"

"They did."

Fay could see the rifle on Billy's back. Even though her gun was lowered, she kept her finger on the trigger.

"Where's the rest of your family?" Fay asked.

"At the farm. It's just me here."

"Why?"

Billy didn't answer, but he didn't need to. Fay knew why. Her finger slid off the trigger. It made sense. Billy killed his own father to save Mike's daughter's life. He helped save all of them, including Fay.

"I just couldn't stand the way they were looking at me anymore," Billy said. "It was too much."

Fay considered her options. She could kill him, but then that might cause more repercussions with the rest of his family. As mad as they were with him now, she was pretty sure that his family would still be upset if he died.

"You planning on staying here?" Fay asked.

"I figured there would be plenty of space available. I don't need any of your supplies. I'll be fine on my own. I just need a place to stay."

Fay slung the rifle back over her shoulder.

"C'mon, we were about to have some lunch," she said.

* * *

THE PRAYER BEADS were lying on the sheets next to Jung's stomach as he was curled up on the bed. He was thankful for Fay. The burden of having to think, to act, to do anything, was lifted from him.

The whiskey was gone, but the numbness still remained. Fay had poured all the bottles she could find in his room down the drain, in hopes of snapping him out of the stupor he was in. It failed.

He would hear his son say his name, call after him over and over, shaking him on the bed. He could hear the desperation in his voice, needing his father to help him with something, but it didn't matter how much his children cried for him. He wouldn't move.

He felt better when Fay would come and take the kids from him. He didn't like to be left alone with them anymore. They reminded him too much of his wife, and they represented his failure as a husband and a father.

Jung rolled onto his back. It took more effort than he thought it would. The past week of drinking with little to no food had left his body weak. He tried pushing himself up with his elbows, but he collapsed back on the bed.

He could feel the strain of his heart from the exertion of moving, the pounding of his chest trying to pump life throughout his body, struggling to keep him alive. His breath accelerated. He could feel his muscles tightening from the stress. He gulped for air.

Finally, his heart rate slowed and the panic subsided. He lay there for a few more minutes before he tried again. This time he managed to sit upright, swinging his legs over the edge of the bed.

One of Claire's dolls was lying on the ground next to his feet. The doll's eyes were staring back at him, motionless, lifeless. He flipped the doll over with his foot and tried standing.

His steps were wobbly, uneven. A sharp pain shot through him when he moved. Everything was so stiff and rigid.

Jung grabbed a paper cup sitting next to the sink in the bathroom. He reached for the faucet absentmindedly, forgetting there wasn't any running water, there wasn't any power, and soon there wouldn't be any food.

He crushed the cup in his hand and threw it against the wall. The moments of helplessness he'd felt since all of this started began to well up within him.

The riots at the airport, the struggles on the road, the events at the cabin—he was nothing more than a pawn in the rest of the world's game. Each member of his family was a pawn, and one of them had already been sacrificed by his lack of power.

When the lights went off, it didn't just shut down the country; it shut him down. All of his wealth, all of his influence and contacts, meant nothing with the power turned off.

Jung grabbed the shower curtain and ripped it down. The ringlets and shower bar crashed to the bathroom's tile. He flung the curtain out of the bathroom and onto the carpet.

Soaps and other cups still lined the bathroom sink. Jung swept his arms over the marble tops, knocking everything off.

He ripped the towel rack from the wall and smashed the mirror with the blunt end, splintering the mirror into hundreds of cracks and broken lines. He sent his fists through the walls, putting holes in the drywall.

He flipped the mattress from the bed frame, smashed the lamps, pulled the drawers out of the dresser, and crashed the impotent television to the ground.

When Jung finally collapsed to the ground, he felt a stinging in his hands from the cuts and bits of glass stuck in them. He yanked out the pieces he could then lay down on the carpet.

The destruction of the room was something he could control. He knew men couldn't come back from the types of things he did, the things he saw. There was only one other thing within his control. There was only one way out.

* * *

CLAIRE AND JUNG JR. munched on some Cheerios. Billy would make faces at Claire, and she kept giggling. It was the first time he let himself laugh in a long time.

"What happened?" Fay asked.

"You know what happened."

"They just kicked you out?"

"I left. Whatever damage I caused will take a long time to undo. My brother won't speak to me. My mother won't look at me. Whatever family I had died with my father."

They were words Billy had been thinking for a long time but never said aloud. It was odd for him, talking about it.

"I'm sorry," Fay said.

She grabbed his hand, and he felt the rush of life flow back into him. The way she was looking at him made him feel things would get better.

"Thanks," Billy said.

"I'm done!" Jung Jr. shouted.

Fay let go. The warmth of her touch lingered on him for a moment, and Billy refused to move his hand, afraid that doing so would cause the feeling to disappear.

"You guys want to go outside for a little bit, while I bring some food up to your dad?" Fay asked.

The two of them squealed with excitement. They ran outside before Fay could say another word.

"Can you go out front and keep an eye on them for me?" Fay asked.

"Sure."

Billy chased the two of them outside. They were both pretty fast, but he was able to keep up with them. He set the rifle down on the fountain and found a few rocks. He grabbed some empty cans and bottles and set them up on the short stone wall that surrounded the courtyard.

He tossed the rock over to one of the cans and knocked it over. Jung Jr. laughed and picked up his own rock. When he threw his he missed, but found that even more fun than hitting the can.

Claire got excited since her brother was excited, and Billy sat back and watched the two of them just be kids.

Billy remembered when his brother was that little. He was always smiling. There wasn't anything that he couldn't make fun.

Out of everything that happened, damaging the relationship he had with his brother was the one thing he wished he could have changed. He still hoped that they could go back to the way things used to be, but it might not be until Joey was older. Until his brother understood the type of man their father really was. He knew the pain would never fully wane, but perhaps it would fade enough for them to be brothers again.

* * *

BETH DUMPED the last of the hay bales into the fields as the cows came trotting over. She knew there was a stockpile in town at the feed store, but she had no idea what kind of shape it would be in.

She also had no idea if Mike and his family were still there. She wouldn't be able to take out their entire group by herself. It would be suicide.

But she knew if she didn't make the trip into town, the livestock wouldn't last much longer, and with her husband gone, Joey would be the only provider of food.

There was always Billy, but she wouldn't allow herself to go down that road yet. She was still too conflicted and upset about what happened. She wasn't sure if she'd ever be able to forgive him.

She left the cows to their food and headed back toward the house. Joey was on the porch when she walked up.

"Get ready for supper," Beth said.

"I'm not hungry."

Joey had his rifle apart, cleaning it. He put a few drops of oil onto the barrel and wiped it down.

"You have to eat something," Beth said.

"I told you I'm not hungry."

He wasn't looking at her. Beth snatched the rifle from his hands.

"Give that back!" Joey said.

"You don't talk to me like that!"

"You don't get to tell me what to do anymore!"

Beth brought her hand to the side of Joey's face. The slap silenced both of them, and each looked shocked at what happened.

Joey's lip quivered. Beth's mouth dropped. She reached out to him, but he backed away. Tears formed in the corner of his eyes.

"Joey, I…" Beth said.

Beth could hear his footsteps thump along the steps as he ran up the stairs inside the house. She looked down at the gun still in pieces on the porch. She bent down and finished cleaning the parts of the rifle Joey left and reassembled the gun.

Beth's hand was on the handle of the screen door when she heard it. At first she thought it was just a bug buzzing around her ear, but when she realized what it was, her eyes found the road.

The truck was slowing down as it approached the farm. When it arrived at the front gate, it idled there for a moment before it finally inched forward onto the dirt road leading up to the house.

The dust from the road flew up and swirled into the summer sky. Beth couldn't see the face of the driver because of the glare of the sun, but from what she could tell, it was a military vehicle of some kind.

The tires were large and ribbed for different types of terrain.

There was a mounted machine gun on the top and heavy armored plates protecting the whole vehicle.

Beth kept the rifle crooked under her arm. She knew it wasn't loaded, but whoever was in that truck didn't know that.

The door to the truck swung open, and Beth brought the rifle up to her shoulder. A boot hit the gravel followed by another. The man that spun around from the door wore beige army fatigues, aviator sunglasses, and had short crew-cut hair with a clean-shaven face.

He also wore a 9mm pistol holstered on each hip, held together with a belt and additional ammo. He kept walking toward Beth, but neither of them said anything. She was still in shock at the sight of a working vehicle in her front yard.

Beth examined his uniform. There wasn't a single fiber out of place. She looked back inside the truck to see if there was anyone else, but the sun's glare still blocked her view. If there were others inside, they didn't step out.

"I can wait for you to grab some bullets to reload if you'd like."

"Who are you?" Beth asked.

The soldier kept his hands behind his back as he walked up the porch steps. He took off his sunglasses, and two piercing blue eyes examined her.

"My name is Cain. I'm a part of the Cincinnati scouting division," he said.

"Cincinnati? You're quite a ways from home."

"Not as far as you'd think," he said.

"What do you want?"

"Are you here alone?"

Beth took a step back and held up the rifle between them out of instinct, forgetting there wasn't any ammo in the gun.

"I'm here to help," Cain said.

"Help how?"

Cain stepped forward, the barrel of the gun pushing into his chest. He leaned forward as far as he could, looking Beth straight in the eyes.

"I can help get back what you lost."

* * *

FAY KNEW something was wrong when she inserted the key into the door for Jung's room and saw that the chain lock had been set.

"Jung? Jung, open up," Fay said.

She tried to peek through the small crack in the door, but she couldn't see anything. She pounded her fist on the door.

"Jung, this isn't funny."

That's when she saw a hand limp on the floor. When the sunlight from the cracked door hit Jung's hand, it shimmered red.

"Jung!"

Fay took a step back and kicked the door in, breaking the chain and flooding the dark room with sunlight. She rushed over to Jung, who was unconscious on the floor. His wrists were cut, and blood was everywhere.

"Oh my God, Jung, no."

She checked his pulse but couldn't feel anything. She bent her face down to check his breathing, but there was nothing. She tore the sheets off the bed, wrapping them around Jung's wrists. She wasn't sure if there was any blood left to stop, but she couldn't think of anything else to do. She tied the sheets as tight as she could.

Fay placed her hands on Jung's chest, trying to remember the CPR course she took a few years back and what she needed to do to try and restart his heart. She placed the heel of her palm on his sternum in the middle of his chest. She pressed down hard, hearing the crack of bones. She didn't stop though. She counted to thirty and tilted his head back, clearing the airway, and pushed two breaths into his lungs.

"C'mon, Jung, c'mon."

Fay kept her arms rigid, pressing down on Jung's chest. She was in the middle of the compressions when she heard Billy running up the stairs. She panicked.

"Billy, don't bring the kids up here!" Fay shouted.

Billy rushed into the room. Fay looked around for Claire or Jung Jr., but they weren't with him.

"Don't worry; I put them in a room downstairs. What happened?" Billy asked.

Fay gestured to the sheets around Jung's wrists. Blood covered her hands and the carpet.

"He wasn't breathing when I came in. He was passed out on the floor. I couldn't feel a pulse either," Fay said.

"Jesus."

Billy started messing with the sheets around Jung's wrists.

"What are you doing?" Fay asked.

"Making a tourniquet."

Billy rewrapped the sheets, twisting them with one of Fay's spare magazines she had on her.

"He's lost a lot of blood," Billy said.

"He's going to make it."

Billy grabbed her arm, but she shoved him off. She wasn't going to let him die. She couldn't let him die. This was her job. If she failed, then the kids downstairs wouldn't have anyone.

The thought crossed her mind that the kids might be better off without him alive, but she didn't want to believe that. She knew Jung was only a shadow of the person that he used to be, but she didn't think that all of him was gone.

She finished another thirty compressions, and when she put her mouth over his and blew, Jung coughed.

"He's breathing. Jung, can you hear me? Jung?" Fay asked.

Fay shook him, but there wasn't any other sign of life. She checked his breath one more time to be sure.

Billy placed his finger on Jung's neck and held it there, still as water.

"It's faint, but it's there," Billy said.

"Thank God."

"We need to get fluids in him fast. Do you have any first aid equipment stored anywhere?" Billy asked.

"Whatever I found is in my room. You stay here with him. I'm going to go check on the kids and then bring back some supplies. What room did you put the kids in?"

"One twenty-three."

"Okay, I'll be back."

Fay headed down the staircase, and when she made it to the bottom, she stopped. Her head felt dizzy, her legs turned to jelly. All of the adrenaline rushed out of her. She grabbed the staircase rail to steady herself and shut her eyes. She focused on gathering her strength, and when she felt sturdier, she found room 123.

Jung Jr. and Claire were huddled together on the bed. Both of them looked frightened when she came inside, but as soon as they recognized her, they both ran to her.

"You guys all right?" Fay asked.

Neither of them would let go of her legs. Fay reached down and picked up Claire. She grabbed Jung Jr.'s hand and walked to the bed.

"Did you guys hear me yelling?"

Jung Jr. nodded his head. Claire wiped her eyes. Fay didn't know how she was going to explain their father's condition. She knew

Claire wouldn't understand, but Jung Jr. was probably old enough to grasp it.

"Your dad's…"

She trailed off. The two faces looking at her had lost their mother, their father was trying to take himself out of the equation, they were stuck in a place incredibly far away from their home, and there wasn't any guarantee that they'd ever see it again.

Fay figured they had other family somewhere. She just had to keep them safe long enough to find them. That would be the first thing she'd speak to Jung about when he woke up. She wasn't going to take any more chances with him.

"Your dad isn't feeling well," Fay finally sputtered out.

"Is he dying?" Jung Jr. asked.

"No, he's going to be fine," Fay replied.

Jung Jr. buried his face in her stomach, and Claire started to play with her hair. Whatever Jung was going through, Fay had to snap him out of. She couldn't let these kids lose the only parent they had left.

DAY 23 (CINCINNATI)

*B*oth Colonel Cadogan and Sergeant Blake escorted Mike to Bram's apartment. He was patted down three different times: once before he entered the building, once before he was allowed in the elevator, and one more time before he was ushered onto Bram's penthouse floor.

Mike stepped out of the elevator and was escorted into Bram's living room.

The furniture was simple but modern. There were a few paintings and pictures placed on various walls. The wood floors were shined and glossy.

There was a table set with fine silverware and a four-course meal. The meal consisted of ham, mashed potatoes, salad, fruit, bread, and green beans, all with steam rising from the plates. Mike let his hands run across the fine lace of the tablecloth.

But everything else failed in comparison to the view that the apartment granted. The entire south wall was a window giving a panoramic picture of the city and the Ohio River.

"It's nice to see civility again, isn't it?" Bram asked.

"The pat-downs on the way up suggested security over civility."

"Well, one has to be careful these days as I'm sure you're aware."

"I'm aware."

Bram gestured to the couch.

"Please, have a seat," Bram said. "How has your family adjusted to their new home?"

"We're fine."

"I hear your daughter has an aptitude for the military."

"Who are you?"

Two crystal-stemmed glasses sat on the small table between them. Bram picked one of them up, pinching the thin stem between his fingers. The rays of sunlight coming through the windows filtered through the crystal's glass, separating the sunlight into different colors on the floor.

"Prisms are remarkable," Bram said. "If you take white light and point it through a crystal prism, the light will separate into all its natural components. Now the degree of separation depends on the angle in which the light enters the prism. It takes a precise measurement to disperse all of the white light."

"That doesn't answer my question."

"Who I am and what I do is much like this prism. I help break down matter into its purest nature."

Two waiters entered the living room and filled the crystal glasses with water, which they served along with a plate of pierogies.

"I'm told they're a Pittsburgh staple," Bram said.

Bram picked up one of the Polish dumplings and popped it into his mouth.

"Delicious," Bram said.

"You obviously brought me here for something. Now, it's either because you think I'm a threat, or you think I can help you. So which is it?" Mike asked.

Bram grabbed the napkin on the table in front of him and wiped his fingers harshly.

"Should I be worried about you, Mr. Grant? From what I hear about your group, you've been through quite a bit, seen a lot of violence. Are you planning on continuing that trend here with us?" Bram asked.

"Not if I don't have to."

"Good."

Bram pulled a phone out of his pocket and placed it to his ear.

"Bring it in," he said.

A few moments later Colonel Cadogan returned with Sergeant Blake. Cadogan carried a briefcase, and the two men joined Mike and Bram.

Cadogan opened the briefcase and pulled out a laptop. When he turned the laptop around for everyone to view, there was a picture of Dr. Wyatt on the screen.

"Do you know this man?" Cadogan asked.

"No, I've never seen him before," Mike replied.

"This is Dr. Quinn Wyatt. He worked for the EPA before the blackout. About seven months ago he was in front of a Senate hearing involving his research on the vulnerability of our country's utilities," Blake said.

"The Senate hearing never finished, and Wyatt was branded a lunatic," Cadogan continued.

"Before the blackout, I was CEO and president of a micpropro- cessor manufacturer. I read Dr. Wyatt's research, and he mentioned that one area where the country was susceptible to attack was an EMP. Due to my business interests, his report caught my attention," Bram said.

"What happened?" Mike asked.

"I brought him on as a consultant in hopes of developing a new processor that could withstand a high-powered EMP attack like the one described," Bram said.

"What was in it for you?" Mike asked.

"If we could prove the danger of an EMP attack and successfully patent an EMP-resistant microprocessor, it would be worth billions," Bram answered.

"So, what went wrong?" Mike asked.

"Dr. Wyatt was still hell-bent on making Congress pay for branding him a lunatic. Instead of developing a prototype, he used Mr. Thorn's facilities to manufacture an EMP device strong enough to take out the entire country," Cadogan said.

"Even high-powered EMPs have a limited range. The only way it would have worked was if the device was detonated in the atmosphere," Mike said.

"I've had some military contracts in the past. Dr. Wyatt forged paperwork with my signature, telling the Pentagon about the work he was performing and how it could be used for military applications," Bram said.

"He then used those military connections to have a mercenary unit sneak into a missile silo in Kansas where he launched the device," Cadogan said.

"We didn't find out that he was involved until after we arrived in Cincinnati. One of my manufacturing plants was located here, and we had started producing some first-generation EMP-resistant chips at this location. We installed them in certain public and private buildings, which is why we were able to get most of the city up and running so quickly after the blast," Bram said.

"I've been in contact with Washington, and we're home base for now until we can ship out repairs to the rest of the country. We have a three-month timeline right now of getting power back on in all major cities," Cadogan said.

"So what does all this have to do with me?" Mike asked.

"Dr. Wyatt's still in Cincinnati, and he's been trying to undermine our operation since he arrived here," Blake said.

"He's held up south of the Ohio River, and he's been preventing us from getting supplies to the southern states," Bram replied.

"He's surrounded himself with extremists who are using the EMP attack as an opportunity to establish a new government. We believe he's running out of resources though," Cadogan said.

"The biggest advantage Wyatt has right now is the river. There's only one working bridge, and he has a stronghold on it. If we can take control of the bridge then we'll be able to hit them on their turf," Blake said.

"And we want you, Kalen, and Sam to be a part of the raid," Bram said.

"Aside from a few military personnel, most of the members of our units are civilians with limited combat experience. You and your group, however, have quite a bit of experience," Cadogan said.

"No, my daughter will not be a part of this. No one from my group will," Mike said.

Mike rose from his chair and headed to the elevator. He didn't have to take orders from these people, and he sure as hell wasn't going to put his daughter on the front lines of a war.

"You realize what this is, Mike?" Bram asked. "We don't stop him, and everything we have is in jeopardy. And not just for your family, but every family in the entire country."

"That's not my problem," Mike said.

"It's not up to you," Blake said.

"My answer wasn't a suggestion," Mike said, hitting the down button of the elevator.

"Your daughter has an assignment, and she will follow her orders," Blake replied.

Mike's knuckles cracked as he squeezed his hands into fists at both sides. He slowly turned from the elevator.

"You're not seeing the bigger picture here. If we lose Cincinnati, it could take years for this country to rebuild," Cadogan said.

There was a sidearm on Blake's hip. Mike could see Blake's fingers itching to grab it.

"Go on," Mike said, gesturing at Blake's gun. "Try it. But you better put me down, because if you don't, my face will be the last one you see on this earth."

Blake's hand was gripped around the pistol's handle now. Mike took a step forward, and he could see Blake's arm tense up.

"Blake, stand down," Bram said.

Blake released his grip and took his seat. Bram ran his hands through his hair and walked over to Mike. His voice was low when he spoke.

"Everyone in this room has made sacrifices. All of us have lost more than we care to talk about, but we're so close. We're almost at the finish line. All we need is one last push, Mike, and then we'll be done. Nobody will ask anything from you or your family again," Bram said.

Mike wanted to believe him. He wanted to believe that everything was almost over, that he just needed to go a little bit further and they'd be in the clear, but Mike knew better. There was always something else, and it always came at a very high price.

"When was the last time you were in combat, Sergeant?" Mike asked.

"November 2013. I was in Afghanistan," Blake replied.

"You have any close brothers that made it out of Afghanistan alive, but never really came home?"

"Yes."

"A month ago I had to ground my daughter for getting a D on her report card," Mike said. "Last week I watched her shoot a man in the head in the middle of the street."

Cadogan rubbed the stubble on his face. Blake didn't know where to look, except the ground. Bram was the only person who still held Mike's gaze.

"I think me and my family have pushed far enough," Mike said.

The elevator door pinged open, and Mike stepped inside. He hit the bottom floor button, and when the doors to the elevator closed, he took in the faces staring back at him. Cadogan looked depressed, Blake was angry, and Bram's was curious.

Mike didn't break his stride as he rolled past the soldiers that frisked him before entering the building. As he walked back to the hotel, he passed couples and families in the streets, enjoying the sunshine.

He should have felt happy at that moment, seeing the normalcy of what an afternoon should be, safe. But the only emotion that overtook him was animosity.

Mike hated those families. None of them had experienced what his own went through. None of them were being called on now to sacrifice more. Just him.

Then he noticed the stares of the people he passed. Everyone was avoiding him, moving out of his way. He couldn't tell why until he caught his reflection in a window. The man staring back at him wasn't recognizable. The look on his face was resentful. Vicious.

He stood there, studying the face until it was one he remembered. His mind went back to his father. He desperately wanted him to tell him what to do, but it wasn't an answer that he was going to get.

Anne wasn't home when Mike made it back to the hotel, so he decided to head to the school to see Freddy.

All of the kids were outside, playing kickball in the small field next to the school. The teams were split up in an even mix of different age groups.

All the children wore smiles on their faces. They were in that moment of pure joy, oblivious to the world beyond the game they were playing.

Mike's stress melted away at the sight of Freddy bouncing up and down, excited about being next up to kick. He couldn't remember the last time that he was able to watch his son just be a kid again.

The look on Freddy's face was the reason why Mike had done all he had to keep his family safe. Because he wanted all of them to be normal again, to be able to return to the life and people they were before the blackout.

Mike knew what he had to do. When Blake and Cadogan led their men into battle tomorrow, he would be there with him. Not for a cause, or for the millions of people counting on the power coming back on; that was too much. He would be doing it for one person, who was still smiling as he stepped up to the plate.

DAY 24 (CARROLLTON)

*J*ung squinted his eyes into the sunlight breaking through the blinds. For a moment he panicked, trying to remember where he was, how he got there. He tried moving his hand to block the sunlight and realized they were tied to the bedposts. He looked down at his feet, which were in similar restraints.

He was completely immobile. When he started to thrash against the ropes, he immediately felt dizzy and stopped. Whatever strength he had left was barely enough to lift his head, let alone break the rope tying him down.

The room started to spin. He felt as though he was going to puke. The taste of hot, sour bile started to fill his mouth. He forced it back down, burning his throat and stomach.

His clothes were gone and the only thing covering his body was a nightgown, leaving him exposed and vulnerable.

The door opened and flooded the room with sunlight. All he could see of the person that entered was their silhouette. When the door shut, it took a minute for Jung's eyes to adjust back.

"How are you feeling?" Billy asked.

Jung was silent. He wasn't sure if he couldn't speak because of the shock of Billy standing in his room or the lack of strength needed to turn his thoughts into words.

Billy placed a bottle of water and a pack of crackers on the nightstand next to the bed. He reached for Jung, who immediately recoiled.

"It's okay," Billy said.

The bandages on Jung's arm had a purple tinge to them.

"Looks like we'll need to rewrap those," Billy said, sighing under his breath.

When Billy went to untie the bandages, Jung finally found his voice.

"No!" Jung said.

Billy jumped. Jung's voice was violent, loud.

"If I don't change those bandages, the cuts will get infected. We need to keep those wounds clean," Billy said.

"Let me go."

"Jung, I can't do that."

"Let me go!"

Jung pulled his arms and legs against the restraints as hard as he could. The brief burst of adrenaline coursing through his body gave him a moment of strength. The bed started to shake from his thrashing.

"Jung, calm down," Billy said.

"Letmego! Letmego! Letmego!"

Billy ran out of the room, leaving Jung thrashing by himself. After a few more moments, the adrenaline left him and Jung's body went limp. His face was covered in sweat, and his breaths were labored.

There was a reason Jung didn't want Billy to take his bandages off. What lay underneath was a shame he didn't want to see. He remembered everything: holding the shards of the broken mirror, digging into his skin, watching the blood flow out of him, and the slow fade of falling asleep.

He just wanted it to end, but someone always kept pulling him back. That was his punishment. He wasn't ever going to be able to escape the world he was in. The fires of hell on this earth were going to continue to burn, and he was meant to burn with them.

* * *

JOEY FOLLOWED Cain everywhere he went. If Cain was outside, Joey was outside. If Cain was in the kitchen, Joey was in the kitchen. If Cain was cleaning his pistol, Joey was cleaning his rifle.

He would watch Cain linger in the living room, moving from picture to picture, or ornament to ornament, examining each of them. Joey noticed that Cain always kept his hands behind his back when he studied something.

The rare moments where he wasn't mimicking Cain's habits were spent exploring Cain's truck. Joey had never seen anything like it. It was like something out of a movie.

The heavy armored doors, the massively thick tires—it was a tank on four wheels. Even the windshields were thick, caked with dust.

When Joey woke up early that morning, he rushed downstairs, wanting to catch Cain at breakfast, but when he made it down the kitchen was empty, except for his mother, who was pulling jars out of the cupboard.

"You hungry?" Beth asked.

"No, I'm gonna go huntin'."

"Take this with you."

Beth tossed Joey a bag of jerky. He caught it and stuffed it into his pocket. He grabbed his rifle on the way out and began his journey into the woods.

The forest was always quiet in the morning, and cool. The sun had yet to burn the patch of land with its summer heat. Joey weaved in and out of the trees, rifle tucked under his arm. He usually had to travel deep into the woods before he found any tracks, but today he caught sight of some deer prints ten minutes into his walk.

Whenever he found tracks, a switch would flip in his head. His feet became lighter, and the rifle became another extension of his arms. He moved through the woods as if he was a part of the trees, swaying in the breeze.

The tracks were fresh. The deer was close. Joey scanned the thick patches of trees. The wind was blowing in his face, so he knew the deer wouldn't be able to smell him coming.

After a few more minutes of a steady pace, he saw him. It was a young buck, its antlers still growing. The deer was fifty yards away, stepping casually between clusters of trees, munching on some grass.

Joey brought the rifle's scope to his eye. The branches kept drifting in and out of the crosshairs, making it difficult to find a shot. He waited patiently. He knew he had the advantage. He just needed to be patient.

He looked up from the scope, still keeping a bead on the deer, and tried looking for any clearing ahead that the buck would be walking into. There was a ten-foot gap between two trees five feet from the path the deer was on. That was his shot.

A few minutes later, the head of the deer found its way into the middle of Joey's crosshairs. He moved his finger gently to the trigger. He gave a slow exhale and fired. The sounds of the shot ringing through the forest and the deer hitting the ground were simultaneous.

Joey smiled, looking up from his scope, and slung his rifle's strap over his shoulder.

"Nice shot," Cain said.

Joey flung himself around, trying to grab the rifle off his shoulder and falling backwards in the process.

Cain was in his usual stance, hands behind his back, looking straight through Joey.

"Need help dragging it back?" Cain asked.

"Okay."

That was the first word Joey ever said to him, and it came out in a whisper.

Joey and Cain both grabbed the deer's antlers and started pulling it toward the house. Joey kept his head down most of the time but would glance up occasionally just to make sure they were still heading in the right direction.

When they made it out of the woods and into the farm's open field, both let go of the deer's antlers. Joey bent over on his knees, taking a moment to catch his breath.

"Why don't you run and get the cart," Cain said.

The cart was on the side of the house, but his mom left a few bags of chicken feed on it. He yanked the bags off and put them back in the barn.

Joey wheeled the cart through the field, and he could see Cain with his back to him crouched over the animal. He couldn't see what Cain was doing, but whatever it was had the deer's carcass trembling.

The cart hit the ground with a thud when Joey dropped it a few feet behind Cain.

"What are you doing?" Joey asked.

Cain was cutting something along the deer's chest.

"It's a special moment, isn't it?" Cain asked.

Cain kept his back to Joey, continuing the sawing motion with his arm. Joey could hear the cracks of bone and the slicing of muscles and tendons.

"Killing something gives you a certain power," Cain said.

Then, Cain finally turned around. Joey's eyes immediately went to Cain's hand, which was holding the deer's heart. Blood dripped from Cain's forearms and onto his uniform.

Joey froze. The knife that Cain used was in his other hand, wet with blood. A hole was left in the deer's chest, where the heart was stolen. Cain stepped forward, extending the animal's organ to him.

"You did this, Joey. Your skill brought this animal down. It will feed you and your family. This is yours," Cain said.

Joey reached out his hand hesitantly. The heart was tough, warm, and wet. It took both of his hands to keep it from slipping out of his grip.

"That is power, Joey. You have it in your hands right now," Cain said.

Joey imagined the heart still beating. He could feel the life and death of the animal in his bare hands.

"Your father understood that power, didn't he?" Cain asked.

"Yes."

"If you could have him back, would you?"

"Yes."

Cain dropped to one knee, keeping himself at eye level with Joey, who was still staring at the heart in his hands.

"There is nothing that will bring your father back. Nothing. All that's left of him is up here," Cain said, his bloody finger tapping Joey on the forehead. "Does it make you angry that he's gone?"

Joey nodded his head. He missed his father more than anything in the world. The anger he felt about the loss of his father, and the betrayal of his brother, still hadn't left him. He found himself squeezing the heart tighter. He could feel the tear running out of the corner of his eye. His entire body was tensing up. The anger was tearing through him like a freight train.

"Use it," Cain said.

Joey's fingers dug into the heart, piercing it, pouring blood and spilling it to the grass. He started screaming as the heart broke apart in his hands. He squeezed harder and harder until the lump of muscle turned to mush.

"Good," Cain said.

* * *

WHEN JUNG TOLD Fay he wanted to go outside, she looked at him as if he was crazy. He knew why, though. He hadn't left the room since they arrived. He never even wanted to get up and leave the bed unless it was to use the bathroom.

"Why?" Fay asked.

It was a valid question. Jung probably could have come up with a lot of different answers for it, but he decided to stick with the truth.

"I need to see my wife, where she's buried," Jung answered.

Jung was still in his restraints. He wasn't sure if she would let him go. She didn't trust him anymore, so he probably figured she thought there was some ulterior motive behind it.

"You eat something, and I'll take you to where she's buried," Fay said.

"Okay."

After Jung forced down an entire packet of crackers, an apple juice, and some chips, Fay finally undid his restraints and walked him outside.

Fay had to guide him and pretty much hold him up since this was the most physical exertion he'd had for days.

Jung and Fay shuffled down Main Street, and Jung's eyes caught the spot where Jenna died.

"C'mon," Fay said. "She's over here."

On the edge of town, there were a few clearings cut in the grass. The larger of the clearings had dozens of rocks circled around the edge.

"What's that?" Jung asked.

"We couldn't identify all of the bodies of the townspeople, so we buried them together. Mike didn't want to leave them to rot where the bikers left them," Fay said.

"How many were there?" Jung asked.

"Count the rocks."

Jung's mouth dropped. He couldn't believe that many people were killed. Then he noticed a few other smaller clearings. His throat went dry.

"Is that…" Jung trailed off.

"No," Fay answered. "Jenna's over here."

It was different than he expected. He could see the dirt was upturned where they buried her. The small stone that rested at the head of the grave was nestled firmly in the ground.

He bent down on both knees, silent. Fay stood behind him, taking a few steps back, letting him have as much space as she could.

Of all the things that happened since the power went out, and after everything that transpired, the first memory that popped into Jung's mind was his wedding day. He could still remember the butterflies in his stomach, waiting to see her.

The moment when he saw Jenna walk down the aisle, time stood still. All he could see was her smiling with her arm tucked around her father's. He remembered the swelling pride that filled him, knowing the kind of woman he was about to commit his life to. She was kind, smart, and loyal. Whatever perfection he could have conjured up in his feeble mind wouldn't have held a candle to his wife.

Jung felt inside his pocket and ran his fingers across the smooth surface of the prayer beads. He pulled them out, clutched them in his hands, and closed his eyes.

"I'm lost, Jen. I failed you. I failed our children. I need you down here with me. I can't do it alone. I miss you," Jung whispered.

The tears rolling down his cheeks were accompanied by the silent sobs of grief. He could feel his shoulders trembling as he hunched over, bringing his forehead to the dirt.

Fay came over and placed her hand on his back. She helped him up, and with her help, he walked over to her headstone.

Jung kissed the beads in his hands before setting them on the headstone. He wasn't just letting go of his wife. He was letting go of whatever soul he had left. The final piece of the man he used to be was left there at Jenna's grave.

* * *

BETH RAN the knife down the belly of the deer, spilling the intestines onto the ground. The deer's pelt was already removed and set aside. The buck yielded a fair amount of meat after it was gutted, around sixty pounds.

Beth wrapped the meat and discarded the entrails to the pig trough. She was stacking the venison in a bag when Cain walked in.

"Need some help with that?" Cain asked.

Before she could answer, he picked up the bag and threw it over his shoulder. On the walk back to the house, Cain stayed close enough to make her feel his presence but far enough away to where she wasn't uncomfortable.

"Your boy's quite the hunter," Cain said.

Beth kept her eyes on the house, ignoring him. Her heart rate accelerated. There was a refined recklessness about him that put her on edge.

"Your husband taught him well," Cain said. "They were very close, weren't they?"

"Yes," Beth answered.

"His passing was recent?"

"About a week ago."

"Probably for the best."

Beth stopped and turned around. She was never a woman who expected to be pitied, or felt sorry for, but even she recognized a certain level of sympathy for someone who had just lost a husband and a father.

"What did you say?" Beth snapped.

"You heard what I said."

Cain's voice was low. There was a threatening tone that went along with it. She felt as though he was challenging her, unafraid of the subject matter and the normal, cordial way someone would handle the situation.

"You needed him to die. If he didn't, you wouldn't have anything to hate. You wouldn't have anything to drive you forward like you do now," Cain added.

Beth yanked the bag of venison out of Cain's hand. She shoved her finger in his face and started screaming.

"You have no idea what's best for me and my family, so don't pretend that you do!"

She turned to leave and Cain grabbed her shoulder. The move was violent, and it was the first time he'd touched her since his arrival. Beth thrashed against him, but he was too strong. Her efforts were as fruitless as water breaking onto a rock.

"Is that why your other boy's not here? Because you knew what's best for your family?" Cain asked.

"Stop it."

"I wonder why he left?"

"Let me go."

"Where is he, Beth?"

She could feel Cain's grip harden around her arms. It was like a vise clenching down on her. The more she fought it, the harder he squeezed.

"Did your son leave because you were weak?" Cain asked.

"No."

"Could he not stand the sight of his pathetic mother and younger brother begging him to save them?"

"He was the weak one!"

Cain let go of her arm. Her entire body was shaking now. The emotions of everything that happened were finally catching up with her.

"I drove him out because he killed his father! Because he couldn't survive like I could! Because I hated him for being weak!" Beth screamed.

The smile that cut across Cain's face was like watching a miner cut through stone, revealing a precious metal that he'd been searching for his entire life, and now he had finally reached the reward for all those years of laborious efforts.

Cain grabbed the bag of meat back from Beth's grip and continued walking toward the house. Beth just stood there, frozen. She couldn't believe the words that left her mouth.

The terrible, burning truth that had waited patiently to escape was now out in the open. Beth hated Billy for what he did. She didn't want to forgive him, and she didn't want him to come back. All she wanted was to make him pay for what he did.

* * *

BILLY KEPT an eye on the kids while Fay took Jung to visit Jenna's grave. The children hadn't visited the grave yet, but Fay didn't want them to go with their father when he was in such a vulnerable state. She didn't think it would be good for either of them. Billy agreed.

Jung Jr. pushed a small truck along the floor, and Claire kept crawling after him.

Billy and his brother used to be like that. Joey would follow him wherever he went. Billy never had a moment alone. It got to the point where it was annoying. Now, he'd give anything to have his brother look at him the way he used to.

The door to his room opened up, and Fay poked her head inside. She motioned for him to come outside. He closed the door behind him and noticed Fay still had Jung's room key in her hand.

"How'd he take it?" Billy asked.

"Hard to tell. He didn't say anything to me."

"Did you tie him back up?"

"Yeah."

"What are we going to do about the kids, Fay? We can't keep them from their father forever."

"We might not have to."

"What?"

"He's giving up, Billy. We can't force him to eat or drink. If he wants to waste away, then that's what he's going to do. It's not like we can sedate him and put him on life support."

"How can he do that?"

"He's broken, Billy. He has been for a while now."

"That doesn't mean you give up! That doesn't mean you quit! You keep pushing!"

Billy caught himself. He didn't realize how loud he was, or how much he was shaking until he saw Fay backing away from him. He relaxed his hands and exhaled.

"I'm sorry. It's just…"

"Your family will forgive you, Billy. It'll just take time," Fay said.

"I know."

* * *

CAIN SAT at the kitchen table with Joey and Beth. The sunlight still shone in through the windows. The rays caught the dust floating through the air. He sat there watching the small particles dance, drifting back and forth and swirling in unorganized patterns.

He'd been on the road for weeks, searching for people to recruit for Bram's cause. While most of his other colleagues focused on larger cities, Cain took a different approach. He spent his time traveling through smaller towns, looking for soldiers who didn't realize the war they were already a part of. Once Cain found them, all he had to do was polish them up.

"So it's true?" Joey asked. "The power's on in Cincinnati?"

"Yes," Cain answered.

"When can we go?" Joey asked.

"You haven't earned it yet," Cain replied.

There was a test, something Cain administered to every prospect he came across. It required no skill or training, simply a certain frame of mind.

All of the people that Cain had come across were survivors. They could all hunt or were prepared with supplies to last them years. Most of them were competent with some kind of weapon, but every single one of them failed the test.

He'd all but given up his search until he stumbled across the Murths. When he found them, he was able to put most of the pieces of their puzzle together himself. He spent a lot of time studying them, watching them. They were creatures of unyielding habit. They pushed forward, no matter what, and that's what made Cain believe they were the right fit.

He knew he would get chewed out once he made it back to Cincinnati. Bram would have a fit that he'd been gone for weeks and managed to bring back only two new recruits, but Cain knew that whoever passed his test would be in it with their life.

Cain rose from the table and walked over to the wall where the large cross hung, watching over the house.

"'Have I not commanded you? Be strong and courageous. Do not be terrified; do not be discouraged, for the LORD your God will be with you wherever you go,'" Cain said. "Do you know what that's from, Joey?"

Joey shook his head. Cain reached for the cross and took it off the wall. He walked back over to the table, standing between Joey and Beth.

"It's from the book of Joshua. After Moses died, the Lord commanded Joshua to lead the Hebrews across the river Jordan, and promised him that whatever ground his foot touched be his," Cain said.

Cain gripped the cross with both hands. His forearms tensed up, squeezing the cross.

"What a crock of shit," Cain said.

He snapped the cross in half and tossed the pieces onto the table. Beth jumped from her seat, and Cain backhanded her across the face. Joey lunged after him, and he tossed the boy on the floor next to his mother.

"Where is he?" Cain demanded. "Where is your God? What has he given you? Your husband is dead. Your brother has exiled himself. You're running out of food and time. You've placed your destiny in the hands of a man you cannot see or hear."

A welt was growing on Beth's cheek where he struck her. Cain's eyes softened. He grabbed a rag from the kitchen and dipped it in a bucket of water in the sink.

"Come here," Cain said, motioning over to Beth.

Beth went to him timidly. He dabbed the welt gently and looked down to Joey. Beth closed her eyes. Cain bent down to Joey's level.

He knew he could convince him. He knew the boy would have it in him.

"Your brother killed your father, Joe. That's not something you can let him get away with. If you want you and your mother to survive, you have to take action," Cain said. "Can you do it, Joe?"

"Yes," Joey answered.

"Good."

* * *

"I'M HUNGRY," Jung Jr. said.

Billy was drifting off. Jung Jr. had been tugging on his arm for the past ten minutes, but he was too tired to do anything about it.

"We just ate, buddy," Billy said.

"But I'm hungry again."

Then the jumping up and down to demand attention started, followed by Claire attempting to emulate her brother, only adding to the noise.

"Okay, okay. Let's go grab something," Billy said.

Both kids squealed with delight. Billy led them outside and over to Fay's room, where the food was stored. The sun was sinking low in the west, and when Billy first heard the sound, he thought he imagined it, but it was growing louder in the distance.

"It's a car," Billy whispered to himself.

He picked Claire up and grabbed Jung Jr. by the hand and sprinted toward Fay's room. She was out the door before he could knock.

"You hear that?" Billy asked.

"Which direction is it coming from?"

"East, I think."

"Take the kids inside."

"What? Why?"

"We don't know who's coming. You have your rifle on you?"

"It's back in the room."

"Grab it. Quickly!"

Billy dashed to his room. The rifle was leaning against the corner. He grabbed it, checked the magazine to ensure it was loaded, then headed back over to Fay and the kids.

"Stay in here until I say it's safe to come out. If something happens, stay hidden. Your best bet is to stay here and hope they keep going," Fay said.

"But—"

"No exceptions. Now, get in there and stay quiet."

Billy hurried the kids in the room, and he locked the door. He sat the two of them on the bed and put his finger to his lips.

"You guys need to stay quiet for me, okay?" Billy said.

Jung Jr. and Claire both brought their fingers to their lips. Billy smiled.

"Perfect," he said.

Billy stepped softly over to the window, staying low to remain out of sight. He could see Fay crouched behind one of the cars, her eyes glued down the road.

The vehicle's engine grew louder, and it sounded as though it was slowing down. Whoever it was planned on taking a look around.

It was some sort of military vehicle. It stopped directly in front of the motel, and the engine cut off. The windows were tinted, but even if they weren't, Billy wasn't sure if he'd be able to see who was inside.

His hand pressed against the window, almost breaking the glass, when he saw who stepped out. It was his brother, and his mom, with a man he didn't recognize. All of them were armed.

Before Fay could aim her rifle, Beth brought her down with a shot that echoed through the courtyard.

Billy dashed out of the hotel room, forgetting the kids in the room.

"Mom, stop!" he screamed.

Then, when his mother saw him, he watched the barrel of her rifle point at him, and he ducked for cover behind the staircase. The bullets ricocheted off the concrete. Billy peeked through the spaces of the stairs and watched both his mother and brother advance on him.

He didn't know what to think. Was it this man they were with that was making them do this? Were they acting on their own? What was happening?

The thought of Jung Jr. and Claire suddenly flooded his mind. He couldn't let his family hurt them. Billy brought the rifle's stock to his shoulder. He closed his eyes, exhaling slowly.

When he opened his eyes, he jumped from behind the staircase and fired a few rounds in his mother's direction, causing her to jump behind one of the small stone walls in the courtyard. He tried looking for his brother, but he couldn't see where he went.

He used the wall behind him as a guide and kept his sights on his mother as he backtracked to the room where the kids were. He finally made it to the door and backed inside.

Before the door was shut, he felt hands grip his neck and face. The rifle hit the floor as Billy tried to free himself from Cain's hold, but it was useless. The more he struggled, the tighter Cain squeezed.

"Shhh," Cain whispered.

It took Billy a moment for the scene in front of him to sink in. Both Jung Jr. and Claire were on the floor, crying and holding on to each other while Joey stood next to them with his rifle aimed at both their heads.

Joey was looking at him, but it wasn't his brother's eyes staring at him. It was some other creature's gaze. They looked like their father's eyes.

"Your brother wanted to come show you something," Cain said.

Billy screamed through Cain's hand, trying to talk to his brother, but all that came out was mumbled cries. His eyes moved from Joey's finger on the trigger to Jung Jr.'s and Claire's crying faces.

"Show him, Joey. Show him who you are," Cain said.

This wasn't his brother. This wasn't any type of reality he knew. How could it be? It was a nightmare. He just had to wake up.

The barrel of Joey's rifle pressed against the side of Jung Jr.'s head. Billy started to feel light-headed. The room started to go black.

Claire's face was beet red from crying. Her screams were piercing, scared. She clutched onto her brother, whose face was just as red and afraid. Joey's hand was shaking.

"Do it," Cain said.

Claire screamed again, louder than she had before. Billy couldn't take his eyes off his brother's finger hovering over the trigger. One small movement was all it would take to transform his brother from innocent to murderer.

"Do it!" Cain screamed.

The sound of Joey's rifle going off seemed as if it was far away, in another world, in another life. When it was over, all Billy could hear was a solid ringing in his ears, and the last thing he saw before he passed out was the blood splattered across his brother's face.

* * *

WHEN BILLY WOKE UP, he tried moving his arms, but he felt the tight

371

grip of rope around his wrists, keeping his hands tied behind his back. His ankles were bound together as well.

He looked to his left and saw that Jung was tied and bound next to him. Jung had his eyes open, but they were glazed over.

"Jung," Billy said. "Jung, what's going on?"

Jung didn't respond. He just sat there, a dead look on his face, staring at something. Billy followed Jung's line of sight, and when he saw what Jung was looking at, he turned his head and puked on the ground.

The acid from the vomit burned his throat, all the way from the pit of his stomach to the roof of his mouth.

Both Jung Jr. and Claire were piled on top of each other. The blast from Joey's rifle had left their heads and faces unrecognizable. Their small hands, arms, and legs were tangled together and motionless.

Billy's body convulsed as sobs escaped him. They were silent at first and then grew to painful moans. The cries were rooted in not only the children's deaths but also the actions of his brother.

Billy just lay there on his side against the rough, granular concrete, staring at the two tiny, lifeless bodies on the ground in front of him when a pair of boots blocked his vision.

"I'm glad you finally came around. We were starting to worry," Cain said.

Cain grabbed Billy's shoulders and sat him upright. He tapped the side of Billy's cheeks and then wiped the tears off them.

"There, there now. It's okay. Those kids won't have to suffer anymore. Your brother did a very brave thing, you know," Cain said.

It was Cain's eyes that threw Billy off. They were crystal blue, clearer and richer than any eyes he'd ever seen before, eyes that hid the twisted mind that stole his brother's childhood.

"You know he didn't say a word when we brought him down here?" Cain said, gesturing to Jung. "Now, there's a man who has lost all connection with who he used to be. I'd bring him with me if he weren't a complete zombie. Such a waste," Cain said.

Cain pulled a knife from his belt. It ran six inches in length with a solid black handle. He placed the tip of the blade gently on the toe of Billy's shoe.

"You know your family is very special. I can't tell you how many towns I've been to like this one where people are barely surviving, trying to hold on. Each time I tried to help them, convince them that there was a better way, but none of them could go the distance.

They couldn't leave behind the one thing stopping them from flourishing," Cain said.

Cain ran the knife along the fabric of Billy's pants with enough pressure for Billy to feel the blade's presence but light enough to not cut the fabric.

"Where's my brother?" Billy asked.

"Oh, he'll be here in a minute. I'm sure he won't want to miss the show," Cain answered.

"You're sick."

"You know what I just realized? I haven't properly introduced myself."

Cain laughed, shaking his head. "I'm so sorry about that. My name is Cain."

"I don't give a *shit* what your name is."

"See! That's the spark! That's what you need! But you're missing the sense of detachment that your friend here has. If I could just combine the two of you, I think you'd be a great addition, but I'm afraid we're running out of time," Cain said. "Ah, here she is."

Billy looked to his right and saw his mother walking toward him. She had dark circles under her eyes. They were deeper than usual. More hollow.

"Mom?" Billy asked.

She didn't respond. Cain stood up and handed her the knife.

"Don't take too long," Cain said.

Cain patted her on the back and disappeared behind Billy. Beth knelt down in front of him, her eyes looking at him but not seeing him.

"Mom, what are you doing? I don't know what that man did, but listen to me, this isn't right. Mom, you're not thinking straight," Billy said.

"I loved you," Beth said.

Billy started crying. His whole body shook as the flow of tears opened up again down his face. His head tilted down. He tried stopping, but he couldn't.

"I'm sorry, Mom. I'm so s-sorry. I'm sorr-ry," Billy said.

Beth lifted Billy's head. Her face was calm. The blade was still clutched in her other hand. She smiled, and Billy caught a glimpse of how his mother used to look at him before all of this, before the blackout and the death of his father.

"Billy," Beth said.

Her words were soft like when she used to come and tuck him in at night when he was a child. He was always afraid of the dark, but whenever she came in before he went to sleep, he always felt better, safer.

"I don't care," Beth finished.

Billy felt the cold steel thrust into his neck. His whole body seized. The pain was quick, and he immediately gasped for breath. He could feel the blood spilling from his neck onto his chest. Everything felt warm at first, then cold, empty... tired.

Beth held his gaze the entire time. Her face was twisted with anger. But even with that face staring back at him, the last image Billy saw was him and his brother playing in the yard. It was sunny outside, and there was a slight breeze in the air. They were chasing after each other, playing tag.

The pain finally subsided and Billy smiled, hearing nothing but the sound of his brother's laughter echoing through the field in his mind.

* * *

JUNG DIDN'T PUT up a fight. When he saw Cain open the door to his room he thought that was the moment, this man was the one to end everything for him, but he was wrong.

He thought that'd he lost all ability to feel anything, but when he saw his children dead, something inside of him was screaming, demanding to be let out, but it couldn't escape.

It was trapped deep within him, like a man lost at sea, screaming through the storm to another ship in the distance for help, but no one was able to hear him.

The only emotion that came out was the steady flow of tears tumbling down the side of his cheeks. When he felt Billy's body collapse next to him, he looked down to see blood spilling into the cracks of the concrete.

Jung could smell the blood and feel it sticking to his shirt and arm. Everything was red. He felt himself panicking. The world around him seemed to be folding in, suffocating him until he couldn't breathe anymore.

He tried to regain control and went back to the sight of his children. He couldn't understand why they piled them on top of each other. They were discarded like a broken appliance.

Cain was saying something to him, but all Jung could see were Cain's lips moving. He couldn't hear their sounds, or what he was telling him. Jung knew it was because of this man's actions that his children were dead.

But Cain was just the instrument, not the source. The real murderer was Jung. He pulled the trigger on his children long before Cain showed up. It had been there lingering in the back of his mind. He knew the moment would come, but Jung's one wish was to be dead before he saw it happen.

Whatever God he'd given up on had decided to return the favor, punishing him for his lack of faith and devotion to his family and fellow man. His mind went to the book of Revelation, and the first words he'd spoken were from the very book he'd forsaken.

"Every eye will see him, even those who pierced him; and all peoples on earth will mourn because of him," Jung said.

Cain bent down on his knee and met Jung's eyes, smiling. The blade Beth had used to kill Billy was in his hand still dripping with blood.

"So shall it be. Amen," Cain said.

The slice of Jung's throat was quick. The blood drained from him like an open faucet, and Jung's eyes fixed on his children until the last bits of life vanished from his face.

Cain wiped the blade on Jung's shoulder, cleaning the red off the silver steel. He tucked it back into his belt and clapped his hands together.

Beth's and Joey's hands were stained red. That was the sight Cain was looking for, there in front of him. They were hungry now, purged of whatever ties to the past they were holding on to.

"Now, the fun begins," Cain said.

SIX MONTHS AFTER THE BLACKOUT

*T*he computer screen on Ben's desk was the only source of light in the office. His eyes were bloodshot, strained from looking at files for the past nine hours.

Ben leaned back in his chair and attempted to rub the dryness out of his eyes. He looked over at Mitch, who was passed out on the sofa. So far the only thing Mitch offered in the research was the occasional snore.

Through all of the files that Ben searched, he couldn't find anything on either Dr. Wyatt or Mike. Both of them were squeaky-clean. Aside from Wyatt's bumble at the Senate hearing, he hadn't made any waves.

The only thing he could find on Mike was a speeding ticket under his wife's name, and their marriage license.

Ben kept staring at the marriage license, studying it. There was something about it that didn't sit right with him, but he couldn't place it. He wasn't surprised that Mike had been married.

Whenever Ben pried into Mike's past in the interrogation room, he'd never get anywhere. Mike wouldn't talk about anything.

Even if Dr. Wyatt was telling the truth and there was a journal that chronicled what happened and proved Mike's innocence, why would he give it to him? The man obviously believed he was guilty, but Ben didn't think it was of the crimes Mike said he committed. There was something more.

* * *

"You really think this is going to work?" Mitch asked.

"We've tried everything else. If this doesn't get a response out of him, then I don't know what will," Ben answered.

Mitch let out a long sigh and then opened the interrogation room's door. Mike was inside, shackled to the chair and floor, and dressed in orange.

Mike kept his head down as usual, and Ben took a seat across from him. Ben laid the manila folder gently onto the table and folded his hands together.

"How are you doing today, Mike?" Ben asked.

The only answer Ben received was the shuffling of chains. Ben opened the file but made sure Mike couldn't see the contents of what was inside. He flipped through the pages, just examining them.

"You know we had a friend of yours pay us a visit yesterday," Ben said.

It was the first time Mike actually looked at him. Whatever secrets Mike was hiding, having an "old friend" stop by was bound to make him nervous.

"Did you ever spend any time in Washington, DC, before the blackout?" Ben asked.

"I don't have any friends," Mike said.

"I actually lived there, before the EMP blast. Most of the city was a dump, but it wasn't without its charms."

Ben continued to examine the pictures in the file, glancing up every once in a while to see Mike's eyes glaring at him.

"The monuments there are incredible. It's a great destination for families," Ben said.

Mike pulled hard against the chains, but they were so tight that the only thing Ben noticed was the flex of Mike's arms.

Ben set the folder down and pulled out pictures of Freddy, Kalen, and Anne. Each picture slid across the table's smooth surface and stopped abruptly at Mike's arm.

"Were they in on it too, Mike?" Ben asked. "Did your family help you break into that military base and launch that EMP? Did they even know who you were, what you were planning on doing?"

Mike didn't say anything. He just glanced down at the pictures. Ben tried reading the emotions on Mike's face, but it was blank.

"Do they know you're here?" Ben asked.

"We thought you'd be happy to see them," Mitch said.

Mitch leaned on the table, his large belly digging into the table's edge.

"You couldn't protect them, could you? You weak piece of shit," Mitch said.

"AHHHHHHHH!" Mike screamed.

Mike snapped and turned on Mitch, but the restraints did their job. Curses and spit flew from Mike's mouth as he screamed at both of them. It was a stream of adrenaline that lasted for fifteen minutes, then finally subsided with Mike exhausted and slumped in his chair, looking numb as he stared at the pictures on the table.

"Mike," Ben said, "I don't think you did any of what you said happened. I don't believe a family man who was married for twenty-five years at a job you'd been at for just as long would snap like this. Tell me what happened. I can help you."

Mike's eyes were red. Ben could see the tears he was holding back, ready to burst at any moment. Ben picked up a picture of his son and held it up for Mike to see.

"What happened, Mike?" Ben asked.

Mike gently grabbed the picture from Ben's hands. It was Mike's shoulders that started to shake first, then his arms and hands, and the picture wobbled back and forth. The first tear hit the table, and with the dam now broken, the rest of the tears fell like rain.

After a minute of letting himself go, he started to regain his composure, drawing in deep breaths.

"Who is he?" Mike asked.

"Who is who?" Ben asked.

"The man who came to see you."

"He identified himself as Dr. Quinn Wyatt."

The picture of Freddy fell from Mike's grip. His eyes darted from Mitch to Ben.

"Where's the journal, Mike?" Ben asked.

"Whatever he told you is a lie," Mike said.

"The journal, Mike. What did you do with it?"

"Take me back to my cell."

It wasn't going to work. Wherever the journal was, whatever happened, Mike wasn't going to tell him. Ben called for the correction officer, and Mike was escorted back to his cell.

Mitch patted Ben on the back.

"C'mon, kid. You need a drink."

* * *

OUT OF ALL of the businesses that started back up after the power came back on, the ones that had the quickest success were the bars. People wanted to forget whatever terrible things they did during the blackout as fast as possible.

Mitch ordered a whiskey and coke, and Ben sipped on a beer. The bar wasn't too busy, but then again it was twelve thirty in the afternoon on a Wednesday.

"I don't know what he's scared of," Ben said.

"This place is a dump."

"He knows he didn't do any of this, and he's still punishing himself for it. Why?"

"Hey, barkeep! Where's the bar nuts?"

"If we could just reach out to his family. Maybe they could help us."

Ben rested his head on his arm and then felt a nudge in his side.

"Hey," Mitch said. "You can't save someone that doesn't want to be saved, Ben."

"What'd you do?"

"What do you mean?"

"During the blackout. I know you weren't stationed in DC. You said you were from Philadelphia, right?"

"Yup."

"That place was a madhouse. How'd you survive?"

"Hey, it's the city of brotherly love."

Ben laughed, and Mitch gave a chuckle. Both of them took another sip of their drinks. Ben placed his beer on the small white napkin.

"Ben, the things that happened during the blackout were bad. People... they lost who they were. I saw people stab each other over crumbs. Fuckin' crumbs," Mitch said.

Mitch drained the rest of his drink and slammed it down on the counter. He called the bartender over again and asked for another.

"Did you kill anyone?" Ben asked.

Mitch grabbed a handful of the bar nuts next to him and shoved them in his mouth, then washed them down with another swig of his fresh drink.

"We all did what we had to do, Ben. There's not a person out there that doesn't have dirty hands."

Ben knew Mitch had a point. Everyone was without power for too long. People will stay calm for only so long before they riot. The dependency on technology became abundantly clear when none of it worked.

History books would record this time period as one of the worst in American history. The stories would surpass the Great Depression, both World Wars, 9/11, all of it. It was as if the entire nation lost its sanity with the rest of the world watching, and now we were waking up from the nightmare, looking around at the damage and trying to sweep it under the rug.

That's why Ben wanted the proof so bad. He had to pull one truth out of all the lies being peddled to everyone. There had to be one beam of light out there.

"I killed someone," Ben said.

Mitch stopped chewing and set his drink down.

"Ben, you don't have to—"

"It was in the middle of the day, about three months in. I was on guard at the food bank in DC. You should have seen the lines of people waiting. It stretched for miles. You couldn't even see the end. We moved on to the emergency reserves at that point. You could see the hunger on everyone's faces. The food bank was handing out the bare minimum. The tension running through the crowd was thick, and there was this guy, a dad with his family, and they were close to the front of the line. His little girl was crying, and she just wouldn't stop. He walked up to me, saying that his daughter hadn't eaten in three days. He begged me to let him cut in line, just to grab food for her. He was even willing to give up his rations just to feed her, but we had protocol. No one could skip, no exceptions. Then other people started pleading, arguing why they should be able to eat first. The guards were outnumbered a thousand to one. If they rushed the gates, then it would have been over. I pulled my gun and told him to get back in line, but he just wouldn't stop. He kept screaming for me to let him through, and the crowd around him was getting restless. I couldn't let the chaos break out. I couldn't let one person destroy what little we had left. I warned him one more time to get back in line, and he made a move on me so I pulled the trigger. One shot through the head. The rest of the crowd backed down after that. I can still hear two things from that day when I close my eyes to fall asleep. I can hear the sound of my gun going off, and the screams from his wife, cursing me as she wept over her husband's corpse."

Ben took another sip of beer then clutched the drink in both hands as he closed his eyes, letting out a breath that was soft and slow.

"The supplies from Europe arrived the next day," Ben said.

"You followed your orders, Ben. There was no way of knowing

what would happen if you hadn't pulled the trigger. You knew what you had to do. It was a hard choice, but one that had to be made."

"Yeah… orders."

* * *

EVEN THOUGH DR. WYATT volunteered to come to the investigator's unit, Ben and Mitch housed him in an apartment building onsite. He was impressed with the size of the facility they were able to use. It looked like an old university that swapped housing bright young minds for suspected criminals.

Dr. Wyatt unpacked his suitcase and placed what spare clothes he had into the small dresser at the foot of the bed. There was a TV on top of it, which he didn't use. He found himself not using any piece of electronics out of habit. He managed to make it as far as he did without it and realized just how much of a time waste it was to spend your free hours glued to a television numbing your mind.

His room was on the eighth floor of the building, and he had a decent view of the surrounding area. There were cars moving on the roads, traffic lights changing from red to green, and he could hear the hum of the electrical transformer from the power lines just outside his window.

It was such a different sight than the one he experienced just a few months ago. The frozen cities had been thawed and were now beginning to teem with life again.

Dr. Wyatt sat on the edge of the bed and ran his fingers along the fabric of the comforter. The sheets on the bed were clean, the floor in the room was vacuumed, and the A/C was blasting through the vents.

All of this was brought back for mankind, the same mankind that ignored him, shunned him, and tried to bury him. He started to think that him being there was a bad idea. Even if he had a chance to speak with Mike, there was no guarantee that he'd be able to help him, and even if he was able to help him, there was no promise that Mike would accept it.

Every time he thought about it, a sour feeling hit the pit of his stomach and spread throughout his body. He reached for his bag and pulled out the bottle of pills he kept with him to ease the stress.

He washed the pill down with a cup of water he filled from the sink and lay down to let the medicine take effect.

* * *

BEN CALLED Dr. Wyatt first thing in the morning and told him to come to his office immediately. He didn't tell him why though.

Ben was still hung over from the day before. Mitch just kept feeding him drinks, and before he knew it, he was hunched over in the toilet puking his guts out. Ben took a taxi home, and when he woke up in the morning, his head felt as if it was on an anvil being pounded by a sledgehammer.

When he saw Mitch come in the office looking as fresh as a newborn calf, he shrugged his shoulders in disbelief.

"How the hell are you not dying right now?" Ben asked.

"My liver's used to that sort of punishment."

Mitch offered him a little hair of the dog, which Ben emphatically declined. He couldn't even look at alcohol without wanting to vomit.

One of the office assistants came in a little later to let Ben know that Dr. Wyatt was there. He met Wyatt in the interrogation room alone.

"I appreciate you coming in on such short notice," Ben said.

"Well, the armed guards you sent to collect me were quite convincing."

Ben could feel the strain of trying to focus on the conversation at hand. He rubbed his eyes.

"Long night?" Dr. Wyatt asked.

"You could say that."

"We all have ways of coping, Agent Sullivan."

"Is that why your pupils are dilated?"

"What can I help you with?"

"When you came in, you said you wanted to help Mr. Grant, correct?"

"That's correct."

"And it's something you're still interested in pursuing?"

"Yes."

"Why?"

"As I told you before, he—"

"Suffered a great deal, yes, I know that, Dr. Wyatt. But how did he suffer? I know he had a family. Do you know where they are?"

"You need to let me speak to him."

Ben let out a sigh. He was exhausted. He was running out of

time, and patience. Whatever Dr. Wyatt believed he could do to help Mike involved speaking with him.

"He doesn't want to be saved," Ben said. "I've tried reaching him, but it's just no use. He believes he's guilty. The evidence we have suggests that he is, and my superiors are breathing down my neck to close this case."

"Besides your drinking, have you turned to anything to help you cope with the things you did during the blackout, Agent Sullivan?"

"Yes."

"And what was it?"

"My family."

"It's nice to have something to help pull you out of the darkness. Myself, I didn't have any family, so as you can see from my 'dilated pupils,' I've coped in other ways."

"Dr. Wyatt, I don—"

"Do you know how Mike Grant coped after what happened in Cincinnati?"

"No."

"Well, I do. And if you don't let me speak with him, a good man is going to die."

Ben didn't know what else he could do. He researched every possible lead, checked every scenario, but he still couldn't shake the feeling that through all of those procedures something was wrong. Maybe it was time to try something a little unconventional.

"All right, Dr. Wyatt. I'll bring him in," Ben said.

53

CINCINNATI (DAY 25)

ike kept Kalen close the entire morning. He was next to her when they were grabbing their gear, loading their ammo, and boarding the trucks to take them to the rallying point where they would try and take the bridge from the rebels.

He tried making a case for her to stay in the city, but it fell to pieces when she spoke up demanding that she be a part of the raid. Once Blake heard that, the discussion was over.

The brief was simple. The rebels were running low on supplies and ammo. They were outnumbered, and this campaign was to be the last push to get them back over the river and take control of the bridge, allowing the rest of Bram's men to connect with his other units in Lexington.

Blake and the rest of his men outnumbered the rebels two to one, so the tactic would be to drive a wedge between the rebels. Divide and conquer.

The rebels hadn't used any heavy artillery for the past week, so it was believed they'd run out. Everything would be handled on the ground, with man-to-man combat. Mike, Sam, and Kalen were a part of Unit One and charged with taking out the left flank.

When the truck came to a stop, Mike's heart was pounding out of his chest. His hands felt like bricks holding the rifle. He tried massaging them earlier in the morning, but it didn't really help.

Blake gathered everyone around him once the trucks were emptied. Mike watched them turn around and head back to the city, toward safety. All he wanted to do at that moment was throw his daughter in the back of one of those trucks.

"All right, everyone, listen up!" Blake said. "We'll be joining up with the rest of the troops at the front line. We have them on their heels, so this is it. You all know what needs to be done. Let's move out!"

There were only thirty of them, but from Blake's description, that was more than enough to overrun the enemy. They broke off into five groups of six. Mike's group consisted of himself, Sam, Kalen, and Blake. Two other guys rounded out the group, Steve and Jimmy. Both were hunters before the blackout, and both were excellent marksmen. Mike's group could've done a lot worse.

Gunshots rang out the closer they moved to the river. Mike could smell the mixture of water, gunpowder, and dust swirling in the air. The scent grew stronger as the sounds of guns and screams increased.

Up ahead Mike could see the forces already there, advancing on the bridge. The rallying point for the unit was a small office building just behind the front lines. Blake led the group inside, and they had a front-row seat for the bloodshed.

"Listen up! We push whoever we can to the west. No hesitation," Blake said.

Mike clicked the safety off the rifle. He looked to Kalen, who was still staring out the empty window frame where the glass was shattered. He pulled Sam close and whispered in his ear.

"Don't let her out of your sight," Mike said.

Sam nodded and moved over to Kalen's right side. When Blake finally signaled they were heading out, Mike gave Kalen one last glance and took a deep breath.

The firing was sporadic, and Mike could hear the shouts of men on both sides. He kept Kalen in his field of vision the entire time, while scanning for anything that would harm her.

Blake was leading them toward a small cluster of soldiers on the outside edge of the bridge. He was the first to open fire, followed by Jimmy and Steve.

The rebels immediately returned fire, and Mike shoved Kalen down behind a car for cover.

"Dad!" Kalen said.

"Stay down!" Mike screamed.

Mike rested his rifle on top of the trunk and squeezed the trigger, firing off some rounds into the rebels, then ducked back down as they returned fire.

Kalen crawled to the front of the car by the engine. She rested her rifle on top of the hood and opened fire.

"Kalen!" Mike yelled.

Mike jumped up, but was pinned down by more rebel fire. Kalen took off running, and he crawled to the front of the car to see where she was heading. He saw her up against another abandoned car, parallel to Blake, who was waving everyone forward.

The rebels were slowly realizing they were being flanked, and he could see them retreating not to the west but across the bridge. There was a lull in gunfire, and Mike sprinted toward his daughter.

His shoulder slammed into the car door as he caught his breath. Kalen continued the assault on the rebels. He yanked her down.

"What are you doing?" Mike asked.

"Our mission."

She yanked his hand off her and moved back into a firing position. Mike watched her with a blended sense of admiration and fear. The swell of pride came from watching his daughter so focused, thriving in a moment of chaos where most would crumble. The stroke of fear came from the knowledge that getting to that point of focus came at a cost of her old self, one that she wasn't going to get back.

"They're retreating across the bridge! Move forward!" Blake yelled.

The gunfire coming from their team was relentless now. The rebels were sprinting as fast as they could across the bridge. The other units were converging at the bridge's entrance, picking off as many of the rebels as they could.

"We need to move across and secure the other side before they regroup!" Blake said.

"Anybody that goes across that bridge is a sitting duck. It's too exposed," Sam replied.

Mike looked around. There were three abandoned cars close to the bridge's entrance. One of them had the tires blown out, but the other two were good.

"We can throw those cars in neutral and roll them across," Mike said.

"That's our cover," Blake replied. "Let's move!"

They opened all of the car doors and rolled them forward across the bridge, shielding them from the gunfire raining down on them.

Another unit followed their lead and began pushing their own car across the bridge. Both Mike and Blake were on the front doors. Sam was behind Mike, and Kalen was behind Blake on the rear doors, while Jimmy and Steve were pushing from the bumper.

As they crept their way across the bridge, Mike noticed the gunfire had let up. He looked up and saw that most of the rebels had disappeared. In fact, he couldn't see any of them. Mike scanned the shoreline and the end of the bridge, but there was nothing.

"They're gone," Mike said.

"Keep pushing forward," Blake ordered.

Something was wrong. After all of the fighting and protection of the bridge, why would they give it up so easily? From everything that Mike had learned about the bridge, it was a pivotal, strategic point.

They were past the halfway point, and the bridge started its downward slope. The car started picking up speed. Mike jumped in the driver's seat and tapped the brakes so they wouldn't end up crashing into anything on their way down.

Then, just to his left Mike could see a tarp on the sidewalk. The end was flapping open from the breeze. He looked over to his right and saw another tarp directly parallel to the one on the left.

Mike slammed the brake pedal hard. The open doors flopped forward a bit, and everyone slammed into them.

"They're gonna blow the bridge!" Mike yelled.

Everyone's heads went up. Mike slammed the car's shifter into park and tried rolling out of the driver's seat, but someone grabbed his arm, stopping him.

Mike looked over, and Blake had his fingers digging into his skin. He tried to break free, but Blake had a really good hold on him.

"We push forward," Blake said.

"The tarps!" Mike said.

"We can't lose this bridge," Blake yelled, running to the tarp.

Kalen followed him, and Mike sprinted after her. Blake lifted the tarp off and revealed enough plastic explosive to blow the bridge sky-high.

"Jesus," Blake whispered.

"We need to get off the bridge now!" Mike yelled.

"If we lose this bridge, it'll set us back months and it'll give the rebels time to regroup. We can't let that happen," Blake said.

"Toss it over the side!" Jimmy yelled.

"No, if it goes off underwater, it could damage the bridge's pillars," Blake answered.

Blake pulled his radio to his mouth.

"We need an ordnance expert on the bridge. Now," Blake said.

A few minutes later, a man came jogging up toward them. He was an older gentleman, probably late fifties, and had thick-rimmed glasses. He wasn't dressed in the normal military fatigues like Blake had on, so Mike figured he must have been a recruit like himself. He introduced himself as Brian.

"What do we have here?" Brian asked.

"Can you disarm it?" Blake asked.

Brian walked around to the back end of the explosive device. There was a wire that ran from the back of the C-4 along the bridge wall leading to the opposite side. When Brian saw the configuration of the bomb, he sprinted in the other direction without saying a word.

Jimmy and Steve followed him. Blake tried to corral his unit, but once the other soldiers saw them sprinting away, it was a free-for-all.

"We have to get this explosive off the bridge!" Blake said.

Kalen went over to the other side where the other tarp was. She flung the tarp off, revealing an equal amount of explosive as its counterpart.

Mike grabbed her by the arm and tried pulling her backwards. She kept wiggling out of his grip.

"It's not worth it. Let it go," Mike said.

"I'm not going to fail!"

Kalen was punching his chest, struggling to break free. Mike's hands were starting to ache from her thrashing. She wasn't going to give up. He'd seen that look before. It was the same look he had when he was on the road from Pittsburgh to the cabin, traveling to get to his family.

Mike flung her on the other side of the bridge away from the explosive. He scooped up the bomb and sprinted down the slope of the bridge. He set the bomb in a clearing away from the bridge's entrance. When he started to make his run back to the top of the bridge, the other bomb left on the bridge detonated.

The concrete and metal flew through the air and landed all around him. Mike coughed and rolled around on the ground. A solid ringing ran through his ears, and his vision was blurred, straining to focus on the shapes around him. When the ground stopped spinning, he managed to focus on what was left of the bridge.

Only a few thin pieces of concrete and steel connected the two sides. Mike scanned the bridge, looking for Kalen, but he couldn't see her.

Then a distant thumping sound began to replace the ringing in his ears. He couldn't tell where it was coming from, but it was quick and sporadic. It was as if it was coming from all directions.

Mike was still on his belly, crawling forward, trying to stand but unable to get his legs underneath him. The ringing started to clear, and the foreign thumping sounds became more recognizable. They were gunshots.

Mike looked behind him and could see rebel forces moving back toward the bridge and firing along the bank. Mike stumbled forward, attempting to stand, but then landed face-first on the concrete.

He heard shouts behind him, and the last thing he saw before he blacked out was the butt of a rifle smacking his forehead.

* * *

"What do you mean we can't go after him?" Kalen screamed.

One of the field nurses was sewing Blake's arm up from the blast wound he suffered when the bridge exploded. There weren't any casualties, but a few of the men were banged up pretty bad.

"You saw the bridge. It's gone, and we don't have any navy to speak of, so unless you want to swim across the river with our supplies on a raft, I suggest you calm down," Blake said.

"How long till we have boats in the water?" Kalen asked.

"Boats weren't a priority in our rebuilding efforts. It'll be a while."

"How long's a while?"

"Will you give us a minute?"

The nurse left the room, leaving Blake and Kalen alone. The stitches in his arm were poking out, and blood streaked down his skin.

Kalen wasn't without her own injuries. A piece of concrete had knocked her unconscious and left her with twelve stitches across her forehead. There was a constant throbbing in her forehead, but she ignored it.

"Look, kid, I know how much you want to get your dad, but we have to be realistic about this. We don't have any way of getting over the river right now, and even if we did, there's no guarantee that he's still alive. That's something you're going to have to be willing to accept," Blake said.

Kalen grabbed hold of the frame at the foot of the bed. She felt as if she could squeeze through the metal, crumpling it into flat pieces of lead.

"We're going to get my father back. Dead or alive, he's coming home," Kalen said.

Anne and Freddy were in the waiting room when she got out. They had been there all day, waiting to see her. She had been done with her checkup hours ago, but she wasn't ready to face them just yet. She needed more time to gather her thoughts.

She thought she'd know what she was going to say when she saw them, but the moment her eyes landed on her mother's face, whatever plan of action she had disappeared.

She found herself running into her mother's arms, feeling the embrace and warmth she hadn't allowed herself to feel for what felt like a very, very long time.

"It's okay, sweetheart," Anne whispered.

Kalen squeezed her mother tighter and could feel Freddy coming in on the side of her, wrapping his arms around her waist. She held the back of his head and just allowed herself to be vulnerable again.

Once she finally gathered the strength to let go, Kalen wiped her eyes on her shirt, and Anne examined the stitches on her forehead.

"What happened?" Anne asked.

"The bridge we were sent to take over was destroyed. Dad was on the other side when it blew. I don't know if—"

Kalen cut herself off. Freddy was looking up at her with the fearful eyes of a child, wanting to know more but afraid of what that knowledge meant.

"They don't know when we'll be able to cross the river to get him back. They don't have any boats prepared," Kalen said.

"There's no other way across?" Anne asked.

"No, the other bridges were blown up a while ago. I guess the rebels wanted to bottleneck everyone. Have one way in, and one way out."

Kalen could see the same words Blake had said etched across her mother's face. The chances of her dad being alive were slim, and even if he was, there wasn't a guarantee they could get him back.

* * *

MIKE'S HEAD WAS POUNDING, and he was drifting in and out of consciousness. He caught glimpses of different images when he was able to keep his eyes open. Brick walls, people in surgical masks, soldiers with rifles—all appeared and disappeared.

When Mike finally came to, he was in a bed. His head was still pounding, and when he tried to touch his forehead, he realized both of his hands were restrained. His feet were also tied down around the ankles.

He strained against the cuffs, but he couldn't break them. There was an IV set up next to him, and he could hear voices just behind the curtain, accompanied by footsteps. Mike's heart pounded harder with each step, and when the curtain finally swung open, a doctor with a clipboard was looking down at him.

"How are you feeling?" the doctor asked.

"The bridge. What happened to the other soldiers on the bridge?"

"Calm down. You're going to be all right, but you need to rest."

Mike started thrashing violently against the restraints, shaking the entire bed.

"My daughter! Where's my daughter?"

"Nurse, sedate him."

The nurse shoved the needle into Mike's arm, and he could feel a weightlessness fall over him. The faces staring down at him dissolved as he drifted off into a dreamless sleep.

* * *

WHEN MIKE WOKE AGAIN, he was still in the hospital room, but this time the curtain had been flung open and he was in the room by himself. There were two other empty beds with their sheets neatly made.

The drugs had left him tired, woozy. He was having a hard time concentrating.

"Hello."

The voice was cordial but firm. The figure Mike was staring at in the doorway was blurry. He could tell that he was in a suit, but he couldn't see the features of his face.

"I apologize for what happened earlier. It's not something I wanted to do, but my men told me you were being very... difficult."

The old man moved to the foot of the bed. Mike could make out his face now. It was kind but weary. Lines of stress creased along his forehead, under his eyes, and along his mouth.

Mike shook his head, trying to clear his thoughts. He recognized the old man, but he couldn't remember from where. Whatever drugs they had him on were fogging his mind. Mike checked his limbs. He was still tied down.

"What happened to the other soldiers on the bridge?" Mike asked.

"Most of them survived the blast, but the bridge did not fare very well. It wasn't a move we wanted to make. It hurt us just as much as it hurt you, but we couldn't allow your men to advance."

Mike wasn't sure how many questions he was going to get out of him, so he wanted to pick them carefully.

"Where am I?" Mike asked.

"You're in south Cincinnati."

"Who are you?"

"My name is Dr. Quinn Wyatt."

54

DAY 25 (COLUMBUS)

*B*eth watched Cain drive. She hadn't taken her eyes off him since they left Carrollton. She was drawn to him in the most unexplainable way. Everything he did seemed so effortless yet calculated with tremendous intention.

Cain kept his eyes on the road and hadn't glanced her way the entire trip. In fact he hadn't said a single word. She wasn't sure if Joey had said anything. All she could focus on at the moment was what he made her do.

Every once in a while she'd glance down at her hands and see the stains of blood, the blood of her son. It was dried now, flaking against her skin.

She was indifferent to it all. Whatever, or whoever, she believed in before was a forgotten memory.

Beth looked out the window. The street signs were signaling that they were close to Columbus. Then the car turned onto one of the exits for the city.

"I thought we were going to Cincinnati?" Beth asked.

"We're just going to make a quick pit stop here," Cain answered. He looked over to her for the first time on the trip and smiled. "I need to show off my new weapons."

Beth hadn't been to any major city since she was a little girl. Her jaw dropped when they entered downtown Columbus. The skyscrapers and buildings towered over her. There were abandoned cars and trash everywhere. It looked like a war zone.

They weaved in and out of the parked cars through the streets until they made it to a blockade of men in uniform with guns. Cain stopped the truck.

"Stay here," he said.

The door slammed as he left and walked toward the soldier. He was greeted with a handshake and smile. He kept gesturing back to the truck, and Beth could see the other soldier squinting into the window to get a look at her.

Joey poked his head through the space between the two front seats.

"What are we doing here?" Joey asked.

"I don't know."

"I'm getting hungry."

"I'm sure we'll eat something soon."

Once they were past the blockade, the rest of the city seemed so neat. The cars had been cleared from the streets, and the trash had been picked up. People were walking back and forth casually, as if nothing was wrong.

In one of the windows of the stores they passed, she could see a fan plugged in, blowing air across someone's face.

"The power is on?" Beth asked.

"What?" Joey said, jumping out of his seat.

"Yes," Cain said.

"How?" Beth asked

"We turned it on," Cain said.

They pulled into a space where some other military trucks were located. "City Hall" was printed across the sign in front of the building.

There were more guards stationed at the entrance, and all of them saluted Cain as he passed them.

Inside, there were rooms filled with people. None of them had uniforms on. All of them were in regular street clothes, and they varied in age and ethnicity. Cain brought them to a room where most of the inhabitants were young men.

"Wait here, and I'll come to collect you in a little while," Cain said.

Before Beth could say anything, Cain closed the door. Two empty chairs were alone in the corner, so that's where Beth and Joey headed.

There were whispers as the two of them walked by, and understandably so. The men in the room looked strong, healthy. An old woman and young boy didn't fit the room's standard.

Beth had no idea what'd she gotten herself into. For the first time since she left Carrollton, she could feel doubt creep into her mind.

* * *

CAIN KNOCKED on the office door, and a hoarse voice greeted him from the other side.

"Enter!"

The old man behind the desk looked up from his paperwork.

"Ha! Cain, my boy! I was starting to think you wouldn't make it," Major Griffin said.

Griffin embraced Cain in a hug, and Cain took a seat across from Griffin's desk.

"What took you so long?" Griffin asked.

"I wanted to make sure that I got what we needed."

"Always the perfectionist. How many did you bring back?"

"Two."

"Two? That's it?"

Cain nodded.

"Jesus, Cain. Thompson brought back at least a dozen. You really couldn't find any more than two?"

"I found plenty, but I only found two that fit what we need."

"Well, they must be something. Nothing wrong with quality over quantity. Did you drop them off in the training room?"

"Yes."

"The drills should be starting soon. Let's go take a look."

Cain and Griffin snaked through the hallways. A few other soldiers joined them as they walked out the back and headed across the street. The group of recruits they brought in exited the side of the building and spilled into the training yard.

The officers around Cain and Griffin pointed out the ones they recruited.

"So where are yours, Cain?" Thompson asked.

"There in the back corner," Cain answered.

Laughter rippled through the group, but Cain didn't flinch.

"Stopped at a daycare on your way in?" Thompson asked.

Griffin grabbed Cain by the arm and leaned him in close.

"Is this some kind of joke, Cain?" Griffin asked.

"Just watch."

The group of recruits went through a few exercises on the field. Beth and Joey struggled with some of the drills, while the rest of the group brushed through them with ease. It went on like that for about an hour.

After the final physical drills were completed, Thompson slapped Cain on the back.

"We can't all bring home winners," Thompson said.

"No, we can't," Cain said.

The group of recruiters started to disperse, and Griffin shook his head in disgust. Everyone had turned their backs to him.

"Anyone care to place a small wager?" Cain asked.

Thompson was the first to turn around.

"And what's the bet?" Thompson asked.

"That my recruits can get the job done, but yours can't."

"We've already seen what the recruits can and can't do, Cain, but I'm always up for watching you embarrass yourself."

"Bring your two best recruits to the shooting range in an hour."

"What do you say, boys?" Thompson asked, glancing around at the other recruiters. "Anyone up for a little target practice?"

* * *

When the hour was up, the recruiters gathered their two best marksmen. It was an inside range, with targets set at different intervals. The first was close, only five yards out, but the farthest was thirty yards, used for rifle practice.

It was decided that everyone would be using the same rifle for consistency. Thompson went to set the targets down the field but stopped, turning back to Cain.

"Maybe we should start at the five-yard mark? That way your recruits have an easier time," Thompson said.

"The ten-yard mark will be fine, but I brought my own targets," Cain said.

Cain disappeared into one of the rooms. When he came back, he was pulling the arm of a young woman. She was blindfolded and had a gag in her mouth. Cain stood her in front of the ten-yard target and whispered in her ear.

"Stay still."

He gave her a kiss on the cheek, and she shuddered as he removed the blindfold and pulled the wad of cloth out of her mouth.

"What are you doing?" Griffin asked.

"Winning a bet."

Cain brushed Griffin off and picked up the rifle.

"First person to shoot wins," Cain said.

The only sound that was heard was the gasp from the woman. She was shaking. Tears were running down her face. She struggled for breath when she spoke, choking on her own spit.

"P-please, d-don't do th-this," she said.

"This is insane," Thompson said.

Thompson moved toward the girl, and Cain aimed the barrel of the rifle at him. Thompson froze.

"Out in the field, we won't be shooting thin sheets of paper with rings around them. We'll be shooting people like her. People who oppose us and what we're trying to build. Or did you forget that on your trip, Thompson?" Cain asked.

Cain pressed the rifle's barrel into Thompson's chest.

"This isn't a rebuilding effort we're putting together. We're still tearing down the old country to make way for a new one. Where the weak-willed and weak-minded, people like that," Cain said, pointing at the girl, "are no longer part of the problem."

The recruits started to speak out all at once.

"I didn't sign up for this."

"This is crazy."

"You can't be serious?"

Cain fired a round into the ceiling, silencing everyone. He motioned to Beth, who came over and grabbed the rifle from him.

Beth aimed the rifle at the girl, who was screaming hysterically now. She kept backing up, pressing into the stand behind her, trying to dissipate through the wood and metal.

"Fire," Cain said.

Beth squeezed the trigger. The bullet flew through the woman's head, and she hit the floor. The only sound after that was the bullet casing rolling on the concrete.

Beth handed the rifle back to Cain and rejoined the other recruits. Cain kept the rifle in his hands and walked over to Thompson.

"I win."

SIX MONTHS AFTER BLACKOUT

*D*r. Wyatt's palms were sweaty. It didn't matter how many times he wiped them on his pants, they just wouldn't dry. He'd been sitting in the interrogation room waiting, and dreading, for Ben to bring Mike through the door.

When the door finally opened and Ben escorted Mike in, Dr. Wyatt's insides twisted all at once.

"I'm not speaking with him," Mike said.

"You can do whatever you want, but you're in this room for the next twenty minutes," Ben said.

The chains around Mike's ankles rattled against the floor when he walked.

"You don't need to keep those on him," Dr. Wyatt said.

"Yes, you do," Mike replied.

"I'll be watching on the other side, so I don't want anyone trying anything stupid," Ben said.

The door clicked shut after Ben left. Dr. Wyatt had rehearsed this moment in his head a million times. Each time he'd run through it there would be a different ending, but the moment he opened his mouth he couldn't find the words he practiced.

"What are you doing here?" Mike asked.

"I've been trying to find you," Dr. Wyatt said.

"You shouldn't be here."

"This isn't your fault."

"Enough of it is."

Sweat was collecting under Wyatt's arms. He undid the button on his collar, feeling the steam escape out of his shirt.

"You're punishing yourself for something you had nothing to do with," Dr. Wyatt said.

"But we both know why I'm here."

"Mike..."

"You broke your promise, Doctor, so now I'm breaking mine," Mike said.

Dr. Wyatt said nothing. He simply rose from his seat, shaking slightly as he walked past Mike and out the door.

Once he made it out of the interrogation room, he ran for the bathroom. He shoved the stall door open and made it to the toilet just as the vomit sprayed from his mouth.

One arm shook, resting on the toilet seat while he collapsed to the cold tile. He grabbed a piece of toilet paper and wiped his mouth.

* * *

BEN ESCORTED Mike back to his cell. It took him twice as long to go anywhere because of the chains. All he could do was shuffle down the halls, and each time he moved his feet, the steel would cut deeper into his skin.

"Want to explain what all that was about?" Ben asked.

Mike didn't answer. They made it to his cell and Ben dropped him off, undoing his shackles. The steel door clanked shut. There was a small opening in the middle of the door for meals to slide in and out. Ben opened it, so Mike could hear him speak.

"Let me help you," Ben said.

Mike sat down on the edge of the cot, rubbing his hands and wrists. He kept his head down, looking at his feet.

"Make sure I don't see him again," Mike said.

The moment Ben slid the food hatch closed, Mike's hands started to shake. The pain stopped coming and going weeks ago. They just hurt all of the time now.

He just wanted it to be over. He'd tried before, but he couldn't stop the will to live. He needed someone else to do it for him. That's what he wanted to find here. That's why he turned himself in.

He stroked his beard slowly. It was thick and matted. He ran his shaking fingers through the tangled knots. He lay down on the cot, resting his head on the flat pillow. The springs of the bed squeaked as he shifted, trying to find a comfortable spot.

He didn't try closing his eyes. It wouldn't have made a difference if he did. He couldn't fall asleep anymore, and the rare moments when exhaustion finally caught up with him, he didn't stay asleep long. There were always bloody faces to wake him up in the night.

DAY 26 CINCINNATI

*M*ike hadn't been able to leave the hospital for almost twenty-four hours. The straps around his feet and hands were driving him mad. His visit from Wyatt didn't provide him any answers, but then again he wasn't able to stay awake for very long to speak to him.

Now that Mike was awake, he couldn't sit still. The nurses came and checked on him periodically. The faint, random screams of other patients echoing through the halls outside his door were starting to get to him.

Finally, later in the evening, a pair of soldiers came and escorted him out of the hospital. They returned the clothes he was wearing when he was captured, but not his weapon.

The majority of this part of the city was wrecked. Buildings were crumbled; trash and smoldering fires occupied the streets. It wasn't a city in the United States he was looking at—it was something he would see on CNN from a third-world country. Whatever beating Bram and his soldiers gave them, it seemed to be effective.

Mike was brought to a small building farther south of the river, which he got a good look at from one of the streets that led to the bridge, or at least where the bridge used to be. There was a humming coming from behind the building. It sounded familiar, but Mike couldn't put his finger on it.

"What is that?" Mike asked. "That noise?"

"Generator."

"You have power running here?"

"Move."

They waited outside the door of an office. Mike could hear some mumbling on the other side, and when he was let in, there was a group of three men. Two were dressed in military uniforms, and the other was Dr. Wyatt, who was also the only one that smiled.

"Gentlemen, this is the soldier we captured from across the river," Wyatt said.

One of the men leaned into Wyatt's ear, and Wyatt waved him off.

"We'll let you two get to it then," the man said.

The two men exited, leaving Wyatt and Mike alone. There was a single table in the room, and on top of it was a massive map covered in small figures.

"I hope you're feeling better?" Wyatt asked.

"Head still hurts."

"Mine too."

Mike kept glancing down at the map and around the room. The whole place was run-down. The one lamp they had in the room was flickering, struggling to perform its simple task of lighting the space.

"It doesn't look like much, but we make do," Dr. Wyatt said. "Have you had an opportunity to eat?"

"No."

"Here, we still have some sandwiches from lunch."

Dr. Wyatt pulled a tray off a chair in the corner and extended it to Mike. He took one hesitantly.

"I guess the easiest way to start this is asking how much you know about us?" Dr. Wyatt asked.

"Besides learning your entire military strategy?" Mike asked, looking at the map.

"Yes, besides that."

"Why did you bring me here?"

"Because you're the first soldier that we've been able to capture since all of this started."

"I'm the first?"

"Yes, all of the others killed themselves, but not you, which makes me think that you actually value your life. And someone that values their life tends to value the lives of others."

"In my experience it's usually the opposite."

"Sadly, these days you're probably right."

Dr. Wyatt picked up a few of the pieces on the map then set them back down. From the position of the figures on the table, it looked like Dr. Wyatt and his side were on their heels.

Mike took a bite of the sandwich. By the taste of it, they were scraping the bottom of their food rations.

"Have you spoken to Bram?" Dr. Wyatt asked.

"I have."

"Then I need you to tell me everything he's doing. How many men he has, when he's planning on his next attack."

"And just why should I trust you?"

"Because you're still alive."

"And I suppose I have you to thank for that?"

"No, not me. Every man and woman on this side of the river."

Mike swallowed the last piece of bread.

"Let's take a walk," Wyatt said.

Dr. Wyatt led Mike through streets and buildings of what was left of their side of the city. The farther away from the river they walked, the less damage there was. The ordnance that hit the city was powerful but had a limited range.

The power from the other side of the river didn't seem to be trickling over. A few places had generators, but most buildings were still dark.

The only vehicles that were working were those that had some sort of military application.

"Bram's powerful, and he knows it. And his reach is far because he feeds on the ambition of other people," Dr. Wyatt said.

"Sounds like a politician."

"Yes, in a matter of speaking, he is," Dr. Wyatt said, his face turning a little more grave. "And he's a very good one."

They walked for another hour, talking about what each of them did before the blackout. They spoke of family, friends. Mike never opened up to people outside of his family, but he found himself unable to keep his mouth shut.

Dr. Wyatt stopped in front of a small building. It hadn't been touched by the bombings, but was old, and derelict. Mike watched him stand there in silence, examining what was left of the ancient structure.

"Four walls and a roof," Dr. Wyatt said. "But it doesn't have its beating heart."

"The building is only as good as the men that occupy it," Mike said.

"When the power shut off, I'd never seen people in such a state. I watched humans devolve right in front of my eyes."

Mike thought back to Jung and the blind will of survival that made him forsake everything he believed in.

"Men who don't have a value in their own lives can't see the value in others," Mike said.

Dr. Wyatt smiled.

"That man you were fighting for, he's not who you think he is," Dr. Wyatt said.

"I wasn't fighting for him," Mike answered.

"I wouldn't ask anything of you that I wouldn't do myself."

"What do you need, Quinn?"

"I'm going to give you something. I give it to every man I've spoken with since the blackout. After you read it, I'll know which side you're on."

Dr. Wyatt pulled a small journal out of his pocket and handed it to Mike.

"Come find me when you're done," Dr. Wyatt said.

* * *

KALEN WAS CROUCHED behind a building in an alleyway, waiting for the guards to disappear. She'd been squatting there for over an hour, and her knees were aching. When the guards finally disappeared for their shift switch, she almost fell over from getting up too fast. Her knees popped and cracked as she ran for the door.

When she made it inside, she rushed to the back and hid between two aisles. She'd been waiting to get inside the armory supply since she got back from the bridge.

Once she was sure the coast was clear, she started stuffing ammo, pistols, magazines, grenades, anything she thought would help her, into the duffle bag she brought. The last weapon she grabbed was an AR-15 that she slung over her shoulder.

Kalen snuck out of a window on the side of the building and landed in an alleyway behind a dumpster. She started heading to the back when someone covered her mouth from behind.

"Shh," Sam said.

Sam grabbed the bag from her and opened it up. He sifted through the contents and threw it in the dumpster.

"Hey!" Kalen cried.

"What are you thinking?" Sam asked.

"My father's alive."

"And how were you planning on getting him? Going to swim across the Ohio River with all that gear dragging you down?"

Kalen slammed her back against the wall of the building and slid down.

Sam let out a sigh and joined her on the ground. He put his arm around her, and she rested her head on his shoulder.

"From what I've seen, your dad is one tough bastard. If he is alive, then he'll find a way back, but for now you have to do the hardest thing anyone in your position can do," Sam said.

"Which is?"

"Wait."

She knew he was right. Her mind went back to all of those nights when she was out late with friends. Her dad was always up when she made it home, no matter what time it was. His face always had the same look each time. It would be relieved and then, depending on how late it was, upset.

Kalen couldn't imagine the thoughts that went through her father's mind during those nights, waiting for her to come home. She couldn't comprehend the worry when he was separated from his family for almost a week as he trekked from Pittsburgh all the way to their cabin in Carrollton.

She had caused more stress in her father's life than anyone she knew. And now she was sitting on the other end of it.

"I'm afraid I won't see him again," Kalen said.

"You will."

Sam helped her off the ground and walked back with her to the hotel where her mother was waiting for her.

Anne squeezed Kalen tight.

"What were you thinking?" Anne asked.

"That I had to do something."

Anne shook her head.

"Stubborn like your father."

"Have you heard anything yet?"

"No, whatever they're planning on doing isn't a rescue mission. They're acting like he's—"

"Where's Freddy?" Kalen asked.

"He's down in your guys' room. He won't let anyone in," Anne said.

Kalen knocked on the door, but Freddy didn't answer. She

jiggled the handle and tried pushing the door open, but something was blocking it.

"Freddy?" Kalen asked.

She pushed hard, muscling the door open. Freddy had moved the dresser haphazardly into the small foyer in the room.

There was a fort in the corner. Kalen flipped up one of the sheets, and Freddy was tucked in a ball. He clutched the watch that Mike had given him in his hand.

"Hey, bud," Kalen said.

He didn't say anything as she crawled inside. She sat down next to him, and he cuddled up into her lap. Kalen stroked the back of his head, and his body started to shiver.

"Is Dad dead?" Freddy asked.

"No, he's not dead."

"Then where is he? Why hasn't he come back?"

"You know Dad. He has to make sure everyone's safe. That's what he's doing. Keeping us safe."

"You really think so?"

"I know so."

Kalen kissed the top of his head. She pulled the pocket watch from his hands and held it out in front of the both of them to see. It spun from the silver chain, twirling around and around.

"Is this the one that belonged to Grandpa?" Kalen asked.

"Yeah, Dad gave it to me when we were still at the cabin."

"You've been keeping it in good shape?"

"Yup. I found some silver polish at school and cleaned it the other day."

"Dad will be proud you're taking good care of it."

"When will he come back?"

"As soon as he can."

Kalen handed the watch back to her brother then wrapped her arms around him. When she looked up through the opening in the sheets, her mother was standing in the room, watching both of them.

Anne got down on her knees and entered the small fort with her children. The three of them curled up together under the sagging sheets.

* * *

MIKE CLOSED the journal and set it on the nightstand next to the bed he was lying on. Everything he'd just read was racing through his mind: the Senate hearing, Bram's partnership with Dr. Wyatt, the EMP device, the missile launches.

Mike shoved the journal back into his pocket. He found Wyatt in his room, reading by the glow of a single light next to his chair.

"When did you find out?" Mike asked.

"When did I find out what Bram was really planning on doing? When it was too late. I tried stopping him, but at that point everything was already in motion. Most of his men didn't realize what was going to happen either, and a few of them joined me here in Cincinnati where we knew he would gather. We knew he had one of his major facilities here and it was close enough to his other resources to stage a formidable stand for a coup against Washington."

"That's why you blew up the bridge."

"He already has men stationed in Columbus and Indianapolis. He's been recruiting men since the power's gone out to join his... cause. If he connects with his units in Nashville and Charlotte, then he'll be able to essentially divide the country in two with no organized forces to stop him."

Mike sat down on the arm of the only other chair in the room. He lost his legs. During the entire time he was reading that journal, he could think of only one thing: He left his family with that madman.

"What's his play?" Mike asked.

"He's manufacturing missiles at his factory here in Cincinnati. In Nashville they're manufacturing the guidance chips. They're planning on meeting in Lexington where there is a military base with launch capabilities. He already has men there preparing for both parties to arrive. I know their original timeline was to have everything up and running a week from now, but with the bridge gone, I don't know how long we've stalled him. I also don't know how long it'll be before his forces from the south make it up here to press us on both fronts."

"How do we stop him?"

"We don't need to take out all of the components of his plan; just one of them will cripple everything. We've been repairing boats in preparation for blowing up the bridge. We have enough to get everyone across, but we have no way of locating the factory or an understanding of their security structure."

"That's why you captured me."

"Yes."

Mike wasn't sure if he could trust Wyatt or not. For all he knew, this guy was playing him too.

"Why should I believe you and your journal?" Mike asked.

"Because there is enough evidence in that journal to put me away for a very long time. Usually, bad guys don't incriminate themselves like that to the people around them."

"If I do this, I want a guarantee that my family will be taken care of. That they are a priority for extraction when you make it across the river."

"I promise."

DAY 27 (CINCINNATI)

*T*hey drove west for almost thirty minutes. The road was in bad shape. It had been cracked and split into pieces from the weeks of bombardment from Bram and his men.

Dr. Wyatt sat in the back with Mike, while two soldiers rode up front. The top of the Jeep was open, and they had to yell over the engine and wind to be heard.

"It's just up the road here," Dr. Wyatt said.

"How do you know Bram doesn't know about this place?" Mike asked.

"His ordnance would have the range to take it out. If he knew, it would already be destroyed."

They pulled into a small marina. There were dozens of boats lining the docks, ranging in size and function. Most of the boats had men still working on them, but a few were being tested in the water.

"You're sure there are enough to get all of your men across?" Mike asked.

"Yes, but it's taken longer than we thought. We only had two marine mechanics. They've been working day and night and teaching our other mechanics as much as they could to help out," Dr. Wyatt answered. "What we've really been short on are welders."

"I can help with that."

The welding equipment they had wasn't the best, but Mike was used to working with older models. The steel mill back in Pittsburgh was always hesitant about spending money on anything that was new or worked properly.

Mike lit the welding torch. It felt good to have familiar tools in his hand. He brought two pieces of metal together, and sparks flew from the bonding. He could feel the heat through his gloves. He never thought he'd be happy to feel the singe of those sparks again. The focus and precision brought him a sense of normalcy that he hadn't felt for a long time.

After a few hours of finishing up some projects that were high priorities, Mike took his gloves off and started rubbing his hands. Dr. Wyatt came over and extended two pills and a bottle of water.

"How long have they been like that?" Dr. Wyatt asked.

"The past couple years."

"We could have one of our doctors take a look at them."

"I've had all sorts of doctors look at them, and they all tell me the same thing."

"And what's that?"

"Stop using them."

The drive back seemed considerably shorter. They entered Wyatt's headquarters and finished ironing out the details for the assault tomorrow.

"Bram's men are going to vet you, and they might even try to kill you," Dr. Wyatt said. "They won't be giving you the benefit of the doubt, so we won't have much time. You have to stay alive. If you can't lead us to the factory, then we're dead in the water."

"Right. Well, when I left they still had the bridge heavily guarded. Most of the buildings within the city had two guards per structure. The armory, training facility, and heavy artillery are located here, here, and here," Mike said, pointing to different areas on the map.

"As soon as you know the location of the factory, press this."

Dr. Wyatt handed him a small remote, no bigger than his pinky.

"What is it?" Mike asked.

"It's a low-frequency radio transmitter. You hit that button, and we'll know the mission is a go. From there we'll meet you at the rendezvous point along the bank," Dr. Wyatt said. "We'll have multiple teams landing in different locations, but we have some radios working now, so we'll be able to communicate once you tell us where the factory is. All of our men have been briefed backwards and forwards on the blueprint of the city."

"And what about my family?" Mike asked. "When do they get out?"

"When you rendezvous with our men after you've found the

location of the factory, bring your family with you. We'll have a craft waiting to take them across the river, away from the fighting."

"So, how do I get back over there now?"

"Well, that's where it gets tricky."

Mike was led to the shore, over two miles north from the bridge, and given a small flotation device. He would have to swim for it.

"It's about half a mile. The current shouldn't be too bad," Dr. Wyatt said.

"Right," Mike answered, looking to the other side.

"It could be worse," Dr. Wyatt said. "At least it's not winter."

"The chip will be able to survive the swim?"

"It'll be fine. Good luck."

* * *

KALEN COULDN'T SIT STILL at her post. She was paired with Sam, at Sam's request, and both were on security for one of the housing buildings.

She hated it. It gave her too much time to think. The brainless motions of checking ID cards for everyone that walked in for six hours was driving her crazy.

"What time is it?" Kalen asked.

"We've still got twenty minutes before our shift is over," Sam said.

"We shouldn't be here. We should be out looking for him. This is a waste of time."

"Until they have a way to move a unit of men across the river, then there's nothing we can do."

She knew he was right, but she didn't like hearing it. As soon as their shift was over, they beelined for Cadogan's office.

The colonel was sitting at his desk when his assistant ushered both Kalen and Sam inside. He was jotting down something on a piece of paper.

"Well?" Kalen asked.

"Same story as yesterday. We don't have the boats to get across the river," Cadogan said.

"You've got to be kidding me. How have you guys not put anything in motion for that?" Kalen asked.

"Take it easy," Sam said.

"If you just look at it from a strategic point, it's insane not to be scrambling to put a plan together."

"Kalen."

"But you're just sitting in your office with your thumb up your ass waiting for something to happen!"

"Kalen!"

Cadogan didn't lose his composure. He rested the pen on the desk, folded his hands together, and pushed the piece of paper he was writing on aside.

"Ms. Grant, the only reason I've allowed you this type of leniency is because of the delicate nature of your situation. If you talk to me like that again, I will have you shot," Cadogan said. "Is that clear?"

"Let's go, Kalen," Sam said.

She wanted to kill him. She could do it. She'd done it before. The strap of her rifle was still slung over her shoulder. It wouldn't take long; just one quick motion, a squeeze of the trigger.

Every muscle in her body was tense. Her adrenaline was pumping so hard that she could barely feel Sam's hand gripped around her arm.

Once they were out of the building, Sam kept trying to talk to her, but she ignored him. The only thing she could focus on at the moment was not running back into the building and spreading Cadogan's brains over the back wall of his office.

"It's not smart to pick a fight with a guy who has hundreds of men at his disposal," Sam said.

The adrenaline was subsiding. She could feel herself getting tired. The strap on her rifle was slowly sliding off her shoulder. She didn't realize it was falling until Sam caught it.

"Are you all right?" Sam asked.

"It's not fair, Sam."

"I know."

"This shouldn't be happening to us. My family didn't do anything. My dad didn't do anything. I didn't do anything to have this happen to me."

Everything was becoming overwhelming. She looked down at her hands. They always seemed to have a red tinge to them now, as if they were permanently stained with blood.

Sam pulled her in close. She didn't want to fight anymore. She didn't want to be a part of this war. All she wanted to do right now was collapse into nothing. She didn't want to think about her family, or where she was, or what she'd have to do tomorrow. She wanted to go back to the place where everything was normal, but she knew that part of her life was broken.

* * *

NELSON PULLED a wrench out of the toolbox and tightened the nut on the water heater. He wiped the grease off his hands and headed back upstairs.

There was a young man in a shirt and tie standing at the sink in the kitchen when Nelson walked in.

"Try it now," Nelson said.

The young man turned the handle of the faucet, and the water came rushing out.

"It's getting warmer. Thanks for coming down and looking at it," the young man said.

"You're welcome."

This had been what most of his days had consisted of since he'd been in Cincinnati. There were more broken things to fix than he had time in the day, but he did what he could. He was one of only five other maintenance workers in the city.

When Nelson made it back to his office building, there were guards stationed out front along with one of the military vehicles he remembered seeing when they first arrived.

Inside, all of the other maintenance workers were corralled in the break room. Each of them had his head down. The guards had their rifles aimed at Nelson's coworkers.

"You're part of the repair team?" Sergeant Blake asked.

"I am."

"Have you had any experience with infrastructure damage in factories?"

"A little. There was a bad storm that came through Pittsburgh five or six years ago that damaged some of the buildings the company I consulted for were working on."

"You're coming with us."

The guards with Sergeant Blake grabbed Nelson by the arms and pulled him out to the vehicle.

They drove through the streets of Cincinnati toward the north entrance where Nelson and his group originally came in. From there they headed west for ten minutes and parked outside a factory, heavily guarded.

Nelson had never seen this part of the city. It looked more like a military base.

The soldiers led him around the back of the factory and through one of the side doors. The area where he entered was an office space, but he could hear the humming of large machinery and the shouts of men beyond the office walls.

"Through here," Blake said.

Nelson followed him through one of the doors and into the factory. Massive cylinders were being hauled around then fed into an assembly line. He tried getting a closer look, but the soldiers kept blocking his view.

The back of the factory was completely sectioned off. All of the equipment in the area was destroyed, and part of the wall had collapsed with crack lines running all the way up to the ceiling.

"What happened here?" Nelson asked.

"I need you to check the stability of the wall. Make sure it'll still stand," Blake said.

"I'll need the original blueprints to have something to go on, and I'll also need to inspect the rest of the building."

"How long is this going to take?"

"Depends on what I find."

Nelson laid the blueprints to the building across a table they set up for him in the back. He walked along the perimeter, doing a quick visual inspection on both the inner and outer walls.

While he was on the inside, his eyes kept wandering to the workers in the factory. The more Nelson saw, the more he understood what the factory's purpose was.

They made bombs.

He could see the stockpiles of weapons poking out from the tarps that concealed them. There were hundreds of missiles, all ranging in different sizes and shapes. Some of them were small, but the majority of them were massive.

All of the damage he could find seemed to be contained to the back wall. The rest of the building was intact. Whatever had happened didn't affect the rest of the factory.

"I should come back in a few days, make sure everything's stable. You'll have to completely tear down that back wall, though, if you want it repaired," Nelson said.

"That won't be necessary," Blake answered.

Blake nodded to his men, and they grabbed Nelson by the arms and started pulling him outside. The soldiers were rougher with him than before.

Once they were outside, the soldiers shoved Nelson to the ground. He caught himself on the palms of his hands and the skin tore against the concrete, causing them to bleed.

"Hey!" Nelson said.

Sergeant Blake aimed his pistol at Nelson's head. Nelson's hands flew up in the air.

"Whoa, just, listen... You don't have to do this," Nelson said.

Nelson crawled backwards on his hands and feet, his palms stinging each time he moved.

"We have our orders," Blake said.

Three successive shots left Blake's gun and sent bullets flying into Nelson's chest. Nelson fell to his back and gargled what last few breaths of life he had left.

* * *

MIKE WAS SOAKING wet when he crawled up the seawall on the other side of the river. He tossed the flotation device back in the water and ripped his shirt off and wrung it out.

He checked his pocket for the remote that Wyatt gave him. It was still there. He had to get to his family and let them know what was going on.

There weren't any soldiers on patrol in the area Mike arrived in. He wanted to avoid any contact with anyone other than his family as much as possible. He didn't want to waste time being questioned by Bram's men about what happened.

After twenty minutes of walking north, he decided to turn east and head closer to the epicenter of the city where his family was located. He was hoping his clothes would have dried a bit, but he was still soggy.

There was a men's clothing store along the way, and he managed to find a dry pair of pants and shirt. He snagged a hat off one of the shelves and pulled it low over his forehead.

The closer he moved to the center of the city, the more people he saw. Luckily most of them were civilians. He kept his head down, not looking anyone in the eye.

The hotel where his family was located was only a few more blocks down the road. He was still tired from the swim, but the knowledge that he was so close gave him a burst of energy that he didn't have before.

Then, right before he made it to the hotel, he stopped. He couldn't go through the front door. The guards would check him. He'd have to sneak in, but he had no idea if there were any other entrances to the building. He'd only been in and out the front exit.

The fire escape.

But he knew he couldn't get to it from the ground floor. Mike walked to the building next to the hotel and checked the gap between both structures. The alley couldn't have been more than four feet wide. If he could get to the top of the other building, he could jump for it.

Mike went down the side of the adjacent building. The fire escape there was still intact. He started the climb up, and when he made it to the top, the dry shirt he changed into was soaked with sweat.

His boots crunched against the grainy roof, and when he made it to the edge of the building, he looked down.

"This is a terrible idea."

Mike backed up and sprinted as fast as he could. He pushed off the edge of the building, and when he landed on the other side, his feet slid across the roof and he hit the ground hard.

"Jesus."

Mike got up, his legs still wobbly, and then headed for the fire escape. He descended until he made it to his family's floor.

There weren't any latches on the windows, so he took off his shirt and wrapped it around his fist. He peered inside, checking to make sure the hallway was clear. Then he smashed through the glass as hard as he could. He stepped through the hole, making sure to avoid the sharp edges, and landed on the carpet.

The ding of the elevator door opening made his heart drop. When he looked down at the end of the hallway, he saw Freddy walking out, followed by Kalen and Anne.

"Dad!" Freddy screamed.

He ran toward his father, and Mike scooped him up in a big hug. Kalen and Anne weren't far behind, and the four of them just squeezed each other tight.

"We thought you were gone," Anne said.

"So did I," Mike replied.

"I knew you'd come back," Kalen said.

Mike pulled everyone into Mike and Anne's room. Freddy and Anne sat on the bed, while Kalen leaned against the wall. He went through everything with them. He told them about Wyatt, what Bram did, and what he was planning.

"As soon as I find that factory, I'm taking you guys down to the river and getting you as far away from this place as possible," Mike said.

"I'm coming with you," Kalen said.

"No."

"Dad, I can help."

"You can help by keeping your brother and mother safe."

"How are you going to find the factory?" Anne asked.

"Nelson," Mike answered.

Mike knew that Nelson was pulled into the maintenance unit, so if anyone had an idea of the layout of different buildings within the city, it'd be him. He just needed to find him fast.

"They're on the floor below us," Anne said. "I'll go grab him."

"I'll go with you," Kalen said.

The girls left the room, leaving Mike and Freddy alone.

Freddy wrapped his arms around his father's legs and buried his face in his knee. Mike lifted him up and gave his son a kiss on the forehead. Freddy reached into his pocket and pulled out the watch Mike gave him.

"I cleaned it yesterday," Freddy said.

"Wow. It looks great, buddy."

Mike held the end of the watch's chain and let it twirl. The light in the room caught the silver and made it shine.

"Thanks for taking good care of it," Mike said. "Grandpa would be proud."

"I miss him."

"Me too."

Kalen came back into the room. She was alone.

"Dad," she said.

She motioned for him to come in the hallway. Kalen shut the door behind her and kept her voice low.

"Nelson's dead," Kalen said.

"What?"

"Two soldiers came and told Katie that there was an accident at one of the buildings Nelson was working at. A piece of machinery malfunctioned and collapsed on top of him. They said there wasn't anything left of the body."

"How?"

"That's all they told her, and we didn't press her for anything else. She's still pretty upset."

"Where did it happen?" Mike asked.

"They didn't say."

* * *

KATIE'S EYES WERE RED. Her cheeks were still wet with tears. Nelson's son, Sean, was in the corner, silent. He was the same age as Freddy, and now he was fatherless.

ANNE WAS on the bed next to Katie, holding her hands.

"THEY DIDN'T TELL me what he was working on," Katie answered.

"WHAT ABOUT WHO he was working with?" Mike asked.

"THERE WERE a couple of guys that did the same job as him, but Nelson said they would always go to the job sites alone. There was never any need for two of them to be in the same place."

"WHERE WAS HE STATIONED?"

* * *

FOR A BUILDING that housed the maintenance team, it was pretty run-down. The workers were just leaving for the day when Mike showed up.

"I need to speak to you guys for a second," Mike said.

"Any repair requests need to go through your building supervisor."

"It's about Nelson Miller."

The old man paused for a moment then looked around to see if anyone was watching. He grabbed Mike's arm and pulled him inside the building. The old man locked the door behind him.

"Who are you?" the old man asked.

"I was a friend of Nelson's. Do you know what happened to him?" Mike asked.

The old man gave a snort and ran his liver-spotted hands through what white hair he still had left.

"Maintenance accident," he said.

"You see a lot of those accidents around here?" Mike asked.

"More than I care to notice."

"What's your name?"

"Fred."

Fred and Mike sat down at a small table in what Mike assumed was their break room. It wasn't much to look at. A yellow fridge hummed in the corner, while a toaster covered with bread crumbs sat alone on the counter.

"How long have you been here?" Mike asked.

"Since this whole thing started."

"You're from Cincinnati?"

"Lived here all my life."

Mike wanted to choose his words carefully. He felt as though Fred knew what was happening, but he couldn't risk exposing what he already knew.

"What do you know about the man that's running this place?" Mike asked.

"I know that he came in with his men, killed a lot of people, established order, and turned the power back on."

"And everyone was okay with what he did?"

"Once the power came back on, people were okay with pretty much anything."

"I need to know where they sent Nelson to work today."

"It's on the report."

"I need to know where he really went today."

"Whenever the military show up here, we know that whoever goes with them isn't coming back. We don't know where they take them, but I have a feeling it's up in the northwest part of the city. That's where the factory district is, and that's where we hardly ever get called to," Fred said.

"What are they doing up there?"

"I don't know. But whatever it is, they don't want anyone seeing it."

58

SIX MONTHS AFTER THE BLACKOUT

"*A*gent Sullivan, I don't give a shit what this guy's telling you. We have a signed confession. The prosecution is moving forward, and if the bastard doesn't want to defend himself, then we're not going to give a reason to delay the trial," Mack said.

Ben could feel the spit flying out of his supervisor's mouth. Mack Field wasn't one for trying to push the boundaries. He knew what his superiors wanted, and he made sure that he delivered.

"I understand that, sir, but with Dr. Wyatt willing to testify—"

"Do you have his testimony in writing?"

"He hasn't given me a confirmation in wri—"

"Then the hearing is going to happen tomorrow."

"But, sir—"

"You're dismissed, Agent Sullivan."

Mitch was slumped in a chair with his hands on his belly, waiting for Ben to come out. Ben didn't make eye contact with him when he passed. Mitch pushed himself up out of the chair and followed Ben back to their office.

"I told you he wouldn't go for it," Mitch said.

"I had to try."

"And how much longer are you going to 'try'?"

Ben spun around and pinned Mitch up against the wall. Mitch's cheeks flushed red, and the fat under his chin squished up into his face.

"As long as it fucking takes!" Ben said.

The entire hall was quiet. Everyone was looking at him. Ben let Mitch go and walked back to the office alone.

The walls shook when Ben slammed the door shut behind him. A pile of papers sat on the edge of his desk, and he sent them flying into the air with one sweep of his arm. He pulled the filing cabinet off the wall and shoved it to the ground.

It didn't matter if he went to his boss's boss's boss. Nobody was going to get in the way of this. Everyone was looking for somewhere to place blame about what happened, and Mike was giving himself up on a silver platter. He couldn't help the man if he didn't want to help himself.

There was a knock on the door, but Ben didn't answer. After a few more minutes, the door opened. Ben expected it to be Mitch, but when he saw the face of Dr. Wyatt, his half smile turned into disgust.

"What do you want?" Ben asked.

Dr. Wyatt came in, stepping over the pieces of paper scattered across the carpet. He knelt down slowly and joined Ben on the ground.

"You know I wasn't sure what I expected to happen when I saw Mike yesterday. When I saw the way he was looking at me, I just lost my nerve," Dr. Wyatt said.

"The trial's tomorrow, and Mike will be dead before the week's over."

"Maybe not."

Dr. Wyatt slid his hand into his pocket and pulled out a small object wrapped in a white cloth. He dropped it in Ben's lap.

"What is it?" Ben asked.

"Something that might be able to buy a good man a little more time," Dr. Wyatt said.

* * *

BEN WAS ESCORTED by a corrections officer down the hallway where the dangerous inmates were housed. These were the people who committed violent crimes. Mike Grant was in a cell on this row. He was sandwiched right between a serial rapist and a triple homicide.

Mike was lying on his cot when Ben stepped inside.

"You get two minutes," the guard said.

The officer kept the door open, and Ben leaned up against the wall. The space was cramped with just one person, let alone two.

"Come to say your last words?" Mike asked.

"Wyatt came to see me today."

"I told you I'm not speaking to him again."

"I know. He gave me something. He wanted me to give it to you."

Ben pulled the white handkerchief out of his pocket and set it on the foot of Mike's cot.

"I don't want anything from him," Mike said.

"Then don't open it," Ben said, leaving the cell.

* * *

MIKE JUST SAT THERE LOOKING at the cloth bundled by his foot at the end of the cot. Whatever was inside was something Wyatt believed could change his mind.

Mike paced the confined space, staring the cloth down. He reached out his hand a few times to grab it but then abruptly pulled it back.

"Stop it," he said.

He turned his back to the cot and pressed his hands up against the wall. He tried to bury his hands in the concrete. The flesh around his fingers and knuckles turned white from the pressure.

When his hands finally felt as if they were going to break off, he stopped. He turned around and slammed his back into the wall.

Mike reached for the cloth, and when he felt the outline of the object, he knew what it was. He backed up quickly, running into the wall again. His entire body was shaking.

The silent sobs that came were followed by low cries. His head hung heavy between his shoulders, and the tears hit the concrete floor.

"You son of a bitch," Mike said.

Wyatt must've known there weren't enough words he could say to make him change his mind. He had to bring something that was personal, something from home.

59

DAY 28 (CINCINNATI)

*O*nce Mike knew where the factory was, he pressed the button on the transmitter, and when he took his family to the pickup point, Dr. Wyatt's men were right where they said they'd be. He brought Katie, Sean, Mary, Nancy, Erin, and Sam along with him, but the soldiers were giving him trouble for the extra weight.

"We were told there would be three. This is nine," the lieutenant said.

"I know what was supposed to happen, but things changed. You're taking these people with you," Mike replied.

He wasn't going to let Katie and Sean stay here, not after what happened with Nelson. And he couldn't leave Mary and her sisters to fate. He trusted Sam to keep everyone safe.

"I can't guarantee Dr. Wyatt will take them in," the lieutenant said.

"He'll take them."

Anne was holding Freddy's hand. Mike gave his wife a kiss and knelt down to his son.

"I need you to take care of Mom for me. Okay, buddy?"

"Okay."

Kalen was off to the side, standing by the rubble of what was left of a store. She had her arms folded across her stomach and was looking out over the river.

"Hey," Mike said.

"I should be going with you."

"Kalen, we're not starting this again."

"I can help, Dad. I'm a better shot than any soldier that came across the river, and you know it."

"I do know it. That's why you're staying with your mom and brother."

Kalen uncrossed her arms and hugged him. He could feel her face buried in his chest, and he held the back of her head gently.

"I love you," Kalen said.

"I love you, too."

The lieutenant signaled to Mike that it was time to go.

"Once I take them to the factory, they'll radio to send you guys across the river," Mike said.

"Be careful," Anne said.

"I will."

On the way to the factory the lieutenant wanted to stay south to allow the rest of the units coming across the river to catch up, but Mike insisted on keeping north.

"There will be more of a chance of Bram's men seeing us if we stay south," Mike said.

"It's a good thing they don't know we're coming then," the lieutenant said.

"How long have you been in the military?"

"Since I turned eighteen."

"So that was last year then?"

"You don't think I know how to do my job, do you?"

"I think you're cocky. And that doesn't work in the world now," Mike answered.

"You know how many men I've lost in my unit since this whole thing started?"

"How many?"

"None."

"Well, I hope it stays that way."

* * *

BETH WAS GIVEN a post at the factory along with the unit of men that came with it. When Cain introduced her, there were no questions asked. Everyone accepted her as their officer in charge.

WHEN BETH WALKED around the factory, the soldiers would salute her then go about their duties. They respected her simply because Cain told them to.

HER MIND KEPT GOING BACK to Cain in the moments she was alone. She wondered what he was doing, what he was planning. His eyes concealed a mind that was constantly active, preparing for what was next.

BETH HADN'T SEEN her son since they arrived. She wasn't sure where he was and felt no sense of urgency to try and find him. She didn't feel like a mother anymore. The only person she had to look out for now was herself.

THE ONLY OTHER distraction in her mind was trying to find Mike. She knew he had taken his family here, but she hadn't seen him yet.

IT WAS a slow burn inside her, constantly pushing her forward. The steady anger never seemed to grow or fade. It was an anger that was at peace, perfectly balanced and designed to accomplish whatever she wanted to do. And she wanted Mike and his family dead.

* * *

BLUEPRINTS WERE PILED over Bram's desk. They were stacked on top of each other, and Bram was shuffling through them.

"If we can't override the silos, then we can't launch, and if we can't launch then we lose the one strategic advantage we have," Bram said.

"Sir, we'll find a way to do it. Our men are working on it as we speak," Cadogan said.

"Well, tell them to work faster!" Bram said, knocking the blueprints off his desk.

He'd come too far for this to happen. All of the preparation, the planning, the blood that was spilled to get to this point, couldn't have been for nothing.

"I'll take care of it personally, sir," Cadogan said.

Bram let out a sigh.

"I'm sorry, Andreas. I know you'll make sure it's done. You can tell Sergeant Blake to come and collect the blueprints," Bram said.

"Yes, sir."

"Andreas."

The colonel turned around, and Bram walked over to him. He rested his hand on Cadogan's shoulder.

"You've done well," Bram said.

Cadogan bowed his head. Bram didn't toss out compliments on a regular basis, so he knew what it meant to the colonel.

"Thank you, sir," Cadogan replied.

As Cadogan left, Cain walked in.

"Bram, we have a problem," Cain said.

"What is it now?"

"I need to see the files of everyone that's arrived in the city over the past week that wasn't brought in by a recruiter."

"All of those records are in the administration building. What's going on?"

"The woman and boy I brought with me from my recruitment trip told me of a man and his family that were on their way to Cincinnati."

"So?"

"I need access to those files."

"Why?"

"Because they're a threat to our cause."

* * *

PAUL PULLED OPEN the filing cabinet and thumbed through the folders inside. He pulled out one labeled "Mike Grant" and handed it to Cain.

"You cleared him yourself?" Bram asked.

"I did," Paul answered.

"This profile is shit," Cain said, thumbing through the pages of Mike's file.

"I followed protocol in every are—"

"Where is his family?" Cain asked.

"The hotel on Seventh," Paul answered.

Cain left without another word. Bram followed him out of the office, jogging to catch up with him.

"Tell your men to hold his family," Cain said.

"I was told that Mike Grant was killed at the bridge. Holding his family won't accomplish anything, Cain."

"Not according to his profile."

* * *

Sergeant Blake busted down the door to Mike and Anne's room.

"They're not here," Blake said through his radio.

"And the children's room?" Bram asked.

"Empty."

Bram slammed the radio on the ground. He knew that if the family was gone, then Mike was still alive, and if Mike was still alive, then Wyatt had got to him.

"Son of a bitch," Bram said.

"We need to gather whatever resources we have and comb the city. According to the reports, his wife was at her job yesterday, so the earliest they could have left was last night. Unless they managed to steal one of the vehicles, they can't be far," Cain said.

Bram gritted his teeth and shoved his finger into Cain's chest.

"Find them. Now."

Sergeant Blake exited the hotel and met Bram on the street.

"I want this city turned upside down. If they're still here, then I want them found, understood?" Bram asked.

"Yes, sir."

"And double the men at the factory. I don't know how much Mike knew, but if he found out about the factory, that's something Wyatt would have pried out of him."

Blake ran off, and Bram hopped back into his Jeep.

"Take me to the factory," Bram said.

* * *

Freddy's legs were swinging off the edge of the seawall. His heels smacked the concrete. Kalen was sitting next to him. All of a sudden he gasped, making Kalen jump.

"Jesus. What was that?" Kalen asked.

"I left it," Freddy said.

. . .

"Left what?"

"Kalen, we have to go back."

He was grabbing her hand, pulling her toward the city.

"Freddy, go back for what?"
    "I left the watch Dad gave me in our room."

"It's okay. Dad won't care. Trust me."

"I care!"

He started crying. He couldn't believe he left it there. His dad trusted him enough to let him have it, and he'd taken such good care of it. He couldn't lose it now.

"Freddy, we can't go back," Kalen said.

"Kalen, please."

His hands were folded together, begging her to take him back.

"It won't take long," Freddy said.

"You know exactly where you left it?" Kalen asked.

"Yes," he said, nodding emphatically.

. . .

"ALL RIGHT, we don't have a lot of time though. Come on."

* * *

THEY WERE ALMOST to the factory. Mike had over one hundred men behind him. He did his best to keep them out of the paths of what traffic still existed in the city, but it was harder with the larger numbers.

The lieutenant joined Mike at the window of the building they were hiding behind. Mike nodded to the end of the street where the factory was located. There was a lot of activity going on, more so than when he located it earlier.

"There it is," Mike said.

"Shit."

"What?"

"I knew it'd be guarded, but I didn't think they'd have that many men."

"Your guys can't handle it?"

"A lot of the men that Bram has were men I used to serve with. Even with everything they've done, it's not easy killing your brother. I was hoping we could avoid as much death as possible."

"It's impossible to avoid that these days."

Mike held up his part of the bargain. He brought them to the location. Now it was time for the lieutenant to hold up his end of the deal.

"All right, I brought you to the factory. Now, you get me and my family out of here," Mike said.

The lieutenant nodded and radioed the unit watching Mike's family.

"We're good here. Take the Grants and the others across the river."

This was it. Mike was so close to getting out of here, getting his family somewhere safe.

"What?" the lieutenant asked. "Well, find them."

"What's going on?" Mike asked.

"Your kids ran off."

* * *

FREDDY AND KALEN kept to the outskirts. Kalen didn't want to turn deeper into the city until she absolutely had to.

They finally made it to the cross street where their hotel was located. She could see a few military vehicles sitting out front.

"They know we're gone," Kalen said.

She knew how much Freddy wanted to get that watch, but this was too risky. There was no way they were going to get inside that building. It was locked down.

"Freddy, we should go back. We can't—"

Kalen turned around and he was gone. She panicked. She looked down the street and could see his figure sprinting down the sidewalk toward the hotel.

"Shit."

He was fast for a kid, but she was gaining on him. She could feel the stitches on her forehead throbbing. It felt as though they were going to burst and blood would just pour out of her, but she pushed through it.

Freddy was fifty yards from the hotel, and Kalen was ten yards from Freddy. The soldiers had their backs to the both of them. Kalen reached out her hand and grabbed Freddy's shoulder.

She yanked him into an alleyway, concealing them from the street. He squirmed, but she had a good grip on him.

"Are you crazy?" Kalen asked. "Those soldiers are there because of us. If they see you, you're a goner."

"I'm not leaving it behind."

Freddy pushed Kalen off him. She recognized that stubborn look and realized he wasn't going to give up.

"C'mon then," Kalen said.

Kalen led Freddy down the alleyway of the building with the fire escape next to the hotel.

They climbed the metal stairs as quickly as Freddy's legs would let them, and when they made it to the top, Kalen walked to the edge of the roof.

"We'll have to jump for it," Kalen said.

Freddy tiptoed to the edge and peeked over. His eyes were as wide as watermelons. She knew he wasn't going to jump.

Freddy took a few steps back, and when Kalen walked over to him, he sprinted off.

"Freddy, no!"

Before she could grab him, he leaped over the edge and barely landed on the other roof.

Kalen's feet skidded to a stop right before she reached the edge herself.

"Jesus Christ! What were you thinking?"

"You said we had to jump. So I jumped."

His answer was so innocent and matter-of-fact that she had to chuckle a little bit. She backed up and jumped over to join him.

Kalen tussled Freddy's hair and shook her head.

"You're one crazy kid."

The two of them descended the stairs and found the window where their dad snuck in. Kalen poked her head through first to make sure the coast was clear then went back for Freddy.

Once they were in the room, Freddy made a beeline for the table next to the bed and pulled the drawer open.

"Got it!"

"Okay, now let's get the hell out of here. Mom's probably losing her mind."

When they made it back to the window to leave, the sirens went off. Kalen wasn't sure which direction it was coming from, but when the gunfire echoed in the distance, she was afraid that she and her brother missed their chance to get out of the city.

* * *

"Concentrate fire on the west side!" the lieutenant ordered.

The moment Mike heard that his kids disappeared, he ran back toward the river, but the lieutenant stopped him.

"I have to get back to my family," Mike said.

"I can't let you go in the middle of this."

"It's not your decision."

"You see that!"

The lieutenant pointed over to Bram's forces who were gathering at the end of the road. Some of the vehicles were being mobilized.

"I need every available man to stop those bastards from getting to us. And you're available."

He shoved a rifle into Mike's chest. Mike flipped the rifle around and aimed it right at the lieutenant's head.

"You gonna shoot me, Mike?"

"That's why the gun's aimed at your head."

"You're not gonna shoot me. If you do that, you'll never see your family again. But they'll see you, or what's left of you after my soldiers pump you full of lead."

Mike's finger itched over the trigger. He wanted to pull it. He was sick and tired of the shit that he had to go through in order to be with his family. Maybe this was the only way out.

No.

He lowered the rifle, and the weapon was taken from him. His hands were tied behind his back, and he was shoved down onto the ground, hard.

"Now, we can do this the easy way, or the hard way. You help us, and I make sure to get you back to your family as quick as possible. The sooner that building is rubble, the sooner you can find your kids."

Mike knew what Anne would want him to do, so he just decided to go along. And he figured if he managed to take out some of the soldiers who would be looking to hurt his family, then that was a plus.

"I'll need both my hands to help," Mike said.

* * *

BRAM SPOTTED the rebels through the streets on his way to the factory. He radioed for soldiers immediately and almost crashed through the gate when he arrived.

Beth met him out front with a group of men and immediately started to mobilize against the rebels.

Bram made his way into the factory and met with the head engineer.

"Where are we at with completion?" Bram asked.

"We weren't scheduled to load the missiles until tomorrow, sir."

"Well, I want them loaded now! Do you understand me?"

"Sir, we don't have anywhere to take them."

Bram grabbed the engineer by the throat and slammed him against one of the piles of missiles. He was choking the life out of him, and the engineer clawed at his arm.

"Anywhere but here will do just fine."

* * *

JOEY HAD the radio close to his ear. He was waiting for any sign of action. Cain never assigned him a post. All he was told to do was scour the city and look for any signs of the people from Carrollton.

He wanted to find them more than his mother did. He was

consumed by it. Ever since he killed Jung's children, he needed more.

When the radio call went out for soldiers to head to the hotel to gather the Grants, Joey followed them to the address given.

His short legs pumped as hard as they could against the pavement, and his rifle was tucked tight under his shoulder.

It took him twenty minutes to make it to the hotel. The soldiers were already out front when he arrived. He recognized a few of them, but when he saw Bram, he knew it was serious.

Cain had introduced him when they first arrived. Out of all the people Joey met, including Cain, Bram was the one who frightened him the most.

He couldn't put his finger on exactly why. It was the combination of his expensive clothes, the massive apartment, the way he spoke. Bram embodied a way of life that Joey had never seen before. He didn't like it.

Joey tucked himself in an alleyway two buildings down from the hotel. He was glancing north when he saw Freddy, running as fast as he could toward the hotel with his sister right behind him, and then they disappeared in an alleyway themselves.

Time to hunt.

* * *

THE ARTILLERY from Bram's forces blasted the buildings the rebels had scattered to for cover on their march toward the factory.

Dust, concrete, and rebar scattered the ground. Chunks of asphalt were sent flying into the air, landing on cars and smashing through windows, when the explosives hit.

Mike was covered in dust. He could barely keep the rifle in his hands. His fingers felt as if they were made of steel. He wasn't even sure if he'd be able to pull the trigger.

"We need to get the hell out of here now!" Mike said.

The lieutenant was still by his side, barking orders to his men.

"We can't turn back now," the lieutenant replied.

"You told me you've never lost a man in your unit. We're sitting ducks here. We need to get out."

Mike could see the turmoil in the lieutenant's eyes. He could tell the man wanted to pull out, but his orders overrode his instincts. They couldn't retreat.

Mike crawled over to the front of the building. The military trucks were pushing forward down the street. It wouldn't be long before they were right on top of them. He went back over to the lieutenant and grabbed his shoulder.

"Have one unit stay here to continue pressing fire. Tell the rest to retreat to the rear of their buildings and head up the streets behind us to the factory," Mike said.

"Our building doesn't have an exit. We checked," the lieutenant answered.

Mike yanked one of the grenades off the lieutenant's belt and put it in his hand.

"Make one," Mike said.

* * *

ONCE THE SIRENS WENT OFF, Anne pulled Sam to the side. She begged the soldiers to go in and look for her children, but they wouldn't budge.

"I HAVE TO FIND THEM, SAM," Anne said.

"WE DON'T EVEN KNOW where they went," Sam replied.

SHE HAD TO DO SOMETHING. She couldn't just sit there and wait, not with everything that was happening.

"SAM."

"ALL RIGHT. Where do we start looking?" Sam asked.

* * *

BETH WAS RIGHT UP FRONT, leading the soldiers and vehicles down the street. Her rifle was up, firing into the group of rebels to the left.

SHE PICKED off as many as she could. That focus that fueled her was still burning slow, steady. It marched over her, stepping in unified rhythm.

EACH TIME she pulled the trigger, the burn intensified. With every bullet that flew from the rifle's barrel, the desire to kill grew.

THE PIECES of lead flew through the air, slicing the flesh of the rebels. In her head she pictured the faces of all the people she'd ever wanted to hurt. All of the individuals who belittled her, any who thought they were above her.

EVERY REBEL that fell to the ground was someone from her past. Now she was in control. Now she had the power, and she wasn't afraid to use it.

BUT WHEN SHE heard the gunfire behind her, that power she held so dear began to fade. The rebels had flanked them from behind, and while some of her men ran for cover, Beth moved forward to meet them head-on.

THE SUCCESSION of her shots became faster. Her heart was pounding. In between each pull of the trigger, she could hear screaming. It wasn't until her clip was emptied that she realized that the person screaming was her.

* * *

KALEN DIDN'T KNOW why she ran toward the sound of the gunfire, especially with Freddy still with her. As soon as they heard the sirens go off, she grabbed her brother's hand and jumped onto the fire escape.

She knew whatever was happening must have been bad when the soldiers at the hotel drove right past them and didn't even stop to wonder why a girl and young boy would be headed in the same direction.

"Slow down, Kalen!" Freddy yelled.

She heard him, but she couldn't stop. She had to keep going. If she slowed down, she felt she would be caught. And she couldn't let that happen.

The gunfire was becoming louder. She could feel the blasts from the artillery that shook the ground.

Then there was another gunshot that sounded as though it came from behind them. Freddy's grip went limp in her hand, and she felt herself get pulled back from the weight of Freddy hitting the ground. When she turned around, there was a red stain on his back.

"Freddy?"

He wasn't moving. She bent down and flipped him over. His face was pale. His skin was clammy.

"Kalen?"

His voice was quiet, weak. Before Kalen could do anything, another shot rang out that ricocheted off the ground next to them.

Kalen looked up and saw Joey a few blocks down the road behind a car. She picked Freddy up in her arms and carried him into the store next to them.

She laid him down gently on the floor and ran her hand along his cheek. His small body started to shake. He was going into shock.

"Hang on, Freddy."

They were in an old electronics store. Kalen looked around for anything she could use to stop the bleeding. She found a pack of cleaning cloths used for computer screens and tore it open. She tilted Freddy on his side and stuffed the small rags into the wound.

"I feel cold," Freddy said.

The tears rolling down Kalen's face landed on Freddy's shirt. Her arm was shaking as she tried to keep pressure on the wound.

"It's going to be okay. You're going to be okay."

"Where's Mom? I want Mom."

"She's on her way. She's looking for us right now."

The shock was wearing off and the pain was starting to set in as Freddy started wailing. Each time his body convulsed from the cries, Kalen could feel more blood spill out of the wound.

The boy who was always so filled with laughter and love was experiencing the most painful moment of his life, and she couldn't do anything to help.

"Kalen?"

She wiped the tears from her face, trying to compose herself.

"Shh, it's okay."

"Don't tell Dad about the watch."

Kalen couldn't help but smile. Through all of this, Freddy was still worried about disappointing their father.

Freddy's eyelids started to flutter. Kalen grabbed his hand.

"Freddy, stay awake. You have to stay awake, okay?"

He didn't respond. He closed his eyes, and his hand and head went limp in her arms. Kalen shook him.

"Freddy!"

Her brother, whom she loved and fought with so much, was no longer with her. He would never date a girl, learn how to drive, go to prom, graduate from high school, or experience anything in life again. His future was gone.

Kalen's breathing accelerated. She could feel the rage burning through her, igniting every cell inside her body. A chain reaction had been set off that couldn't be stopped now.

Whatever commitment tied Kalen to the rest of the human race was severed the moment Freddy's heart stopped beating.

Kalen closed her eyes, took a few deep breaths, and kissed her brother on the forehead. She set him down gently and grabbed the watch out of his pocket.

* * *

IT WASN'T HARD TRACKING them. When Joey realized what they were running toward, it was pretty simple. When he saw them heading down the street, he parked himself next to an idle car and brought Freddy into his crosshairs.

He knew if he could bring him down, then it would slow Kalen up. *Wound the weak, and the strong will follow.* Those words from his father echoed in his ears.

The moment Joey squeezed the trigger and Freddy hit the ground, he knew he had them. They wouldn't be able to go anywhere, and he knew the sister would stop to save him.

That's when he realized what Cain was trying to tell him. That type of love and attachment is weakness. It was a weakness he didn't have, and that's why he was so strong. That's why Cain chose to bring him here. To purge those that had weakness.

When he saw Kalen on the ground with Freddy, he lined up another shot. He had his elbow on the hood of the car, and Kalen fell into his crosshairs.

Just before he fired, his elbow slipped on the hood and he missed.

Joey watched Kalen carry Freddy into the store next to where he was shot. He inched along the sidewalk close to the storefronts and made his way to the building she'd entered.

He didn't see a weapon on her, and he felt that if she did have one, she would have fired back. Regardless, he still wanted to be careful. There wasn't anything more dangerous than a wounded animal.

There was an alleyway right before the building she entered with a side door that led to the store that Kalen dragged Freddy inside.

Joey kept the rifle tucked under his arm as he pulled the door open. He stood frozen as his eyes adjusted to the darkness.

Once he had a better look he could tell he had entered some type of stockroom. There were rows and rows of shelves with boxes on them.

He stepped lightly, rifle up, scanning the room. When he made it to the end of the aisle, he could see the outline of another door.

Joey knew that's where she was. He knew she was just sitting in there, exposed, crying over her brother's body.

He figured Freddy would be dead by now. The shot was right in the back, and the .223-caliber bullet would create a hole too big for that small body to contend with.

Joey's hand reached for the doorknob. He turned it as quietly as he could. The barrel of the rifle was the first thing that poked through the door. When Joey took another step forward, pushing the rifle farther into the room, he felt a force knock the gun upward.

* * *

KALEN YANKED the rifle out of Joey's grip, and he fell to the floor. She swung the butt of the rifle and brought it down on his face.

Joey's cheeks immediately swelled up, and his nose was broken and bent. She watched him crawl around on the ground, grasping at anything to help pull him up. She brought another smashing blow into his gut, which stopped him from moving again.

"You little bastard!" Kalen screamed.

She brought the butt of the rifle down on him again, smacking the back of his head. Each time she hit him, the force of the blow was harder. Her screams grew louder. Joey's blood splattered across her shirt and face.

When she was finished, she couldn't recognize the boy's face anymore. It was nothing more than a bloody stump.

Kalen's screams of anger were replaced by silent sobs. She looked down at her bloodied hands, and they started to tremble.

Kalen crawled back over to Freddy, lifeless on the floor. She picked up his body and cradled him in her arms. She stayed like that for a few more minutes.

Once all of the tears in her were gone, the only thing she could focus on was the gunfire echoing in the distance. She rested Freddy on the ground gently and then picked up the rifle. She racked the chamber, making sure it was loaded, then walked out the door.

* * *

THE FIRST PLACE Anne thought to look was the hotel. When they arrived, it was empty. Even the guards had left.

"Where else could they have gone?" Sam asked.

Anne could hear the gunshots in the distance. She was afraid she knew the answer to Sam's question.

"Come on," Anne said.

Sam pulled her back once he saw she was heading in the direction of the fighting.

"We can't go there, Anne," Sam said.

"That's where they are."

"Why would they run into a war zone?"

Anne wanted to tell him that it was because her daughter had changed. That it was because of the types of atrocities the world allowed, and that they had scarred her daughter, but she didn't.

"I just know," Anne said.

Anne led the two of them up the street, and after a few minutes of jogging, Anne slowed down.

"What's wrong?" Sam asked.

Anne's eyes were focused on a pool of blood staining the sidewalk. She stood there frozen, then sprinted toward it.

A streaked trail of red flowed from the sidewalk into the store.

"Anne?" Sam asked.

When Anne pushed the door open, she fell to her knees. Freddy was on the floor, motionless. His skin was white, drained from the blood that no longer pumped through his veins.

"No," Anne said.

The tears were welling up in her eyes. She crawled on her hands and knees to her little boy. Sam tried to pick her up, but she smacked his hands away from her.

"Anne, he's gone."

"My baby."

Sam went to grab her shoulder, and she spun around. She kept hitting him, again and again.

"Leave me alone!" she screamed.

She was sobbing hysterically now, cradling her son in her arms, bathed in red. Everything she and Mike had done to keep their children safe was shattered. There wasn't anywhere evil couldn't touch them, no matter how hard they tried.

* * *

MIKE WAS the first in the factory. Most of the workers had scattered. Judging by how fast they ran away, they weren't volunteers of Bram's forces.

"We need to get the charges in place before more of Bram's men arrive," the lieutenant yelled.

The other soldiers ran around, placing the explosives in various positions around the factory. Mike stayed with the lieutenant guarding the front entrance to ensure the enemy couldn't enter.

"We should get the rest of the men in here," Mike said.

"Why?" the lieutenant asked.

"If this factory is as important as Wyatt says it is, then Bram won't risk putting it in danger by firing at it. It's the safest place to be right now."

"Yeah, until we blow it to bits."

Bram's men didn't expect the fight from behind, so the rebels had them on their heels. They had managed to destroy most of the vehicles, and Bram's men had scattered to the surrounding buildings for cover.

All they needed was a little more time and the factory would be destroyed, Mike could get to his family, and all of this would be behind him.

"How much longer is this going to take?" Mike asked.

The lieutenant pulled up his radio.

"Where are we at with the explosives?" he asked.

"Just six more to place, sir."

The lieutenant clicked off his radio and cocked his head to the side.

"There you go."

But Mike wasn't listening to him. He was squinting down the

street, looking at a young girl working her way down the road, firing her rifle at anything that moved.

* * *

Whatever was in her path, Kalen shot. She didn't know who they were, or what they were trying to do, but if they had rifles on them, that was reason enough for her to make sure they couldn't use them anymore.

Kalen had never felt so focused before in her life. Her movements were so precise and fluid. There wasn't a separation between her and the rifle. The weapon was just an extension of her body.

One of the military vehicles was still operational, and it started heading in her direction. She ducked inside one of the storefronts for cover.

The fifty-caliber on the roof of the armored truck shattered the windows and tore through the concrete of the building. Shards from the glass landed on her head and sliced her hands and face.

Kalen moved to the far side of the store but stayed close to the front to see where the truck was heading. She saw it circling around and aimed for the tires.

The tires exploded from her gunshots, and the truck careened out of control, smashing into one of the buildings along the street.

Then, crouched behind one of the disabled military trucks, Kalen saw her. Beth was barking orders and building up her own body count.

The moment Kalen saw her, she sprinted in her direction. It didn't matter how barricaded Beth was, Kalen was going to take her down.

One of the soldiers around Beth finally noticed Kalen running at them, but it was too late. Kalen sent a bullet flying into his temple.

Before Beth could do anything, Kalen barreled into her and slammed her to the ground. The soldiers around the two of them tried to help, but Beth ordered them to stop.

Kalen got Beth in a chokehold. She was squeezing the life out of her. Beth grasped at her arm, trying to free herself from Kalen's grip, but she couldn't.

Beth's fingers crawled along her leg, trying to reach for her knife. Kalen didn't see Beth reaching for the blade. Beth grabbed it and jammed the five inches of steel into Kalen's leg.

The blade went in deep. Kalen could feel it scraping against her bone. She gripped her fingers around the blade's handle and slowly pulled it out. Every inch the blade came out sent screams into the air.

When the blade was finally removed, she stuffed her hands over the wound, trying to stop the bleeding, but something was wrong. No matter how much pressure she applied, the blood just kept coming.

She could feel herself getting light-headed. Then, as Beth pulled a pistol from one of the soldier's belts around her, Kalen watched a barrage of bullets fly into Beth and the soldiers next to her.

* * *

MIKE PICKED up his daughter and ran as fast as he could in the other direction to the factory. He could see the blood pouring out of her leg and her eyes drifting in and out of consciousness.

He burst through the door and set her on the ground.

"I need a first aid kit, now!" Mike yelled.

The lieutenant called over one of his men, and they started working on her right away.

"Kalen, stay with me, baby. Stay with me."

"Dad."

"Shh, it's going to be okay, sweetheart."

Her voice was so soft. Mike could see the life draining from her face.

"I'm sorry, Dad."

"Oh, honey, you don't have to be sorry for anything."

"She's lost too much blood," the medic said. "I think she hit an artery."

"I tried, Dad. I tried…"

"Kalen," Mike said.

Her head went limp, and her eyes closed. The medic grabbed Kalen's wrist, then looked over to the lieutenant and shook his head.

"Kalen?" Mike asked.

Mike pulled his daughter close. Whatever pain he endured, whatever loss was suffered, didn't matter because Mike knew that it was to make sure his children survived. Now, a piece of that was dead, and with it… him.

* * *

CAIN WAS on the second floor of the factory. He watched everything from the large window in the office upstairs.

He was disappointed. He thought Beth would have survived longer than she did.

"What a waste," he said to himself.

He could see Bram down with the rest of his soldiers, scrambling to keep the factory, but it was a losing battle. Once the rebels had the explosives in place, it wouldn't matter.

Cain slammed a magazine into his pistol and racked one into the chamber. He picked up a file on the desk.

When he opened it, there was a picture of Anne. Cain smiled and tucked it into his pocket. He picked up a rifle from the desk as well. He peered through the scope and looked down the street.

He saw a large man, dressed in civilian clothes, holding a rifle. He wasn't shooting anyone, but Cain thought he recognized the face.

He grabbed another folder from the stack of files he found and flipped through the pages. He looked through the scope again and watched Sam turn around and head back to where he came from.

"Now, where are you heading off to in such a hurry?"

* * *

SAM WATCHED Mike carry Kalen to the factory, and the fighters from across the river seemed to have Bram's soldiers pinned down. Sam knew that the objective was to get rid of the factory, so he figured it would just be a matter of time.

SO MUCH LOSS. So much death for one family. He wasn't sure how much more Mike and Anne could take. Everything around them was falling apart.

RIGHT NOW THOUGH, the best thing he could do was to get back to Anne. If he could keep her safe, then maybe there would be some chance of normalcy for her and Mike.

HE KNEW what happened to a person who lost the things they held so close to their heart. A part of them died. It got lost forever in a sea of despair, the waves constantly tossing and turning the small raft that was barely keeping them alive.

SAM KNEW Mike and Anne's raft was barely strung together. And there were more waves coming their way.

* * *

ANNE STILL HADN'T MOVED. She just sat there on the floor, in the middle of the pile of blood, holding her son.

"My baby," she whispered.

There was a documentary on television she had watched earlier that year. It was about mothers from different countries who had lost their children at a young age.

All of them were crying hysterically, clutching their dead children in their arms, not wanting to let them go.

Some of the women had gone mad, completely losing their minds and the will to live. The burden of losing a child had ended marriages and ripped families apart. It was a void that could never be filled, no matter what someone tried stuffing inside it.

She remembered wondering how she would react if that ever happened to her. Would she lose her mind? Would it end her marriage?

Anne couldn't fathom what losing one of her children would do to her. Now, what every parent fears more than anything had happened to her.

All she felt was empty. Everything about her son that she loved looped constantly in her mind. But the images of him laughing, playing, sleeping, only added to her pain. It hurt because she knew there would never be any new memories to draw from. There was no more hope, no more chance of what could be.

When Sam came back, she just stared at him. She watched his lips move but couldn't hear what he was saying.

Anne remained speechless when she watched a man with cold blue eyes walk up behind Sam and knock him out.

Cain dragged Sam out of the doorway entrance and looked down at Anne, who was still rocking her dead son in her arms.

"Hello, Mrs. Grant," Cain said.

* * *

BRAM WAS ON HIS HEELS. The soldiers around him were starting to shrink. Everything was closing in on him, and there wasn't a way out.

This wasn't how it was supposed to end. He was going to rewrite the country's future. He was going to bring people into a new era of ideals. Now, with every bullet that flew into one of his soldiers that hit the ground, so did those aspirations.

With the fight going the way it was, he was shocked when Cain turned up with a woman covered in blood.

"Where the hell have you been?" Bram demanded.

"Finding you a bargaining chip. Say hello to Anne Grant. Wife of Mike Grant, who is in your warehouse right now getting ready to blow it up," Cain said.

"What?"

Bram looked the woman over. She looked nothing like the photo he saw earlier that day. Her eyes were empty. Her face was grave. She looked as if she was already dead.

It was Bram's last play. If this didn't work, he knew it was over.

"Cease fire!" Bram yelled.

The men around him echoed his orders. A few moments later, the firing stopped and Bram could hear similar shouts from the rebels.

"Get me a bullhorn," Bram said.

* * *

"THE EXPLOSIVES ARE SET, SIR."

"ALL RIGHT. We're all set here. Let's get the hell out of Dodge," the lieutenant said.

MIKE STARED at Kalen's face on the stretcher they set her on. At that moment he wasn't in Cincinnati, in the middle of a war, standing in a factory with soldiers and missiles.

RIGHT NOW HE was back in Pittsburgh. He was just getting ready for work, making his rounds to everyone's room. He was opening Kalen's door to give her a kiss on the forehead before he left for the day, taking a moment to watch her sleep. She always looked like her mom when she slept. It was so peaceful.

BUT WHEN THE lieutenant grabbed his shoulder and spun him around, that moment was gone. He wasn't in Pittsburgh. He wasn't watching his daughter sleep. He *was* in the middle of a war.

"MIKE GRANT."

MIKE RECOGNIZED BRAM'S VOICE, and when he looked outside through the scope of his gun, he could see his wife standing right next to him.

* * *

THE LIEUTENANT GAVE Mike a rundown of the situation. Bram would trade her life for his factory.

"Take the goddamn chargers down," Mike said.

"Mike, it's not that simple."

"Take them down!"

"If you talk to him and buy us some time, then I can position some of my snipers to take him out."

"They better have good aim."

Bram had himself surrounded by his men. When Mike got close, Bram told his men to make a small opening so Mike could see him.

Anne was stained with blood, and Mike had no idea whether or not the blood was hers.

"Anne, honey, are you okay?" Mike asked.

"She'll be fine when my men finish a clean sweep of the factory and the rest of the rebel bastards that are here have gone back over the river," Bram said.

"Let her go, Bram," Mike said. "If you want a bargaining chip, then use me. I'm the one who led them here. I know where you can find Wyatt."

"And where is our mutual friend?" Bram asked. "Still having others do his dirty work for him? Wyatt always had a problem with the execution."

Mike didn't know how much time the lieutenant's men needed.

"I'm going to give you till the count of ten, Mike. If my factory isn't cleared out and the rest of the rebels aren't hightailing it out of here, then your wife dies."

Cain handed Bram his knife, and he put it to Anne's throat. She didn't move. She didn't scream. The only noticeable change was the tears streaming down her face.

"One," Bram said.

"Bram, look around. It's over," Mike said.

"Two."

There had been plenty of time to take the shot by now. Mike didn't know what the lieutenant was waiting for.

"Three."

"Let her go, Bram."

Mike's hand reached for his gun, but he didn't grab it. He was afraid if he tried to make a move then Bram would too. The knife was too close to Anne's throat.

"Four."

What is he waiting for?

"Five."

Mike looked over to the lieutenant's men, still aiming their guns at Bram's soldiers. Nobody was moving.

"Six."

"Lieutenant, tell your men to back down. Tell them to do it now!" Mike said.

"Seven."

Mike rushed up to one of the lieutenant's soldiers. Mike pulled out his own gun and put it to the soldier's head.

"Clear the factory now!" Mike screamed.

"Eight."

Mike looked back to Anne. His body was churning with grief and rage. He couldn't watch another one of his girls die.

"I will kill this man if you don't get the hell out. Do you hear me, lieutenant?" Mike yelled.

"Nine."

Mike squeezed the grip of his gun hard. Either his fingers would break, or the rifle's handle would.

Bram's mouth looked as though it was about to form the word "ten" when a bullet split the side of Cain's head open. The moment that happened, Bram slid the blade of his knife across Anne's throat and she fell to the ground.

Mike aimed his gun at Bram and squeezed the trigger. He pulled it repeatedly. He couldn't tell how many of his shots got off, because once the first bullet went into Bram's body, every other soldier with a weapon fired.

Once Mike could hear the click of the firing pin signaling that his magazine was empty, he felt the pieces of lead tear through him.

The hot bullets flew into his chest, sending him backwards and hurling him to the ground.

* * *

When Mike woke up, he felt as if a car was sitting on top of his chest. His vision was blurry as he looked around. There were tubes stuck into his arm, and it was difficult to breathe.

He was dressed in a hospital gown, and when he tried to move, a sharp pain shot through his entire body.

He could hear a beeping somewhere next to him. It was growing louder. A woman came in and pressed a few buttons on the machine next to his bed.

"Where am I?" Mike asked.

"Take it easy, Mr. Grant."

She pressed her hand on his shoulder. Mike started to feel dizzy.

"I need to see my son," Mike said.

"You need to rest."

The nurse plugged another needle into his arm. He started to feel sleepy again.

"No, I need… to… see…"

* * *

When Mike woke up again, his chest still hurt, but he was propped up in the bed. The first face he saw when he opened his eyes was Dr. Wyatt.

"Hello, Mike," Wyatt said. "You've been out cold for a few days now. It's good to see you awake."

Mike tried to remember the events before the hospital. How he got there. Where his family was. Slowly, everything came back to him.

"Where is Freddy?" Mike asked.

"How are you feeling?" Dr. Wyatt asked.

Wyatt kept dodging the question. Mike could feel panic rush

over him. There wasn't any anger left. It was just fear. Fear and grief. He started crying.

"Where's my son?" Mike asked, tears pouring down his face.

Dr. Wyatt rose from his seat slowly. He reached into his pocket and pulled out the silver pocket watch that Mike had given his son.

When Dr. Wyatt placed it in Mike's hand, the scream that came out of him was so primal, so harrowing that it caused three hospital staff members to rush into his room.

Mike thrashed on the bed. His chest felt as if it was going to rip apart, but he didn't care. He'd lost everything. There wasn't any type of pain left in the world that could hurt him.

60

DAY 56 (CINCINNATI)

*M*ike put on the shirt the hospital staff gave him. He buckled his pants, tied his shoes, and ran his fingers over the scars on his chest.

The doctors took out four bullets. Even though it had been a few weeks, Mike still couldn't push himself. The doctors told him it would take another three months of rehab before he could do anything physical again, but Mike didn't have any plans on staying here.

He knew the doctors couldn't make him stay once he was able to start getting up and moving around on his own. The only time he'd left the hospital previous to this was when he buried his family.

It was a few weeks ago. He declined to speak during the funeral. What little hope he held onto was that his family knew how much he loved them. And he knew they couldn't hear him anymore anyway.

Dr. Wyatt requested to see him before he left. Mike didn't want to speak with the man, but that was the one condition upon his release. This place was as much of a prison as it was a hospital.

Mike walked into the waiting room, and Dr. Wyatt was there, reading a magazine.

"What do you want?" Mike asked.

Mike's tone was dry, heartless. If he had a weapon on him, he would have killed Wyatt on the spot.

"I'm asking you to stay. You're still not well enough to travel and be on your own yet. We're just now starting to set up supply routes to get the rest of the country up and running, but it'll take a few more months. It's still not safe out there," Dr. Wyatt said.

"It's not safe anywhere."

Mike reached into his pocket and pulled out the pocket watch that belonged to his father, which he passed down to his own son. Now both his father and his son were dead. Mike tossed the watch to Wyatt.

"I don't want it," Mike said.

"It's something you should keep. It belongs to your family."

"Then bury it where the rest of my family is."

Mike turned to go, but Dr. Wyatt stopped him.

"Here, take this," Dr. Wyatt said, handing him the journal.

"Why?"

"Because I didn't hold up my end of the deal. This journal has enough evidence for you to do whatever you want to me."

Mike grabbed the journal, stuffed it into his bag, and left. As he walked down the streets of Cincinnati, he realized there wasn't anything left in this world for him. He decided to go back to the one place where he could be alone. The cabin.

The only thing he had to worry about now was how he was going to choose to leave this world. That was one choice he wasn't going to let anyone else make for him.

SIX MONTHS AFTER THE BLACKOUT

*T*he judge brought the gavel down hard.

"Order. I will have order in this courtroom," he said.

Mike still had his handcuffs on, and he was sitting next to his appointed attorney.

"Mike Grant," the judge said, "you have pleaded guilty and provided a written statement to the crimes against the United States government and its people, correct?"

"Yes, Your Honor."

"At this time, you are able to make any opening statements before the proceedings take place."

The courtroom was small. The only people that were allowed inside were a few high-ranking government officials, the attorneys, the judge, and sitting directly behind Mike was Agent Sullivan.

Mike dug his hand into his pants pocket and felt the cool outline of his father's silver watch. When the guards patted him down, he was allowed to keep it.

"I have done terrible things. Things that have cost me everything I hold dear. When the power went out, we didn't just lose the lights in the cities, we lost the light within ourselves. We became dark, and twisted. We killed each other. We lost our way," Mike said.

Everyone in the room was looking at him, staring, waiting for him to finish so they could walk through the dog and pony show and get to the execution, delivering him to justice.

"I watched my father, my wife, and my daughter die in front of me. I've felt their blood on my hands. It's a stain I still haven't been able to wash off. And when I found out that my son had been murdered, I didn't think I had anything left to live for."

Mike gripped the pocket watch harder. He was holding onto it for dear life.

"I thought I wanted to die. That's why I came here, why I turned myself in. But then I remembered something my father told me a long time ago. He said that as long as one member of a family is alive, the rest live with them. They live on through the choices you make," Mike said.

"What are you getting at, Mr. Grant?" the judge asked.

"Every single event that I listed in my statement happened—the EMP explosion, the planned coup to overthrow the government, all of it. But I wasn't the one who planned it."

Mike's attorney started typing furiously at his laptop. Everyone started talking. The judge banged the gavel hard again.

"Order! Order! Mr. Grant, do you have any proof of your statements?" the judge asked.

"Yes, I do. There is a small cabin just outside of Carrollton, Ohio. It belonged to me. Inside you'll find a desk, and in the bottom drawer is a journal. The journal belonged to a Dr. Quinn Wyatt. In it you'll find all the evidence you need of who planned the attacks."

Mike turned around and looked at Agent Sullivan. Ben was smiling.

"In light of these recent events, I move that we take a recess. I would like both counselors to join me in my chambers," the judge said.

Mike's attorney disappeared, and an officer came and escorted Mike out of the courtroom. Before Mike left, Ben grabbed his arm.

"What changed your mind?" Ben asked.

"My son."

* * *

ONCE THE AUTHORITIES confirmed the journal was at Mike's cabin, a new investigation was launched. Agent Sullivan was hailed for his thoroughness and diligence, and Mike was told that he would be set free.

Up until his release, Mike was allowed to see visitors. This time he chose to see two.

"Mike," Katie said, wrapping him in a hug.

Sean was by her side. He gave Mike a slight smile.

"I can't believe you're alive. All of this is… crazy," Katie said.

"How did you know I was here?"

"The trial was on the news. The government was comparing catching you to catching Osama bin Laden."

"Except I turned myself in."

Katie gave him another hug, and the three of them sat down.

"How have you been holding up? How are Mary and her sisters?" Mike asked.

"We've been okay. Mary and the girls have been staying with us. My company is finally getting back up and running. We're going to be moving out to California in a few weeks so I can start heading up the West Coast division. It'll be a nice fresh start."

"That's good."

Katie grabbed Mike's hands.

"Mike, I… We're alive because of you. What you've been through, the price you paid… It's not something I can ever repay. I am in your debt for the rest of my life."

"It's okay."

"No, it's not. If you ever need anything, and I mean anything, it's yours."

"Thank you."

* * *

MIKE WAS GIVEN his personal effects when he was released. And when he walked outside, Dr. Wyatt was waiting for him.

"I'm surprised you're not locked up yet," Mike said.

"They cleared me on a few conditions."

"What are you doing here?"

"Mike, I can't fix what's already been broken. We both know that, but the reason I wanted to come find you was because I want to prevent these types of disasters from happening again."

"People don't want to change. They just want things to be back to the way they were."

"Not everyone."

Mike cocked his head to the side.

"What do you mean?" Mike asked.

"As part of the terms of my 'pardon,' I've been asked to be a part of a new agency that would be in charge of preventing these types of attacks and disasters from happening again. I want you to be a part of it."

"And why should I trust you?"

"How about me?" Sam said.

Mike turned around, and the two men smiled and embraced each other in a hug.

"It's good to see you, Mike."

"You too, Sam."

"Mike," Dr. Wyatt said, "you're not the only man who wants to work off the debt of death that we accumulated during the blackout."

"So what do you say?" Sam asked.

Mike pulled out the silver pocket watch. He flipped open the cover, and inside was a picture of his family.

"When do we start?"

Made in the USA
Columbia, SC
10 January 2021